A THOUSAND TEXAS LONGHORNS

Westerns by
Spur Award–Winning Author
Johnny D. Boggs

RETURN TO RED RIVER

MOJAVE

VALLEY OF FIRE

WEST TEXAS KILL

THE KILLING SHOT

A THOUSAND TEXAS LONGHORNS

JOHNNY D. BOGGS

PINNACLE BOOKS
Kensington Publishing Corp.
www.kensingtonbooks.com

For Max McCoy & Kim Horner McCoy

"Live through it," Call said. "That's all we can do."
—LARRY MCMURTRY, *Lonesome Dove*

PART I
Winter

CHAPTER ONE

The first thing he noticed were the trees.

Not a leaf, not a branch, not a twig, and nary a pine needle in sight. Nothing. This high up in the Rockies, with plenty of water, Virginia City, Montana Territory, should have been lumber rich, but Mason Boone turned his head and spit. Log cabins dotted the hills, and wooden-frame buildings lined the main street, with some picket, board-and-batten, and clapboard shacks mixed among a few stone structures. Wood had to be around here somewhere. Smoke puffed out of brick chimneys and iron pipes, and Boone smelled woodsmoke, not coal.

Boone stepped out of the way as a mule-drawn wagon headed toward Nevada City. Wooden wagon, too. The driver didn't look altogether friendly, and his blue overcoat reminded Boone of damn Yankees. Boone looked in every direction.

Not even a shade tree.

That didn't matter, because there wasn't any sun here, either. Just dark clouds, closer to the ground than they ought to be, but although Virginia City sat in a bowl, the elevation topped five thousand feet. For the time being, the only snow could be found in the shady parts, caused by the buildings, or in the dirty piles shoveled off walkways and boardwalks, or swept over any flat-roofed structure. Boone figured his toes had frozen solid after trudging through drifts on his hike here. Around the city, clouds, threatening more snow, obscured peaks of most of the surrounding mountains.

One tree. That's all I want. Just one tree. Just to sit under. Rest my feet. Scratch my back.

Another wagon driver hollered at Boone to get the hell out of the road.

"Ride around me." Boone's tone and eyes must have warned that cackler that Mason Boone wasn't one to trifle with. Boone looked down one boardwalk—if anybody would actually call those planks a boardwalk—and across the street. Over the rooftops at the hills. Nary a tree. Maybe higher up, behind or above the gray clouds, but not here.

Virginia City, Mason Boone figured, might as well be in Kansas.

"Pies. Fresh-baked pies."

Discovering the source of the voice, Boone forgot all about trees. What in God's name had gotten into him? Trees? He was no lumberjack, no carpenter, could barely tell the difference between a sweet gum and an aspen. It might have had something to do with that dream from the past night, another one of those he barely remembered—like most of his dreams, the rare times he ever dreamed—but, more than likely, this preoccupation with trees could be attributed to walking from a piss-poor claim in the Gravelly Range all the way to Virginia City. His feet hurt. Not enough left of his socks to darn. Holes in both boots, if you could call them boots. If some Quinine Jimmy told him that his nose was frostbit and had to be cut off, Boone wouldn't have cared. He didn't even stop to look at the wares in the window of the Mechanical Bakery.

He forgot about how much his feet hurt. He forgot about trees. He walked, picking up the pace, when the woman with the pies turned down another street. Boone didn't catch up with her until she stood in front of the Planter's House. His focus trained so hard on the raven-haired woman hawking pies, he didn't even notice the sign above the building on the other side of the street.

BARNARD, SLAVIN & CO.,
at the
~ Liquor Emporium ~
PURE RYE & BOURBON WHISKEY
Brandy, Gin, Rum,
Stoughton and Plantation Bitters,
Port Wine, Claret Wine, Heidsick Champagne,
Sparkling Catawba, Carbon Oil,
ETC., ETC., ETC., ETC.

She saw him, though, yet did not step back, even though Boone knew he stunk to high heaven. His nose might have been frozen by the wind, but he could smell. Yet penetrating his stench came the delectable aromas of delicacies that had eluded him at that boar's nest where he had been mining.

He hadn't seen a woman since Easter.

"Ma'am," he managed.

"Would you like a pie?"

The voice might have been guarded, and the eyes colder than the wind, but she managed a smile. At least, Boone convinced himself she smiled.

He stared without blinking.

"Ma'am?" This time, many seconds later, it came out as a question.

"A pie," she said. "Dried apple today. That's all we have."

"Dried apple," he repeated, which came out as if he were speaking Blackfeet. Black hair. Parted at the middle. Dark eyes. Round face. Coat of winter wool. He saw the tray she carried, pies with golden crusts lined in a row. Four pies. Not very big, but deep-dish. From the vacant spots, she must have already sold nine.

"Would you like a pie, sir?"

His eyes came up again. A horse, hitched in front of a business up Jackson Street, began to urinate.

Boone found his voice. "How much?" His right hand reached into the pocket in his denim britches.

"Five dollars."

He stopped reaching. His hand had gone through the big rip and his fingernails began scratching his thigh. He had used the remnants of his underdrawers the previous night to get a fire going.

Boone stared. "Five . . . dollars?"

She did not debate him.

For a puny pie?

Fellow come all this way, nigh two thousand miles—most of that on the ankle express—well, Boone figured, a man who traveled that far, he deserved a pie. But nobody ever charged five dollars for a pie back in Texas or Tennessee. Besides, Boone didn't have five cents. Hadn't seen a dollar in a coon's age.

"Five . . . dollars?" He stopped scratching his leg, removed his hand from the pocket, stared at his fingernails, noticed the filth. He also saw people stepping out of the Planter's House, and even more from the building across the street. That's when he finally saw the sign.

All of a sudden, he felt real thirsty.

"Five dollars." The raven-haired beauty spoke again.

"Maybe you'll have sufficient funds tomorrow." She moved back toward Wallace Street.

The men in front of the Liquor Emporium laughed.

Later, Boone figured, he must have gone crazy. All those months on the Ruby, all that hard work—for nothing. The long walk to Virginia City. Not to mention all the miles he had traveled just to get here. Sure, that'd be more than enough to drive a fellow loco. Mason Boone wasn't the kind of man who'd let some walking whiskey vats drive him to do something stupid. Then again, later, when his brain became less addled, he would also remember that folks back in Smith County had said Mason Boone wasn't the type of man who'd quit his country and desert.

The pie-selling angel stopped when Boone caught up with her.

"Yes?" There was no warmth in her voice, no humor in those deep, dark eyes. He noticed a slight scar above an eyebrow. Wondered how she had gotten it.

Laughter from the far boardwalk reached him.

Mason Boone smiled. "Maybe," he said, "we could work out . . . a . . . trade?"

The eyes did not blink. His face suddenly warmed, and he knew why. Damn it all to hell if he hadn't blushed. The woman should be blushing, or turning red with rage, but it was Boone who felt embarrassed. And now the laughter across the street angered him, and if he had not been so captured by those dark eyes, he would've charged across the street like he had charged at Missionary Ridge. Instead, he just looked into eyes like the darkest, deepest mine.

He hated himself.

A kaleidoscope of colors replaced the beautifully shaped face, and pain blinded him, shooting from the top of his head to his toes. Someone had to be screaming, and blood ran between his fingers as Boone tried to squeeze the split in his skull back together.

Maybe Boone let the oaths fly. If anyone still laughed, the roaring in Boone's ears drowned out that noise. He thought he had drawn his legs up, smelled the mixture of manure and gravel in the dirt, felt as though he had rolled himself up into a ball.

He prayed that he hadn't messed his britches.

He swallowed snot.

He tasted blood.

For a brief moment, he remembered Kennesaw Mountain and beginning that long, stupid walk.

Then he pictured the pine trees, even saw his ma and pretty Janice Terry, and smelled the scent of pine trees, pine sap, and felt the warmth of a fireplace back home in Tyler. Folks up here in Alder Gulch thought Texas was just like Kansas and Wyoming, some flat, treeless plain. They'd never seen the Piney Woods. Boone wished he had never left.

He heard that woman's voice.

"Nelson. *Don't*." The last word came out as a scream.

Just before Boone disappeared into blackness darker than that pie-seller's eyes.

CHAPTER TWO

Dried-apple pies toppled onto the boardwalk and streets. Four of them, ruined—twenty dollars' worth of baking, lost—but Ellen Story could not, would not, think about that. She let the tray she had fashioned rattle on the stones, brushed past her husband, and knelt by the stinking, bearded young man who clutched his bleeding head. His hat—if one could call it a hat—rolled over toward the groggery. His hands turned crimson before they slipped from that fine, dark hair. His eyes fluttered, eventually rolling up and out of sight, and he let out a heavy sigh.

"Get up, Ellen . . . And you . . . *you* best go about your business."

Looking up, she found her husband pointing the Navy Colt's barrel at the men lounging in front of the Liquor Emporium's entrance. They must have stepped out from their afternoon of idleness to witness the fun. Most of them disappeared for more drinking, but two moved down the street toward hobbled horses. Even the men standing in front of the Planter's House began to find safer climes.

"Ellen. I said, 'Get up.'"

There he stood, king of the world. Times like this, she

wondered what she'd ever seen in him back in Leavenworth, Kansas.

Well, that wasn't quite the truth. She knew exactly what she'd seen in Nelson Gile Story. About an inch under six feet tall, nigh two hundred pounds, with blond hair and blue-gray eyes, he wasn't hard on the eyes like most of her would-be Jayhawker suitors. "Got a head for business," Pa had told her. "And the Midas touch," said her older brother, John. Nelson Story worked hard; of that she had no uncertainty. Any man who hauled wood for her father couldn't fear calluses or be allergic to sweat. Back then, eastern Kansas, spitting distance from Missouri, could be the devil on courtships.

Nelson Story came from Ohio. The Trents started off in Kentucky before Ellen's pa moved to Platte County, Missouri, when John was a youngster. Ellen was Missouri-born, but Pa moved the family to Kansas Territory in '54 so when it came time to vote for statehood, the more Kentuckians and Virginians casting ballots, Ma explained later, the better chance Kansas could become a slave state. Well, that hadn't worked out, but Pa never had been the luckiest or smartest man Ellen had known.

Nelson Story, on the other hand, was something else. So her father decided to forget about his Southern leanings, Democratic tendencies, and that forlorn hope of becoming rich enough to own a bevy of slaves.

In those years, Ellen rarely saw this side of Nelson Story, though a few gossips let stories slip out about him knifing a neighbor's forearm up in Ohio, beating a man half to death in Monticello Township, using a Colt to buffalo a drunkard in Liberty—much as he had just done to this poor fellow.

"Ellen . . . I won't tell you . . ."

"Shut your mouth, Nelson." Her black eyes burned. Her husband blinked. "Hand me your bandanna."

First he pouted, started to say something else, thought better of that mistake, and finally slid the Navy into the holster on his left hip. Another .36 remained holstered on the right hip. "For balance," Thomas Dimsdale, editor of the *Montana Post*, often joked. "Montana wind would spin Nelson like a top if he didn't carry two revolvers."

She took the piece of frayed calico and pressed it against the man's head, trying to be gentle yet hard enough to stanch the flowing blood. A wave of nausea struck her, and she hated herself for this. Her husband despised weakness, but, closing her eyes, she drew in a deep breath, held it as long as she could, and hoped she would not throw up black tea and fresh biscuits onto this poor man. When her eyes opened, Nelson Story squatted beside her, his hand out, eyes maybe a tad softer now.

"Here," he said. "I'll do it."

Their gazes locked.

"It's my bandanna, Ellen," Nelson said.

Without waiting, he moved his right hand down and pressed the rag tighter on the man's wound. Withdrawing her hand, Ellen looked away from the stranger, but the wreckage of her morning's baking made her sob, "Oh." She hadn't meant to say anything.

Nelson Story glanced at the busted pies. "It's all right," he said.

"No, it is not."

Not in a town like Virginia City, Idaho Territory. No, it was Montana Territory now, since the federal government had carved Montana out of Idaho and who knows what other territories. She still had trouble remembering that they now lived in Montana Territory, not Idaho Territory, but

Nelson always told her it didn't matter the name, hell was hell no matter who claimed it. Ellen had been selling pies since they had arrived in Bannack City, due west, back in the early summer of '63. She figured to earn her keep, and in this country, where a pie could sell for five bucks, a husband and wife needed to work together or go bust.

Twenty dollars' worth of pies. Gone to dust.

She looked at the stranger, still breathing at least, and the bleeding appeared to have slowed. She remembered the shock on his gaunt face when she had told him how much a pie of hers would cost. Man had to be a greenhorn. A hundred-pound sack of flour cost twenty-eight dollars these days, and folks thought that was a blessing. A year ago, a person would have thought he had haggled his way to glory if he paid under ninety bucks for a sack. Butter still went for a buck-fifty a pound; that same price could fetch you an egg, providing it wasn't as big as a goose egg. Onions went for forty-five cents a pound, and when Nelson had learned how much merchants were charging for potatoes, he had hitched up a wagon, driven all the way to Fort Hall, and returned with a wagonload of spuds that he sold for two bits each.

Midas touch. Nelson still had that. Sometimes, though, that touch landed a little harder. The stranger moaned.

Still wearing sleeve garters and a visor, Mr. Bagley eased his way down Jackson Street and cleared his throat before he knelt. "I'll take care of him," he said softly, and lowered his right hand toward the blood-soaked bandanna. He did not look at Ellen, but he nodded at Nelson. "You get Miz Ellen back home." He slowly removed the bandanna. "Iffen he needs a stitch or two, I got some fishing line that should fix him up." The rag returned. "Don't worry. He won't die. Not with a head this hard." He winked at her husband. "Hard as you buffaloed him, Nelson, I thought you'd done cleaved his head down to his gizzard."

Nelson rose, thanked the merchant, and extended his right hand toward Ellen. She let him lift her to her feet, and after another wave of nausea passed, she gave Mr. Bagley an appreciative nod. God bless him. Relief swept through her whole body. She could have kissed him on the streets, harelip and all.

Nelson picked up the tray she had dropped, and moved to his bay gelding, which was looking bored at the intersection of Wallace Street.

"I'll take care of your horse, Mr. Story," someone called out from in front of the newspaper office on the corner. The youngster weaved between a pack mule and a farm wagon, and gathered the reins. "You boarding him at Montee's place?"

Nelson nodded. "Yes, at the Big Horse Corral. Thank you, bub."

"My pleasure, sir. My pleasure." Boy and horse moved down Wallace Street.

"Let's go home, Ellen," Story said.

As cabins went in Virginia City, theirs was, well, a cabin. This evening, it still smelled of flour and dried apples, and the winter kitchen remained a mess. As Nelson hung his gun belt on the elk horn, she pulled out her purse and laid gold dust, nuggets, silver dollars, and even some U.S. scrip on the table.

"A hundred and eighty dollars," she announced. "Or close to it."

He laid his hat, crown down, on the desk, and moved to the table, fingering a gold nugget.

"You don't have to bake pies anymore, Ellen," he said at last.

"I like to . . ." she started. She was about to say *help*, but Nelson would not like to hear that, so she changed her ending. "Cook."

"Yeah." He ran the back of his hand against his face. He needed a shave. "But maybe you'd like someone to cook for you, for us, for a change."

She moved away from the table.

His right hand reached inside a coat pocket and slowly pulled out a leather pouch. He loosened the drawstring and shook out nuggets that spilled into the mixing bowl. The stones—much bigger than the ones Ellen had earned for her pies—glittered in the candlelight. Ellen's lips parted, but she found no words.

Nelson laughed. "And that's not the half of it. That there . . ." His chin jutted toward the mixing bowl. "That's just from Alder Gulch. The half interest I put in with Ben Christenot's claim in Pine Grove. And over at Oro Cache. You wouldn't believe what those are assaying at. I scarcely believe it myself."

Midas touch. In Ellen's head, her brother John's words rang like the Liberty Bell.

Sweeping her into his arms, Nelson kissed her hard.

Then someone knocked on the door.

He cursed softly, stared at her briefly, then crossed to the door, his hand resting on the butt of a holstered revolver.

"Yes," he called.

"Nelson," came the muffled voice. "It's Ben."

The right hand slipped off the walnut butt and moved toward the door, which he pulled open slightly, glanced at Ellen, and stepped through the opening. The door remained partly open, but Ellen did not eavesdrop. She tried to think of what Nelson had just told her. Were they rich? She fingered one of the nuggets, rubbing off sugar and flour.

Once the door opened, Nelson stepped inside, pulled on his hat, and found the gun rig. As he buckled the belt, he looked at Ellen.

"Don't wait up," he told her. "And pull in the latch string."

The door closed behind him.

CHAPTER THREE

The potatoes on John Catlin's plate were cold. Same with the gravy. Even the beef. The waitress at the La Porte Dining Palace refreshed his coffee and moved on. Catlin broke the dam of mashed potatoes with his spoon, but no waterfall broke free, no flood of brown drenched his beef, for the gravy had congealed. Which didn't surprise him. For at least fifteen minutes, he had just stared at the food.

Chair legs scraped the floor as Steve Grover sat, uninvited, holding his own cup of coffee. Sipping, Grover shook out a copy of *Daily State Sentinel*. Catlin looked across the small café—*Palace* was a misnomer—to see if he knew anyone else in the restaurant. He hadn't thought to look when he first sat down, but unless someone was hiding, Grover and Catlin were the only ones here. No, there was a gent with a silk hat by the table near the window that looked out onto the alley. Spooning lemon cake.

"How long you been here?" Catlin asked.

"Just got here, got a cup of water dyed with coffee. You were so focused on your chow you didn't even hear me say 'Afternoon, Captain.'"

"Oh." Catlin eyed his food. Grover studied the newspaper.

"At two dollars a year," Grover said, "a man would think there'd be something worth reading."

"You subscribe to an Indianapolis newspaper?"

"No." He turned the page. "Found it on a bench outside of Marston's."

"You getting a photograph or ambrotype taken?"

"Neither." Grover flipped to another page. "Just walking past. He's closed on Sundays anyhow." He peered over the top of the paper. "You ever get a likeness made of yourself?"

Catlin nodded. "Indianapolis. Before we marched south. Tintype. Mailed one, no, must've been two, to Ma and Pa in Michigan. I got four. Must have kept one for myself. Don't know what I did with the other."

"How much did that cost?"

He shrugged. "Two bits. Four. Dollar. Don't rightly recall."

Grover returned to the newspaper, went to another page, looked at Catlin again. "How'd you know it was an Indianapolis newspaper?"

"I left it on the bench outside Wallace's Grocery House."

"You subscribe to the *Sentinel*?"

"No. I found it in the trash box outside of Culver's."

"You buying a book or crockery?" Grover asked.

"Where?"

"At Culver's."

"No. He's closed, too. It being Sunday. I just looked down by chance, saw it, picked it up."

"Wonder how it got all the way up here. The paper, I mean."

"Drummer, I warrant."

"Most likely. Wonder how it got from Culver's to Marston's."

"That's a mystery for sure." Catlin looked at his plate, sighed. "You don't read the *Herald*?"

"Charlie Powell don't put nothing in his paper except advertisements for blood pills. You?"

Catlin was too late trying to cover his yawn. "Excuse me. I'll pick one up now and then. When I find one at the grocery or Culver's store."

"How'd your winter wheat make out?"

"Slim. Yours?"

"About the same. Spring wheat was average."

"Mine, too."

"Figure this spring'll be better."

Catlin nodded. "If we get some decent rain."

Silence.

"Come to church?"

"Got here too late. You?"

"I just got here."

A month, or maybe just a minute, passed.

"Well, I know why you left this on the bench. Nothing worth reading in Indianapolis, either."

"There's always something worth reading," Catlin said.

"What?"

Sighing, Catlin took the paper, turned to the second page, and tapped at the quotation below the paper's name and the date.

THE UNION—IT MUST BE PRESERVED.
—JACKSON

Grover nodded, took the paper, and slid it to the side of the table.

Catlin plowed the potatoes with his fork, preparation, he figured, for spring. If spring ever returned.

Grover slurped. Catlin farmed the mashed potatoes. The

gravy hardened. The waitress walked by without checking on either.

"You know what I like to read in any newspaper?" Grover asked.

"What?" Catlin said.

Grover picked up the paper again and tapped a column on the front page. "The railroad schedules. Bellefontaine Railway . . ." Catlin feared his friend would start reading the whole damned table, trains arriving from the east, and the west, the expresses, plus everything else, but, no, Steve Grover condensed things considerably, and even Indianapolis lacked a bevy of railroads. "The Atlantic and Great Western Railway . . ."

"You plan on taking a trip?"

"Where would I go?"

Catlin shrugged. "Lake Michigan?"

"Wouldn't need to pay money for a train ticket to see that. Could march there if I had a mind to. I sure know how to march."

Catlin smiled with understanding.

"You ever seen Lake Michigan?"

Catlin looked up, surprised at the question, and his answer. "Can't rightly say I have. You?"

Grover's head shook.

Another round of silence.

"Funny," Grover said.

"What's that?"

"Lake Michigan." Grover sipped his coffee. "The two of us. We saw so much of the South. Even Washington City. And we haven't seen a big lake that's, what, twenty miles north of us? If that."

Catlin grinned. "You want to go?"

"Where?"

"Lake Michigan."

Grover shook his head. "Not in winter."

"Maybe come spring."

The head shook again. "We'll be plowing." Another taste of weak coffee. "Besides. It's just a bunch of water."

Catlin thought about tasting the meal he'd paid for. Decided against it.

"Ran into Missus Yoho at Alvord's store yesterday," Grover said.

"How's she doing?"

"Got the catarrh."

"I see."

"Getting better."

"There are remedies."

Grover tapped the newspaper. "Papers are full of advertisements for cures. Especially in Charlie's *Herald*. Last time I saw a copy, anyhow."

"Must be an epidemic."

"You ever caught it?"

"Don't think so. But I don't rightly know what the catarrh is."

"Me, neither."

Two months passed. Or maybe it was just a couple of minutes.

"It's just a cold," Grover said. "Something like that."

"What's that?"

"The catarrh."

"Yeah. Congestion. Runs down the back of your throat."

"Huh?"

"Catarrh."

"Yeah. I know what it is."

"Most people do."

"Old Banash seemed to have it from Louisville to Atlanta."

"Likely still has it. Where did he hail from?"

Grover thought. "Union Mills?"

"I thought it was Unionville."

"Might've been. Union-something."

"Or maybe Rensselaer."

They grinned. Sipped coffee. Which still wasn't good. Catlin wondered how his dinner would taste if he'd bother to eat. Then again, he knew how it tasted. Hell, that's all everyone ate here whenever they came to town to splurge on a meal, something they didn't have to cook themselves. And when they ate at home, this is the same blessed meal they'd cook.

"She asked if I'd speak to the Unconditional Union Girls of La Porte," Grover said.

"Who?"

"Missus Yoho."

Catlin had to reconnoiter to figure out where Mrs. Yoho came into the conversation. "Speak about what?" he asked after a moment.

Grover smiled and tapped the folded newspaper. "How I preserved the Union."

"Oh." Catlin wondered if the beef might be halfway decent. "I got asked to speak once."

"To the Unconditional Union Girls?"

Catlin shook his head. "St. Rose's Academy."

"What did you say?"

"Nothing. I told the headmistress to ask me another time. After the wheat crop was in."

"Oh. You get asked to talk a lot?"

Catlin looked at his friend. "I don't get to town often."

"Yeah. What brought you into town today?"

"Run some errands."

"Not much open on a Sunday."

"I know."

"Is anything open in La Porte on a Sunday?"

Catlin shrugged. "The Dining Palace. Church. Livery."

"What I figured. What errands did you run?"

"I run . . . away from the farm."

Grover smiled. "Yeah. Me, too."

The bell above the door jingled. Cold air came in. Hot air came out.

"See you, hon," the waitress told the fellow with the silk hat.

The door closed. The waitress went back to reading a penny dreadful.

"What did you tell her?" Catlin asked after another season came and went.

"Who?"

"Missus Yoho."

"Oh." He slurped more coffee.

Catlin waited.

"Well?"

"What?"

"What did you tell Missus Yoho?"

"Nothing." He wiped his nose. "Oh, I guess I told her to ask me next time, when I had more time."

"It's December, Steve. You won't have less time than right now."

"Well."

They drank. Catlin gave up on his dinner and slid the plate toward Grover. "You hungry?" Catlin asked.

"You aren't going to eat this?"

Catlin shook his head.

"Off your feed?"

"Just not hungry."

"My pa wouldn't let me get up from the supper table till I'd cleaned my plate." He raised his head, suspicious. "You want me to pay for . . . ?"

"No, Steve. Eat. It's cold. But it's on me."

"Well, I can't say I'm hungry." But the plate was empty three minutes later, and Steve Grover wiped his mouth with the sleeve of his coat.

"They know how to make good roast beef and mashed potatoes here, that's for sure."

"It's their specialty."

"Maybe it's the catarrh," Grover said.

Catlin looked up, his face blank.

"What's ailing you," Grover explained.

"Nothing's ailing me, Steve. Except . . ."

"What?"

Catlin smiled. "Boredom."

Grover's face surprised Catlin. His old friend—friend for something that felt like twenty years now, when it would be just four come spring—knew what he meant, when half the time, John Catlin couldn't figure that out himself.

"Remember what you said?" Grover asked.

"When?"

"In Washington City. During the Grand Review."

Before Catlin's head shook, Grover answered his own question. "You said, 'Steve, we're going home at last.' Remember? That's exactly what you said." He drained the coffee with two final slurps and set the empty mug beside the plate. "Here we are, walking past President Abraham Lincoln, Sherman, Grant, Sheridan, ladies throwing flowers at us, swooning, men cheering, and after all we'd been through, you just wanted to get home."

Catlin smiled. "All I wanted to do was get home after we first saw the elephant."

"Me, too," Grover said. "Best time of my life, but I was too scared to know it."

"Me, too."

"Horse apples."

Catlin looked up.

"You were born to soldier, John. Captain Sabin said you took to infantry faster than crap flowed through a goose. Made fifth sergeant before I could shoulder a musket. Captain after Atlanta. Missus Yoho ought to ask you to speak about . . ." The words trailed off.

Catlin remembered. Twenty-five years old when he had joined the fight in August of 1862. All that marching and drilling in the Indiana summer. Meeting Steve Grover. Meeting hundreds of other men.

"Lake Michigan," Catlin said.

"Huh."

"I was just thinking. I'd never seen anything before we enlisted. Well, Ohio. Maybe I ought to go see Lake Michigan."

"You seen Ohio, John?"

"I was born in Ohio. Can't say I remember much about it. Pa and Ma had the wanderlust. They're living in Michigan now. Never seen Michigan, either. We sure saw a lot of country."

Grover drank coffee. "I don't think you'd want to see Lake Michigan now, John. It's colder than a witch's teat outside."

Spring, summer, and fall came and went, and here they sat, ten minutes later, at the Dining Palace in La Porte. Most likely, the waitress had started her fifth half-dime novel.

The cook was probably on his third marriage. The owner might have sold his interest and taken the Bellefontaine to . . . anywhere.

"What would you tell them?" Grover asked.

"Tell who?"

"The Union Girls. Or St. Rose's Academy, were they to ask you again."

"Oh." Catlin shrugged.

He finished his coffee.

"Coffee was better in the 87th," he said. "Grub was, too."

"That's what you'd tell them?"

"Who?"

"Missus Yoho, you dern fool. Charlie Powell at the *La Porte Herald*. The headmistress at St. Rose's. The governor. President Johnson, were he to give you a medal. Your ma. Your pa. Anybody who asked."

"Oh. No. I don't talk about it much. When I do get asked, I just shrug, say, 'We won the war, saved the Union, freed the slaves.' If I say even that."

"I'm the same."

The clock ticked. The waitress stared at them long and hard, before she turned another page in some yellow-covered book.

"Well." Catlin stretched. "Guess it's about that time."

"Yeah."

"Getting late."

"Yeah."

"Ought to get my wagon, head back home."

"Yeah."

"Might come a good snow."

"Maybe. Moisture would help."

They waited.

"We did it, though. Didn't we?" Grover said.

"What's that?"

Grover punched at the newspaper. "'The Union—It must be preserved.' We sure preserved her."

Catlin nodded. He made himself stand, otherwise they might be here till the century turned. The waitress looked their way, relief washing over her face. Catlin found his watch in his vest pocket, checked the time, sighed.

"You know what I'd tell them?" A sadness filled Steve Grover's eyes.

"Tell who?"

"The Unconditional Union Girls."

"Oh," Catlin said. "What?"

"I'd tell those ladies this: I never knew how gol-durn boring Indiana was till I went off to war."

CHAPTER FOUR

When he came to, the first thing Mason Boone did was vomit. During a pause between his retches, he heard a snigger and a laugh. Once his eyes finally focused, he realized that he wasn't in the cold street and that that black-haired, dark-eyed angel had vanished. From his own stink, he knew he hadn't had any peach pie. No, the woman had been hawking apple pie. Dried-apple pie. The thought of pie left him dry-heaving.

Another aroma eventually reached him, and Boone lifted his eyes toward a tin cup. Past the cup, he made out yellow teeth grinning between a brown mustache and goatee.

"This'll cure you," the voice said.

Groaning, Boone lifted his head as much as he dared and took the tin cup. The liquor practically burned his eyes as he brought it to his lips. It didn't go down any better, but it stayed down. For now. The forty-rod took away the headache, though, until Boone gently fingered the pulpy knot on the top of his head.

The man with the goatee splashed more rotgut into the cup, then brought up the jug to his own lips. Another voice in the shadows said, "Looks like you got tomahawked with a Cree war club."

"Story swings it like an ax," Goatee said.

This time, when Boone lifted the cup, his stomach recoiled and bile started climbing up his throat. He rested the cup on his knee.

A horse snorted.

Hooves stamped.

He smelled wet hay, grain, leather. Figured he had to be in a livery stable or barn.

"Story?" Boone asked.

Goatee nodded. "You were accosting his wife."

Boone had to think. Bits of memories came to him. He remembered the woman, and the pies, but not any husband.

"You don't remember?"

"He never saw the bastard," another voice, more mouse than man, whispered from the darkness. "Story ain't one to give a body no chance."

Goatee drank more home brew. The jug found a spot on a bale. The man found a more comfortable position. "From the looks of them butternuts and brogans, or what's left of shoes, I say you fought for the South."

Boone delicately traced how big the scalp injury was. No stitches that he could detect, but he knew from experience just how hard it was to stitch a head wound. At least no one had tried to cauterize it. They had just packed it down tight with some sort of salve, or maybe mud. For all he knew, it could have been bandaged with horse apples. He ignored Goatee's comment. He had been in Montana Territory, or Idaho Territory, or whatever the damned government wanted to call it these days, long enough to realize more Yankees mined up here than Johnny Rebs.

"I like a man who don't talk much," Goatee said. "They call me Plummer."

Boone looked harder at the man.

"So you been here long enough to hear that name."
Goatee nodded. "I figured it's a name to be remembered. It
ain't my real name. You don't need to know that. Hell, I've
practically forgot it. You just call me Plummer."

"Damn fool alias to use if you was to ask me," one of the
voices said. "Get your neck stretched just like ol' Henry."

"You got no imagination, Freddie," Goatee told the mousy
voice behind him. "That's why I took the sheriff's name.
What are the chances two men using the same handle would
get killed in the same district?" Grinning, he tapped his
temple. "Brains. That's what I got. Brains." He wet his lips.
"Was you here when they stretched the sheriff's neck?"

Boone's head shook. All he had heard were the tales—
he didn't know what he ought to believe—about one Henry
Plummer, who not only had been sheriff and, simultane-
ously, leader of an outlaw gang. Until the folks around Bannack began to suspicion the lawman, persuaded a captured
bandit to give up some names, and then lynched the sheriff
and other brigands. That had been early back in '64. And
in Bannack. Boone hadn't reached Alder Gulch until the
following fall, and he'd never even seen Bannack.

"I'm gonna let folks think I'm Henry Plummer's kid
brother. Put the fear of God into the vigilance committee.
Let them worry if the sheriff's brother plans to getting his-
self a little revenge. You savvy what I'm saying?"

Boone didn't understand a thing. But at least he was out
of the cold. He asked, "Was it Plummer that buffaloed me?"

"Plummer's dead, you idiot." Goatee turned his head,
spit, and swore. "What have we been talking about? I asked
you if you were here when the sheriff got killed, you said
no, and then you ask me . . ."

"Leave him be," said a voice, the one more Virginia than
mouse, and not slurred as much as Goatee's. "Fellow gets

his brains knocked to his bowels, a four-inch gash in his noggin, and you interrogate him like you're the professor at the *Post*. Man ought to be dead, hard as Story hit him."

"Story hit me?" Boone said.

"That's right," Plummer said. "You got your head practically cleaved in two by N. G. Story—and that N. G. stands for 'No Good.' So me and the boys are gonna put Story in his place, and we figured—since it was Sandy yonder who got your head put back together . . ." The nod was too vague, Boone's vision still not quite adjusted to the light, whiskey, and headache to determine which voice belonged to Sandy. ". . . we figured you'd like to get a chance to get even with the damned head-splitter. You game, boy?"

His stomach had settled, he hadn't vomited, so Boone figured he might have nodded in agreement. He reached for the forty-rod. Not that he remembered doing it, but his hand held the cup, the fumes almost disintegrated his nose hairs, and he drank.

"That a boy, Reb. We'll show Story and his vigilantes just who runs Virginia City and Alder Gulch these days. Rest up, pard. Drink up. Ain't nothin' gonna happen till dawn."

"They giving Timmy, Mikey, and Mark that long to get right with God," the mouse squeaked.

"We'll see who's meeting St. Peter first in a couple of hours," Plummer said.

"Story's got balls," the deeper voice said.

Plummer took another pull from the jug. "Yeah. But come dawn, all of Alder Gulch will find out if Story's balls are brass . . . or papier-mâché."

CHAPTER FIVE

There were five of them, not including Goatee, who called himself Plummer. Not including Mason Boone, either, since Boone didn't consider himself a member of the gang, or posse, or whatever they were. His head hadn't cleared up enough to savvy much of what was happening. If he understood anything at all.

Light began creeping through the open door of the barn, though Boone wouldn't call it morning. Outside, what looked like snowflakes swirled in the wind.

When was the last time it snowed back home in Tyler, Texas? Boone couldn't recollect, but at least he remembered he grew up in East Texas. That meant he didn't have anemia. No. That wasn't right. Not anemia. What was it?

"I know how it is, pard." Goatee slurred words even worse now. "You come up here expecting to find the mother lode and get nothing but tailings and tailrace." The man who wanted to be mistaken for a dead thief and lawman tried to suck the last drops out of the jug.

Boone felt the knot on his head. He could touch it now. *Mother lode,* Goatee had said. The fool didn't know much about Alder Gulch. There might be some lode mining going on somewhere in these hills, but all Boone had seen were placer outfits. Boone wouldn't call himself an expert, but . . .

The man named Sandy came over with a pot of coffee, filling Boone's cup and ignoring goateed Plummer.

"About that time, Ambrose," Sandy told the boss, which triggered Boone's memory.

"Amnesia," he said aloud, causing Sandy, Plummer, and the three others to stare in his direction.

Boone almost grinned and held his cup up. "Thanks."

"Drink up." Plummer, or Ambrose, or Goatee—whoever he was—pitched the empty jug into the nearest stall and tried three times before he climbed to his feet.

"We got business. Time for us to save our McGee cousins. Time for us to show Virginia City who runs Alder Gulch." He unbuttoned his coat, revealing an old horse pistol stuck inside the waistband. Plummer seemed to sober up instantly. "Sandy, you and Robin back me on the street. Donnie, I want you and that Colt's revolving carbine at the corner, and you make enough noise so the vigilance boys think they's fifty of you right behind you. Howard, you stand on the other side. When I nod, send a blast of bird shot into the sky. When those pellets start raining down, you train the barrel with the buckshot at the crowd. If they start the ball, you finish their dance. You savvy?"

All but Sandy nodded. Boone's head started hurting again, so he kept still. Besides, Plummer hadn't given him any directions. Now that he could see better, Boone realized that the leader of this gang couldn't be out of his teens, and that the mustache and goatee were pasted on like a young thespian playing Shakespeare in some chintzy troupe.

Plummer said: "And you, iron head, you hold our horses. We ain't got that many, so we'll be riding double."

With that, the men walked outside. Boone was the last

onc out of the barn, and to his surprise, he found several horses tied up at hitching rails. He counted five mounts. He watched the men marching toward the main street, and did some math. Three McGee boys. Plummer with the Goatee. Sandy and the four others whose names he had already forgotten. And Boone himself. Ten men. Mrs. Mary Alma back at the Tyler Subscription School would be beaming with joy, at least, if Boone's ciphering was right. Boone could figure which one wouldn't be riding double. The men didn't look back. They had already turned the corner.

Mason Boone walked after them, but he left the horses in the alley.

If he hadn't already figured out that Ambrose, alias Plummer with the Goatee, was a damned fool, he understood that before he climbed halfway up the hill on the northwest side of town. A crowd had come out this fine, if snowy, Monday morning to watch the hangings. Not that Virginia City was as big as it had been when Boone had briefly passed through on his way to that god-awful mining camp fourteen months or so back, but Boone figured at least fifty people braved the cold to watch the show.

Fifty against five? Boone had already dealt himself out of this hand. Plummer with the Goatee had gumption. No brains. But Boone watched those men keep right on up the hill, and it wasn't an easy hill to climb even without snow and wind. Plummer's group didn't seem to care that the hangings weren't happening in town, but up at the pauper's cemetery.

Three wagons had brought each of the McGees up, and the teams had been unhitched, and the tongues pushed up, with ropes attached and hangman's nooses ready. The

McGees, already hooded with hands tied behind their backs, had been hoisted atop separate crates, and now three businessmen in greatcoats and mufflers began tying their legs with short ropes.

Plummer with the Goatee drew out the Dragoon, cocked it, and the other men spread out on either side of him.

I wonder if these McGee boys know what fine fools they have for friends. A horse's snort and a squeaking wheel interrupted Boone's thought, and he turned and stepped aside as a surrey made its way up the hill. Boone reached for his hat, only to realize he hadn't seen his hat since the previous evening. The cold wind and snow seemed to ease the pain in his head.

"Stop."

The rig's driver obeyed. A woman leaned out. Boone's heart leaped.

"Are you all right, sir?"

God must have rendered him mute, but Boone nodded at the lovely woman.

"I apologize for any inconvenience, any injury," the angel spoke. "My husband has . . . well, if you are in town tomorrow, see me. The pie will serve as payment and apology."

She vanished. The whip lashed. The surrey continued its climb.

Boone followed, no longer trailing the friends of the McGees, but the fancy rig.

"My word, Missus Story, you should not be here, not to witness this." A pale man with a thick mustache, and dark hair combed back to hide his thinning locks, with the palest eyes Boone had ever seen, and a delicate English accent, hurried up to the rig. He turned his head and coughed.

"And you, Professor Dimsdale," the black-haired woman said, "should not be here in this weather."

The hacking cough almost doubled the slim man over, but he straightened, glanced at his silk handkerchief, which he used to wipe his pallid lips before slipping it into the outside pocket of his gray coat.

"Mr. Story will be having a benny if he sees you," the man pleaded.

"I know of his temper, and I live here. This is something I should see."

The man started to protest, but he detected Boone easing up the road.

A shotgun's roar turned the attention of the weak English gentleman, Mrs. Story, the driver of the rig, Mason Boone, and everyone at the edge of the cemetery to Howard, the skinny redhead with the shotgun. He now stood next to Plummer with the Goatee, after thumbing back the hammer of the barrel holding the buckshot. Pellets must have been falling harmlessly to the hilltop now, but the only sound Boone heard was the wind moaning through wagons and over remnants of shoddy crosses. Howard's shotgun pointed in the direction of the men closest to the three wagons that had been turned into hangman's scaffolds.

"First one of you sons of bitches that even looks crossways gets killed." Plummer with the fake mustache and goatee took center stage. "You yellow dogs ain't hanging nobody because it'll be you who gets buried. My name's Plummer, if that means anything to you. So here's how we're playing this hand. I got me a hundred and fifty men at Daylight Creek. And another fifty over yonder." The wave seemed vague. "And if one more gunshot sounds, those boys are riding up here like Quantrill done at Lawrence." He waved the heavy pistol. "So which one of you's got the guts to take on another Plummer?"

The wind stopped as though ordained by God.

A voice near the wagons said, "Come on, Ben."

A tall man wearing a black hat stepped out of the sea of bearskins, sheepskins, and dark wool. The woman by the surrey and the lunger gasped. The man with him, the one named Ben, stopped, turned, and put his hand on a holstered revolver, but did not draw. The other man walked to the first McGee and kicked over the crate.

As the man danced, twisted, and died kicking, the man moved to the second wagon. This particular McGee was pretty heavy, and the man in the wagon grabbed the tongue with both hands just before Nelson Story—Mason Boone had no doubt who had taken on the job of executioner— kicked over that crate. The snapping of the man's neck sounded like thunder. He didn't kick at all, just twisted on the cord.

The last of the McGees started singing, sobbing, crying, and praying at the same time. Story kicked over the crate and moved down the hill as the last McGee kicked so hard, his pants fell down. The man called Ben drew a pistol and put a bullet in the kid's head, then yelled, "Cut the bastards down."

Nelson Story stopped about twenty paces in front of the quiet Plummer with the Goatee and the shaking Howard with the shotgun.

No one spoke. Plummer turned around slowly, lowered the pistol to his side, and moved back down the hill. No raiders swarmed up the hill from creek beds or streets. Howard laid his shotgun gently on the ground, then hurried after his leader. The other once-vengeance-minded men mingled ever so discreetly with Virginia City citizens.

The wind resumed. So did the flurries.

The professor named Dimsdale said, "Bloody hell. Bloody hell. Bloody hell."

And as Howard and Plummer with the fake mustache and goatee walked past the surrey, Mason Boone cleared his throat and said: "They're brass."

CHAPTER SIX

Molly McDonald was in her cups, but she wasn't drunk enough to ignore the woman's scream down by the privies— even if her comrades were.

"What you stop for, Mickey?" the Bulgarian said, nodding toward the wagon yard.

"You hear that?" Molly asked.

"Yeah, Mickey, we heard it," said Harvey Coleman. "I sound like that when I take a shit after eatin' at Michener's. C'mon, we're three sheets to the wind and gotta pull out of this pigsty before daybreak."

"You bitch!" came a curse in the blackness behind the privies, followed by a thud against wood.

"Ain't no concern of ourn," Coleman argued.

"You boys go on," Molly told them. "I gotta take a piss."

"Mickey," the Bulgarian said. "Not your affair."

"Get to the wagons," Molly ordered. "I'm just taking a piss. Give you my word of honor."

Reaching behind her back, she withdrew the bung starter. Never had been much of a hand with revolvers. Knives, either, but give her a blacksnake whip, and she could guide a freight wagon across the North Platte and to the banks of the wide Missouri without working up a decent sweat. Twenty yards into the darkness, she stopped, turned, and glanced at the street. Coleman and the Bulgarian, true to their word, were out of sight. Now Molly felt her heart slamming against her rib cage, and the wooden handle of the weapon she'd stolen from a Leavenworth saloon felt clammy in her hands.

Three years she had been doing this, living in a man's world like a man. Chewing tobacco, drinking the worst liquor in the territories, having to sneak away to empty her bladder, but her parents hadn't found her, and unless she slipped, probably never would. Hell, they'd likely given up on ever seeing their beautiful Southern belle again. Besides, if they saw what she had become, they'd disown her—much as she had disowned them three years ago.

Her blond hair had been shorn tightly, linen kept her breasts tight beneath her coarse muslin shirt, the wind and sun had bronzed her face, and she had learned not to take a bath very often. She wore a black patch over her left eye, but had the Bulgarian or Coleman ever borrowed it, they would see right through it.

Somewhere beyond the adobe village and Fort Kearny, a coyote yipped. Molly stepped to the first privy, thankful that the Nebraska cold kept the stench down in the two-holer. Well after midnight, with just a sliver of a moon, the alley in Dobytown remained dark.

Another noise reached her ears, and she wondered why the hell she had decided to be so brave. She certainly didn't need to impress the Bulgarian or Coleman. A figure lurched around the edge of the picket structure, and Molly choked back a shriek before she swung the bung starter up. She had to swing up. Molly didn't stand much taller than five feet in her short-heeled boots, and the man coming at her had to be five foot eight.

Her blow landed solid. The man let out a yelp, fell hard to the ground, and did not move.

Knees buckling, Molly sank beside the son of a bitch she had just laid out cold. The rye almost made its way up her throat, but she choked most of it back into her gut, turned, spit the rest onto frozen sod.

When her chest stopped heaving, she managed to say, "Shit."

The man groaned. Molly brought up the bung starter and quickly dropped it. "Shit," she said again, and rammed her left hand into her coat pocket, brought out the lucifers, and struck one against her thumbnail. Wind blew out the flame, so she cursed again, fingered another lucifer, and this time cupped her hands as soon as the tip flared to life. On her knees, Molly moved closer to the man.

"Son of a bitch," she said. "You're a woman."

Men didn't wear dresses. Molly laughed at the thought. *And women don't wear trousers or chew tobacco*. She started to bring the match closer to the woman's face, saw the knot and blood the bung starter had left on her forehead, and then glimpsed something else, closer to the privy, reflecting the match's flame. Walking on her knees, she moved toward the other body on the ground and brought up the match just as it blew out. Another curse, another match, and the fire cast an eerie glow on . . .

She whispered a series of profanities toward the corpse.

Molly McDonald might have clubbed a woman by mistake, but there was no doubt that the man with the butcher's knife stuck just below his rib cage, angling upward, buried all the way to the hilt, was none other than Brevet Major Warner Balsam. Deader than President Lincoln himself.

Swearing again, she shook out the match, pushed herself into a standing position, and said, "Wait here, lady."

Then she took off down the alley, back to what passed for Dobytown's main drag, for she remembered the mule tethered in front of the crib next to the Bona Fides. The jack was still there, didn't even resist when Molly loosened the reins and led the lethargic but otherwise cooperative animal a tenth of a mile to the alley, then down toward the privies. That's when the mule started braying.

Must've smelled the blood, Molly figured, since an animal's sense of smell was stronger than her own, especially after all that rye she had consumed at the Jack of Diamonds.

"Stay," Molly told the mule, as if ordering a dog.

She dropped beside the woman, still breathing, now groaning. She saw her ripped blouse, the two fingernail scratches along her neck. Easy to figure out what had happened, for Molly had seen the major at work before. Some poor wayfaring lass on the Overland Trail. Maybe a widow, though Molly saw no ring. Maybe . . . anything. That cretin Balsam deserved what he had reaped. But Molly also understood the temperament of a place like Dobytown and of soldiers stationed at Fort Kearny. Hanging a murderess sure would break up the monotony of a Nebraska winter.

Molly moved to the corpse and reached toward his blouse. Months had passed since she had touched a dead man, and that had been some poor wayfarer who got filled with arrows and scalped by Cheyennes. At least, that's how Coleman figured it, and Coleman had been moving up and down this trail since the Oregon rush. She tried to avoid the dead man's eyes. Yeah, he had to be dead. Eyes hadn't moved one way or tother since she had first spotted him. Her fingers touched the cold chain of a watch, and she ripped it up, watch and all, though the fob broke off and fell somewhere. It didn't matter. Bringing the watch, still ticking, toward her face, she could feel its weight. Maybe gold. It was hard to tell in the darkness, but it kept right on ticking. So she swung it hard against the privy door. The noise stopped. She filled her lungs, held her breath, entered the outhouse, found the opening, and dropped the busted watch into the stinking depths.

Next she found his billfold, from which she withdrew the government scrip. These she stuffed inside her left boot top. The Remington revolver and pouch of leaden balls and percussion caps she deposited into another privy.

All right. Molly could breathe now. But what about the knife? Would a thief and murderer leave a knife in the murdered victim's body? Probably not. She sat beside the dead man, gripped the freezing handle, and tugged.

"Son of a bitch," she said. Damn thing didn't budge. She started again, but out of the corner of her eye, saw the mule begin to wander back toward Dobytown's main drag.

"Hold on." She sprinted forward, grabbed the reins, and tied one to the unconscious woman's ankle. Now she had to catch her breath, but not for long, because voices sounded. Maybe from the Jack of Diamonds, but possibly closer. Men who drank eventually urinate. So do women. With everything going on now, Molly thought she might piss her britches.

Another curse, and she left the blade buried inside the major and moved toward the woman.

She lifted. A woman just over the five-foot mark usually wouldn't be able to jerk the dead weight of a woman six or seven inches taller up, but Molly "Mickey" McDonald had put on some muscle all these years.

The woman's head titled, and she puked all over Molly's coat.

She called the woman an unpleasant name.

"C'mon," Molly said. "They catch you here, both of us'll be swinging in the breeze." She tugged. At length, Molly managed to drop the upper half of the tall blonde's body over her shoulder. Even managed to stand and stagger toward the borrowed mule. She never quite figured out how she got the woman draped over the packsaddle, didn't figure it would be comfortable, but that bung starter had likely sent this pretty little thing to another world for the rest of this evening.

Now all Molly had to do was get the lady and the mule as far away from the privies as she could. Get her to the wagon yard, convince the Bulgarian and Coleman that this was the right thing to do, the only thing to do, the Christian thing to do. Maybe she could tell the Bulgarian that the man this damsel had stabbed to death was a Turk. The Bulgarian, for some reason or the other, didn't care too much for Turks.

Turn the mule loose, get some shut-eye, see what happened outside Fort Kearny on the morrow.

She tugged the reins. The mule brayed.

"Your mind's gone," Coleman told her.

"No," Molly countered. "I—"

The Bulgarian interrupted. "She roll Major. Kill him. Kill him dead. That what they say in Dobytown."

Coleman added. "It's what they say at Fort Kearny, too."

Molly found the coffee, refilled her tin cup, then spit tobacco juice onto the coals. "That ain't what happened."

"It's what Cap'n Jessup says happened," Coleman said. "How do you know the major was trying to take advantage of this woman?"

Because . . . Molly didn't have a chance to make up a

good lie for the Bulgarian, who added, "She not even wake up. You hit her?"

"Yeah, I hit her. Scared the tar out of me."

"I told you not to go down that alley," Coleman reminded her.

"Look here," Molly said. "There's scratches on the woman's neck. Her blouse is ripped."

"Could be from the major defending himself," the Bulgarian said.

"We've made this haul too many times to count," she reminded her pards. "You know how Balsam worked. Remember that whore from eight months back?"

"Sergeant O'Brien said the major's watch was gone. And his revolver."

"So it would look like the sumbitch was robbed and killed. So they'd be looking for a man. Not a woman."

"A man," the Bulgarian said. "Like us."

"He had a poke on him, too," Coleman said. "Poke." He grinned. "Poke like a sack of money or gold dust. Not poke like . . ." The smile broadened. It might have been the best pun, or joke, or whatever the hell it was, Coleman had come up with in thirteen years west of the Missouri.

Molly's eyes rolled. "Those army boys aren't gonna be going after us. Not back to Leavenworth. And you leave it to me, and I'll have this petticoat looking worser than me. She'll pass for a man, sure as I'm sitting here."

"I don't know," the Bulgarian said.

"You want to let a bunch of vigilantes lynch a pretty girl? Well, I thought I rode with men. You want to turn her over, go ahead. I've made my play. But you've been riding for this outfit a trifle longer than me. It's your call, men."

The Bulgarian studied Coleman, who turned toward Molly. "What about the major's poke?"

Molly slipped her fingers inside the boot top, drew out the scrip, and waved it in front of her partners' eyes.

"We split even?" the Bulgarian inquired.

"Just like always," Molly said.

Coleman's head bobbed as he reached for the paper currency. Molly let him take it, but snatched a couple of bills from his fingers and held them up. "This is for the lady. She'll need some new duds. Men's clothing."

"What about her hair?" Coleman stared at the woman, still unconsciousness.

"While I'm at the sutler's, you cut it off. Short."

The Bulgarian sighed. "A shame. Pretty golden locks."

"Ain't it, though." After stuffing the scrip in her trousers pocket, Molly started for Dobytown.

CHAPTER SEVEN

"Looky here, youngster." The bearded man withdrew the meerschaum pipe, blew smoke toward the loft, and pointed the stem toward the stalls on the right. "What do you see there?" The wooden stem turned to the left. "Or there?" He stepped out of the barn and nodded in the general direction of the community of Summit, then gestured toward the cemetery, old mining claims, and the hills overlooking Virginia City. "Or anywhere?"

Mason Boone blinked. All he had done was ask the man if he had any work needed done. Boone wasn't quite sure when he had last eaten, and homemade liquor couldn't keep a body going forever.

"You know what I see?" the old man began.

Boone realized he had picked the wrong place to ask for a job.

"I see a big city that's missin' one thing: People."

He hacked, spit, and tapped the pipe's plain bowl on a hitching rail. "Ain't just here, boy, it's all up and down the Fourteen Mile City. Ever' camp from Alder to here and gone's seein' the same dad-blasted thing. Gold gets found up in Last Chance Gulch. Same ol' story, son. They find pay dirt on Grasshopper City, and Bannack City sprouts up overnight. But then when we find a bonanza here, in Alder Gulch . . . You been to Bannack lately? Know what you'd find if you done so? I'll tell you, boy. You'd find a big city without a whole lot of people. And now . . . we got folks lightin' a shuck up north to Last Chance Gulch. And that ain't a fittin' name for a minin' camp, boy. Last Chance? There'll be hundreds of other chances. Gold's everywhere. Hell, boy, folks here ain't just pullin' out up that way. Some are gallopin' over yonder way, to Emigrant Gulch by the Yellowstone. I've half a mind to flip a three-cent nickel, and if she turned up with the lady's head, I'd move northeast to Emigrant Gulch, and if she showed the three columns, I'd mosey up that way, to the Last Chance. And if she landed on her side, straight up, I'd move back to Bannack. Or Idaho. Or the Pikes Peak country. And if I had one iota of brains in my noggin, I'd just say to hell with it all and go back home to Springfield, Missouri. Most days, I wish I'd never left anyhow."

He sucked on the pipe, realized it was out, and shoved it into a pocket in his mackinaw.

The old man stared again at Boone, sighed, and asked, "Where you from, boy?"

"Texas."

"You traveled all that way . . . for this?"

Farther, Boone figured. He had deserted the 10th after Kennesaw Mountain. Still, he let his head bob a couple of times.

"Well." The big boots shuffled. "You asked to work. That says somethin' 'bout you. Most of the bummers just beg for enough to get a dram of beer. Man with a charitable streak could go broke. We ain't got a bad town. Not yet. Still the territorial capital, though I reckon we'll see how long that lasts. I've seen better-lookin' gents, though you might clean up if you'd shave and . . . Jesus . . . taken a bath. Wind must've just shifted directions. You stink worser than goat piss." He spit again, looked Boone up and down, and, at length, sighed. "I tell you what, buster, I ain't forgotten St. Vincent de Paul. Ain't much to muck, but you clean out the stalls, feed and grain the three horses I got here—but not the bay. Bay gets hay only. She don't take to grain. Probably a Kootenai pony, I don't know. Water 'em all. You do that, and I'll pay you two dollars."

Two dollars. Boone could hardly believe it. Two whole dollars for half a day's work. Then he recalled where he was and how much two dollars would buy a man in an expensive place like Virginia City. That might buy him as much as a three-cent nickel would back home in Tyler.

The man kept talking.

"You can sleep in the stall. No, no. Best not sleep in a stall. Stinkin' the way you do, you'd drive off any business that might come my way. Sleep in the loft. Back of the loft. It's warm enough up there. I'll see if I can't find an extra saddle blanket you can use. That suit you?"

Boone nodded.

"You get paid in the morn." The old man stiffened. "After I've graded your work. You do a pissant's job, you get a kick in the pants."

Boone remembered the first mine boss he worked for. And the second. All this codger had to say come morning was that the work wasn't up to his standards, now scat. But, hell, it was cold outside, and at least Boone had a place to sleep for the night. Mucking stables, feeding horses, that would at least take his mind off the emptiness in his belly.

"All right." Boone held out his hand.

The man stared at it, started to shake, but suddenly

stepped back, raising his hand, grabbing the brim of his slouch hat, and whipping it off his head.

"Missus Story," he said past Boone's shoulder. "It's mighty nice to see you, ma'am."

Mason Boone instantly detected the aroma of pies.

Turning around, he reached to remove the hat he had lost, realized his mistake, and took a step back, suddenly aware of just how ripe he was. Maybe . . . maybe he could take a bath in the livery. Without freezing to death.

"I have been looking for you," she said. He saw the pies on the tray.

"Take one," she told him, smiling.

She wore a dress of cornflower blue crinoline, striped with thin black lines. Beige hat. Dainty gloves. A black scarf tight around her throat, and a shawl of dark blue wool. He hadn't seen a dress like that since . . . since, well, he and some of the boys had purloined a copy of *Godey's Lady's Book and Magazine* back before Pumpkin Vine Creek, to admire the women pictured, not the latest fashions.

"Please," the woman said, and smiled. "A gift. An apology. Please."

His stomach grumbled audibly, and his face flushed with embarrassment.

"It's not a handout, sir," she said. "It's payment for . . ." Her head tilted toward his, which began to throb again.

"If you like, consider it a grubstake," she said.

Boone looked, swallowed, could not figure out what to do.

"It's peach," she said. "Not peaches from the States, but Salt Lake. Dried peaches, of course. That's about all I could find at Rockfellow's. No raspberries, no cherries, and he had just sold out of currants. I will not pay a dollar a pound for blackberries and detest canned fruits, especially when he's charging twenty-two dollars for a case of peach airtights."

She tried again. "Please."

His trembling right hand reached out and took the nearest pie. He almost dropped it. Swallowing, he looked briefly at the young woman, nodded, and stared at what remained of his brogans. "Thank you, ma'am," he whispered.

"You take care of yourself," she said. "And good day to you, Mr. Brill." Boone heard her lace-up shoes leave the boardwalk, cross the street, reach the other side of the road. After a few footsteps, her voice sang out, "Might I have your name, sir?"

Across the street, the angel stared at him.

"Boone, ma'am," he answered without thinking, a whisper at first, then he called out loud enough for her to hear. "Boone. Mason Boone."

"What a charming name, Mr. Boone. A good day to you, Mr. Boone. And to you, Mr. Brill."

He watched her walk to the corner, turn on to Wallace Street. A moment later, her fine voice called out, "Pies. Dried-peach pies. Five dollars. Pies. Pies. Fresh-baked pies."

"I'll be a clubfooted bastard," the old man whispered.

After lifting his gaze, Boone turned toward the livery owner, who fished the pipe from his mackinaw and fumbled in a shirt pocket for a match. "Today's your lucky day, Mason Boone. Five-dollar pie. And a two-dollar job. You ought to try your hand at faro over at Esterhouse's layout."

He started to strike the match, stopped, stared at the pie, then at Boone's face. "You ought not ruin that pie eatin' it with your filthy fingers. They's a spoon in my office. Top drawer on the right-hand side. Wash it when you're finished. I'm goin' to the Liquor Emporium. Today just ain't my day."

CHAPTER EIGHT

"Keep your hair on," Professor Thomas Dimsdale yelled at the tramp printer standing over the Degener & Weiler printing press in the back of the *Montana Post* office.

The Irish printer muttered an oath.

"Your job is to set type, Patrick, and run a proof. If anything is incorrect, I shall make the necessary corrections as I read the copy." He sighed, ran his fingers through his dark hair, and shrugged at Nelson Story. "Sorry, Nelson. You were saying?"

Story smiled and sipped the tea the editor had brewed.

"I said I've made a fortune in my mining investments."

The editor reached for the pencil that rested over his right ear.

"This isn't for you to print in the *Post*."

The young man's pale face seemed to drain of even more color.

"We're talking, businessman to businessman, friend to friend," Story told him.

"As you wish."

Story set the cup on the saucer. "The Monson, Julia

Ferina, Farragut, Oro Cache did well. The half interest I owned in Christenot's mine over in Pine Grove did fine, too."

"Bully for you." Dimsdale found the silk handkerchief in the pocket of his waistcoat and dabbed his mouth.

"But the pickings get smaller every day. Meaning my profits get smaller, too."

The Englishman sighed. "Alas, this is a story I hear wherever I travel up or down the Fourteen Mile City." He straightened, and spoke in alarm. "You don't mean to pull out of Last Chance Gulch, do you?"

"Not yet." Story's head shook.

"How's your store in Summit doing?" the professor asked.

Story let out a short laugh. "When you can charge nine dollars for a hammer, and no one tries to haggle, I'd say you're doing all right. But I came here to mine."

"And you have succeeded."

"Yeah. So far."

"If you mean that legislation being bandied about in Washington City, Nelson, I don't think you have much to fear. Justice Hosmer left to straighten out these foolish politicians. And others are joining him, not to quash a law that would make miners bid on claims they already, and rightfully, own—ridiculous, asinine, an absurdity—but to promote statehood. Imagine, Nelson. Virginia City, state capital of Montana. Not territorial."

"Are you smoking opium these days, Professor?"

The befuddled look on the journalist and schoolteacher's face bemused Story, who chuckled. Nelson Story, everyone in the territory would say, rarely attempted a joke.

"Oh, I see. But let me point out that Nevada got statehood just last year."

"Last year, we were fighting a war."

The handkerchief returned to Dimsdale's pocket.

"Paris Pfouts left for the East. Hoping to secure investments."

Story waited, and the Englishman continued. "There's money back East, Nelson. Lots of money. You should go to New York City. Philadelphia."

"I'm considering it."

"Is that for publication?"

"After I depart, you can print it. Not before. There are still some in the gulch who would like to see me dead. Robbing a stagecoach is a pastime for many banditti."

"Surely we have rid the Fourteen Mile City of the last of the nefarious brigands."

Story chuckled. "Professor, half the population of Virginia City still think I'm a nefarious brigand. N. G. Story. No Good Story." He nodded at the newspapers rolled up on Dimsdale's desk.

The editor studied the papers, confused, and looked back at Story.

"You read papers from all over the territories and the states, Thomas," Story explained. "Where do you think the money is?"

Now life returned to the newspaperman's eyes and his face seemed to flush. Dimsdale laughed heartily. "Nelson, you should never ask a newspaper editor for financial advice."

"That's the damned truth," the tramp printer yelled from the back.

Ignoring the Irishman, Story repeated his question.

Dimsdale sighed again, shook his head, and said, "I don't know, Nelson. There's grain. Farmers are moving into the Gallatin Valley. But that likely means the price of grain will decline, dramatically. And I don't believe farming is a wise investment. A hailstorm. A drought. Too much risk involved. Have you thought about opening a bank?"

"I *think* about everything."

"Well, what is it that you truly desire?"

"That Ellen didn't have to sell pies on the streets."

"I think she just does that for joy."

"A wife of mine should not have to work."

Dimsdale turned his head, probably because a professor like him, from England to boot, didn't understand Nelson Story's way of thinking.

"She's pregnant, Thomas," Story said.

The man whirled, stunned, blinking repeatedly. "And, no," Story told him, "you aren't printing that in your paper, either. What I'm looking for from you, old friend, is what all these newspapers you get are reporting. About what people want. About what's gonna make a man with ambition his pile."

When the Englishman stopped blinking, and after he found his piece of silk to dab his mouth, he sipped his own tea, swallowed, and said, "Nelson, a newspaper prints what its editor believes. If the name of the newspaper is the *Republican*, you can bet it's leaning toward the party lines. If its banner reads *Democrat*, there you have it. And if it says *Independent*, the editor is a damned liar."

"Yours says *Post*."

"Because that's what John Buchanan named it when he started this rag back in '64, and I was just too lazy to give it another name after I bought him out."

A silence filled the office, except for the printer as he set type.

"Professor," Story said after a long while. "You know me for what I've done since I came up here with Ellen. Want to hear my biography? I started college, never finished. My pa died. So did my sister. But that's not what I'm telling you. I freighted in Kansas. Chopped wood. Hauled wood. Hell, that's how I first met Ellen. I'd buy a calf and sell it, buy a hog and sell it. Clerked in a mercantile. Pushed a broom. Mule skinner. Sold fence rails, posts, worked for a farmer or two. Drove a wagon to Denver during the Pikes Peak rush. Tried mining. Tried selling stuff to miners. Even ran a mercantile. Did just about everything and hardly cleared a dollar."

"You've cleared more than a dollar now, Nelson."

"And I'd like to keep what I've earned. And make more. So my wife, when she's in the family way, doesn't have to sweat over an oven and walk the streets selling pies."

With a shrug, Dimsdale reached for the nearest rolled newspaper, tore off the wrapper, slid it out from the string, unrolled it, and laid it across his desk after moving the cup and saucer to the far side. He pointed. "This is the Galveston, Texas, newspaper, but this article is from a Dallas paper. Says Missourians and Kansans are ruining the beef market because of this egregious lie about Texas cattle killing off local cattle with something they call Spanish fever." His finger moved down the column, up to the top of the page, and partway down until stopping. "Here . . . no . . . this just decries the actions of the Freedmen's Bureau. What could you expect from an improvident Texas newspaper?" The finger moved again. "The pecans are lovely." He looked up. "Pecan pie. Oh, my, fresh pecans."

He slid the Galveston paper to Story and found another newspaper delivered by stagecoach. "Here. The *Tribune* from Chicago. Likely more reliable. Well, here's a report on the progress of the transcontinental railroad. Railroads, Nelson. Now there's something to consider."

"I think those railroaders would rob me blind before I knew what I was doing."

"I would not try to counter that argument. Beef prices are . . . interesting. I did not realize beef was in such demand."

Dimsdale leaned back in his chair, swiveled, and sighed as though he were dreaming of eating peach pie after a supper of beef à la mode. He pretended that the silk handkerchief was a napkin.

"When's the last time you ate a steak, Nelson?"

Story grinned. "That wasn't elk?"

Dimsdale returned to the *Tribune*, scanned down the column but stopped, and raised his head. "Did not you say one of your previous enterprises involved selling a calf?"

"Two calves," Story said. "Bull calves, to be precise."

"And you profited from this initiative?" the editor asked.

CHAPTER NINE

José Pablo Tsoyio tried to lift his face out of Texas caliche, but the sole of a boot pushed his head back into the gravel, then twisted, tearing out the old man's fine hair, bending his nose back and forth, ripping his lips even more.

"When I let you up," Big Bobby Cupid said, "you gonna go back to that cook shed and you gonna cook up something fit to eat. Like I hired you to do, greaser. You savvy that, Heliot Ramos?"

Heliot Ramos was the name José Pablo Tsoyio had chosen to use for this job. Perhaps had he picked another name . . .

The boot rose. Men chuckled. And Big Bobby Cupid moved away.

Slowly, José Pablo Tsoyio rolled over. The back of Big Bobby Cupid—now there was a man undeserving of his name. He was neither big, nor—definitely—Cupid. The Texan reached the porch of the bunkhouse, took the plate from the hands of the cowboy named Chase, and dumped the contents onto the earth. "This slop ain't fit for hogs," Cupid said as he turned around and tossed the plate. It landed on the side, spun, rolled, and toppled not far from José Pablo Tsoyio.

Chase and the three other cowhands laughed.

"Get up, bean-eater," said one of the men, a tall hombre who thought his mustache to be a masterpiece. He twisted its ends, then took the bottle of rye another cowboy passed his way. "And make biscuits this time. Your corn bread tastes like sand."

They laughed again, guzzling their whiskey, as José Pablo Tsoyio sat up. He wiped blood, sweat, and caliche from his face, spat out more blood, and tried to smooth and straighten his long, black and silver hair.

"Mis buenos amigos, perdóname . . ."

"No, no, no, no, no." Big Bobby Cupid shook his finger as though he were scolding a child. "We gone through this before. Speak English. You want to go back to your home country, you can speak all the Mex you want. But on my place, you talk English, boy. You savvy?"

Whispering, *"Nací a treinta kilómetros de donde me siento . . ."* he looked to the southwest, remembering his home, remembering when this country was, indeed, his own country, and when no one spoke English.

"What's that you just said, Heliot Ramos?" Chase asked.

"Nada. Nothing, my friends."

"Didn't sound like nothin'," said the pockmarked one with the powder burn on his right hand, the one whose name José Pablo Tsoyio could never remember, perhaps because he used so many. That caused a bloody smile to form on the old man's face. For likewise, José Pablo Tsoyio often changed his name with the seasons.

"I will cook your supper again," José Pablo Tsoyio assured the men, and spit out more blood.

"Be sure it's something fit for white folk to eat," Big Bobby Cupid said.

"And leave out your damned peppers," Chase said. "They give me the trots."

The *norteamericanos* laughed. The bottle made its way back to the curly-haired man who did not look like much, but was more than good with a running iron. Never had José Pablo Tsoyio seen a gringo so good at changing another man's brand as this youngster. An artist. He could have made a fortune working for someone other than Big Bobby Cupid.

"You got an hour," the boss man said. "And it better be good. Else we'll kick your ass all the way down to the border, and there's a passel of mesquite thickets between here and the Rio Grande."

Laughing, the men entered the adobe cabin, while José Pablo Tsoyio loosened his bandanna, wiped his face gingerly, and wondered how a man like him, who had ridden with pride as one of Don Sebastian Degallato's vaqueros for so many years, could wind up here, like this, on a hard-scrabble outfit working for pesos and being abused by ruffians with no manners, and no taste for fine cuisine.

Groaning, he tried to stand, couldn't, and had to crawl all the way back to the porch bunkhouse, where he used the railing to pull himself to his feet. He found his hat on the warped floor, dusted it off, set it gently on his aching head, and moved toward the cook shed, slowly, always limping. He stopped by the plate Big Bobby Cupid had tossed aside, and had to slide his right leg out before leaning down to pick up the tinware. And that, José Pablo Tsoyio knew, was why he was here, cooking for a place to sleep and maybe, *por favor*, a little money to get by instead of dressed in refined clothes, riding as gentlemen, as caballeros . . . dancing at the balls with the prettiest señoritas in the villas.

One bull. One horse wreck too many. One leg that could

no longer bend. One gringo who laughed once too often, only to lie on his back while trying to hold in his guts after the knife of José Pablo Tsoyio had ripped the fool from bowel to ribs, in San Felipe del Rio. And this is what had become of that magnificent caballero, José Pablo Tsoyio.

As the *norteamericanos* liked to say, "What the hell." José Pablo Tsoyio lifted his right leg through the opening of the cook shed and struggled inside.

Most days, José Pablo Tsoyio thought, have bad moments, but as long as you end the day with a prayer on your lips and remember that you are blessed by the Virgin Mary and her Son, you will not remember the bad things that have happened, only the good. And thus you will know that tomorrow might bring wonders you have never seen.

His mother often said that. Or something like that. José Pablo Tsoyio was too old to remember much of what his mother had said, but it sounded nice. Sounded wonderful. Like the stew he had been sweating over for the past thirty minutes. He brought up the ladle, sniffed, grinned, and set the ladle on the counter before moving outside, finding the cast-iron rod, and using it to lift the cover of the oven. Yes, the biscuits were ready. Browned on the top. He hoped they were cooked thoroughly, for the man named Chase was particular about biscuits. Ah, but only if a man like Chase, or any of those who rode for Big Bobby Cupid's rawhide outfit, could have tasted one of José Pablo Tsoyio's sopaipillas, then he would have understood what Jesus served his disciples at the Last Supper, and what awaited everyone who walked the streets of gold.

He moved back into the shed, found the heavy towel so he could lift the stewpot and limp his way from here to the

bunkhouse. There was a stove in the bunkhouse, but Big
Bobby Cupid said that stove was for heat—as though anyone
ever needed to warm up in this country of hell—and for
white men only.

Carefully, José Pablo Tsoyio moved out of the shed,
straining, limping, daring not to spill any of the mouthwa-
tering stew as he moved. Someone must have been watching, waiting, from inside the bunkhouse because Chase and
Big Bobby Cupid stepped outside and moved to either side
of the open door.

"Stop," Big Bobby Cupid said after José Pablo Tsoyio
managed to climb onto the rough porch. He obeyed the
order, and the big gringo stepped closer, looked at the cook's
battered face and then down into the pot.

"Smells good," Chase said.

Cupid spit into the pot.

"Jesus," Chase said.

Laughing, Cupid stepped back. "Why didn't you fix this
to begin with?"

"My apologies," José Pablo Tsoyio said.

"Yeah." Big Bobby Cupid turned and yelled, "Chow's on,
boys. Goat stew. With onions."

A rebel yell sang out from inside, and José Pablo Tsoyio
gingerly made his way to the heavy table, where he set the
pot on a pad. He moved toward the door.

"Where you goin', buster?" the magician with the running iron yelled.

"For your biscuits, compadres," José Pablo Tsoyio told
them.

"Biscuits. Hot damn. Biscuits and stew. Run fetch 'em,
Ramos. I'm practically starved."

José Pablo Tsoyio, alias Heliot Ramos, made his way
back to the Dutch oven, put the biscuits on a platter, and

returned to the bunkhouse. The biscuits were snatched up in a moment, but José Pablo Tsoyio found a bowl while the other men settled into their chairs and began to eat.

When José Pablo Tsoyio dipped the ladle into the remnants of stew, Chase said, "What are you doin'?"

Sadly, the old man turned. "I . . ." He offered the smile of the meek. "I am hungry, too, my friends. It has been a long day. A very hot day. I . . ."

"This meal is for white folks, greaser," Chase said.

Big Bobby Cupid laughed. "I think I left your supper out by the porch. In the dirt."

The men around the table giggled over their bowls. One dipped a biscuit into the stew, and bit off a chunk.

"Forgive me," José Pablo Tsoyio said. "I forgot."

"Yeah."

"Tastes good," one of the gringos said.

"Make sure breakfast is even better," Big Bobby Cupid said.

"Hey," one of the cowboys said, "you didn't bleed in this stew, did you, boy?"

"No." José Pablo Tsoyio's head shook. "No, señor."

"Good. I don't like blood in my goat stew."

"I don't care for spit in mine," Chase mumbled.

"Huh?"

"Nothin'."

"Well, go on, Ramos," the one with curly hair said. "Adios. See you in the morning."

After a slight bow, José Pablo Tsoyio stepped out of the bunkhouse and into the fading daylight. He looked at the barn, where he slept in the loft, and moved in that direction.

"Hey, you ignorant bean-eater," Big Bobby Cupid said. "Shut the damned door. I don't want flies in my stew."

"*Sí*. Yes." The right leg hurt as José Pablo Tsoyio turned around, limped, and pulled the door shut.

Slowly, he moved toward the barn, looking at the horses in the corral, picking the one he would take, the high-stepping dapple whose brand had been altered by that artist in the bunkhouse. José Pablo Tsoyio knew which saddle he would steal, too. Just before he stepped through the barn's open door, he glanced again at the bunkhouse. Studying the sky, he lifted his wooden crucifix, kissed it, thanked the spirits for their wisdom. Closing the door was a most wonderful thing, something José Pablo Tsoyio had not considered. He fingered his split lip, which no longer hurt so much, and went to the peg that held the good saddle, the saddle that would befit a caballero riding for Don Sebastian Degallato. Yes, this would do nicely. Even the stirrup lengths would not need adjusting. He climbed to the loft, gathered his gear, bedroll, stiletto, and the .44-caliber Dance revolver he had won in a game of Spanish monte.

Once back down, he moved to the corner of the door and looked toward the bunkhouse. To wait. Maybe till sundown. If no one came out by then, he would saddle the dapple and ride. North. Yes, north. North and perhaps he could go back to using the name his *madre* and *padre* had blessed him with: José Pablo Tsoyio.

If he thought about it, he would find a church on the ride north. A priest who would hear his confession. But not about what happened here, this evening, for José Pablo Tsoyio had not sinned. Closing the door had saved him from that mistake.

Imagine, he thought as he began to roll a cigarette. What a tragedy it would be for some coyote or wolf to be lured by the scents from the bunkhouse, enter, and eat the flesh of the dead men inside. Would the poison have also killed some poor, innocent animal?

José Pablo Tsoyio did not know. But now it did not matter, for it would not happen. Striking a match, he lighted his cigarette, inhaled, held the smoke, and blew a smoke ring toward the loft. The Dance rested on his lap. No sound came from the bunkhouse.

CHAPTER TEN

Mason Boone's eyes popped open, and he listened in the darkness, smelling hay, and himself—for he had voted against that bath, what with the snow coming down again— and decided he had been dreaming. He reached up, smoothed what he could of his mustache, and plucked something from the hair. Holding it between forefinger and thumb, he brought it to his nostril and sniffed.

That, he thought as he grinned, was not a dream. He popped the morsel into his mouth.

That black-haired woman sure knew how to bake a pie.

"Man's got a comeuppance coming."

The voice came from below. And this, Boone understood, was no dream. It belonged to Plummer with the Goatee. If the kid still donned theatrical makeup.

"We all got a comeuppance coming." That would be Sandy.

"Not as much as No Good Story," Plummer said.

"The McGees fought a good fight. They just lost. I ain't one for revenge, not when revenge can get me kilt." That voice, that was something new. Didn't sound like any one of the fools who had tried to stop the vigilance committee from stringing up those three criminals at the potter's field overlooking Virginia City. But Boone figured most of that crew had likely made a beeline for Canada, Fort Hall, maybe Tyler, Texas—as far away as they could get from a hangman's noose.

"This ain't about vengeance, boys," Plummer said. "It's about profit."

"Meaning?" That voice was spoken too softly, and the wind had started to pick up, so Boone didn't know if that came from one of the original gang, or some conglomerate.

Plummer didn't answer, or if he did, he just whispered.

"Well?" Sandy said.

A cork popped. Boone wondered what they might be drinking. Rye? Bourbon. Taos lightning. He frowned. *If those sons of bitches mess up that stall so that skinflint won't pay me my two dollars, I'll fix their flints something good.*

"He's cashing out," Plummer said.

"You mean he's leaving Vagina City?"

Chuckles echoed the joke.

"Leaving," Plummer said, "on the next stage for Salt Lake."

"This gossip?" one of the new voices said.

"Straight from the mouth of the mule himself," Plummer answered.

A snort and a laugh. "He up and tell you that directly?" Again, that was Sandy.

"I pay attention when I'm swamping a saloon," Plummer said. "I ain't just trying to earn enough for a meal."

"And a poke," one of the conglomerates added.

A few laughed. Plummer ended that with a savage curse.

"He was talking to Mr. Nowlan."

"The banker?" Sandy asked.

"Yep."

"Story didn't recognize you?" someone asked.

"Nobody pays mind to someone pushing a broom in a saloon," Plummer said.

"They ought to. Lucius Matthews collected a right smart of gold dust sweeping out saloons."

Again, Plummer cursed. His gang fell silent. "He's taking his gold, and most of his money, to New York City."

"Ain't the Salt Lake banks good enough for him?"

"If you peckerwoods read the *Post*, you'd know that every politician and businessman is bound east, trying to get the politicians to make Montana a state."

Someone laughed. "They'd do that in Washington City, pal, not New York."

"But the banks are in New York."

"Well, San Francisco's a mite closer," Sandy said.

"He ain't getting to San Francisco. Or New York. Or Salt Lake City. He's going to hell. And I'm gonna send him there. And all of us will be richer than kings."

Boone raised his right hand to his head, felt along the top, found the tender spot where Nelson "No Good" Story had tried to split his skull. He pictured the tall man, showing not a flitter of fear, moving from one wagon to another, kicking out crates, hanging three men. Boone didn't even know what the McGee boys had been accused of. His stomach seesawed.

A man like that, Boone thought, *wouldn't have skedaddled after Kennesaw Mountain.* He changed that thought. *If he was so brave, how come he has been up here during the whole damned war and not fighting for one side or the other?*

He smoothed his hair, grimacing a couple of times, and

brought his hand down his face, stopping at the end of his nose. He sniffed, but found no fragrance of dried-peach pie, just horse dung, straw, and the wretched stink of what had become Mason Boone.

"I don't know," someone was whining below the loft. Sandy. Boone recognized the voice. "We ain't never done nothing like this before. Nothing this . . . bold."

"Yeah," said one of the newbies. "I don't know, either."

"I do," Plummer said, and a revolver cocked.

"You done all this?" Old man Brill shook his head. "After I left? Your . . . ownself?"

"Yes, sir," Boone answered impatiently.

"Huh." The man spit into a bucket. "Well, I'd say that's two dollars' worth of cleanin'." He gestured to the office. "Come on inside, bub. I'll pay you in gold dust."

Once settled, Brill opened a drawer, pulled out a key, started to shut the drawer, laid the key on some papers, and withdrew the spoon. He held it up. "You wash this, too?"

"Yes, sir."

"Pie any good?"

"Yes, sir."

"You in a hurry, boy?"

"Yes, sir."

The spoon rattled as it fell back in the drawer, which the old man slammed, and muttered, "Ever'body these days is in such a dad-blasted hurry. All they're doin' is hurryin' 'emselves into a hole six foot deep." He rose, turned, and whirled around. "Close your eyes. Tight. All right. No peekin'."

Feeling like an idiot, Boone stood there, sighed once, but kept his eyes shut. Something rattled. The old man grunted.

Footsteps sounded, and metal slammed on wood. "All right, bub. You can look."

When Boone's eyes opened, he stared down the barrel of a Colt Dragoon. "Now, don't you try nothin' fancy, bub. I'm payin' you what I owes you, and that's it. You think you deserve a bonus, you'll get that in lead. Savvy?"

"All I want," Boone said steadily, "is two dollars."

"Comin' up." The man laid the cocked revolver by a tin box, found the key, opened it, and withdrew a pouch. Then he opened a larger drawer, slammed it shut, and cussed, "Where the hell did I leave 'em scales?"

Boone waited till what felt like February, but the man finally cried out, "Eureka," and brought the scales to the desk. He nodded at Boone and began tapping dust onto one side. Boone stepped closer, just enough, and kept his hands wide apart. Old Brill barely noticed, and Boone could have swept the Dragoon off the desk, crushed the old-timer's skull, and walked out with a fortune—a fortune anywhere but Virginia City. Instead, he watched the old man's thumbs. Just waited for Brill to cheat him. Like most of the bosses Boone had worked for in Montana Territory.

Finally, Brill dropped the pouch back into the tin box, pulled another pouch from another drawer, and carefully brushed the dust into it, after which, he drew the string and tossed the small pouch to Boone.

"Paid in full."

Boone just stared.

"Don't tell me you want a receipt."

Boone felt the pouch, looked at the scales, and finally at the old man, who shrugged and locked the box, tossed the key into a drawer, reached for the Dragoon, and lowered the .44's hammer.

"This is more than two dollars."

"Well, arithmetic never was my strong suit."

"I don't understand."

"Blame it on St. Vincent de Paul. And them damned nuns."

Boone blinked.

"You didn't take a bath," the old man said.

"It was too cold."

"You sleep all right?"

Boone shrugged.

"Well, there's enough in what I paid you for a bath. Maybe some clean duds. And money for breakfast. After that, I'd say you maybe have two dollars. You done a good job, boy. But you could save yourself some money if you was to take a bath here. I know, it ain't much. But it cleans me good enough. And don't think I'm some deviant. I'll be outside, watching this town dry up and blow away. Not lookin' at you, all envious, in your birthday suit."

Boone shook his head. "I don't understand."

"It's called charity, bub," the old man roared. "That's what St. Vincent is all about. It's because I'm an old man and a damned poor businessman. And this here place ain't never been so clean. Go on, I'm expectin' a busy morn'. Gonna count my farts. Get out of here. And stay away from the roulette wheels. But if you strike a fortune, come buy me out. I got me a hankerin' to see what Mexico looks like. Might be a good place to thaw out."

Numbly, Boone stepped outside. The blast of cold wind slapped the senses back into him, and he hurried toward Wallace Street.

CHAPTER ELEVEN

"Nelson?"

No answer. *Good*, Ellen Story thought, before she slipped through the doorway to their cabin, pulled the door closed, dropped the empty platter, pitched her pouch filled with profits onto the settee, and shed shawl, coat, hat, and gloves. The room spun, and she leaned against the rough log wall, praying for the dizziness to pass. She never would make it to the outhouse behind the cabin. She'd never even reach the winter kitchen. She tried for the fireplace, but barely got to the kindling bucket before dropping to her knees, bending over, and retching.

She had only her blouse sleeves to wipe her mouth, after which she lifted her head and stared at her cabin. It wasn't much. Spartan, like many Virginia City homes, but better than the tent they had in Bannack City after first reaching the territory back in '63. Anticipating the San Francisco of Idaho Territory, they had found a rough-hewn village practically deserted, causing Ellen to snap at Nelson. *Three months of suffering on the trail to come to . . . this?* This time, Nelson had reined in his temper before leaving to investigate, so eventually, they had followed the miners to this new strike in Alder Gulch.

"He don't drink," her father says. "Not much, nohow. Got a mind for business. Ambition enough for an army. And I see his eyes holding on you when he's loading wood for me. Worse men in Kansas, daughter."

"Are you trying to marry me off, Papa?"

"I'm just thinking aloud, daughter. Go bring him some water. He's sweating like a field hand."

The memory passed. She leaned forward toward the bucket, but this time, God spared her the ignominy of vomiting on kindling.

Everyone in the Fourteen Mile City proclaimed Nelson Story as one proud man, ramrod straight, utterly fearless, but few understood just how deep Ellen's pride reached. So the last thing she wanted to hear was someone tapping at the front door. God help her, she prayed whoever stood outside had not heard her gagging and vomiting and, being neighborly, just wanted to check on her.

Dear Lord, her silent prayer continued, *send this visitor somewhere else. Please, in all your mercy, spare . . .*

The door pushed open. "Anybody home?" a voice drawled.

"Ohhhh." The groan was audible. The door had failed to close all the way. She had been in too big a hurry.

Ellen wanted to die. Instead, she dropped her head and vomited. Again.

Shaving tonic almost gagged her, and she started to slip into a void, but strong hands caught her. Squeezing her eyes shut, she swallowed down bile and made herself look into the face of a young man, clean-shaven except for a mustache.

"Ma'am, I got to get you to a doctor," the man said. Dark eyes. Like her own. But brown hair, not black.

"No," she managed. "I'm fine."

"You're sick, ma'am."

"It'll pass. It's . . ." Well, there was no need to bore a total stranger with any particulars. And if Nelson happened to come in, he'd thrash the man before she could explain what was happening.

What was happening? What was a complete stranger doing in her house? Maybe . . . perhaps . . . yes, he must have been passing by when he heard the . . .

Ellen almost vomited again.

"I'm gonna get you . . ."

"The chaise." Feebly, she gestured.

The stranger's head turned. She whispered, "Just get me there."

He lifted her and carried her to the daybed, that wedding present from her father, of burl walnut and yellow fabric. Nelson had wanted to sell it in Denver, for it had taken up most of the tent they had pitched on their journey west, but her will could best his on particular points. The stranger, knight, figment of her imagination, he eased her onto the sofa, resting her head on the side. His knees were on the rug, and she saw the top of his head.

"Oh. I know . . . you're . . ."

"Can I get you something to drink, ma'am?" he asked as he rose, still on his knees, but straightening. "You got brandy?"

"Water, maybe." Her breathing had not steadied. "Pitcher. Table."

When he moved toward the dining table, she tried to get up, to run for the door, but she couldn't even lift an arm. He was back, tin cup in his hand, and he held it toward her. She smiled weakly, and he understood, sat on the edge of the chaise, lifted her head, and brought the cup to her lips.

"Thank you," she said.

"You're welcome." He looked around the cabin. To see what was worth stealing? Not much. No money here, not enough worth stealing, anyway. No weapons. About the only thing of value Ellen happened to be lying on. In the cabin, Nelson had finally gotten around to tacking muslin, smoothed and stretched, on the inside walls, to hide the logs, make it look like these walls were plastered. And sometimes it did seem that way, but only in darkness. When you were bone-tired. Other homeowners had put up false fronts outside of their houses, some had managed to add columns, or what resembled columns, and arches. A few had nailed medallions.

The man's dark eyes landed back on Ellen. He still held the hat, a new hat, hardly a speck of dust on brim or crown, in his left hand.

He wore tan woolen trousers stuck inside tall boots, a blue shirt, and a long woolen scarf—maybe a sash used as a scarf—of reddish orange with thin white stripes trimmed in blue. She couldn't tell if he wore a vest, or a gun belt, for the double-breasted, maroon greatcoat remained buttoned. As her father had once told Nelson, "You clean up pretty good, young fellow." She was about to tell him that when she felt it. She gasped, her eyes widening, and brought her hands to her stomach.

"I'll fetch a doctor . . . or somebody." The man's hat slipped to the rug, and he started to rise, but she grabbed his arm with her left hand.

"No."

"You're sick."

"It'll pass."

Feeling it again, suddenly giddy with excitement, she

brought his hand to her stomach. "Wait," she ordered. "Do you feel it?"

"Ma'am?"

"There." She laughed, and from the look in his dark eyes, she knew he had felt it, too.

"He kicked. He kicked. That's as hard as he has kicked yet."

The man's face lost all color, and he let his hand slip from her stomach and drop to his side.

"You're . . ." He could not finish.

"Don't you think it felt like the kick of a son?"

Now he sprang to his feet. "I'll get you . . . midwife . . . doc . . . ummmm . . ."

"No." She laughed as though forty days had passed since she had thrown up. "It's not time yet." Tears of joy welled in her eyes. "It is the kick of a son."

He stared at her with a child's eyes.

"How's your head?"

"Ma'am? Oh." His right hand went toward his scalp. "Fine. I reckon."

"You look well."

"Ummmm."

"Did you like the peach pie?"

He blinked. His lips parted. Closed. He glanced out the door he had left open, too. "It was . . . good. Real . . . good. You . . . you want me . . ." He gestured vaguely. "Close the door?"

"No, not yet. The cool air feels good."

"It's getting colder."

"I'm not an invalid. Just morning sickness. You wouldn't understand such things."

"No, ma'am."

She brought her right hand over toward him. "We have yet to be introduced properly. My name is Ellen. Ellen Story."

"Yes, ma'am. I know."

She waited.

He looked at her hand, glanced out the open door, and rubbed his hand against the coarse wool of the greatcoat before swallowing her tiny hand in his giant one. He wet his lips.

"Boone," he said. "Mason Boone."

"It's a pleasure to make your acquaintance, Mason Boone."

"Yes, ma'am."

"Might I have another sip of water?"

He knew she was stalling—of that she had no doubt—but he raised her head, let her drink, and lowered it gently on the cushioned side. "Ma'am," he said, "I'm looking for your husband."

"He is not here."

He waited more than he needed to, but when he knew for certain she had no intention of adding anything else, he said, "Well, ma'am, might you happen to know where he is? It's quite important."

Nelson, she realized, would never have shown this much patience. Those brown eyes, she thought, so deep, mysterious. The baby kicked again. She smiled.

"It's a boy," she told him. "I know it."

"I'm sure he will be, ma'am."

Back on the farm in Platte County, Missouri, before they had moved off to Leavenworth, friends had told Ellen that her eyes were blacker than the pits of Hades, with not an ounce of kindness showing in them. Her eyes, it was said, could scare a drunkard to sobriety or a sober person to drunkenness. But his . . . she found safety in those deep brown eyes.

"I mean him no harm, ma'am." He drew in a deep breath, exhaled. "But I really need to find him."

Trust someone, she told herself. She frowned. She had trusted Nelson Gile Story, and look where that had gotten her. But the baby kicked again, and she regretted such mean thoughts about her husband. She made the mistake of looking up at Mason Boone again.

"He's leaving town," she said. "Taking the stagecoach to Salt Lake City."

The man rose. "Would you happen to know what time that stage is leaving town, ma'am?"

She answered with a shrug.

"Or . . . where the stage leaves from?"

"Down Wallace Street," she said. "Big sign. Next to the mercantile."

After pulling on his hat, he took the cup and refilled it from the pitcher on the table, brought the cup back, setting it gently in her hand. "You sure you don't need a doctor, ma'am?" he asked.

"I'm fine, Mr. Boone. Thank you."

"Yes, ma'am. Should I close the door for you?"

"That would be nice of you, sir."

When she heard the door begin to close, she called out, "I hope to see you again, Mr. Boone."

But he did not answer. The door settled snugly, and she heard the sound of his boots until the crunching of snow ceased.

CHAPTER TWELVE

The pong of sizzling salt pork made Constance Beckett bilious, but a sudden terror removed any chance of throwing up. She opened her mouth to scream—yet only a soft gurgle rose from her lips, and her lips burned with pain.

Her heart pounded. She felt cold, clammy, but imagined beads of sweat popping out on her knotted brow. She pictured the beads, red like blood, and that reminded her of . . .

She tried to sit up, but couldn't. Swallowing down bile and fear almost left her gagging. Her throat felt raw, as though someone had crushed her voice box. She tried to talk again, but couldn't.

Where was she?

In a wagon. That much was certain. The canvas tarp overhead popped in the wind. She couldn't move to see what lay in front of the wagon, but through the oval opening in the back saw the grayness of . . . of . . . of . . . Nebraska. Fort Kearny. The pounding inside her head rang out like a smithy's hammer, and she reached up to touch her skull with trembling fingers. A bolt of pain shot from her head down her spine, and she gasped.

Once she could breathe again, found feeling in her fingers, she realized something was wrong. Trembling, she probed the rest of her head.

Her hair.

What had happened to her hair?

Voices interrupted that thought, outside, probably by the fire where someone was ruining a piece of salt pork—if any piece of salt pork had not already been ruined. Her throbbing head prevented much focus on what anyone near the wagon had to say. She looked to her left, carefully, and saw an empty sack, a bedroll. Moving her head or eyes more would have killed her, so she just stayed like that, and slowly began to realize that her hair was not the only thing missing.

What happened to my clothes?

Her right hand drifted down to find hard duck trousers. Fingered a heavy woolen shirt. She couldn't see her feet, but from the feel she knew those black sateen lace-ups purchased at Mr. Miller's store in Nashville were history. Coarse woolen socks between her feet and the leaden weights someone had nailed into her heels itched like mad.

Hoofbeats clopped outside. *Maybe,* Constance thought, *I am to be rescued.* If only her throat, her mouth, could make some noise. She tried. Nothing.

A conversation began outside. She tried to sit up, but that just sent her back onto the thin woolen blanket her captors must have thought would feel like a bed. It felt like iron.

"Captors," she mouthed, and slowly understood. *I have been kidnapped.*

"Murdered, you say?"

The raw voice outside numbed her.

"And robbed."

"No fooling?" the first voice, nasal but musical, sang out.

"Dupree said the major had maybe a hundred dollars on him when he left Taggart's."

"You bluecoats got paid already?" another voice drawled.

"Hell, no. Listen, I ain't standing here bandying words in this teat freezer. Y'all seen anybody?"

"Anybody?" The nasal voice laughed. "We seen everybody, Lieutenant. Which in Dobytown and Kearny in December ain't a whole lot."

"McDonald, you and Major Balsam weren't exactly on the best of terms," this lieutenant said.

"Because Major Balsam was a cock—"

Constance Beckett's mouth dropped open. "Not only that," the nasally man continued, "he was . . ."

Her blush deepened. And turned pale an instant later.

Balsam. Major Balsam. Major Warner Balsam. That's when she remembered. Which caused her to scream.

But no sound came out. She turned her head and began sobbing without control, wishing she could forget.

WANTED: *Correspondence*

A simple enough request, an advertisement she had seen in the *Nashville Daily Union*. She had even asked the reverend at the Congregational church what he thought, if it would be proper for a widow like herself to correspond with a complete stranger. Her memories galloped ahead of their correspondence, his love of Tennyson, her fondness for Byron, her life in Tennessee, his in Iowa, her work with the church and children orphaned by the recent unpleasantness, his love for duty and his command in the 7th Iowa Volunteer Cavalry.

Could she fall in love with a soldier who had fought against her late husband?

Well, it turned out that Major Balsam's command had seen no action against the Confederacy. Mustered in in 1863, Balsam had been sent north to the Dakotas to campaign against the Sioux. Later, Balsam's command was stationed at Fort Kearny on the Oregon-California Trail in Nebraska Territory. He wrote about watching the cranes in the Platte River, the buffalo, the savage Indians, people and more people migrating westward. He wrote that he would be overjoyed if she might travel west. He proposed marriage.

She talked it over with the reverend and with her closest relative, even though Aunt Charlotte despised the color blue, the Stars and Stripes, anything Yankee. Yet Aunt Charlotte told Constance, "Warner seems like a nice young man. He might help you forget about Leland."

Who, please God, did Warner hire to write those letters? Surely this could not have been the same man.

The conversation by the fire—the scent of salt pork no longer prevalent—snapped her from her memories.

"Ain't getting any argument from me on that matter, Lieutenant. If Major Balsam's face was to catch fire, I would have put it out with an ax. But I surely wouldn't stick a knife in his heart. Cut his throat, maybe? Cut off his balls? Well, if I thought he had any."

The officer said, "Perhaps I should search your wagons."

Constance looked through the opening. No place to hide in this freight wagon, but could she roll over, move to the driver's box, hide . . . ?

"Help yourself, Lieutenant. But if you find a low-down skunk of a man-killer, can we split the reward for the capture of that son-of-a-bitching asshole killer?"

The wind made the lieutenant's reply incomprehensible.

The nasally voice chuckled. "How come I ain't surprised? You hear that, Coleman? There ain't no reward posted for the capture or killing of the major's murderer. Yeah, I bet it would be damned hard to get anyone to put up even a Pawnee scalp, popular as Balsam was."

Constance heard the lieutenant's profane response.

"If you gonna search the wagons, get to it, bub," the person Constance guessed to be Coleman interjected. "So I can have another cup of coffee. If you ain't . . ."

Saddle leather squeaked, traces and spurs sang out, a horse snorted, one must have bucked, and the lieutenant gave some command that Constance could not understand. The sound of hooves moved away, and now, through the oval opening in the wagon, Constance could see dusty, blue-clad soldiers trotting away. She mouthed her thanks to Jesus and God for her deliverance.

By the campfire, the blasphemous bullwhacker shouted at the retreating soldiers: "Hey, Gibbons. If you capture the fellow who gutted Balsam, bring him to Leavenworth. That way, before y'all hang him, we can give the son of a bitch the medal he deserves."

From cold, relief, tension, fear, revulsion . . . a combination? . . . Constance began to shake. After trying to lift her head, to make sure the bluecoats were indeed returning to Fort Kearny and not doubling back to drag her out of the wagon, kick her to the gallows, and stretch her neck before she could tell them why she had killed Major Balsam, Constance tried to control her breathing. Her head propped on the blanket and wood. Through the opening, she saw only the cold gray of Nebraska. The voices of the man who spoke through his nose and his companions had stopped.

The image of Major Warner Balsam suddenly filled the opening. Big, bearded, breath stinking of tobacco and whiskey. This man knew nothing of Byron or Tennyson; he understood only brutality. As soon as Constance realized this, she had asked him for money to buy passage back to Nashville.

That was the first time he struck her.

Then . . . she had wanted to kill herself.

A week later, Balsam said he was tired of her, but he knew she still might fetch a decent price at Charlie's cribs, so he was dragging her out of the laundresses' quarters and into Dobytown—the miserable village of soddies and earthen buildings in a raw, ugly country where the cold burned your skin, stiffened your hair, and stopped blood from flowing.

When he shoved her against the privy's door and put his tongue in her ear, saying something about one more trip for memory's sake before she whored herself to death, she spit in his face. He slapped her savagely, kneed her savagely between her legs, doubling her over. She had reached out to break her fall, landed against him, laughing, and found the wooden handle of something sheathed in his boot top. When he jerked her to her feet, the weapon came out of his boot. He pushed her against the privy. She tried to scream, but his big hand grabbed her throat and began to squeeze. Harder. Harder. She could not breathe. She could barely see him. He pressed his palm tighter. He laughed.

God, she remembered praying.

And He gave her strength. And Major Warner Balsam looked down and now saw the knife in her hand, yet still he laughed. He dared her, "Use it, bitch."

Then his hand fell from her throat, and he staggered back.

And that was all she remembered.

Yet it must have been a dream. The knife. The major. The man with the nasal voice and a vocabulary that was 79 percent vulgarities, and the salt pork, and the lieutenant saying that the major had been murdered.

Because Major Warner Balsam had climbed into the back of the wagon. And Constance Beckett screamed and wanted to keep on screaming till a nasal drawl silenced her.

"Shut up, woman, or Lieutenant Gibbons and his boys will be loping back here and you'll be lynched before sundown." The voice added profanity Constance had never heard, even from Balsam's lips.

"That's better."

A little man squatted beside her.

"The Bulgarian is brewing some tea," the runt said. Maybe that meant something. Perhaps he spoke in code. "Coleman's hitching the teams, and we should be lighting a shuck in fifteen, twenty minutes. That'll give us time to get acquainted. I'll talk." He pulled out a writing tablet and a pencil. "You can write. I trust you learned your letters and such. If not, well, I'll teach you Injun sign. So here's the deal. I'll speak first. You're coming with us to Leavenworth, Kansas. It ain't that I want you owing me your life. It ain't that I figure I can get half your earnings because I know you killed Major Horse's Arse. Let's just say we're two peas in a pod, lady. You can call me McDonald. Mickey McDonald. And I know it ain't polite, at least not here on the frontier, but what the hell can I call you?"

CHAPTER THIRTEEN

He walked over to the Eagle Corral on the corner of Jackson and Cover streets, to ask Foster how much he was getting for beef, so Foster showed him the three corrals—empty. "How much would you pay for a steer?" Story asked.

"Same rates as horses, mules, oxen, and donkeys," Foster answered.

"I mean if you had a steer to sell?"

Foster rubbed his chin. "Well, selling steaks isn't what we do for a living. This is a livery. Not a butcher shop. Or the Stonewall Store." His expression changed. "What do you mean by *steer*?"

"You run a livery and a cattle yard, Foster. You know what a steer is."

"You giving up gold for cattle, Story?" The liveryman chuckled. "Thinking about becoming a rancher? No profit in that. Tried my hand in Texas. Learned my lesson. That's why I went into the livery business."

Story hadn't expected that bit of background. "Where in Texas?"

"Southern tip of Tarrant County. South of Fort Worth."

"Good cattle town, Fort Worth?"

"Well, you got to understand, Story, there wasn't much

of a market for cattle in Texas. Not back when I was there. Hides. You sold the hides to a tannery and ate the beef. That's changed some now, I hear. Got a letter from a cousin who went up the Shawnee Trail with a neighbor. Through Dallas, across the Indian Territory, into Missouri. Planned to sell a hundred head." He stopped and blew out a long breath.

"Planned?" Story asked.

"You were in Kansas, Story. You remember bush-whackers and Jayhawkers during the war. Well, Missouri-ans jumped the drovers, killed two, took the herd. Like I say, I'm glad I got out of ranching. And if you're thinking about bringing cattle to Montana, you'll want to stay out of Missouri and Kansas. Which will be damned hard to do, because most of the cattle you'll find is in Texas. You seri-ous about ranching?"

"I'm thinking about diversifying my interests. Cattle markets are good in Kansas City, better in Chicago. And I bet a man could do right well with a herd in the Gallatin Valley."

"By Jehovah, Story, you sound serious."

"Ever heard me tell a joke, Foster?"

The man studied Story harder. "Wait till I tell Culver about that. Nelson Story. Rancher."

"Now, you haven't answered my question. How much would you pay for a steer?"

"To eat?"

Story nodded.

"Whatever the professor over at the *Post* says beef's sell-ing for in Chicago, we'd match that, I'm sure. Then Culver and me would quadruple the price and sell it to Solomon Star, who'd triple that price before he sold it out of his store. Like I said, Story, it's economics."

"And what would you pay for a steak?"

"You mean a beefsteak that didn't come from an ox that broke its leg and got butchered by a freighter or neighbor?" He laughed. "Top dollar, man. Top dollar."

"Well, Foster, that's good to know." Story started figuring how many head the three cattle yards would hold, how much Foster and Culver would really charge him, and how much he could charge to sell steers to Mr. Star, or Mr. Rockfellow's store on Jackson Street, and every restaurant in the Fourteen Mile City.

The man slapped his livery apron. "You really think you could get cattle here, Story?"

"If there's profit in it," he answered.

"Story, you're a wonder. But are you a betting man?"

"Only on sure things."

"What I figured. See, I was thinking about betting that you won't have beef to sell in Virginia City by the end of next year."

"How much?"

The liveryman blinked. "Well, five hundred dollars?"

"Double it." He held out his hand.

Foster's Adam's apple bobbed. "I mean, more than one steer. Real cattle. Not an ox. And not something you brung in from Fort Hall."

"I'll make it specific. A Texas longhorn."

The Adam's apple stopped moving. Foster rubbed his palms on the apron. "No, no, not for a thousand dollars. One longhorn. Some dern fool might bring one up on a boat."

"Minimum of twenty. Driven by me right down Wallace Street." Story's right hand had not moved once during the conversation.

Foster chuckled. "Story, it's a pleasure doing business with you."

* * *

Sitting in the Concord, waiting for the jehu to get the mules moving, Story thought about that conversation. And what Ellen would say if she learned he had bet a thousand dollars that he could get a herd of cattle up here before the start of 1867, a little more than a year. He was already out $350 for the price of a ticket on Ben Holladay's stagecoaches that would take him as far as Atchison, Kansas. That included up to twenty-five pounds of luggage—for Story, two grips stored in the coach's rear boot—but not the strongbox on the floor. No way in hell, Nat Stein had told him at the station, would Holladay insure or be responsible for any gold bullion, dust, or notes from either a bank or the Treasury. Stein said they'd store the box up top. *Over my dead body,* Story had countered. After all, Stein had already assured Story that this strongbox was Story's responsibility, not the Benjamin Holladay Stage's.

Three of the four male passengers stared at the padlocked box on the floor of the Concord. Story didn't figure his boots, resting atop the iron box, interested the men. The box didn't, either. They wondered what would be inside such a box. The fourth man looked at the woman by the window, but Story knew the banker, and the banker already knew what was in the box. The woman focused her attention on the crack in the leather curtain, probably to avoid cigar smoke fogging the coach's interior. The banker smoked the cigar.

Story stared ahead, his arms folded, the pair of holstered Navy .36s in plain view.

He exhaled with satisfaction as the jehu called down, released the brake, and lashed out at the mules. The Concord pulled forward. Everybody moved. The strongbox didn't.

Bannack City, Boise, Salt Lake City. That would be the first leg. In Salt Lake, he would take another Holladay stage. Once in Atchison, he could cross the Missouri River to Winthrop, then ride the Hannibal & St. Joseph Railroad east and start making his way to New York. It was, he understood, a long way to carry a box containing 140 pounds of gold. At the going rate of $18.93 a troy ounce, that would total better than $40,000.

Almost as soon as the coach had started rolling, it slowed to a stop, and the driver called out, "That's a good way to get run over, boy."

"I need to speak with one of your passengers."

Swearing, the banker tossed his cigar out of the window.

"You best write a letter, boy, because I got a schedule to keep. Out of my way, or you'll be tastin' Habakkuk's and Zephaniah's hooves."

"Then I'll ride with you."

"Not without payin'."

"Here."

The woman sighed in irritation. The man closest to the door swore, then removed his hat and apologized to the woman. Story kept listening.

"Bub, as puny as this poke is, you won't get no further than the first station before Bannack City."

"That's fine with me."

"Get in, and be quick."

The coach was already moving, the door banging open, and a man in a black hat and greatcoat the color of a good Madeira gripped the sides and swung up, tried to pull himself in. The coach turned sharply to the road toward Nevada City. Story figured the man would fall out then, but only his hat rolled off, and that fell to the floor and stopped beside the strongbox at Story's feet.

One of the men yawned. The other grinned. The banker ignored the dark-headed man as he tried to pull himself inside.

"Won't someone help this wayfarer before he breaks his neck?" the woman said softly.

Outside from the driver's box, the jehu cursed, snapped his whip.

Story considered helping the man, but the one closest to the door reached over, grabbed the tawny coat, and jerked the man inside. The wayfarer fell with a thud, gasped, pushed himself into a seated position on the floor, and found his hat. He nodded at the woman, turned to thank the man who had jerked him inside the coach, while the banker mumbled something underneath his breath, before leaning over and slamming the door shut.

The newcomer started to get up, to find a seat, but before he could inch his way up, Nelson Story reached across his body with his right hand to draw the Navy Colt on his left hip from the holster. He thumbed back the hammer and aimed the long barrel at the young man's nose.

CHAPTER FOURTEEN

"Speak your piece."

Mason Boone looked above the barrel of the revolver and at the man holding it.

The woman gasped.

"Nelson," said a well-dressed gentleman by the window. "How do you know this stranger desires an interview with you?"

The Navy's barrel waved just a bit.

"That gash atop your head gave you away." Story's smile revealed no mirth. "Next time, buy a hat that fits tight."

The stage slid in the snow, and everyone lurched to the other side of the Concord before it straightened.

"Well," Story demanded.

Straightening and lowering the dainty handkerchief, the woman came to Boone's rescue. "Sir, this man has paid his fare and appears to be unarmed. Surely you remember your Bible, sir. This horrible country may be without law, but it is not without God."

"I'm well aware of the Golden Rule, ma'am." Neither the Navy nor Story's eyes wavered. "Do unto others, but do it first."

Gasping, the woman quickly paled and bounced up and down when the coach's right-front wheel hit a rock of substantial size.

When the coach stopped swinging on its thorough braces, Boone still found himself staring down a revolver barrel.

Hell's fire, Boone thought, *this is what I get for trying to be a Good Samaritan. About to get my brains splattered across a stage being driven by a crazy old fart, and even if I don't get murdered, I'll have a long walk in the bitter cold from the swing station to wherever I wind up.*

"This stagecoach is going to be robbed," Boone said.

"Not by you," Story told him.

"I came to warn you," Boone said.

"Why not warn the driver? Or Nat Stein at the station? Why wait till we're leaving town?"

"Because the men who plan to rob the coach also plan to kill you."

Something flickered in Story's eyes, but the gun remained steady.

"And you know this because . . . ?"

"I slept in a loft at a livery last night, maybe early this morning. They were downstairs—"

"Who?"

Boone started to answer, but the banker cut him off. "Christ's sake, Story, he was in the loft. He couldn't have seen them, in the dark. And I haven't seen this gent in town."

"You might have," Story answered. "I wouldn't have recognized him if not for the split I put in his skull. How'd you get cleaned up? Roll a drunk? Rob a store?"

"They were friends of the McGee brothers," Boone answered.

Story's eyes narrowed, and he nodded.

"Which livery?" the man asked.

Boone had to think. "Brill," he said.

"That figures," one of the male passengers said. "That crazy old coot isn't particular about who he lets put a horse in one of his filthy stalls."

"They're not filthy now," Boone said.

That caused something else to shine in Story's eyes. The hammer clicked, then lowered as Story brought up the Colt's barrel and rested it on his thigh.

"Where's the robbery to occur?" he asked.

"The leader didn't say."

"It could be a ruse, Story," the banker said. "He gets inside, so they have someone inside the coach."

"How many road agents have you known to pull something like that?" one of the other men said, as he reached inside his coat and withdrew a hideaway gun. "If it's one of the old McGee gang, they'd hit us at the slide rock—like every other bandit who has held up one of our stages."

"My goodness," the woman said.

Story looked at Boone.

"You fight in the war?" Story asked.

Boone nodded.

"North or South?"

"Texas."

"Which regiment?" the gent with the hideaway gun asked.

"Tenth Cavalry."

"Hood's Brigade?" the man asked.

"No. We were assigned to Ector."

Now the hideaway gun pointed at Boone's left eyeball as the man told Story: "He's a liar. I was an adjutant in the 7th Texas Infantry under John Gregg. He took over the brigade after Hood got shot all to hell at Chickamauga. The 10th got transferred to our brigade after Atlanta."

Hell, Boone thought, *even when I tell the truth I get guns stuck in my face.* Story was considering him, but his revolver remained pointed at the coach's door. "I wouldn't know about that," Boone said. "I quit after Kennesaw Mountain."

The man with the hideaway pistol leaned back, and his face began to redden. "You . . . deserted . . . ?" He raised the hideaway gun to drive the butt deeper into the gash Story's Navy had carved, but his colleague grabbed the man's arm, while Story's Navy began to move in the general direction of Gregg's former adjutant.

"Hell, Billy Ray," the man's partner said, "I wish to hell I had flown the coop after Sharpsburg."

A calmness settled over the coach. The woman managed to whisper, "Should not we warn the driver and guard?"

"We got a ways before we get to the slide rock, ma'am," Story said.

"But what if they decide to ambush us before we reach the slide rock?" the banker asked.

"They won't," Story said. "If they rode with the McGees, intelligence and ingenuity are not in their makeup."

Boone decided to ask a question. "What did you do during the war?"

Story said, "Taught school some."

Billy Ray's partner laughed. "Not in Texas, from how you talk."

"Ohio," Story said. "Kansas."

"I hear Kansas was bloodier than Franklin, Tennessee," the levelheaded friend of the one with the hideaway gun said.

"I have no interest in politics or history." Story leaned closer to Boone. "Why do you want to help me? That's the puzzlement I have. If I got my head split open, I'd want revenge."

"I'll give it back to you with interest." Boone didn't mean

to spit out the words with such anger, but could not stop himself. Hell, now he wished he had never deserted the Cause. He could have avoided that long hard journey from Georgia to Montana, could be cracking pecans and sipping corn liquor back home in Tyler. "But . . ."

Story waited for the answer Boone could not give. *But . . . your wife . . .*

"A few more questions," Story said, and the Navy began moving back toward Boone's face. "I ran errands all day. You could've tracked me down long before I got on this stage. What took you so long to warn me?"

"I was busy," Boone said. "Haircut. Shave. Dinner. Duds. It took me a while to decide maybe your life was worth saving."

"That sounds honest. But I didn't buy my ticket from Nat Stein till today. How'd you . . . and how did McGee's morons know I was leaving town this afternoon?"

Boone wasn't about to mention his visit with Ellen Story, although part of him thought Story might like to know his wife was sick. No, that would take too much explaining, and Story did not like long explanations. Besides, Story's question had given him an alternative to the truth.

"I saw one of the men from the barn on a horse kicking up mud down the road. Then I asked . . ." He took a chance. ". . . the newspaperman where you were. So I ran down here and stopped the stage."

"Convenient." The Navy cocked again, and the barrel moved to Boone's nose. "But you said you didn't recognize the boys who were talking about killing me while you were spying on them in the loft."

"I didn't recognize him from the loft." Mason Boone had never thought so fast, but a .36 caliber revolver six inches from one's head made a man a real quick thinker. "I recognized him from the hanging the other day."

Story raised the barrel slightly and told the banker, "Holler up and have them stop this coach."

When the banker complied, the jehu shouted back, "Piss up a rope. I got a schedule."

The Navy roared in Story's hand, filling the coach with white powder, and punching a hole in the roof.

"Halloran," Story thundered above the driver's and messenger's yells, "you stop this rig right now or the next ball goes up your asshole."

CHAPTER FIFTEEN

"You're chickenshit," Story told the jehu.

"And you're a hard-ass," Halloran fired back, "but I'm a livin' chickenshit, and I intend to go on livin' as long as I can. So I ain't drivin' myself up to slide rock. Been held up enough times by road agents. Don't aim to get kilt if I can help it."

"Then I'll drive," Story said.

"They'll recognize you," the banker pointed out.

Story frowned at the banker. "I take it you'll wait here, too?"

The banker smiled. "Someone has to protect this lady from New Hampshire."

"How about you two?"

The two other men glanced at each other and climbed into the Concord, and Story turned to the messenger, who spit out tobacco juice, grimly nodded, and moved to climb back into the driver's box.

"Frank," Story said.

The messenger turned around.

"I'd rather you stayed here."

The old man frowned. "Why?"

"I'd feel better if someone protected this lady from Mr. Saunders."

The banker started to puff up, but quickly deflated and forced a theatrical smile.

"They'll be expecting someone to ride shotgun," the messenger said.

Which is when Story turned to Mason Boone. "Yeah. They will."

With a sigh, Boone shed his new greatcoat, gave it to the woman to hold, while the guard named Frank handed his double-barrel shotgun to the driver and removed his buffalo-skin coat. Next, they swapped hats. The messenger's was too small for Boone, but he used his woolen scarf and tied it over his head, bringing down the worn, ripped, and stained sides to cover his ears. That might disguise his face enough.

"Chaw?" The messenger held out his plug.

"I'll pass, but thank you," Boone told him.

"Don't got the habit?"

Boone chuckled. "I like a good chaw—just not when I'm getting shot at."

Frank laughed. "Smart fellow."

"Not too smart," Story said as he pulled on the jehu's tan coat. "He's riding up there with me."

Boone put a foot on the front wheel's hub and began his climb into the box. Once seated, he reached over and took the shotgun from the messenger. "You got two barrels of buckshot," Frank told him. "Make 'em count." The answer was a silent nod. Frank carried a pistol in a holster, but did not offer it to Boone.

Story came up next, found the lines, and looked down at Halloran.

"We'll get back here as soon as we can," he said. "I'd get a fire going in that depression. Keep you warm."

"Try not to get my hat shot off your head, Story. It looks ridiculous on you. And you better bring my rig and my mules back here, real quick," the jehu said. "I got a schedule to keep."

"You haven't been on time once in eighteen months," Story told him, and called into the coach. "You two ready?"

One of them answered with a rebel yell that made Boone smile ever so slightly. Then he pulled up the woolen muffler Frank had handed him and drew in a deep breath. A moment later, Nelson Story brought the jehu's bandanna up over his mouth and nose, released the brake, and whipped the lines. The four mules began pulling the Concord up the track.

To Boone's surprise, Story knew how to handle a team, and the stagecoach moved faster up the hill. Story's Navy Colts lay on the bench, on either side of him. Extra cylinders, fully capped, rested beside the revolvers, for quicker reloads.

"We're making good time," Boone said, just to say something. His stomach roiled, his heart pounded, his throat turned raw, and the palms of his hands sweated inside his gloves.

"Because we're a hundred forty pounds lighter," Story said. It was much more than that, but now Boone understood why Story had left the messenger behind. Story had dragged the strongbox off the coach. Plummer with the Goatee and the other highwaymen might wind up killing Story, Boone, and the two men inside. But they wouldn't get Story's gold.

"It's rude to ask a man his name," Story said, "but I'm a rude bastard."

"Mason Boone," Boone said.

"All right. You know my name."

The coach rolled.

"How far?" Boone shouted. "To the slide rock?"

"Two miles. Now shut up."

The wind blew cold as the coach climbed, hugging the side. The track remained narrow, and as Boone saw the approaching curve, trees on both sides of the road, he decided that—for this moment—he hated trees. A bandit could hide behind any one of them, and in the gloaming, he would have a hard time spotting anything except a muzzle flash. The road climbed through, not quite a pass, but up a fairly steep rise. A small woods of frozen trees to the right gave the appearance of a mountain. Story's face—what little Boone could see—hardened with anticipation. Was this, Boone wondered, the slide rock? He couldn't see anything resembling rocks. The coach made its turn, and suddenly Story worked the lever on the brakes, cursing, pulling hard on the lines to steer the Concord toward a gap in the woods.

"Hang on," Story sang out, whether to Boone or the two men in the coach, he didn't know. Only at the last second in the coming darkness did Boone find the danger. Another wagon, pulled by two dark horses, sped downhill. Boone didn't have time to see too much, just the outline of a thin man pulling desperately on the lines—having no effect on the horses. Boone glimpsed the wagon, small wheels in front, rear wheels maybe twice as big. The wagon wasn't a stagecoach, or a farm wagon, but a big box, like a rectangular house on wheels. That was it. The next thing Boone felt was a savage blow that tilted the Concord and sent Boone flying over the side.

Tree branches ripped off the ill-fitting hat, carving scratches across Boone's nose and cheeks. He tasted sap, then blood. Horses and mules screamed. Wood splintered. Curses followed a deafening crash. Boone must have hit the ground, but didn't remember that. Didn't feel it, either, until he tried to push himself up.

Rolling over onto his back, he squeezed his eyes tightly, opened them to see tree branches.

"Son of a bitch." That sounded like Story.

A door squeaked. Profanity followed.

Boone rolled over, spit a mixture of tree bark and blood onto the ground. The coach rested in the woods, the mules hidden by the trees. Story lifted himself out of the driver's box. The Texan from Hood's Brigade helped the other passenger from the Concord. Boone couldn't see the strange wagon that must have collided with the stagecoach, but the tortured scream of a horse from the other side of the road sickened him.

A bullet ricocheted off the rim of the rear wheel—Boone saw the spark, heard the zing, and grasped for the messenger's twelve-gauge. He couldn't find it. Didn't recall if he still gripped it while flying through tree branches. Another shot slammed into wood. The two passengers tumbled into the softness of dead grass and needles. Toward the driver's box, Boone shot a look as he crawled on hands and knees toward what might have been the double-barrel. No sign of Story. Another gunshot rang out.

"Hands up," a voice cried out. "Hands up. Don't move or you're dead."

Boone kept moving. He dived, rolled, and gripped . . . a rotting log.

Two figures rushed out of the thicket to Boone's left. A muzzle blast blinded him, and Boone dropped to his chest. Hooves pounded the road, not from Virginia City, though, not from where they had left the banker, the jehu, and the messenger, but over toward Twin Bridges.

A gun roared. Wood disintegrated from the stagecoach's door.

"Move and we kill you, Story," one of the charging gunmen shouted. Although his ears rang from the din of the cannonade, Boone thought he recognized that voice as Sandy's. He saw the Texan and his pard raise their hands. The galloping horses slid to a stop, and Boone slowly turned his gaze toward the road. Two more men leaped from their saddles. One fired a revolver, and the lantern on the coach, just beneath the driver's box, exploded.

"What the hell." That came from Plummer with the Goatee.

Boone dropped his head to the softness of earth. *Play possum,* he told himself. *There's nothing you can do.* Still, he looked at the box, wanting to find the silhouette of Nelson Story.

"We got 'im, Ambrose," Sandy called out. "Ambrose. Over here."

The horse screamed.

"Shut up," answered Ambrose, alias Plummer with the Goatee.

"What the hell happened?" said the man who had ridden up with Ambrose alias Plummer.

"Damnedest thing I ever saw," said the man with Sandy, who, if Boone remembered correctly, was called Donnie.

"We thought you planned it," Sandy said.

"Where the hell's Story?" Ambrose yelled.

"We got him over here. Him and some other gent."

The horse screamed.

"Where's the driver? The shotgun?" Ambrose's partner yelled.

"Probably throwed all the way to Ruby," Sandy said.

"Look for them," Ambrose ordered.

Boone flattened his head. Tried to remember the prayer his mother taught him as a boy.

The horse screamed.

"Robin, put that horse out of its misery," Ambrose ordered. "And if that damned fool driver of that funny rig is still living, kill him, too."

He had not recalled that prayer, but God must have heard his thoughts, because a few more steps, and Robin would have walked right over Boone. The man turned. Ambrose made his way to the stagecoach.

"This isn't the way I planned it," Ambrose said, "but it didn't turn out half-bad."

Boone looked for a rock, a stick, anything he could use as a weapon.

The report of a pistol almost made him shriek.

"Horse is dead." Robin called Ambrose by his Plummer handle.

"The driver?"

"I don't see him. Getting too dark."

"Keep looking," Ambrose said. "Now, Story, you're . . . You, show me your face. Son of a bitch, Sandy, neither of these is No Good Story."

"It's gotta be. Hell, it's the stage from Virginia City. He's gotta be . . ."

The door opened, slammed shut. "That box of gold ain't there." Ambrose ran to the back of the stagecoach, worked the straps for the rear luggage compartment. He yelled, "Donnie, see if it's in the driver's box."

Boone fought to keep his control, tried to formulate a plan. Retreat or attack. Whichever would work, but nothing he could come up with seemed to give him a chance at survival.

Donnie took hold, stepped up onto the wheel's hub,

pulled himself to the driver's box. The back of his head became silhouetted by a muzzle flash, and the brigand fell like a sack of potatoes onto the road. The mules snorted.

"What the hell?"

"Oh, my God!"

Boone made out the shape of Nelson Story as the dark outline of a figure rose out of the box like some monster in a five-penny dreadful. Sandy took a step toward the corpse on the ground, tripped, and pulled the trigger of his revolver. That flash illuminated the coach gun lying on a tree root, and Boone started crawling. Profanity. Another gunshot. Boone lunged, grabbed the Moore & Co. twelve-gauge, hoping, praying that the percussion caps had not been dislodged during the wreck. He heard the roar of a large-caliber revolver, answered by two lighter discharges, and a panicked gasp from Sandy: "Ambrose . . . I am killed."

Sandy pulled the trigger as he toppled forward, and the inches of flame belching from the weapon provided enough light for Boone to see the boots and legs of a man moving on the other side of the coach. Robin. Boone pulled both triggers. Only one barrel roared.

CHAPTER SIXTEEN

"I would have killed you, you filthy bastard," the road agent named Ambrose said, "but you shot my damned hand off."

Not quite, Story could tell from the torch of pitch pine Wilkinson, the Texan, held, but the thief's right hand would never be any good, not that the outlaw had much time to fret over being a cripple.

"I got a question for you," Story said.

The man attempted to spit, but the spittle merely dripped down Ambrose's chin.

"Was this man part of your gang?" With a nod, Wilkinson moved the flame closer to the vagabond named Boone.

"Damn right he was. Been with me for three years."

Story nodded. "What I expected," he said. "You're as bad of a liar as you are a highwayman." Story moved to the one whose right ankle and calf had been torn apart by buckshot from that cannon Frank usually carried. Story might not have come through this fracas alive if not for that lucky shot. The man was sweating and bleeding, bleeding and sweating, and trying not to cry.

"Make your peace with your Maker, boy," Story said. "Your time is at hand. Come on."

He walked past the boot of the coach.

"You want one of us to stand guard?" the Tennessean, Rees, called out.

"No," Story said. "They're not going anywhere."

"But to hell," Wilkinson said, chuckling.

Texans. They disgusted Story. He wouldn't give two cents for the lot of them. There was nothing amusing about hanging cutthroats, but then Story never found much humor in anything. He stopped at the dead horse and stared at the giant box of a wagon that lay on the side of the road.

"Ever seen any conveyance like that?" Story asked.

The Southerners shook their heads. Story turned to Boone. "You?"

Boone started to answer, but stopped and came up to Rees. "Let me borrow your torch," he said, took the flaming wood, and moved to the wagon. The back door was open, and there was another small window behind the driver's box, but that part of the wagon seemed to be canvas, much of it now crushed from the wreck.

"Looks like a What Is It," Boone said. The Texan and the Tennessean shot each other a quick glance. Boone leaned, pushed the door open, and stuck the torch inside.

"Don't set the damned thing on fire," Story told him.

"Maybe it is . . ." Boone withdrew the torch and let the door swing back down. "A What Is It. Saw them during the war. You could get an ambrotype, tintype, photographs. That's what it looks like, but, well, there's no camera, no plates, none of those things those photographers carried with them."

"You got a likeness made of yourself?" Rees asked.

"No. Other fellows did." Boone climbed up the wreck, raised the torch, and dropped back down to the ground. "But there's stenciling up there that says 'O'Brien's Photographic Van.'"

"All right," Story said. "Let's see if we can find O'Brien."

"Or what's left of him." Wilkinson took a few steps and picked something up, holding it like a dead snake in front of the flame.

Story stepped closer. "Stethoscope," Rees said. "Sawbones use those to hear your heart."

"Huh." Wilkinson pitched the instrument as though it were a dead rat and wiped his fingertips on his trousers. He turned. "What would a photographer need with a stethoscope?"

Boone shrugged. Rees chuckled. "Well, if you drove a rig like he did, one of them stethoscopes would be quite handy."

"Split up," Story said. "He couldn't have gotten far."

"Especially if he's dead," Wilkinson said.

Boone found him, lying between two small lodgepole pines. Story and the others came closer to stare down at a rail-thin, young man with a beard like Abraham Lincoln's, only reddish, and a now-busted, bleeding nose, and myriad other injuries. Boone glanced up. "He's alive."

Squatting beside the driver, Story held the back of his right hand underneath the man's nose, felt the breath, then fingered the man's throat. "Heartbeat's strong." His hands moved along the man's body, where bruises already began to show, and blood flowed freely from cuts. "Knot on the top of his head the size of a coffee cup." He glanced at Boone. "Reckon you know how that feels."

Boone's face did not change.

"Let's get him back to the coach, see what our prisoners are up to," Story said.

"When do we go back to get Frank and Halloran?" Rees asked. "And the other passengers?"

"Those bastards shot out our lantern," Story said. "I'm not driving that rig down the mountain in pitch-dark. We'll head down come first light."

"That jehu will be furious," Wilkinson said.

Story's reply would have made most women, and some men, blush.

The campfire roared, and the men, including the two prisoners, huddled by it. Boone used the flask taken off the corpse of one of the road agents, and splashed the rye over a silk handkerchief Story had found in the What Is It's driver's coat pocket. He dabbed the wounds with the liquor. For the serious, though not life-threatening, wounds, Story wrapped strips torn from a silk shirt they had found in the back of the wrecked wagon. The minor cuts and scratches, he figured would clot soon enough. Or the damned fool driver would just bleed to death.

"That's enough," Story told Boone. "You look like you could use a bracer."

Boone sipped, sighed, and handed the pewter container to Rees, who drank and passed it on to the Texan. He took the longest swig and offered it to Story.

"No, thanks," Story said, but when the Texan grinned and started to drink more, Story added: "Let's leave some for this damned fool."

"How 'bout us." Ambrose was not asking, and Story was not about to reply.

"He's coming to," Boone said.

The man blinked repeatedly and looked toward the fire. Flames reflected in the man's eyes, he groaned, and slowly moved his head. The eyes found Story first, then Rees, and finally the Texan. He did not look at Boone, who sat behind the What Is It driver.

"What happened?" the man finally asked. No trace of an accent that Story could detect.

The Texan answered, "You damned near killed yourself and us, as well."

The man blinked. "Oh." Tears welled in his eyes. "Oh, yes. My horse. Something . . . spooked her. She . . . bolted."

"Where were you bound?"

"Virginia City," he said.

"Photographer?" Story asked.

He might as well have been speaking Russian.

"Sir?" the stranger said after at least half a minute.

"Are you a photographer?"

His eyes squinted, he wet his lips, cringed in pain, and finally answered. "No. No. I . . . Oh . . ." He smiled. "The wagon. I see. The wagon. I bought it . . . in . . ." He swallowed. "In Boise."

Boise. That old mining camp along the Snake River. It hadn't been much when Ellen and he had traveled up to settle here, but from all Story had heard, it was booming now. Territorial capital of Idaho with an army fort and gold strikes popping up. Story said, "Any way you go, that's around four hundred miles, mister."

The man grinned. One of his incisors had chipped. "Well, I almost made it. How far am I from the territorial capital of Montana?"

"Depends," Story said.

"On what?" The man's face showed horror.

"If you can walk. If you can walk, it's not that far. If you can't, you better hope you got some grub in that What Is It. Because this time of year, people don't travel much, and the stages only come through three times a week. And you might have noticed that we can get snow measured in yards."

The man's laugh died slowly. "Surely, you're not serious."

"About the weather?"

"About getting me to Virginia City, sir." The man snapped with the haughtiness of an easterner.

"I'm not one for jokes, mister." He offered his hand. "Name's Story. Nelson Story." He introduced the others.

"I am Seth Beckstead," the dumb ass said. Mason Boone lifted the handkerchief he had used to cleanse the man's wounds, holding it closer to the fire so that Story could read the initials. *S.R.B.* In lavender thread.

Story reached inside the pocket of Halloran's coat—he wished he had not traded with that damned jehu—and withdrew the stethoscope he had retrieved after they had discovered the injured man.

"Is this yours?" Story asked.

"Yes." The man smiled. "I might have use of it. I've never had to examine myself. As the saying goes, 'A doctor who treats himself has a fool for a patient.'"

Story didn't laugh. "You're a doctor?"

"Indeed, Mr. Story. I was graduated from the University of Maryland School of Medicine six and a half years ago."

That's when Story handed Dr. Seth Beckstead the flask of rye. "Get some rest, Doc. We'll chat more come morning."

CHAPTER SEVENTEEN

Seth Beckstead limped that snowy morning. The man named Boone, though he had sprained his left wrist firing that menacing shotgun, held the door to the What Is It open, while Beckstead crawled through the wreckage.

"Aha." Beckstead smiled and tossed a sack toward the opening. *This should make peace with these scoundrels.* "There's coffee, my good man." Boone grunted. He must be freezing. Beckstead sighed when he found the bottle of brandy, shattered. At length, he spotted a satchel and something else. The red wooden box, his name stenciled in black, and the title he had longed to forget.

MAJOR, 2ND MARYLAND VOLUNTEER REGIMENT

With satchel and surgical kit, he crawled through scattered clothes, books, busted memories, and the tintype of sweet Lucia, through the opening and into the biting wind as dawn slowly emerged over the treetops.

"Got what you need, Doc?" Boone asked.

"Yes. Thank you." He pushed himself up, shivered.

"Need a hand with all that?"

"Just bring the coffee, Mr. Boone. I am certain your comrades will need that, as shall I. It is a grim task we have this morn."

He started limping to the fire, but stopped, cursed himself as a fool, and moved back to the old photographers wagon. "I warrant a coffeepot might be requisitioned by Mr. Story," he told Boone, who lifted the door open again, and Seth Beckstead crawled inside, all the way to the back, although he saw the coffeepot leaning against a bedroll to his left just by the door. At the far corner, he sat, pulled his legs up, wrapping his arms around his shins, and rocked back and forth, shivering.

The dead highwaymen had been laid out beside the horse. Just two men. Two men and a dead horse. He had seen bodies stacked like cordwood. *Two men? That was nothing. There are injured men outside. Those need your help.* He swallowed. The one with the shattered leg—that would require amputation. So would the mangled hand on the other brigand. But men went on without particular limbs. He felt like the fool, shivering but sweating.

"You are a doctor, Seth Beckstead," he whispered. "You are a doctor. Men need your help."

After wiping his brow, he made himself crawl back, grabbed the pot, called out as cheerily as he could fake, "Found it," and emerged onto the frozen, wet Montana road.

Boone brought the pot and coffee to the fire, and the man named Rees cheered Beckstead. "Never thought I'd be glad to see a Yankee sawbones," he said.

Wilkinson laughed heartily, pointing at Boone's plunder. "Now, that's medicine to my likin'."

Cold-eyed Nelson Story nodded at Boone. "Melt some snow in the pot for the coffee." He turned to Beckstead, his eyes locking on the red box and the black valise. "What's that?"

"Medical instruments. Medicines. Bandages. We have a grim morning before us, I fear."

"They won't need your attention, Doctor."

"My God, man. Both of these men require amputations." He paused, aware of what he had just said, with urgency. He balled his fingers and spoke with resolve, hoping his voice would not quiver. "If I do not remove that lad's leg, or that contrarian's right hand, gangrene will spread and they will die. I must perform surgery immediately, and I shall require assistance from at least one of you."

Thanks to the busted bottle, he had no brandy. Nothing to help dull the pain of sawing through bones. With luck, the men might survive the shock, pass out quickly. With God's mercy, they might survive to spend a few years in prison.

"They won't need your attention, Doctor," Story repeated.

"Did you not hear me, sir? These mean will die—"

"They're gonna die anyway, Doc." Rees nodded toward Wilkinson, and Dr. Seth Reginald Beckstead saw the nooses the Texan was fashioning by the fire.

Beckstead remembered carousing with Walter Stephan in Baltimore, quoting from *Twelfth Night*.

"'There lies your way, due west,'" Stephan said, laughing. Both Stephan and he were well in their cups that night before Beckstead boarded the train to begin his journey, his new adventure. And Beckstead had answered, trying to mimic the voice of the actress who had played Viola: "'Then westward-ho!'"

Now, shivering but no longer from the cold, he quoted another line from another of Shakespeare's plays: "'. . . when I was at home, I was in a better place; but travellers must be content.'"

"As You Like It."

Surprised, Beckstead turned to Mason Boone, who stood over the coffeepot. The man apparently didn't like the attention he suddenly received from his comrades. "Troupe came by while we were wintering in Tennessee," he said. "Gave us a respite after Murfreesboro."

"You saw a performance once and remember that line?"

The man bent to check the pot, or maybe to try to hide. "Well, I just thought I'd been in a better place when I was home."

The Texan chuckled. "Didn't we all?"

This moment of peace, of humanity, vanished like the snowflakes falling toward the fire. Rage boiling inside him, Beckstead limped toward Nelson Story, the leader of this mob. "Sir," he said, "these men are entitled to a fair trial, judged by a jury of their peers, and sentenced by a duly appointed or elected judge."

"You study law, too?" Story said.

Flummoxed, Beckstead shouted, "This is vigilantism, not justice."

"It's both," Story told him. "And this is Montana. Not Maryland."

"But they deserve a trial."

"They've had one." Story pointed at Rees. "Did you see these men?"

Rees nodded. He didn't look uncomfortable in the least.

"What were they trying to do?"

"Murder us. Rob us."

Story's eyes found Wilkinson.

The Texan grinned. He held up one noose. "Doc, I wouldn't be makin' these if I thought these boys were innocent."

"You." Story nodded at Boone. "Did you hear these men plan this crime?"

Boone nodded.

"And what else did they intend to do?"

"Murder you." Beckstead had to strain to hear Boone's answer.

"You turncoat son of a bitch," the man with the mangled hand said. "I should have shot you dead the moment I saw you. Filthy, traitorous bastard. You just want to be pirooting hard-ass Story's wife." He laughed. "You—"

Story kicked him in the jaw. Teeth and blood flew from the man's mouth as he slammed into the ground. A revolver appeared in the cold man's hand. "One more word about my wife . . ." He spun toward Boone. "Is that damned coffee boiling yet?"

"It's likely warm enough," Boone said, not looking up.

The Texan and the Tennessean rose and moved to the fire. Story followed.

"Will not any of you show mercy?"

No one answered, or even looked at Beckstead.

"I'll report this to the law. I'll report it to the editor of the newspaper in Virginia City."

"Do that," Story told him. "And while you're in the office, ask Professor Dimsdale to read the book he printed in the *Post*. He calls it *The Vigilantes of Montana*."

"Like Story says, Doc," Rees said as he held out a cup for Boone to fill. "This isn't Maryland. These men are guilty. And most likely, they would have shot you dead while you lay on the ground unconscious had they gotten the chance."

"Which they would've," Wilkinson said. "Had it not been for Story and Boone here."

* * *

He felt as if he were somewhere else, reading about this in a newspaper or *Harper's*, or watching it as some performance at an opera house. It seemed . . . just . . . surreal.

Boone and Rees helped the man with the mangled leg stand, and Story handed him the tin cup he had just used for his own coffee. Beckstead looked down at his own hand, the cup that he gripped, still filled with lukewarm coffee that he had yet to taste. The first condemned man even thanked his executioners for the drink. The man with the ruined hand shook his head when offered coffee, so Story tossed the liquid into the snow and pitched the cup aside.

During the morning, they had moved the stagecoach around, so that it faced the road toward Virginia City, though its back remained off the road, under the grove of trees. They had also, after drinking coffee, dragged the dead horse to the side of the road, next to the dead bandits, as well as the wreckage of Beckstead's wagon.

"Are not we to bury these men?" Beckstead had asked.

"If the wolves haven't gotten them by spring," Story said, "maybe you can come up here and dig them a proper grave."

Beckstead's mouth hung open till Rees came over and put his arm around the doctor's shoulder. "Ground's frozen solid this time of year, Doc, and it isn't like they would've treated us no different."

This was a different world than Boise . . . or Salt Lake . . . or even bloody, war-torn Maryland and Virginia—the world from which Seth Reginald Beckstead had tried to escape.

Story and Wilkinson jerked the leader, named Ambrose— he would not give another name—to his feet, spun him around against the Concord, and tied his arms behind him.

The same was done, though with less aggression, to the other man, who bowed his head and began to pray.

They led the men to the back of the stagecoach, hoisted them onto the edge of the rear boot. Rees had to climb up as well, to hold the other man, Robin Roy McGuinn, age twenty-four, from Iowa County, Iowa—and if someone would write his mother, Mary Burgess McGuinn, general delivery, and tell her that he died of pneumonia while mining for gold in Bannack City, he would be indebted. By then, Story had climbed onto the top of the coach and slipped the ropes over both men's necks. He dropped a placard of some kind, with a silk scarf used for a rope, over Ambrose's neck. At length, Story climbed back to the driver's box.

Boone kicked out the fire, which hissed underneath the mounds of snow.

"Any last words?" Wilkinson called out.

The gimp shook his head and began sobbing.

Ambrose used a vile profanity.

Story released the brake, whipped the lines, and the coach moved forward about a rod.

The two men kicked in the wind, and slowly strangled.

"My God," Beckstead whispered.

"Fetch what you need to bring, Doc," Story called to him. "You can send for the rest or come get it yourself when you get to Virginia City."

"Come on, Doc." Boone was at his side. "It's over. We got to pick up some folks we left behind before they freeze to death."

"And Halloran's got a schedule he thinks he can keep." Wilkinson laughed as he opened the door and climbed inside.

"Let's go." Beckstead felt himself being guided to the

stagecoach. He had enough sense to stop and pick up his grip, his surgical kit. He did not look back at the dead men swinging from the tree limb. But he would never forget the sign hung around Ambrose's neck.

**LET
THIS BE
A LESSON
TO ALL
ROAD AGENTS**

CHAPTER EIGHTEEN

John Catlin never understood how winter wheat got its name. It grew, once you planted the seeds in the fall, a few inches, just before the first freeze, after which it would just sit there, dead like the rest of the county, till spring came along. Only then would it green up.

Some of his neighbors planted red winter, but never expected anything from it. They told Catlin it helped the soil, kept the winter winds and snow from blowing all that good dirt to some damned Confederate state. Corn was the cash crop. Good old corn. Corn grew. So they'd plow up the red winter, plant corn, make a little money come harvest time. Providing no hail beat the hell out of the acres and acres they had planted. Or a tornado blew everything—sometimes even their homes—to Illinois. But, by thunder, if John Catlin planted wheat, he expected to grow wheat, and not just to mix in with cow dung and fertilize cornfields.

So he grew red winter in the winter, same as Steve Grover, and if—sometimes one enormous *if*—he had a crop by midsummer, he'd reap not only the grain, but also take the straw and bale it. Funny how much an Indiana farmer could make baling dry wheat stalks to sell for bedding for cows, pigs, things like that. Then he could plant seed corn, hope it made, before planting the red winter in September.

And here he sat, with his four walls and one door, and a fireplace that gave him enough light to read Dickens, listening to the wolves screaming as the wind moaned. He had a heck of a home, one that befitted a captain in a volunteer Union regiment. Why, before he had enlisted, the only door he had was his grandma's blanket. Now he had a bona fide door of pine. Living like a king. The other day, Catlin had decided to make pounded cheese. He had carved about a pound of goat's milk cheese with his knife, spooned in enough butter with some black pepper and cayenne. His ma always liked to spice hers with sherry, but Catlin figured the beer he had bought in town would be all right. So after he had tilled it smooth as a baby's bottom in a mortar, he pressed it into a jar, covered the top with the rest of his butter, and now he had a snack. But, damn, he sure wished he had that beer now to drink.

Still, he looked across the room, spotted the jar of pounded butter, but to fetch that would mean he'd have to get up from his spot here, move away from the fireplace. Of course, he would have to do that anyway pretty soon, because he needed to add fuel to the fire.

Of course, Catlin did not have to farm. Man like him could go to work for the Haskell-Barker Car Company, help build railroads all across the country. Or go over to Michigan City and work at the Northern Indiana State Prison. Count prisoners. Walk around and make sure convicts didn't get out of hand. Lots of things a former officer in the Union army could do. Well, maybe not. Some of the factories had started leasing inmates from the prison to do a lot of the work there. Pretty cheap labor, too. Not that farming was much better. The war, Catlin kept being told, was over. The U.S. Army kept getting rid of soldiers every day. No need for them, except out west to fight the savage redskins.

"I wonder what Steve's doing right now?" Catlin folded the newspaper on his lap, looked at the fire, shook his head. "You're getting senile, Captain. Talking to yourself." He chuckled. "Which is probably what Steve Grover's doing, too."

Camp Rose, Catlin figures, must have sounded better than the St. Joseph County Fairgrounds, which is where he has arrived with other new volunteers of the 87th Indiana. He asks a man wearing a fancy uniform where he might take his supper, and the man gives Catlin the worst tongue-lashing he has ever heard from a sober man. Tells him to forage for food. Uses salty language, too.

Maybe Mr. Lincoln's army hasn't figured out that soldiers figure on being fed. Eventually, Catlin finds his camp, with other boys in Company I.

"Where do we eat?" Catlin asks a lean soldier studying the brogans on his feet.

"Not sure we do," the man says. He holds his kersey blue trousers in his left hand, a navy blouse in the other, and just stands there in his undergarments, looking at his shoes.

"What you think of these shoes?" the man asks.

Catlin looks down. "You got mighty big feet. No offense."

The man's head shakes. "No, I pride myself on my small feet," and he draws his right foot out. Catlin nods.

"I told the man giving out these duds that my feet aren't big. I think he found these just to spite me."

"Did you ask to get something more suitable?"

"Yeah. And you wouldn't believe the words he used."

"Oh, I might. I asked a fellow with a lot of color on his blue coat about chuck. He might have said the same words. Could've been the same man."

"Nah. Man who gave me these didn't have much color on his uniform. Except some stripes on his sleeves." He shows Catlin the shape of the stripes and where they fit on the man's upper arms.

"What did he say about chuck?" the man asks.

"Said go draft it myself. With some peculiar adjectives before and after, describing food and me."

The man smiles brightly. "So you're telling me he isn't the chaplain."

Catlin laughs. "Well, I don't know. I haven't figured out this man's army yet."

"He said draft?"

"Indeed. Draft. 'Go draft your foul-word supper your own foul-word self, you foulest word, Private. Do I foul-word look like a foul-word chef, you insolent, insubordinate foul-word, fouler word.'"

"Foul. Interesting choice of words. But draft, I'm just not sure."

"I've never heard it used that way."

"I'd use . . . forage. Unless he meant draft in the monetary form."

"Or prepare. Did they give you any cookware when they gave you the uniform?"

"No. Didn't even give me a blessed musket. Said we'd get those issued later." His head shook. "But as we have yet to be paid, I think forage is what he meant. Though I thought about rummage."

"I like that word. Reminds me of Grandma back in Cleveland. You're in Company I?"

"Yes. Bought a farm in the county."

"I've been farming there for three years now."

"I guess that makes us neighbors."

"And here we are in the same regiment. You know." He points to the new recruit's brogans. *"You soak those in water, the leather will shrink. Not that they'll shrink that much, but with two pairs of socks, maybe three, they might not fly off when they start marching us all day."*

"I was thinking the same thing."

"Perhaps we should go draft our supper?"

"That is one foul-word idea. If you'll let me put on the boots I walked here in, I might foul-word rummage around South Bend with you." He turns toward a white tent. *"There's room here, if you have yet to take an apartment."*

"I would be foul-word honored." They move to their temporary home of white canvas. *"I saw some geese about a quarter mile east of here."* He holds out his right hand. *"My name is John Catlin."*

"Delighted." They shake. *"You may call me Steve foul-word Grover."*

Well, that memory had killed about fifteen minutes for Catlin, who reached down to stoke the fire. He made himself yawn, stared at the jar of pounded cheese, and wondered what Steve Grover was doing right about now. Then he settled back into the chair, picked up the paper, and read without really registering any article, any sentence, any word. Until he saw something, a tiny notice in regular type and font, buried between a sentence about something that had happened in Natchitoches, Louisiana, and a larger advertisement about "Vegetable Ambrosia."

<u>WESTWARD TO RICHES</u>
**I am organizing an expedition that will depart
NEBRASKA CITY
in the spring for the goldfields in the
Northern Rockies.
Following Bozeman's trail.
Experienced Bullwhackers needed.**
Apply to: **MAJ. COUSHATTA JOHN NOAH,
The American House, Nebraska City,
Nebraska Territory.**
☞ *Liberty and Union Men <u>Preferred</u>.*

He read the advertisement again. Bullwhacker. Well, his father had been a blacksmith before trying his hand at farming. Catlin had never soldiered until he enlisted, certainly had never been an officer until he got promoted. How hard could bullwhacking be? Besides, he had all winter to figure out what exactly a bullwhacker had to do.

CHAPTER NINETEEN

The sickly journalist flipped a page in his notebook and scribbled a few more words before he looked up from the desk in the *Montana Post* office and studied Seth Beckstead intently.

"You walked all the way down from the slide rock?" Thomas Dimsdale hailed from England. Beckstead had figured that much out.

"No, I guess a couple of miles down from there. That's where they picked up two other men and a woman, turned the stagecoach around, and loped off for Bannack City. And I never saw anything resembling a slide rock."

The Irish printer, also captivated by Beckstead's truthful account of the lynching of those two criminals, chuckled. "Because it took its name after a miner slipped on ice and rolled down thirty feet. That was back in '63."

Beckstead sighed. "I just want to find the marshal's office to report this crime. The first person I asked when I arrived in this city, sent me up the hill to a graveyard. There was no marshal's office or jail there."

Dimsdale's eyes twinkled and he said, "Someone played a joke on you, sir, I am afraid to report."

"That's where most of our hangings happen," the printer

informed him. "And our municipal lawmen, Marshal Deascey or his assistant, Lewis, would tell you they have no jurisdiction outside the city limits."

"The next man," Beckstead lamented, as if he had not heard the printer, "sent me some blocks over to a shack—I dare not call it a house, not even a toilet—a house . . . that stood in the middle . . . of the blasted street."

"We are trying to get most of those houses removed," the editor said.

Of course, another joke. Have fun at a journeyman from Maryland's expense. He had experienced similar attempts at frontier humor in Salt Lake, Corrine, and, especially, Bannack City.

Beckstead sat up straight, demanding, "Who is sheriff of this county?"

"That would be Neil Howie." Dimsdale added in disgust. "A rough Scotsman."

"And where might I find him?"

"Our capital."

Beckstead stressed every word, speaking deliberately, while blood rushed to his head. *"This is the capital of Montana Territory, sir."*

"I meant our nation's capital, sir. Washington City. Most of our politicians and elected officials went there. To lobby for statehood."

Trying to breathe steadily, to avoid dropping dead from an apoplexy, Beckstead clenched and unclenched his fists, rocked back in the chair, gently. Statehood. Like this nightmare of crime and regulators ever had any chance of becoming a state.

"Howie wouldn't have helped you anyhow, me boy." The Irishman screwed off the top of a flask. "Vigilantes are pretty much his deputies, even when he doesn't give them orders. Besides, he gave a scoundrel named Tweed fifty lashes back in March—took quite a few vigilantes with him. Told him he had ten days to get out of Alder Gulch or he would get a hundred. And if he had not vanished by then, they'd hang him. Am I right or wrong, Tom?"

"I rode up there with them," Dimsdale said. "Tweed left, of course."

Refusing to give in to these ruffians, Beckstead tried another approach. "How about the United States marshal?"

Dimsdale and the printer exchanged looks. "You mean George Pinney?"

"If he has been appointed United States marshal, yes, I mean George Pinney."

"Lincoln, God rest his soul, made the appointment," the journalist affirmed.

"Then could you direct me to the territorial capitol? Or wherever I might find Marshal Pinney."

The newspaper editor coughed, laughed, and shook his head. "Bless you, Dr. Beckstead, but the good citizens of this city, and this territory, have yet to build a capitol or courthouse or any official government building. We have plotted out a good spot for the capitol."

"Good-size chunk of land," the printer said. "Lot of baseball games been played over there in the summer."

Beckstead stared in disbelief.

"Let's see, the territorial legislature usually meets above a billiard hall, but which billiard hall, it just depends. The last time the House met, I believe that was on the second story of Stonewall Hall." He rubbed his chin as if in thought.

"There has been talk of constructing a county courthouse," Dimsdale added. "But courts usually are held inside a saloon. Drinks aren't served, of course. Till after a verdict has been reached."

"They ever figure out where to store all those records that got sent up here after they moved the capital from Bannack?"

Dimsdale straightened and scribbled something on the top of his notepad. "That might be worth reporting," he said. "Thank you for the idea, Patrick."

The printer drank from his flask.

"But what about Marshal Finney?"

"Pinney," the Irishman corrected.

Dimsdale was already shaking his head when, with a wry smile, he looked up from his notebook. When he opened his mouth, Beckstead beat him to the answer. "Washington City."

"He is a man with ambition," Dimsdale said.

"He doesn't spend much time here anyhow. Leaves that to Howie, his deputy marshal here. Pinney's a Helena man. Works out of Butte, mostly, but that's because it's closer to here and Helena. Helena's the big to-do right now because of the strike at Last Chance Gulch." He held up a smeared piece of newspaper. "You can read about it Saturday."

"I can hardly wait." The doctor bowed his head.

How long he sat like that, he did not know, but he smelled pipe smoke and felt a shadow over him.

"Sir, you are new to this territory, as was I when I first arrived," Dimsdale said. "But this is, and will be, a vibrant community. Virginia City is the center of wealth, population, and intelligence of the territory."

"You should write that in your paper, sir."

The man patted Beckstead's forearm. "I did. Back in February when the capital was moved from Bannack. Now, might I ask you a question?" Without waiting for an answer, he said, "What brought you from Baltimore, Maryland, to the wilds of Montana?"

"To save lives," he said sadly.

"Noble. And needed. And why did you choose our humble burg?"

"When I reached Bannack City and saw how deserted the town was, the citizens said Virginia City could use a man with my abilities. *Abilities.*" He spat out the word. "Oh, yes, I have refined certainly one of my *abilities.*"

"We have a number of doctors across the Fourteen Mile City already, I am afraid to report, sir," Dimsdale said. "Oh, I mean not to insinuate that the residents of Bannack sent you here as another one of their larks. More than likely, they thought we could use another surgeon. Last year, this city boasted five thousand residents, with another five thousand in the other camps in the Fourteen Mile City. But now, what with Helena booming and the strike at Emigrant Gulch, we have lost more than our share of settlers."

"Most of them, I hope, have been doctors," Beckstead said.

"Good show, lad. A jolly wit. You will do well in our town, sir. And, I will affirm, that some practitioners of the Hippocratic oath have removed their shingles and bid adieu. Let's see, off the top of my head, Tibbetts, he's our undertaker. Cornell, he sets bones quite well—good to know in this town. Dr. Turner prefers horses. I don't mean to say he is a veterinarian, but he likes to race horses. Rarely will one find him in his office. F. V. P. Moore practices next to Clayton & Hale's Drug Store. You might visit A. L. Justice, who offices next door to the City Drug Store on this street. His partner, Mr. Crepin, left recently for . . . sadly, I report, Helena. They advertised regularly, and, lucky for me, Dr. Justice continues to advertise his services in the *Post*. But I should think Dr. Sparhan would be the doctor in most need of a partner. Where is he now, Patrick?"

The printer replied with a snort: "Champion Saloon on Jackson Street."

Shaking his head, Dimsdale sighed. "Alas, Patrick is not merely attempting a witticism. My recommendation, Dr. Beckstead, would be to seek out a doctor that needs a partner. Share expenses. And profits. Two is more powerful than one, and Dr. Justice still advertises in the *Post*, even without Mr. Crepin to help with the rates. Now, I would like more information about these brigands who attempted to rob the Holladay stage . . ."

Beckstead told them what he could, and that proved to be a wise choice. Because when Professor Thomas Dimsdale said he would take a wagon up to the slide rock with some of the vigilantes, he asked if there were anything Beckstead might have left behind that he would like conveyed back to Virginia City. So . . . Beckstead mentioned some clothes and equipment in the back of a photographers van.

"Delighted to assist you, lad." The editor started again, but a ravaging cough ended the conversation.

"Might I assist you?" Beckstead asked when the spell ceased. He saw the flecks of blood on the editor's lips, chin, and handkerchief.

Dimsdale's eyes saddened as he shook his head. "I am afraid not, Dr. Beckstead. My next doctor shall be our good Dr. Tibbetts."

The mortician.

"You can bunk with me, Doc," Patrick the printer said. "I'm at the Weston Hotel. I'll tell the landlord that you're my bunky till you find another place." He sipped from the flask. "Your share of the rent will be ten dollars. A month."

As Beckstead walked toward the front door, he began, facetiously, to figure out how much he would have to charge for . . . leg amputations . . . arm amputations . . . probing for bullets, canister . . . cleansing bayonet wounds . . . telling the orderly to put the soldier by that tree and bring in someone who wasn't mortally wounded. It wasn't until he reached the door, that he remembered.

Turning, he asked Professor Dimsdale, "Sir, would you by chance know where I might find the residence of Missus Ellen Story?"

The journalist lowered the handkerchief. The printer turned and began cleaning the ink off his fingers with a rag.

"You . . ." Suspicion vanished from Dimsdale's face. "Of course, of course, but Nelson would have asked you to check on his wife."

Nelson Story wasn't the only person who asked, Beckstead remembered. The man Story mockingly called his "ward," the dark-haired lad named . . . what was it? Boone. Of course, like Daniel Boone, but not Daniel. Mason Boone. That man had pulled Beckstead aside; in fact, Mason Boone had asked before the woman's husband had.

He pushed prurient thoughts to the back of his head and listened as Dimsdale continued.

"Patrick, would you be a good lad and take Dr. Beckstead over to the Story cabin? I would . . . but this cold, the snow, and my lungs are just not worth a farthing at the moment."

"That shall be a pleasure, Professor. Come along, Doc. I'll point out Doc Justice's place, too, and show you which way to go down Jackson Street to find the Champion Saloon where Doc Sparhan is likely pissing out forty-rod, too."

CHAPTER TWENTY

The last thing Ellen Story wanted this evening was a visitor, but she left Gustave Flaubert's *Madame Bovary* on the table, pulled on her slippers, and crossed the cabin. Before opening the door, she slipped on an overcoat and pulled it as tightly as she could to cover her growing belly.

"Good evening, Missus Story." A tall, dark-haired gentleman removed his hat in one hand and presented a card in the other. "I am Dr. Seth Beckstead, and I met your husband on the trail. He requested that I drop by and see how you are doing."

He seemed to be pleasant enough. She saw the black satchel and a rectangular wooden box of red resting by his worn shoes.

"Ah." She smiled, took his card but did not look at it. "You are that doctor."

The man blinked, and straightened, and finally shook his head and sighed. "I was told the newspaper would not be printed until Saturday."

"There are no secrets in Virginia City, sir. Won't you come inside?"

Closing the door, she offered him Nelson's chair, while

she dropped the business card on the table and settled onto the chaise.

"Would you care for coffee, Dr. Beckstead?"

"No, thank you." He set the red box on the floor, but kept the black valise on his lap. He pursed his lips, locked his fingers together, unlocked them, and cleared his throat. "Exactly what did you hear about me, Missus Story?"

"That you were involved in a wreck at the slide rock. That you helped thwart a daring attempt at robbing the Holladay stage . . . and then walked . . . walked all the way from the slide rock to town. In the snow. That you are a man of gumption."

He wet his lips, rubbed his hands on his trousers, and looked at her with the innocence of a child. "You heard all of that?"

Ellen laughed. "Well, Doctor, I made up part of it." When his eyes dropped, she added: "But not the part about gumption. I should apologize for Nelson's rudeness, but if I did that, I would have no time to bake pies and clean the cabin. He is a hard man, as you know, but he could have and should have returned to Virginia City to report the robbery attempt himself. He's in a hurry." She sighed. "He is often in a hurry."

"The walk provided good exercise, ma'am."

"It could well have provided you with double pneumonia, sir. I noticed your limp, too, when you came inside."

"The limp came from the accident, Missus Story, and blame for the accident rests on me."

"A Good Samaritan would have driven you into town, sir."

"Spilt milk. I am here. I am healthy. And I am at your service."

"Bully for you, Doctor."

He wet his lips again. She thought she should get him coffee, or water, or brew tea, but that would mean she would have to stand.

"Well," he said.

"Well," she said to fill the lengthening pause.

"Your husband, ma'am, he asked me to check on you, but did not give me any particulars. I do not mean to pry, Missus Story, but . . . are you of need of a doctor's services?"

"I am with child."

He paled. Slid back into the chair. His lips parted, closed, and he ran his fingers through his hair.

"I have arranged services of a midwife when the time comes, Doctor. Miss Papadakis. She is Greek."

"I see. I'm sure you will be in capable hands." He swallowed. "And how far along are you?"

She grinned. "Not as far as from slide rock to town . . ." Waited for his smile, which she liked very much. He reminded her, strangely enough, of Mason Boone. "More like from here to Jackson Street."

"Oh. That soon."

"You know where Jackson Street is? And you just arrived in town today? You are a fast learner, Doctor."

"The street was pointed out to me by the man—a printer at the *Post*—who gave me directions to your home."

"Ah, Mr. Walsh."

"I did not know his surname." He laughed. "And we are to be bunkmates for a while. Odd." He stared at the ceiling. "A man offers me lodging—to split the rent, of course— and yet he never even introduces himself. I only know his Christian name because Mr. Dimsdale addressed him as such. He knows nothing about me, except that I claim to be a doctor, and yet he agrees to let me share his hotel room. Odd."

"Welcome to the West, sir."

When he looked at her again, she asked, "Are you a doctor?"

He seemed taken aback. "You said you *claim* to be a doctor."

"Well. Oh. Yes. I see your point. Yes, no, yes, I am a doctor. Graduate of the University of Maryland School of Medicine. Class of 1859. What I meant was that a man could have claimed anything, that I was a remittance man from Liverpool, that I was an investor from Philadelphia, that I . . . But . . . well, Missus Story . . . let me . . . I assure you . . ."

Her laughter cut him off. "Doctor, I jest. I never doubted your credentials. And Nelson would not have sent a remittance man or investor to check on my needs."

Finally, after a heavy sigh, he smiled.

"That's better."

"Do you have a doctor, ma'am? Not for your . . . your . . . well, as you know . . . a midwife, an experienced midwife, will be valuable to you. But . . . in other cases. I'm . . ."

"Nelson and I have been seeing Dr. Crepin."

"Oh." His eyes narrowed as though he wanted to remember.

She helped him along. "But he has left our town for Helena."

"That's right." Excitement filled his voice.

"I supposed Nelson would choose our next doctor," she said. "Although he detests doctors. Refuses to see them. Mostly because he is such a skinflint. But, it is for him to say who will be our doctor of choice."

"Yes. Yes, I suppose . . ."

"On the other hand, Dr. Beckstead, I believe he has already made that choice."

His head bobbed. "Dr. Justice, I presume. Dr. Crepin's former partner."

"No, Doctor. He sent you to see me. The way I read that, is that he has chosen you, sir."

"Me?"

"You are a man of gumption."

"I don't think so, ma'am."

"From the stories I have heard today, while selling my pies, you stood up to Nelson. Not many men have enough gumption to do that."

"I did not win my case."

"There are not many men who do that, either, sir. Not against my husband." A sharp twinge caused her to straighten and clutch her stomach.

"Missus Story?"

Her eyes were closed, but she answered, "I am all right." The voice was tight, and she did not know if he even heard her.

A moment later, she found him on his knees in front of the chaise, stethoscope in his hand, looking up at her.

"Let me listen, ma'am," he said. "If you would unfasten your coat. This will not hurt in the least, and I will not invade any of your privacy, ma'am. I can listen through your clothing. If you are uncomfortable with any of this, I can find Miss Papadakis if you would just tell me where she lives."

* * *

He had the kindest touch, but she saw him blushing all the while he listened with the device.

"How do you spend your days, Missus Story?"

"In the mornings I bake pies. Small pies. Usually of dried fruits I buy at the store. Then I sell as many of those pies as I can. Then I clean the house. I fetch water from the well and bring it inside. I cook supper. I do what I did before I became with child."

"A bucket of water is heavy, ma'am."

"And two buckets are heavier, Doctor. My mother, when she was with Jeanette, my sister, told me that lifting heavy items helps the body prepare for the ordeal of bringing a young life into our world."

Removing the stethoscope, he smiled and rose. "You and your child—"

"My son," she corrected him.

"Undoubtedly, ma'am. Both of you sound healthy."

"Then I think my husband chose wisely for our new doctor."

He bowed. "I have taken up too much of your time, Missus Story."

"I have found our conversation enjoyable, and hope we shall have another opportunity quite soon."

"I would be honored." He found his hat, his black satchel, and the wooden box. She stood and moved to the door, opening it for him. Outside, in the cold, he turned. "Mr. Dimsdale suggested I reach out to a Dr. Sparhan, to see if he might have interest in taking on a partner. Although, if you think Dr. Justice might serve me better, then . . ."

"Sparhan, Dr. Beckstead. By all means, Dr. Sparhan." Her head shook sadly. "His right hand had to be taken off.

That . . . is dreadful . . . as well you know . . . for a man in your profession."

His eyes seemed different then. He started walking toward Jackson Street and talked, more to himself. "It is dreadful," he said, "for any man in any profession. How well I know."

CHAPTER TWENTY-ONE

The blade of the bowie knife slammed down hard, splintering the ice in the bottom of the bucket. Over and over again. Until Molly McDonald figured she had enough, so she overturned the bucket, dumping shards, chips, and bits and pieces of ice into the stewpot.

"There," she said. "Maybe that'll make enough for some coffee."

"It will not be good if the bucket no longer holds water because of this . . . imbecile." The Bulgarian frowned at Constance Beckett, who stared at the harnesses for the oxen, trying to make sense out of a tangled mess.

"Cory's doing fine," Molly said. "Way I remember things, you couldn't tell the difference between an ox's arse and his face when you first landed in Kansas."

"Still cannot," the Bulgarian said. "But that does not make me a fool."

"She," Molly said, "ain't no fool."

"He's not calling her a fool, Mickey," Coleman said.

Molly looked across the fire. "Maybe you think we should've let them soldier boys hang her," she said.

"It would not be so bad for us, Mickey," the Bulgarian said, "if she would lift her skirts for us once in a while."

"Jeee-sus." Molly made herself laugh. "Cory don't wear skirts no more. And there are more whores in Leavenworth than turds in a pigpen."

"That charge money," Coleman said. "And carry diseases with bad names that make one's pecker rot off."

Molly found a twist of tobacco in her coat pocket, brought it up, and tore off a sizable chaw. "Maybe she does, too."

That got a smile out of the Bulgarian.

But Coleman brought out a blue-tinted bottle he had bought at Goldstein's and had his first bracer of the morning. Usually, he didn't start drinking till at least the sun stood midway up the eastern skies. He sipped, swallowed, and did not return the cork.

"Tell her," Coleman told the Bulgarian.

The Bulgarian hesitated, then reached behind his back, and withdrew a folded copy of a newspaper. He opened it toward her and said, "It's the *Daily Tribune* out of Lawrence."

"I'll have to take your word for it, boys. Y'all know I can't read or write." She could read or write better than either of her pards. The Bulgarian turned to the third page, folded the *Tribune*, and pointed to a bold-faced, all-capital headline that read: *BY TELEGRAPH & POST*. His finger went down to a short notice. "This here item, Mickey, says that the soldiers at Fort Kearny haven't got any notion about who done in Major Warner Balsam late last year, and as such they are posting a bounty of seven hundred dollars for anyone who brings the murderer to justice."

That's not what the *Tribune* reported at all. What Molly read was:

A dispatch to Fort Leavenworth from Col.
McCoy at Ft. Karny, Neb. Ty., reveals no
arrests in the murder of Maj. W. Bullson,
stabbed to death last December. Col. McCoy
requested permission to place a reward of up
to $700 to help solve the mystery.

But Molly had to admit that the Bulgarian got the gist of
things pretty damned close. Better than the damned rag of
a paper, which couldn't even spell Balsam's name right.

"I can't believe the two deceitful miscreants I got for
pards," Molly said. "You're willing to turn in poor ol' Cory
Bennett yonder, hard worker that don't even talk too much,
when you know the major got what he deserved."

"What I know," Coleman said, "is that all we have to do
is turn her in on our next trip north, and we get two hundred
bucks apiece, Mickey."

Coleman's math was as bad as his breath, or, more than
likely, he was trying to cheat on the division.

"Turning her in," the Bulgarian said, "does not mean she
swings. She can prove she killed the major in self-defense.
She goes free. We go away . . . rich."

Molly sat back, spit tobacco juice into the flames, heard
the sizzle, and wiped her mouth with the thick sleeve of her
winter coat. "Two hundred dollars each would buy a lot of
tobacco and whiskey. Maybe even a whore without no
pecker-rotting pussy."

Her pards chuckled.

"We might could even testify on her behalf," Molly said.

Coleman and the Bulgarian nodded with enthusiasm.

"Show me that writing again."

The Bulgarian turned the page. Molly stared at the note,
let her eyes wander, and jabbed at an advertisement.

"What do that say?"

The Bulgarian stared, swallowed, and read slowly and carefully. "Hembold's Fluid Extract Buchu." He looked at the smaller typeface of the advertisement, wet his lips and said. "Non retention of . . ."

"That's enough," Molly said. "What does *buchu* mean?"

The Bulgarian looked at Coleman, who ran his tongue underneath his lower lip for a moment before saying, "It's a type of medicine, Mick."

"By golly," Molly said, laughing. "You boys got an education." She looked at Constance Beckett, now Cory Bennett, trying to figure out one end of the harness from another. "She ain't the sharpest blade I've ever seen, but, you know, boys, she ain't that bad of a looker. Even if she don't lift her skirts for us gents."

They laughed, and got the coffee ready.

The boss of the train bound for Lecompton came by to say that he wasn't going to risk setting out until the norther passed. Didn't want to risk getting caught in a blizzard. He would wait until morning and see what the clouds looked like then.

Molly nodded her agreement, even though she found the boss to be a gutless wonder. Lecompton wasn't much more than forty miles from Leavenworth, and if they got caught in a norther, the damned storm would have blown past them in no time. She figured the boss just wanted another night with a soiled dove to keep him warm. She hoped his pecker would rot off.

On the other hand, that was fine with Molly.

"How's that Bennett working out for you, Mickey?" the boss asked.

"Slower than Easter," Molly replied, which wasn't an exaggeration. Maybe it was even an overstatement.

"Well, fine. Just fine. See you in the morning. I'm thinking about having a nightcap at Matilda's."

"We'll join you," Coleman said. "How about you, Mickey?"

Molly shook her head. "Roulette wasn't kind to me. I can't afford what they charge at Matilda's."

When they were gone, Molly picked up the copy of the Lawrence newspaper and moved to the tent, pushed her way through, and shoved Constance Beckett until her half-frozen eyelids opened. "What . . . what . . . is it?"

"What it is," Molly told her, "is my pards is greedy and you're suddenly showing a profit."

"Huh?" The subzero temperatures had frozen her brain.

"Me and you, doll baby, are lighting out. Right now. Pack up your possibles."

"I don't . . . understand."

"The army is considering posting a reward for you. Not you who be Cory Bennett, but you who be Constance Beckett, who put a knife in a major's chest. Right about . . . here."

The frozen face lost even more color. "I'll never get far enough away."

"That's where you're wrong, kid." Molly pulled out the paper, unfolded it, and placed it on the ground near Constance's slouch hat. "See that there notice?" She tapped the advertisement.

WESTWARD TO RICHES

**I am organizing an expedition that will depart
Nebraska City
in the spring for the goldfields in the
Northern Rockies.**

Following Bozeman's trail.
Experienced Bullwhackers needed.
Apply to: MAJ. COUSHATTA JOHN NOAH,
The American House, Nebraska City,
Nebraska Territory.
☞ *Liberty and Union Men <u>Preferred</u>.*

"Nebraska City?" Constance's head shook dully. "How far is that?"

"In this weather, by train, eight, nine days."

Constance shook her head, adamantly. "We'd never make it. *I'd* never make it. We'd freeze to death. And they would follow us, follow our wagons, we'd . . ."

"I don't aim to take these wagons." Molly pulled off the eye patch. "I aim to burn this, as they'll be looking for a one-eyed horse thief and his pard. I aim to steal two fine-blooded stallions. Then I am for us to take off at a high lope as far as we can get tonight. The gents in Leavenworth won't be thrilled about having to go after us in this cold, and the only two who'll want to track our horse-stealing hides and kill us will be afoot. We'll swap the horses with some Pawnees, drift in to Nebraska, wait till the thaw, and see this Major Coushatta John Noah. That'll give you a couple of months, maybe longer, to learn how to pass for not only a man, but a first-rate, Yankee-loving bullwhacker."

Constance Beckett blinked rapidly.

"Unless you'd rather drop from a gallows," Molly reminded her.

CHAPTER TWENTY-TWO

José Pablo Tsoyio left a gringo dollar by the sleeping head of the *mujerzuela* and softly closed the door to the crib before he walked down the alley. The residents of Dallas would call the weather on that February night cold, but José Pablo Tsoyio had been much, much colder, and after a lovely evening with a soft-skinned woman and a glass of tequila—good tequila, not the garbage they poured at most establishments in this poor North Texas town, José Pablo Tsoyio found the evening pleasant. Until he heard his name called by a man in the shadows.

Stopping, José Pablo Tsoyio put his hand on the Dance revolver he carried in the mule-ear pocket of his Mexican denim trousers.

"Me llamo Jorge Sanchez." He made up the name on the spot. A match flared, followed by slow, easy movement as an orange glow faded and flamed while a cigar was lighted.

"Well," the voice behind the cigar drawled. "I don't recollect ever meeting a cook by that name. Or a man real good with a knife. I do remember a gent about your build, your age, your attitude, and your voice. Alfonso Rivas?"

José Pablo Tsoyio had not used that name in three and a half years.

"Carlos Luis?"

That one was more recent, but not exactly timely.

"Heliot Ramos?"

That brought the pistol out of the pocket, and José Pablo Tsoyio slowly cocked the hammer, stepping on the garbage to muffle the sound.

"Antonio Pinero?"

The hammer lowered. José Pablo Tsoyio had used that name only once. He slid the Dance into his pocket. "And what name are you using today, señor Hannah? Besides *hijo de perra*."

Jameson Hannah stepped out into the alley. Smoking his cigar, he moved easily toward José Pablo Tsoyio. He seemed taller, leaner. "Could I interest you in a drink, amigo?"

"Como desées," José Pablo Tsoyio said.

"How about Hardee's bucket of blood by Trinity Mills?"

"They do not let Mexicans in, señor."

"They will if you're with me."

The *norteamericano* at the door did not like it. Neither did the man at the long bar, but none objected, for Jameson Hannah remained a powerful man, in reputation and size. He wore tall boots of a caballero with a green sash around his waist that carried two pistols. His pants were black, as was his vest and cravat, the shirt a heavy blue wool, the hat gray—but not the gray of the old horse soldier that he had been for three or four years. It was a new hat. Jameson Hannah seemed to be doing quite well, which not many former Confederate soldiers could claim.

Hannah ordered brandy. It was not the drink José Pablo

Tsoyio would have ordered for himself, but since Hannah was spending his own money, there was no reason to complain. They sipped, and Hannah dipped the end of his cigar in the amber liquid and drew on it.

"How's your English, whatever you're calling yourself these days?"

José Pablo Tsoyio shrugged.

"You still making beans and bread for your keep?"

Another shrug.

"Way I recollect, you cook *muy bueno, mi amigo*."

José Pablo Tsoyio smiled ever so politely.

"Though I imagine a certain notorious individual and some of his colleagues would not think that was the case. Your being a good cook, I mean. There was a news item I read in Fort Worth, somewhere south of here. Bunch of rustlers got poisoned. All of them dead. Three, four, six. I don't rightly remember the exact number. And this store clerk at the town, someplace south of here, pretty far south, he—this is according to the paper, and it was a Fort Worth paper, so you know the facts might not altogether be true— but the clerk said there was a Mexican cook working for the outfit. Went by the name Heliot Ramos. No Mexican was found among the bloating, poisoned bodies of the rustlers."

"Perhaps they ate bad beans." José Pablo Tsoyio sipped his liquor.

"Maybe. Man I knew down in Millican died after eating bear grease he warmed up in a brass kettle."

"Cholera morbus," José Pablo Tsoyio said softly.

"What's that?" Hannah crushed out the cigar.

"It is of no importance."

"Well, it's the name of the Mexican cook that made me read the little article." Hannah sipped. "Do you remember a tinhorn named Heliot Ramos down Brownsville way? Just before the war broke out?"

José Pablo Tsoyio shrugged again. "Should I?"

"You killed him."

Another shrug. "I have killed many men, señor. As . . ." He touched his snifter against Hannah's. ". . . have you."

"And since Heliot Ramos had no need of his name anymore, you borrowed it . . . just temporary."

No answer.

"What name should I address you by tonight . . . no . . . I guess it's morning . . . what name, amigo?"

"The name my mother and father gave me sixty-four years ago this evening, señor. José Pablo Tsoyio."

"It's your birthday. Damnation, pard. Many more blessed years before you." Their glasses clinked again, and they moved from the bar to a table.

When the brandy was finished, Hannah ordered another round. The bartender frowned. The waiter took his sweet time bringing two more brandies to the table, and when he set them on the table, Hannah motioned him forward, handed him a silver coin, and then shoved the barrel of one of his revolvers into the man's privates. "You tell your boss that my name is Jameson Hannah." The man was already gagging, but the name caused the eyes to bulge even more. "And two things I detest. One is arrogance. One is tardiness when it comes to drinking on my friend's birthday. And the next time I look at the bar, I'm not saying anything, but if there's not another round on my table in half a minute, I'm killing somebody. And maybe more than just one body. *¿Comprende?* That's Mexican lingo for 'Do you understand what I'm saying, bucko?' Because I figure that since these Mexicans owned this here country before you, me, Davy, Jim, Travis, Austin, or General By God Sam Houston ever set foot in this country, it's probably a good language to use." He shoved the man backward, and he toppled over a table, came up, righted the table, plus the chair that had gone over with him, and moved fast to the bar.

"You are still a man of immense patience, *patrón*," José Pablo Tsoyio told his benefactor.

"Well, I like to stir the pot now and again. How have you been?"

José Pablo Tsoyio responded with his patented shrug.

"How about if I spell things out for you, José?"

After reaching into his vest pocket, Jameson Hannah showed him a ripped page from the *Dallas Herald*. An advertisement had been circled.

DUNN, HOWE & CO.
Pork and Beef Packers,
Jefferson, Texas
**Will pay the Highest Market Price for
GOOD FAT CATTLE and HOGS**

"I am no cattleman, señor."

But Hannah pointed toward the east. "It's a hundred fifty miles or so to Jefferson. I figure to drive a hundred head or so of fat Texas beef to East Texas. Sell good fat cattle for the highest market price."

"Why not pigs?" José Pablo Tsoyio grinned.

"Pig dung stinks," Hannah said. "I sort of think cow shit isn't that foul-smelling. Chicken shit, now that's the nastiest."

They finished their cordials. Jameson Hannah did not look toward the bar for another.

"I need a cook to feed my crew. A good cook. And what I would need from the cook is a man who is not only handy with a Dutch oven and skillet, but makes coffee that doesn't taste like muddy water. And, more importantly, can work a musket or revolver like a soldier. Way I remember things, you fill that bill, compadre."

José Pablo Tsoyio bowed with graciousness.

"I'd need you on the other side of the Trinity north of town, come daylight. I've got a crew of five others. I take half of what we get. You get ten dollars extra. The rest is divvied up between you and the other cowhands. Agreed?"

"It would be an honor to ride with you again, *patrón*."

"The honor, José, will be mine." He turned to the bar. The waiter and the barkeep were staring, anticipating, the bottle of brandy and two clean cordials waiting.

Jameson Hannah nodded, and the bartender was pouring when Hannah turned back to José Pablo Tsoyio.

"We aim to drive fast, and February is not always cooperative when it comes to weather. Get those cattle to Jefferson. Maybe spend the rest of the winter across the border in Louisiana."

"Some might find that advisable," José Pablo Tsoyio said.

"Yeah. I figure the rightful owners of those cows will be annoyed."

CHAPTER TWENTY-THREE

He put the old man to bed again, glanced sadly at the wooden prosthetic that had replaced the right hand, and pulled the sheets and blanket over Dr. Sparhan. Drunk again. Passed out—before ten in the morning. Seth Beckstead had never seen a man so hell-bent on drinking himself to death, but on this bitterly cold morning, he did not plan to spend his time moping around, mopping up the doctor's vomit, which would come at some point. He had something better in mind. He grabbed his coat, muffler, and hat, and his black satchel, and left the rawhide cabin, hanging a CLOSED sign on the stag horn on the wall. As though some patient might actually come by.

Fifteen minutes later, frozen numb by the harshest wind he had ever felt, Beckstead pounded on the door while stamping his feet just to get the blood circulating again. Perhaps he heard footsteps inside, but with the howling wind and the wool over his ears, he could not be sure. He tapped again. Even wearing gloves, his fingers ached with cold.

"Yes. Who is there?"

That did not sound like Ellen Story. Then he remembered the midwife. "It is Dr. Seth Beckstead," he yelled.

"One moment."

The moment lasted half of February. He turned, just to keep moving, and stared down the barren street. Barren from what he could see, which was no farther than thirty feet. He didn't think it was actually snowing this morning. The wind was just driving snow that had fallen during the past four days. If the midwife did not open the door soon, they might find him come spring thaw, buried under a mountain of dirty snow.

The door opened, the voice inside said something, but Beckstead could not hear. He slipped inside, then had to help a prim, dark-headed woman push the door closed. "Thank you," he said, and began peeling off his gloves. "Forgive me, ma'am, but I have forgotten your name."

Dark eyes, though not as dark as Ellen Story's, bored through him. "We have not been introduced."

"My apologies. Your mistress, Missus Story, said she had hired a midwife. I . . ." He remembered his hat, removed it, dumping snow onto the bearskin rug. "I am Seth Beckstead. Mr. Story asked me to check in on his wife while he is traveling."

She bowed, though the eyes did not lighten with any trust. "I am Popie Papadakis."

"What a delightful name."

"Surely you jest, Doctor." She turned. "Missus Story is in the loft. Follow me."

It was much warmer in the loft, and Ellen Story smiled as he came to the bed, and sat in the rocking chair where he guessed Miss Papadakis spent much of her time. Slowly she peeled back the white cloth, and Beckstead smiled at the sight of a tiny, pink-faced baby with already a thick mane of black hair on the top of his head.

"Isn't she beautiful?" Ellen whispered.

She. Beckstead looked again at the sleeping newborn. "I have never seen anything more lovely," he lied. He thought the woman holding the child was the prettiest creature God had ever created. "Have you given her a name?"

Ellen laughed softly, and sighed. She wiped a tear that suddenly appeared. "Nelson never considered a girl's name. We were both so certain a son would be born. The way he . . . *she* . . . kicked. You remember, Doctor. Don't you?"

"I shall never forget."

"She was to be Nelson Story Jr." Ellen's head shook. "But I think . . . Montana."

"It is a beautiful name for a beautiful baby." Beckstead began opening his satchel. He pulled out the stethoscope. "And a fitting name, too. The first daughter of Montana Territory."

"I would think not, Doctor," Ellen said. "Bannack City came before Virginia City, and think of all the Indian girls born here. Alice Montana Story and I are newcomers to this land."

Beckstead nodded in fascination. "Alice Montana Story. Well, Mother, I would like to check up on both of you, if you will allow." He was shaking the thermometer in his left hand. "Open your mouth, please, and stick out your tongue."

"Your prognosis, Doctor?"

Dropping the stethoscope into the bag and pulling a handkerchief from his vest pocket, Beckstead turned back toward the bed and smiled. "A long life for two lovely women," he said. "Just do what you've been doing, obeying Miss Papadakis, resting, sleeping, and loving your wonderful—and healthy—daughter."

It wasn't all the truth. The baby's lungs and heart were weak, but that might be expected for a child born in a brutal winter. Ellen had hemorrhaged more than usual and remained fatigued. Yet these things happened often during childbirth, or so he had heard. Bringing babies into the world was not what medical doctors did; they left that to midwives, or just let the mothers do it on their own. Keeping them alive afterward . . . that was a doctor's job.

"Popie, alas, will be leaving us tomorrow," Ellen said with a sigh and a smile at the midwife, still hovering in the corner, dark eyes like a hawk's, waiting for the right moment to swoop down and claw out Beckstead's eyes.

"But . . ."

"I was not the only woman in Virginia City with child. She must attend to Missus Fletcher's needs."

"Twins," the Greek said. "Most likely."

"Well . . ." Beckstead could not think of anything to say.

"I was hoping, since you are our physician, that you might check on us. What would be your fee for this?"

"Missus Story . . ."

"I insist."

"We shall figure that out later. I want you to rest."

"And I want you to tell me about your adventures in our town. How is Mr. Walsh, your roommate?"

He closed the bag, set it on the floor, and laughed with true emotion. "Patrick Walsh is a wonder. But getting a good night's sleep in the Weston Hotel is . . . shall we say . . . ?"

"Impossible," Ellen said. "I have heard the stories, Doctor."

He shook his head. The Weston had four rooms, all about six feet by twelve feet, and there was a kitchen in the back where guests could cook their own meals, and a parlor with a big skylight in the center for entertaining guests or working or reading or just sitting around while waiting and praying for spring. The problem was, well, the hotel had no hallway. You walked into the first room, tried not to disturb the guests, and entered the second room, tried not to disturb the guests, and entered the parlor, proceeded on to the third room, then the fourth, and finally the kitchen. It could make for a long night, what with Virginia City being a twenty-four-hour town, and it proved especially hard for the guests who happened to be in the first room, and the current tenants in that room happened to be Seth Beckstead and Patrick Walsh.

"Patrick snores, too," Beckstead told Ellen after she finally stopped laughing. He also farted, constantly, but Beckstead left that detail out, as well as his frequent use of the chamber pot from the time he staggered in from the saloons well past midnight till the time Beckstead had to get prepared for work around five in the morning. Work. To fix Dr. Sparhan black coffee and gruel and sit around and watch the old man throw up and start drinking the worst whiskey a man could find in the Fourteen Mile City. Until the doctor closed the doors to his office and wandered to the bucket of blood on Jackson Street.

"My lady should get some rest," the Greek watchdog spoke.

At which point the baby awakened and began to cry.

"Well, Doctor," Ellen began, "I guess it is time to part. But you will pay us another visit."

"Every day," he said, already rising and pulling on his protection for the long walk back to Dr. Sparhan's lodging. "Shall we say tomorrow at nine-thirty?"

"Very well, sir. I look forward to our visit."

"No more than I do. Is there anything I could bring you?"

"The *Post*?"

"Easily obtained, as I happen to be on good terms with the printer."

Ellen's laugh sounded like a symphony.

The Greek cleared her throat. The woman knew not the meaning of the word *subtlety*.

He nodded at her hard face as he reached the ladder and started down. "Good-bye, Alice Montana Story. Take care of your mother. It is a beautiful name, Missus Story."

He reached the bottom and finished dressing for the storm beyond the door.

"I think so," Ellen called down, and her next sentence almost broke Beckstead's heart. "I do pray that Nelson does not make me change it."

CHAPTER TWENTY-FOUR

"I've been trying to figure you out, Boone." Nelson Story's hard eyes trained on the dark-eyed, dark-headed young man leaning against the split-rail fence. "You just follow me like a pet dog. I almost invalid you by bashing out your brains, and here you are. Still with me."

Mason Boone turned, stared, and shrugged.

"I didn't give you a choice at first," Story said. "You had to ride that stagecoach out of Virginia City. But once we strung up those road agents, you could have taken your leave. Yet here you are."

"All you had to say," Boone said, "was 'Git.'"

"Just what do you *get* out of this?"

The Texan let out a quick laugh. He pointed to his coat, pulled it open, showed the belt around his waist, the holster on his right hip, the .44 Army Colt. He moved his right leg out, moved his foot left, right, left right, left right. Those boots had cost fourteen dollars back in Atchison, Kansas. He pushed back the black hat.

"I haven't bought breakfast or supper since Alder Gulch, either," he said.

"I meet Andrew Johnson, president of these United States, in Washington," Story said. "I shake hands with him.

I watch Julia Dean Haynes at the Brigham Young Theater in Salt Lake City, playing Juliet. I meet bankers in Philadelphia and New York City, and I take you back to Ohio, my old stamping grounds. You never said a word."

"But I ate well. Slept in some fine hotels." Which Story knew to be true. Boone had enjoyed the food and even champagne at William Ebbitt's boardinghouse in Washington City, and had gotten lost trying to find his room inside the sprawling hotel run by the Willard brothers while Story was meeting with Montana territorial representatives.

Now, here they stood on pastures near Murfreesboro, Tennessee, tombstones and crosses covering much of the ground. Story walked to the nearest grave, turned, studied the Texan. "At first, I figured you aimed to assassinate me."

"It crossed my mind," Boone said, "a time or two."

"Why didn't you?"

"I wasn't completely convinced I would survive the attempt."

With a nod, Story moved to another headstone. "I told you I never fought in the rebellion." He had changed the subject with such abruptness that Boone appeared dumbstruck. "Many of my friends did. I learned about many of their fates when I was back home in early January. Several of the lads I grew up with fell here."

"Several of mine fell here, too."

That caused Story to reconsider the Texan.

He thought about the dead Ohioans. Brothers Ed and Dick Woodard. Story had been trying to court the boys' sister, Rebecca, so the Woodard boys tried to persuade him to leave their sister alone. In Woodard fashion. Jumped him on the porch, slapped his face, buried one fist in his stomach, slammed a heel on his toe. Threw him against the wall, and stepped back while laughing and issuing a few taunts and threats.

Naturally, no one inside the farmhouse dared open the door, or even turn up a lamp inside. Pa was six feet under by then, along with Ma and Story's brothers. All Story had known was that worthless petticoat Pa had married, figuring the widow Ruhamy Russell would be a good enough mother for his surviving son. She even gave Story two stepsisters, though one of those had died by the time the Woodards came calling. Maybe that's what changed Story. He didn't like being ambushed, and he certainly didn't like being called back from Athens to work on a damned farm. Nor did he like the Woodard brothers.

So while Dick and Ed laughed, Story drew the barlow, the one Pa had given him, unfolded the blade, and slashed Ed Woodard from wrist to elbow. Both brothers ran off the porch like scalded hounds.

Now, nine years later, the whole affair seemed so damned silly. But back then . . . hell, the whole world had pissed him off. Once Pa dropped dead, Story had to drop his studies at the university, return to Bungtown, to a stepmother who despised him. And once Ed Woodard's arm was stitched up, Story heard the whispers, from neighbors, workers at the gristmills and copper shops, even his stepmother. N. G. Story. Stands for No Good. So he had lit a shuck for Kansas Territory.

He told himself he came to Tennessee to apologize to the Woodards, let the brothers know they had taught him a lesson he had never forgotten. That Golden Rule he often recited: *Do unto others, but do it first.*

Story moved to another grave. "Most of these are unmarked 'Unknown.'"

"Most of those who fell near me don't even have markers," Boone said.

Story thought about asking Boone about the battle here. He wanted to. But that was not Story's way. It might show weakness. He didn't have to ask. Suddenly, Boone started talking.

"It was damned cold. Not warm like it is today. I mean, warm for this time of year. We'd trade with you boys. They'd send us food or coffee, and we'd send them tobacco, mostly. That was at night. Next morning, we'd be trying to kill each other. Hell of a thing." His head shook. "Hell of a thing."

When they reached the rented carriage, Story snapped the quirt, and the dun began to head back toward town.

"What do you know about cattle?" Story asked as they trotted back to the path.

"Not a whole hell of a lot."

"I thought Texas was cattle country."

"Not where I hail from."

"Well, here's what I know, from talking to everyone I've met in practically every city we've visited. Cattle. Texas cattle especially. There's a fortune to be had. A man with grit and determination can drive beef to Sedalia or Kansas City and ship the herd to Chicago and turn a massive profit. That's where you can make a fortune."

"What do you know about cattle?" Boone asked.

"I just told you . . ."

"You told me about business. About money. What do you know about working cattle, driving cattle? You don't just sell your beef in Chicago. You've got to get that herd to Chicago. So what do you know about cattle?"

Now Story knew why he had brought Boone with him. The man didn't fear Story, and spoke his mind. There weren't many people around these days who would do either of those things.

"I don't know a damned thing about cattle." Story lashed out at the horse. The buggy increased speed. "But here's something else I know. I know that if a man could get a herd of cattle to Virginia City, Montana, he'd make more money than he'd ever see in Chicago."

Boone started to laugh, before realizing Story was serious. "You'd try to drive a herd of Texas steers to Alder Gulch?"

"Not steers. What they call a *mixed herd*. Steers. Cows. Bulls."

Boone pulled down his hat. "What I do know about cattle is that mixed herds are harder to handle. Just like horses. Geldings, you're probably fine. But once you put two stallions and a mare in that mix, you're playing with fire."

They did not speak for a quarter mile. Story said, "I also learned this. The Gallatin Valley would make fine cattle country. Ranching. And a man needs at least a bull and a cow to start a ranch."

Boone let out a long breath. "Here's what I know about you: You have balls. And ambition. I don't know about brains."

Story glanced at Boone: "Here's what I know about you. You're tougher than a cob. With a head of granite. But you lack vision."

The silence lasted until the town came into view. Story said, "You'll come to Texas with me."

Boone shook his head, but when he started to protest, Story was already talking. "You went with me through Idaho and Utah. Across Nebraska, Kansas, and into Missouri. To Ohio. To Washington City, New York, Philadelphia, and here we are, on some whim of mine, in Tennessee. You've been my ward and my manservant. Now you'll be my adviser."

"You don't take advice," Boone countered. "You don't even give it. And I've already told you I don't know a damned thing about cattle."

"But you know about Texans. And that is why I'll be paying you from now on . . . in wages . . . not duds and grub and train tickets and visits to cemeteries filled with dead soldiers."

"Story . . ."

"One hundred dollars a month. Virginia City wages, of course. Starting now."

When Boone sank back onto the seat, Story said, "I see we have reached an understanding."

They did not shake on the deal.

PART II
Spring

CHAPTER TWENTY-FIVE

"I can't believe I let you talk me into this."

John Catlin did not even shoot Steve Grover a glance. He stared at the sprawling, bustling, busiest little piece of nowhere that he had ever seen. They had crossed the Missouri River in Iowa by ferry and found themselves in . . .

"Indianapolis hasn't got a thing like this," Grover said.

Wagons larger than anything Catlin had even seen in the Union army lined street after street. People ran as though fleeing a twister. Frame buildings with false fronts ran up and down the main street, an oasis on a wavy sea of grass. The first freight wagon he passed had five yoke of oxen. A voice barked at them to get out of the street, and Catlin turned to see a mule-drawn wagon digging up mud, four mules to one line. He grabbed Grover's shoulder and they moved to the boardwalk in front of a long, rectangular business named, according to the red-painted letters on the false top floor:

Men's Furnishing House.

A man exited through the door, almost barreling over Catlin and Grover, did not apologize, just kept on walking.

Catlin looked at Grover, who set his valise at his feet and wiped his brow. "I'd keep a hand on that," Catlin told him, nodding at the grip. He kept both hands on his. Silently, Grover picked up the bag, and both men stepped aside as a burly man in buckskins charged past, patting his fringed britches with a shiny-knobbed whip.

Another man turned the corner and made a beeline toward . . . whatever. Catlin got out an "Excuse me, mister, but . . ." before the crowd swallowed the fellow.

"Over there." Grover pointed across the muddy street.

Catlin saw the man in the tan suit, sitting on a bench in front of Markley's Fitting Out House, and they slogged through six-inch-deep mud, let six or seven people pass, and stepped onto that boardwalk. Grover took a step closer to the man, who turned the page of his newspaper, and stopped, glanced at Catlin, and let his sheepish grin remind Catlin that he was the captain and Grover a mere private. After a menacing scowl, Catlin stepped closer to the bench, cleared his throat, and said, "Excuse me, mister, but could you direct us to . . . the American House?" The man finished reading a sentence, looked up at the two, and adjusted his bifocals. "We just got into town, you see," Catlin explained.

The gentleman pushed back his silk hat, smiled pleasantly, and said, "Do I look like a damned city directory?"— and returned to his newspaper.

"Boardwalk is for walkin', not standin'." Now Catlin turned to find another bearded man in buckskins, a brace of pistols in a wide belt. Catlin backpedaled toward the street and let the big man pass. He and Grover followed.

"Friendly town," Grover said.

"Shut up."

The sky remained black from the smoke of the steamboats along the bank of the Missouri River. The sky matched the mood of Nebraska City.

Men barked, cursed, fought. Oxen bellowed. Mules brayed. Whips and lariats popped. When one wagon moved out, another came into its place. The streets stank of dung.

"Must be more folks here than there were at the Grand Review," Grover said as they waited for a giant wagon to turn left and head west.

"I doubt that."

"Folks at the Grand Review sure were a whole lot friendlier."

Nodding, Catlin spit into the mud. He saw all the fresh excrement he would have to cross to get to the next block and, from the sign on the side:

McCord's Outfitting
If You Don't Like Our Prices,
Lump It.

"Reminds me of Camp Rose in South Bend," Grover said.

Catlin sighed. "But our sergeants weren't as rude or profane."

"Difference between a Hoosier and a westerner, I guess. We gotta walk across that?" He nodded at the dung. "Seems like folks would put a board or something across the street. I bet McCord won't like folks tracking any of that filth into his store."

"Lump it," Catlin said before stepping into the quagmire.

A man crashed through the doors of a saloon, slammed into the wooden column, spit out teeth and blood, drew a knife sheathed in his boot, and staggered back inside. Glass shattered. Someone groaned, and the man flew through the doors again, this time missing the column and landing in the muck between two horses at the hitching rail. The knife flew out next, swallowed by the mud. The man tried to rise, but his face planted again in the filth, and another man came through the door, sucking on his skinned knuckles.

Slowly, he turned and sized up Grover and Catlin, lowered his hand, wiped his lips with his left hand, and tilted his head at the man in the street.

"Friend of yours?"

Grover's head was already shaking as Catlin said, "Didn't get a good enough look at him either time, but I doubt it. We just got to town."

"Years back, this was a peaceful town," the man said. "When we got Russell, Majors and Waddell's freighting company to move here, Majors insisted on a few changes. Including the suppression of dram shops and dens of iniquity. As you can see, the suppression did not last." He turned back toward the saloon, lifted his right hand, snapped his fingers.

He wore plaid woolen britches, a gray hat with the left brim pinned up, high brown boots, a long scarf, and a billowy cotton shirt of red with white polka dots, and a big revolver holstered high on his right hip.

One of the doors creaked open, and a hand stretched out with a pewter stein. The man took the stein and sipped. The hand making the delivery disappeared.

Catlin took a chance. "We were wondering, sir, if you might be able to direct us to the American House."

The man smacked his lips, shook his head, and grimaced. "This is the worst whiskey in the territories." He ran his tongue over his lips. "What business do you have at the American House?"

Well, Catlin figured, it was at least a conversation.

"We're looking for a Major Coushatta John Noah."

The man took another drink, spat it out, and then took

another drink, this time swallowing. "*Válgame Dios,* what business would you have with that nefarious scoundrel?"

"We were hoping to hire on as bullwhackers."

The man laughed. "Good luck with that, gentlemen."

Catlin and Grover waited and the man took another drink, swallowed, shook his head, and pointed the stein toward the north. "You boys must have come undone to want to join up with that scalawag, but . . . if you're game enough, cross the street, two blocks up, another block west. Be gone, lads. But don't say you have not been warned."

"I don't see anything that says *American House*." Grover stopped, and tried prying off mud with a busted wagon spoke.

"I don't see anything that looks like a hotel," Catlin said.

The street ended after some privies and cribs, one dilapidated sod hut with the roof caved in, and a wagon yard filled with mangy mules and donkeys with their ribs showing. There were about a dozen freight wagons, empty, rotting, falling apart. Wheels were missing from two, and the axles busted on at least two more. The place reeked of trash, because this had to be the garbage pile of Nebraska City. Beyond that, rolling plains stretched for eternity.

"Maybe we ought to go back to La Porte," Grover said.

"Maybe. After I teach some rude folks in this town manners."

"Oh, shit," Grover said, and tried to catch up with Catlin before he turned the corner.

The man in the mud was gone, perhaps sucked down into the bowels, and the fellow who had directed them to the trash heap was gone. Catlin barged into the saloon and found the man sitting at a table in the center, smiling.

"Don't tell me," he said with a smile, "that you did not find Major Noah."

Laughter filled the saloon as Grover pushed through the batwing doors, trying to catch his breath.

"But I've found you, mister."

"Major," the man corrected. "You should address me as Major." He removed his hat—the top of his head was bald. "Major Coushatta John Noah, at your service." He rose, left the stein on the table, and approached the two stunned Hoosiers.

"A test, gentlemen. First, you followed orders. Second, annoyed, you came back to settle a score. You showed loyalty and grit. Ask any man in Nebraska City and they will tell you that Coushatta John Noah hires only men with loyalty and grit. Do you have horses?"

Both men shook their heads.

"Well, you have a long walk ahead of you. You're hired. If you can make it to my camp by first thing tomorrow morning." He pointed. "Seven miles due west, on the trail, an ash hollow. You'll smell my cook's sourdough biscuits." He held out his hand. "I'm glad to have you with me."

Catlin stared at the hand, then slammed a right fist into the man's jaw, sending him sailing toward Grover, who stepped onto the boardwalk and held the door open to allow the man to pass, slam into the hitching rail, startling the horses, and land on his knees.

"You must take me for a fool," Catlin said as he stepped out.

The man spit out blood and rose unsteadily. "I am Major Coushatta John Noah." He wiped his lip. "Now, I will pardon you once, but lay a hand on me again, boys, and I will answer with lead." His right hand brushed against the butt of the revolver. "My name is Coushatta John Noah. My train is seven miles due west on the main trail." He pointed. "You follow that road. I will meet you there at first light. We will talk over breakfast. How foolish is it for me, a wagon master, to hire two men who haven't even convinced me that they know an ox from an ant?" The hand extended again.

Catlin looked at Grover, then slowly, shook the hand, tensed and ready if the man reached for that revolver while shaking. He didn't. Instead, his hand slipped into his vest pocket and pulled out a coin. "Go. Have a drink on Major Coushatta John Noah. I'll see you in the morn."

He spun, and took off hurriedly down the boardwalk. Scratching his head, Grover looked at Catlin, and then both men heard footsteps. A tall, thin man stepped past them, unleashed a long whip, and let it fly. The blacksnake caught the running man at the ankles. The only thing John Catlin knew about bullwhackers was what he had tried to teach himself in his farmhouse over the winter, but he learned that to make a long whip fly in close confines took more skill than he had.

Next the man started reeling in the leather like a man working a fishing line, approaching the screaming man who, by now, Catlin was convinced was not Coushatta John Noah. Slowly, Catlin walked behind the man, and Grover followed Catlin.

Just as the thin man with the whip reached the dubious Noah, the slickster reached for his gun. The crunching of bones under the thin man's boots caused Catlin to grimace, then smile. The thin man reached down, jerked the bellowing man to his feet—the .44 remained on the mud-slicked planking. He slammed the man's face against the white-washed wall, leaving a stain of blood, hair, and snot. He brought his knee into the man's groin, buried his left fist into the man's gut, and as the man started to vomit, threw him into the street.

"Buster, you use my name in one of your pranks again, and your hide and hair will be drying with your bones from here to the Big Blue." He picked up the revolver, started to throw it into the mud, then examined it, pulled back the hammer, listening to the action, lowered the hammer, felt the gun's balance, nodded with approval, and slipped the Colt into his waistband.

Turning, he looked at Catlin and Grover.

"You two got business with me?"

"Are you Major Coushatta John Noah?" Grover asked.

"More than that pissant." He gestured to the man still lying in the sludge.

"Well . . ." Grover turned toward Catlin.

"We're answering your advertisement," Catlin told him.

The man gathered up the long whip. "Freighting men?"

They glanced at each other. "We're willing to learn," Catlin said.

The man laughed. "I don't teach school, boys. I drive trains."

"Yes, sir," both men spoke.

"If you read that advertisement carefully, you might recall the phrase, 'Experienced Bullwhackers needed.' Remember?"

The saloon door opened, and a man called out, "The big one put Slick Pete on his arse. I thought he busted the crook's jaw."

The coiled whip slid upon the real Coushatta John

Noah's left shoulder. The left hand began massaging the right hand's knuckles. "Is that true?"

"If I wanted to bust the grafter's jaw," Catlin said, "you wouldn't have been conversing with him."

"Well, all right. But again, I need experienced men. This trip will likely get some of us killed."

He started to turn, but stopped when Catlin said, "That advertisement also said 'Liberty and Union Men Preferred.'"

Coushatta John Noah stopped, turned, and stared.

"We weren't teamsters during the war," Catlin said. "Weren't mule skinners or bullwhackers. If you're heading to Montana Territory's goldfields, you might have need of us, too."

"What outfit?"

"Eighty-seventh Indiana."

"Never heard of it. Where'd you see the elephant?"

"From Perryville to the Carolinas," Catlin answered.

The eyes fell on Grover. "Chickamauga. Missionary Ridge. Kennesaw Mountain. Atlanta. More than I'd care to remember."

"Who'd you follow?"

"Colonel . . ." Catlin started.

"I mean generals. If I never heard of your regiment, I likely don't recollect no petty-ass colonel."

"Grant. Sherman."

"Grim warriors." Coushatta John Noah nodded.

"It was a grim war," Catlin said.

"Meet me for breakfast at the American House," the tall man said. "We'll talk then. If I can't hire you, I'll at least feed you some chuck. That sound right by you?"

"Yes, sir," both men said, and watched Major Coushatta John Noah enter the bucket of blood.

His voice bellowed, "So how many of you pissants

thought Slick Pete's joke was funny?" A few men quickly exited through the batwing doors.

Grover turned toward Catlin. "We still don't know where that hotel is. Why didn't you ask the major?"

"We got till breakfast to find it," Catlin said.

CHAPTER TWENTY-SIX

They camped on a hill just outside of Fort Worth, Texas—Story, Boone, and two friends that Story had hired in Leavenworth, Kansas—Bill Petty and Tom Allen. Well, maybe *friends* was a bit of a stretch. Nelson Story couldn't rightly say he had ever had a friend, but he had met Petty and Allen back during his Kansas days. Good men. Loyal men. Knew how to shoot and drive wagons, and Story had made a lot of purchases in Kansas, telling the merchants that he would be back in a few months. Five weeks later, they had arrived in Fort Worth.

It wasn't exactly what Story had expected.

"I don't see one damned cow," he said as they rode their saddle horses into the small town. "I don't even see a fort."

"Yanks abandoned the fort long before the war," Boone told him. "Moved the soldiers to Belknap."

They stopped in front of the courthouse near a frame building, with the sign, J. W. OLIVER: ATTORNEY AT LAW, swinging back and forth in the wind, the right side hanging down, casting a shadow on the FOR SALE notice tacked on the door. Cabins were scattered about beyond the square, but no streets connected the buildings. The only road led around the courthouse and over toward the West Fork of the Trinity River.

"Maybe you ought to just stock your store, Nelson," Tom Allen said. "Go back to Kansas, get the goods there. You'll make a fortune, and selling airtights, harnesses, everything you ordered—you'd make a killing."

"No. I'm going into the cattle business."

"Cattle trail through Dallas." Boone stuck his arm off toward the east. "Thirty miles or so. That's where you'll find herds."

"Herds bound for Missouri," Story said.

"With all the desperadoes, fences, and angry farmers, those drovers might be inclined to sell their herds," Petty said.

"For Missouri prices."

"Come on." Boone pushed his bay gelding ahead. The others followed without comment. While not exactly bustling, the businesses around the square started to show signs of life. A grocery. A drugstore. Café. Hotel with a stable out back. A man in sleeve garters swept the porch to a cabin that doubled as a mercantile. Seeing the four men, he smiled pleasantly and leaned the broom against a bench.

"Mornin', friends," he said. "What can I do for you this fine day?"

"Looking for someone," Boone said. "Jameson Hannah."

The smile flattened. The easiness in the man's face died, and he straightened. His eyes moved from Story to Allen to Petty—men with *Yankee* written all over them—then back at Boone.

"You a . . . friend of his?"

"No. Never met him. But I served with his brother in the war."

"What outfit?"

He certainly had a suspicious nature.

"Tenth Texas Cavalry."

The man plastered a false smile, and let his head bob up and down. "And how is Caleb doing?"

"I don't know any Caleb Hannah. I knew Cody Hannah."

"That's right, Cody. How is ol' Cody?"

"Not so good since Murfreesboro. That's where he was killed. As you likely damned well know." The man's face went back to that doubtful look, and Boone waved his right hand toward Story. "This here is Nelson Story. Yeah, he hails from Ohio, but we came from Virginia City."

"Nevada?" the man exclaimed.

"Montana." Boone figured there was no sense in explaining that Petty and Allen were from Kansas. The man had enough misgivings for an army of secessionists. "We're looking to drive a herd of longhorns to Montana. And from all Cody told me before he stopped a damn Yankee ball was that his big brother was the man to see about anything when it came to cattle, particular cattle, in North Texas. Now, do you know where Jameson Hannah is or not?"

The man picked up his broom, started sweeping, paying attention to every ball of dried mud, leaf, and speck of dust on his porch. Having given up on any cooperation from the clerk, Boone swore, spit, and neck-reined the bay to the right. "If Hannah's not still in Dallas, or hanging from a post oak, or in jail," the man said, still sweeping, "he'll be at Cascade Mary's soon enough."

"Where's that?"

The man's chin jutted out toward a solitary log cabin off to the northeast.

* * *

Boone couldn't call it a whorehouse, but the ladies of the tenderloin sat on the cabin's porch, in loosely fitting clothes, some looking bored, others seeming to be drifting into a laudanum morning. They smiled as the men reined up and dismounted. One chirpy gestured to a crib behind the cabin. A black boy, not even in his teens, stepped through the open doorway and asked, "Take your horses, gentlemen?"

Boone handed him the reins to the bay. The kid led the horses to the corral.

"Reckon they're safe?" Petty whispered.

The pockmarked brunette removed the cigarette from her lips, blew a smoke ring toward the awning, and said, "I'll make sure nobody runs off with 'em, boys." She then opened up her robe, revealing her white skin and small breasts, before drawing a four-shot derringer from a shoulder holster. Petty blushed. Allen's mouth dropped agape. Story removed his hat, said, "Ma'am," and moved into the darkened room.

Boone stopped at the door, looked at the brunette, and asked, "If Jameson Hannah stops by, tell him a friend of Cody's would like to talk over a business proposition."

"I don't know no Jameson Hannah, sonny."

"Then you're the only one in Texas who doesn't."

"How'd you know Hannah wasn't here already?" Allen asked when they found a corner table.

Boone answered with irritation. "There weren't any horses in the corral."

A Mexican stepped out of a back room, looked the men over, and approached, wiping his hands on an apron, but using the apron to hide the pistol stuck in his waistband.

"Coffee," Story ordered.

"Sí. ¿Quieres algo de comer?"

"Just coffee," Boone said.

The man looked to the door, shook his head, and walked toward the potbelly stove in the far corner.

"How long do we wait?" Petty asked.

"You got someplace you need to be?" Story said.

"Well . . ." The Kansan grinned sheepishly and nodded toward the porch.

"Forget it," Story told him.

By four o'clock that afternoon, they had left the cabin just to visit the privy, and their bellies and bowels were sick of what passed for coffee at Cascade Mary's. The back door opened, and a woman walked in, stepped behind the bar, picked up a tray, laid five tumblers on it, grabbed a bottle from the back bar, and moved to the table.

A petite woman with blond hair pulled up into a bun, she wore a one-piece gown of gray silk with a prim-and-proper white collar, fuller skirt, and banana-shaped sleeves. Even carrying a tray, she moved with grace. Smiling, she lowered the tray and slid it to the center of the table.

"You boys are bad for my business," she said in a smooth Southern—not Texas—accent. "Have a drink on the house before you leave."

"Who says we're leaving?" Story said.

"I do." She removed the cork from the bottle of rye, and began pouring. "I'm Mary. This is my place. I'd like to keep it. And most of the menfolk in Tarrant County would be downright agitated if I had to close it."

"We'll be leaving," Story said, "after we meet someone."

The bottle returned to the tray, she picked up the cork, stoppered the rye, and held out her tumbler.

"When Jameson comes by." Her blue eyes sparkled. "I'll tell him to call on you boys. Where are you staying?"

Boone answered. "Hill up by the creek. Lot of shade trees."

"I know where you're taking about." She raised her glass and waited.

Story said, "What if Jameson Hannah doesn't come by?"

"Sir, don't be silly." If a fellow looked just right, he could see lavender in those eyes. "Jameson Hannah always comes by."

Story let a rare grin appear, and he nodded and reached for the glass, and Nelson Story did not drink whiskey often. The others picked up their tumblers, holding them toward the hostess. Glasses clinked, and the rye traveled down with the smoothness of maple syrup.

The blonde set her empty glass on the tray, picked up the bottle, and brushed past Boone, stopping to run her hands through his hair. "If you boys decide to spend some money, stop by again. I enjoy entertaining Texas boys." She winked at Story. "But I can tolerate a Yankee now and then."

They watched her return the rye to the bar and disappear through the back door.

CHAPTER TWENTY-SEVEN

The rider with the green sash and gray hat rode up the tree-studded hill on a wiry buckskin mustang, cradling a Spencer carbine in both hands. A good horse, Nelson Story figured, and a good rider, who had draped the reins over the gelding's neck and controlled the animal with his legs.

"Morning," the man spoke evenly, nodding first at Story, then at the others in the camp. Story had risen from the fire that morning, holding his cup of steaming coffee in his left hand, and his right thumb hooked inside the belt next to the holster on his left hip. "The name's Hannah. Word is you'd like to have a parley with me."

Story nodded at the coffeepot. "Step down."

Tall, lean, and hard, his face bronzed by sun and wind, his hair dark and long, a mustache dropping down toward his chin, Hannah swung down gracefully, ground-reined the buckskin, and strode to the fire. He still held the Spencer, but now smiling, he lowered the hammer and leaned the weapon against Mason Boone's saddle. At that point, Story moved his right hand away from the Navy Colt.

Boone emptied the dregs from his tin cup and pitched it

to Hannah, who caught it with his left hand, and squatted by the fire. Once his black coffee filled the cup, he sat back on his haunches and looked up at Story.

"The word I heard was *cattle*."

"That's right."

Hannah sipped, nodded with approval, and looked at Boone. "I take it you knew my kid brother."

"Yeah," Boone said uncomfortably.

"Told him not to go. Told him this wasn't our fight." He stared at the coffee. "But Cody just had to go and prove himself."

"He proved himself," Boone said. "More than once."

"Well, that's good to know, I reckon." Hannah swallowed more coffee before looking up at Story. "I'm listening."

"I'm driving a herd of longhorns to Montana."

The cup had been coming up toward Hannah's mouth, but it stopped, and wound up resting on a rock by the coals.

"Well, that's certainly a *plan*."

"I didn't say I'm *planning* to drive those cattle. I said I'm *driving*."

"I heard you. And I still say it's a plan. How far is it to . . . where exactly in Montana?"

"Virginia City. In Alder Gulch. By my guess, fifteen hundred miles, but that's from here. We have to go through Leavenworth first. Leavenworth, Kansas."

"I know where Leavenworth is." He winked across the fire at Petty. "There's a Yankee fort there." His head shook, and Hannah sipped more coffee. "All right, let's call it three hundred miles to Leavenworth. Thereabouts. I'd have to see a map to figure out how much more . . ."

"Let's call it eighteen hundred miles or so," Story said. "Thereabouts."

"Mister, it's March already. Late March. We'd be lucky to get your herd moving by the first of April. Eighteen hundred miles? Getting your beef there by November would take a miracle."

"As long as it's before January the first, I'm good."

"You might be, but your beef won't. Cattle eat grass on a trail drive, mister. And grass don't grow in winter."

"Cattle eat grass in winter, too, and the Gallatin Valley's pretty well protected."

"A horse is smart enough to paw through frozen snow to get to some feed. A longhorn just bawls and starves to death."

"A miner in Summit told me it would be a mild winter."

"And how the hell does he know that?"

"I didn't ask. But he hasn't been wrong in three years."

Hannah laughed. "How many head are you thinking about driving?"

Story shot Boone a glance before looking back at Hannah. "First, this will be a mixed herd. Some I aim to sell. But I want some for breeding. I figure if I raise beef in Montana, I can sell beef in Montana, without all this expense and time." Seeing no reaction from the mysterious cattle broker, Story asked: "Three hundred head sound about right?"

Hannah shook his head.

"Six?"

Hannah reached for his cup, drank, and said, "Make it a thousand." When Story hesitated, Hannah grinned and added, "Your miner said it was going to be a mild winter. So this Gallatin Valley ought to be able to support that many head." He passed the cup to Boone. "More, son, if you'd be so kind." Back at Story, he went on, "Rule of thumb here is one cowboy for a hundred head of beef. That's cowboy." He held up his left hand and spread out thumb and fingers as he counted. "That doesn't include trail boss, cook, or wrangler."

"What's a wrangler?" Tom Allen asked.

"The fellow in charge of the remuda. And you're looking at one substantial remuda."

"Remuda?" Allen asked.

"Horse herd. You don't take one horse for one cowboy. A good cowhand'll go through maybe six horses a day. Sometimes more."

"Ten cowboys for a thousand head is a lot more expensive than three cowboys for three hundred," Story said.

By then, Jameson Hannah had the coffee cup back. "Yeah." He sipped, nodded again in satisfaction before adding: "But I'm not talking about cowboys or cattle. I'm talking about guns."

"Guns?" Petty said.

"I work Texas, boys," Hannah said. "Some in the Indian Nations. Missouri a bit. Eastern Kansas. Louisiana." He leaned back and sighed. "There's this sweet gal in Natchitoches." Another sip of coffee, and he straightened. "But from what I hear and from what I read in the newspapers, there's a hell of a lot of tension on the western plains, and I have to think that one cow or a hundred steers would invite some unwelcomed curiosity among the Cheyennes and Sioux."

"All right," Story said. "A thousand head. Ten cowboys. And the others."

"Good enough."

"But you ought to know that we'll be bringing some freight wagons with us from Leavenworth."

Hannah laughed without humor and shook his head. "Well, then we definitely won't see your mecca till mid-November at the soonest. How many wagons?"

"At least two. I'm considering my options."

"I like a man with vision. Why not a couple of omnibuses filled with whores?"

"No, Mr. Hannah. One thing Virginia City doesn't need is another whore."

Chuckling, Hannah twisted his mustache. "Then I just might take a liking to Virginia City."

He rose, finished his coffee, and tossed the cup back to Boone. "I'll hire the crew. If that suits you. How particular are you about your men?"

"You have the reputation, Mr. Hannah," Story said. "Men you choose should be suited for the task at hand. But warn your men: I don't bend at all."

Hannah nodded. "If I thought you'd bend, I wouldn't have stuck around to hear your little fantasy . . . Now, how particular are you about your cattle?"

"No more than nine or ten dollars a head."

"Fair enough."

"You'll want an advance."

To Story's surprise, Hannah shook his head. "No. I'll get the cattle at my price. You'll pay me your price. My top hand is Sam Ireland. Top hand with a running iron, plus he's a pretty good smithy when he wants to be. I'd have him pound out a road brand for you, ordinarily, but if you want to get your herd to Montana before January, maybe we should forget about road brands. I don't think we'll run into many inspectors anyhow. Let's get to the more important matters: Cowboys here earn forty a month. Wrangler the same. Paying in full at the end of the drive."

"I heard it's twenty," Story said.

"Forty. You hire them at twenty, and they'll quit when they find out we're going to Montana."

Puzzled, Boone set his cup down and said, "You don't aim to tell them where we're going when you hire them?"

"If I told them that, they wouldn't hire on. Not at first. They'd have to get used to you. I'll tell them. Hell, I won't have no choice but to tell them. Cowboys are stupid, but they're not fools. So I'll tell them when the time's right. That's why you pay me one-fifty a month. And I'll take a month's wages in advance."

"Agreed," Story said.

"One of you go see Cascade Mary in the morning. Tell her that I said for her to get you horses for the remuda. Pay her. Less than what you plan on paying for these long-horns."

He pointed east. "Follow the West Fork till you come to the Elm Fork. Where the Trinity branches off. Then follow the Trinity. It'll start moving south. When you come to the big crossing, just sit with the remuda and wait for me. Five or six days. If I'm not back by then, figure that I've been killed. Then you're out a hundred and fifty bucks, but you got your remuda. And it'll be up to you to hire another crew, buy your herd, and start this harebrained drive."

He reached down, grabbed the Spencer, and moved to the buckskin.

"What about the cook?" Allen asked.

"Cook's the most important man on the drive. You'll pay him a hundred a month. Same as the others. He gets his money when the job's finished."

"Where . . . ?" Petty started, stopping as Hannah swung into the saddle.

"Don't worry about the cook," Hannah said. "I got just the man to serve chuck." This time, he gathered the reins, kept the rifle across his thighs, and turned his horse back toward town. "Just remember," he said as he ducked under a tree branch. "The worst thing a cowboy can do is piss off a cook. This one in particular."

CHAPTER TWENTY-EIGHT

Montana hated her. Not the territory. Ellen's own baby daughter. Ellen knew that had to be the case. Sometimes, the girl wouldn't suckle. Or sleep. Heaven help her, just an hour, or even fifteen minutes. That's all Ellen wanted. Just to sleep. Sleep. Sleep. She had put the baby to sleep, bundled her ever so gently, and lay down, closed her eyes, and slept so peacefully. Only to wake up, sweating, fearful, her heart pounding, and slowly started whispering a prayer.

"Oh, God, oh, dear God in heaven, please, please, please let my baby be asleep."

Only to roll over so slowly and stare into the wide, stunningly blue eyes of Alice Montana Story.

Before her daughter began bawling, Ellen Story started sobbing.

Well, she certainly knew who to blame. Nelson Gile "No Good" Story. He was off to New York . . . no, the last letter she had received came from Leavenworth, Kansas . . . saying how he could not wait to see his daughter, that Alice Montana was a crackerjack name. Well, thank you very much for your blessing, you hard-rock piece of trash. Nelson Story was the man who brought her to this godless, summerless Hades. Her hand touched the scar above her eye, the scar being courtesy of her husband, No Good Story. Or maybe she should be cursing her father. Oh, yes, Father. Now, Nelson Story, there's a good man. A provider. A man with ambition. Thank you, very much, Papa. A man who was going places. Places? Certainly. Denver, Colorado, and the bitter mining camps in the Rockies. Then on the trail, with two incessantly slow mules pulling the wagon to Utah and on up to what remained of Bannack City. Those mules were so slow, the Storys became a joke of the train. They'd wait, sometimes taking bets, to see how long after dark it would be before Nelson and Ellen Story made it to camp.

Provider? In a pig's eye.

Ellen caught her breath. Told herself that she had not meant what she had been thinking. Or had she been speaking aloud? *God*, she prayed, *you know I did not . . . Oh, yes, oh, hell, yes, I meant exactly what I was thinking.*

Shut up. Damn you, Montana, shut up. I just fed you. I only have so much milk in my breasts. Will you, for the love of God, God in all your mercy, cannot you do just this one little thing for me?

Guilt almost curled her into a ball. She had gone mad. Mad. Completely. Like Aunt Rhonda of Gallatin County. *Montana, just shut up. Just go back to sleep.*

"Missus Story?"

Shut up. Go away. Just let me die.

"Missus Story?"

"I will rip your throat out with my bare hands if you touch me again, Nelson. You and—"

"Missus Story!"

The slap stunned her. Her eyes widened. If she could have freed her wrist from the vise that gripped her, she would have broken . . .

A face came into focus, not the face of the devil, but

the kind face of . . . no. No. It was not the Texan named Mason Boone.

"D- . . . Doctor . . . Becker?"

"Beckstead. But that's close enough."

He swallowed. He held the bundle that had to be Montana tucked in his left arm. His right arm supported her. He sat on her bed. In the loft. She wanted to reach for her robe, cover herself. But . . . was she fully dressed?

"Missus Story, I am going to lay you down on your pillows," the man said, evenly, calmly, a wonder. "Your daughter sounds hungry."

She blinked. "What are you . . . why are . . . ?"

"I happened to be passing. Purely coincidence. I heard the baby. I heard shouts. Are you all right, ma'am?"

"Y-y-yes. It . . . It was . . . a . . . a n-ni. Nightmare." She smiled.

"Yes. Of course, ma'am. Here's your daughter. I will wait downstairs and brew tea. Let me know when it is permissible for me to return to the loft." She felt the warmth of her precious child in her arms. She heard the footsteps as the doctor's boots moved away from the bed. Ellen looked into the face of Montana and felt the love envelop her. Again. But she could not push those savage, ludicrous thoughts out of her mind.

"Do I belong in Bedlam, Doctor?"

Seth Beckstead held the thermometer toward the light. "That is not for me to say, ma'am, but your temperature is where it should be."

He dropped the device into his satchel, smiled the smile of condescension, and asked, "When is the last time you ate?"

"Oh . . . breakfast . . . no . . . dinner."

"If I were to bring in the scales from Foster and Culver's livery . . ."

"You would not dare."

"Drink your tea, Missus Story."

He produced a book from the black satchel, opened it, read, turned several hundred pages deep into the red-leather-bound book, and read more. Sighing, he closed the book after several minutes and returned it to the black bag.

"You have not sipped your tea, ma'am. I am insulted."

She tasted the tea, now cold, drank more, set the cup on the saucer by the bedside table.

"That was a terrible dream I had," she said.

"I imagine it was." His eyes bored through her. She felt like slapping him. He was an intruder. He came up to her loft—her bedchambers—while her husband was away, thousands of miles away, and, uninvited, had taken advantage of her. The pocket pistol Nelson had given her lay under the mattress. No jury in the world, or especially in the Fourteen Mile City . . .

Her eyes closed. "Oh, Dr. Beckstead, I fear insanity is taking root."

"They brought us cadavers. Skeletons. But they did not teach us anything even close to this at the University of Maryland School of Medicine, ma'am." He smiled warmly and refreshed her tea from the steaming kettle he had brought from downstairs. "As I told you before little Montana joined us, this is more for a midwife than . . ." He grinned weakly and set the kettle on the floor.

"But am I mad?"

"No. Your moods tend to swing like a pendulum."

"I am depressed one minute, angry the next, restless . . . it is . . . unlike me."

"Very much so, but this is your first child. Your husband is gone. You are alone. Should I find your midwife, Miss . . . ?"

"No, no, no. Leave Popie alone. Besides, she charges an arm and a leg, and her work here ceased after Montana was born."

"Well." He glanced toward the ladder. "Perhaps . . . The professor, Mr. Dimsdale, you know, at the *Post*?"

"No. He is too busy. And an Englishman, to boot."

"I could ask one of the ladies in town . . . one of the respectable . . ."

"Those bitches." Her hands covered her mouth. "I did not mean that, Doctor . . . I . . ."

And she broke into a flood of tears, sobbing without control, and felt herself being lifted, pulled closer. She felt his warmth, the bones of his shoulder, and his arms around her back, holding her with strength, but gentleness, rocking her on the bed, easily, smoothly, in complete control. His soft whispers assured her. "It is all right, Missus Story. Everything will be all right. You are fine. You are . . ."

In good hands, she thought.

When he laid her back onto her pillow, she brought his right hand toward her face, rubbed the back of it against her check, and then ran her fingers across his palm. No calluses. Not like sand. Smooth, clean, gentle hands. She looked into those deep, dark, inviting eyes. She felt safe. So safe.

You are a married woman.

Her hands dropped to the quilt.

"Where is Montana?" Her head shot left, then right, then . . .

"Sleeping soundly beside you, Missus Story."

She found the baby, so little, so fragile, so beautiful. Her mood became filled with love. "Oh, isn't she so beautiful?"

"As lovely as her mother."

Those words would not register until after nightfall.

Turning her head, she stared up at him. "You have been a godsend this day, Dr. Beckstead. I do not know what would have become of me had you not happened by."

"Someone else would have heard your cries. Your latch-string was out. It was easy to get in. Perhaps the professor would have come to assist you."

She smiled. "Would not that have been an interesting article in the *Montana Post*?"

"Indeed."

She felt content.

"Dr. Beckstead . . . ?"

"Missus Story." He held up his right hand. "Might I, as your doctor, as your friend . . ." He paused, debated in his head, and laughed. "Would you please call me Seth?"

"Seth." She tested the word. "It is a fine name."

He said nothing, just waited.

"Very well. From this day forward, you are Seth."

"Thank you."

Now the debate ran through her mind. "You may . . . you *must* . . . call me Ellen."

"You will not believe this, Ellen . . ." He grinned and rose, bringing his black valise off the bearskin rug. "But I have two other patients that I need to call on."

"By all means, Doc . . . *Seth*. By all means. I hope I have not inconvenienced you, or them."

"Not at all, *Ellen*. I will drop by tomorrow morning. Is there anything I can bring you?"

"No. I feel much better now . . . Seth."

"As do I, Ellen. Till tomorrow."

He bowed, turned, and quickly moved down the ladder. The door opened, closed. The baby still slept. Ten minutes later, Ellen Story cried again. And did not stop until Montana awakened, demanding in tears that her diaper be changed.

CHAPTER TWENTY-NINE

Circling the horse herd, Boone reined in his gelding as Bill Petty rode toward him. The Kansan smiled, pulled off his hat, and wiped sweat off with his shirtsleeve, then withdrew the makings from his vest pocket and rolled a smoke. "This typical for March in Texas?" Petty asked.

Boone shrugged. "I don't know if Texas has typical weather in any month."

"Doesn't feel like spring."

"Spring lasts about four days. Fall about the same."

Laughing, Petty held out the sack, but Boone shook his head. Once the cigarette was lighted, Petty held it out toward the horses. "That's a lot of horses."

Boone nodded.

"And that Hannah said he only needed one wrangler to watch after them." Petty shook his head, returned the cigarette, and started talking, but Boone didn't hear what he said. Twisting in the saddle, he looked over the hill toward the south.

"You hear something?" Boone asked.

Petty went silent. "Yeah. I sure do." He looked at the grazing horses, then back at Boone. "What . . . I'm not sure about . . ."

"Stay with the remuda," Boone said. "I'll see what's behind that hill."

He put the bay into an easy lope, and stopped on the hilltop, removed his hat, and gawked at the sight. There they came, a long line of various colors and massive horns, stretching out perhaps a mile or more. Wind blew clouds of dust off toward the southeast. A covered wagon rolled along on the western side of the cattle, pulled by four mules. Two riders rode along—the beginning of the herd—and another man rode ahead of them. From the gray hat, that must have been Jameson Hannah. Farther down the line, Boone spotted two other riders, again one on each side of the longhorns. There had to be more riders past them, but the dust obscured most of that for several yards, and beyond that, coming up a draw, Boone's eyesight wasn't that good to make out any riders.

If the wind had not carried Petty's shout to the hilltop, Boone might have just sat in his saddle, staring at the spectacle. He blinked, twisted, waved his hat and shouted, "It's the herd. Go fetch Mr. Story." Petty must have heard. Boone wasn't sure his voice would carry that far with the wind blowing toward him, but Petty whipped his horse into a gallop toward the camp. Boone looked back, debated his options, then spurred the bay back toward the horses. Of course, if the cattle spooked the cow ponies and scattered the remuda toward every point on a compass, Boone didn't know what he could do to stop them. And only when he saw Nelson Story, Tom Allen, and Bill Petty riding hard from camp did Boone think of something else.

What if it's not Jameson Hannah but some other drover bringing a herd up the Shawnee Trail?

Story and the others reined up when they reached Boone. "Tom, Bill, you stay with the remuda. Boone, ride with . . ."

He stopped at the sound of hoofbeats, and four riders crested the hill—no cattle behind them—and sent dust rising behind them as they thundered toward them. Boone breathed a little easier when he recognized Jameson Hannah, riding a chestnut with three white feet that slid to a stop.

"You made it," Story said, unable to contain his excitement.

"This far." Hannah glanced at the remuda, then said without looking at the men behind him. "Lopez, there are our horses. Get them moving and moving quick and we'll see you at the camp."

"*Sí, patrón.*" A young, thin, wiry boy still in his teens spurred his spotted horse toward the remuda, but Boone did not have a chance to see how one rider could manage a herd of horses that size because Hannah was calling his name.

"Boone, you and your pards ride to the drag. Tell my riders there to fall back. They'll be watching our back trail."

Hannah must have seen Boone's face because he went on. "There's nothing to do at drag but keep your mouth shut and just push the slowpokes along. I'd pull up your bandannas, boys, and tight. Else grass might sprout from your stomachs and lungs from all the dirt you'll eat and breathe. Ride on the east side. Won't be likely to spook the herd as much. Fabian, you show them the way, then ride back with the drag boys. You know what to do."

Another Mexican, but wearing pants with embroidery and buttons up the legs, nodded, turned his black horse around, and trotted off. Boone didn't know what else to do but follow him. When he caught up with the dark-skinned man with a thin mustache and black hair to his shoulders, the man put his horse into a lope. Once Allen and Petty joined them, they galloped south, a good fifty yards away from the herd, through dust clouds, leaping over a narrow wash, up a hill and to another.

Seeing the end of the herd, the rider named Fabian reined up hard, twisted in the saddle, and gestured toward the crimson silk bandanna around his neck.

Boone understood, pulled his piece of calico up until it covered his nose and mouth. Fabian did not give them time to tighten the scarves, but pushed the gelding into another lope, slowing down when they neared the trail's end.

Four riders, filthy beyond belief, stopped their horses as Boone and the others approached. He would not have bet on being able to say what colors the horses were, either, the dust was so thick. Fabian whistled and three of the riders turned their mounts south. Then the Mexican looked at Boone.

"My name is Fabian Peña, but introductions will come later." The accent was definitely Mexican, but he spoke in perfect English. He nodded at the one drag rider left behind. "This is Jimmy Titus." The ghost in dust raised his pointer finger from the horn on his saddle. "Just do what he does. *Vaya con Dios*." He spurred his horse, yelling, *"Vámanos,"* and the quartet rode south.

Jimmy Titus adjusted his dirty bandanna, nodded, pointed, and eased his horse up to catch up with the longhorns. Boone fell in alongside of him. Dust billowed and built as Petty and Allen moved their horses into position.

Dust and the bandanna, Boone figured before they had ridden a tenth of a mile, helped hide the smell of manure.

They might have driven through Dallas. Maybe they skirted around it. Boone wasn't sure of anything except the constant bawling of longhorns, a world of blinding dust, and the soreness in his thighs, calves, buttocks, and spine. The sun beat down on them. He wondered what Nelson Story was doing. It certainly could not have been as terrible as the job Boone found himself doing. Sometimes he would look to his right to see how Petty fared, but two thirds of the time he couldn't even see Petty, and when he did, he wasn't about to open his mouth. His lips rarely parted except when the wind shifted, and then he would just spit. That made the bandanna heavier as the spit helped turn the dust into small balls of mud.

They did not stop for dinner. They rode. They did not stop for creeks. They forded them. They stopped only when their horses emptied bladders or bowels.

The sun sank. They kept driving until dark.

Finally, the young man named Jimmy Titus pulled down his bandanna and showed them how to bed down the herd. Boone could see a campfire and the outlines of men. Titus nodded.

"Y'all done good." His twang reminded Boone of the boys he had fought with in the 10th. He realized the kid hadn't said anything to him until just then. "Get some coffee. Tell Mr. Hannah I'll keep an eye on these beeves till he sends my relief."

Boone struggled with the knot in his bandanna, but finally got it undone and began shaking it and slamming it against his filthy britches. "You were at this longer than we were. Maybe I should watch the cattle." He had done a fair job, he figured, looking after the remuda for days.

"Yeah, but I know what I'm doin'. Y'all rest." He looked at Boone's legs. "Mister, you really ought to get yourself some chaps. All y'all. Saddle'll wear through 'em denims and ducks in no time and then go to work on your hide."

"It already has," Boone said, and felt a kinship with the kid when Jimmy Titus grinned widely.

"Save me some coffee and a soft spot of earth," the boy said before turning his horse and riding into the darkening night.

He could have kissed the wrangler, Lopez, when the young Mexican took the reins to Boone's bay and led the worn-out horse to the remuda—wherever that was. Boone looked for a washbasin, found none, but he smelled coffee and beans. He tried brushing off as much of the dust as he could, and started moving toward the covered wagon and the fire, but mostly toward that pot of coffee, when Nelson Story's voice rang out.

"Boone. Over here."

Boone sighed. Story and Hannah sat on a tree stump, drinking coffee, pewter bowls, empty, at their feet. Slowly, stiffly, Boone approached his bosses. Story brought the coffee up toward his mouth, but stopped when he saw just how dirty Boone was.

"How you like riding drag?" Jameson Hannah asked.

Boone wanted to drive a fist through the twinkle in the man's cold eyes.

"Hannah says we need to push the herd hard the first few days," Story said. "It'll tire them out."

"Less likely to run," Hannah added, and sipped more coffee. "It's eighty miles to the Red River. Usually, we'd make it there in ten days. We'll make it in six, no more than seven. Get that river behind us, slow down a wee bit. Where's Titus?"

"With the herd," Boone said. His mouth felt as if it was coated with dirt. "Says he'll stay there till you relieve him."

"Good kid, Titus." Hannah dumped out the dregs of his cup and tossed it to Boone, who was too worn out. The coffee cup bounced off his fingers and hit the grass. He groaned as he knelt to pick it up.

"Course, I won't be relieving the kid. You will."

Boone stared.

"You need chaps," Hannah said. "Or you'll be crippled. Better pants. But we'll get you outfitted once we reach the Indian Nations."

"Should we get proper clothes before we leave Texas?" Story asked.

"No. We're not doing any shopping till we're out of Texas. We'll get supplies for our cook in the Nations there, as well." Hannah nodded. "Drink up. Fill your stomach with José's chow. Then pick out a good night horse. Or, better yet, let Lopez get your horse." He looked across the camp. "Ward. You and Boone here are spelling Titus and Barley in two hours." He looked back at Boone. "You'll get spelled around one or two." He stared again at the fire. "José. Breakfast at four-thirty. Just biscuits and coffee. We'll be pulling out before daybreak."

"When do we sleep?" Boone asked.

"In Virginia City, Montana," Jameson Hannah told him.

CHAPTER THIRTY

On most days, Story rode ahead of the crew with Jameson Hannah, checking out watering holes, possible camping sites. He knew little about cattle, and less about driving cattle, but he kept learning. Nelson Story always prided himself as a fast learner.

Sam Ireland—the one Hannah called a "top hand"—and Fabian Peña rode point. Those were the lucky ones. The only dust they had to eat was whatever the covered wagon driven by the cook, José Pablo Tsoyio, and Story and Hannah kicked up. The wagon had been moving alongside of the herd before the crew caught up with Story and the remuda. Now, the young Mexican Cesar Lopez kept the horse herd moving on the western flank of the long line of beeves.

Farther back, where the line of cattle appeared to swell rode Dalton Combs and Luis Avala. Hannah called that spot "swing," and beyond that came two men at the "flank" position, Jordan Stubbings and Kelvin Melean. The most miserable job fell upon the drag riders, which for the past few days had included Jimmy Titus and Story's men: Allen, Petty, and Boone. Hannah's regular drag riders, Ryan Ward, Ernesto Martinez, and Jody Barley, still trailed the herd.

Hannah said that they likely would take over their regular positions after they crossed the Red River at Rock Bluff.

This afternoon, Hannah had loped off ahead, leaving Story behind. Not that Story minded that one bit. His legs were stiff. Miners walked more than they rode, and most of Story's riding had been in buckboards and freight wagons. Spending fourteen or more hours in a saddle took some getting used to. Men like Sam Ireland and Fabian Peña—indeed practically all of Hannah's hires—looked as if they had been born in a saddle. Even Jimmy Titus seemed unfazed by all this riding, and Titus couldn't be much older than fifteen.

Dust rose ahead, and a moment later, Hannah loped back. He rode a dun this afternoon—the fourth horse he had taken out of the remuda. After reining in, he turned the dun around and pulled alongside Story.

"River's just a little more than two miles ahead." Hannah found his canteen and took a drink.

"Do we rest them today and cross at first light?"

"No, we'll just push them across." He offered the canteen to Story, who shook his head. "Let's ride back. You and I will take point. I want to send Peña and Sam up ahead, scout out the best crossing for us, make sure we steer clear of quicksand."

Galloping past, Hannah told the cook that they'd be at the Red River soon. He issued his command to the point riders, and took the left side of the herd. As Story rode over to the right, he noticed the cattle. Every day the same steers led the herd. Cattle, he figured, were like men. Leaders and followers. He decided to name the brindle George Washington and the chocolate and white one Grandpa William, the first Story to leave Norwich, England, for Massachusetts back in 1637. How many *greats* came before Grandpa, Story couldn't quite remember, but Grandpa William was the one Story male with grit. Till now.

"Luck's with you," Hannah called out over the bawling cattle. He pointed to the west, where thick clouds blackened the sky. "Rains have held off. River's not high. Should be able to get them across without losing too many."

"I'd hate to lose one."

Hannah laughed. "Any head we lose crossing the Red, we'll likely pick two up once we move through southern Kansas. Providing the Texas fever doesn't kill them. And you wanted a mixed herd, so you got bulls, cows, and heifers. Real good chance we'll have some calves before we reach Montana."

Deciding to continue the conversation, Story called over, "You still haven't asked for your payment for this herd."

"In a couple of days, I'll have Luis and Peña run a tally. Nobody counts better than Mexicans, Story. That's one thing I've learned."

Story had learned something, too. He once figured Texans were all Southern trash. After all, they had fought to keep the Negro in bondage, but here, on a trail drive, Mexicans and Texans worked side by side. No one here remembered the Alamo, or if they did, they never brought it up. Even more remarkable, the two men of color on this drive—Dalton Combs and Jordan Stubbings—worked alongside white men, even men who—since Sam Ireland wore a rebel shell jacket, and Jody Barley's butternut britches still ran the blue leg stripes of an infantry soldier— had fought for the Confederacy. Combs had won Ryan Ward's spurs in a poker game two nights ago, yet Combs had allowed the Texan to keep them until they got paid in Kansas City, Missouri.

Kansas City, Missouri. Story ground his teeth. No. That wouldn't even be the halfway point.

Hoofbeats sounded, and Story turned in his saddle as Hannah spurred his horse to reach a fast-riding cowboy. The galloper was Ryan Ward. Story recognized him from the bowler hat he wore with a purple scarf tied around the crown and under his chin to keep it from blowing off.

"Keep the herd pointed toward the river," Hannah called out as he rode.

Story kept glancing back as the men met. Ward pointed down the trail. That was about all Story saw, until both men parted, Ward returning south, Hannah galloping but slowing down as he moved back to his position at the point.

"Let's hurry these along," Hannah said. "That way they won't slow down when we hit the river."

"You sure you don't want to wait to cross at morning?" Story asked.

Hannah pointed toward the clouds.

"And are you sure you don't want me to pay you for this beef?"

"Like I said, in a day or two."

"What I figured." Story dropped back, then urged the lead steers ahead a bit faster.

"What do you mean?"

"Well, if you gave me a bill of sale, I could just show that to the county solicitor, sheriff, and judge and plead my ignorance as a dumb Yankee from Ohio, who happened to be taken in by a cow-stealing son of a bitch. That paper would be my evidence. But this way, no bill of sale, I'm just another dumb rustler. So when you finally got around to telling me that a posse was hot on our tail, I really wouldn't have much choice but to fight for my life."

Hannah laughed. He pointed north.

"We might not have to fight. Ward said that sheriff is pretty far back, but you never know how a herd will swim a river. Especially the Red. She can be a bitch. And that sheriff, I'm not so sure he would want to risk a trial again. Juries tend to like me."

The pace increased.

Story could see the darkness of a muddy, deep, fast-flowing river.

"I sure hope you know how to swim." Hannah was pulling out his revolvers and sliding them into his saddle-bags, then shedding his linen duster . . . all without slowing down. Story didn't have a duster, but he quickly unbuckled his gun rig and let it hang over the horn. Got rid of any unnecessary weight, or anything that would make it harder to get across that river if his horse panicked and pitched him.

"I can swim," Story yelled back.

"Good," he heard Hannah shout. "Because I can't."

Chapter Thirty-one

The full moon had risen over Rock Bluff by the time the drag riders, and the armed guard at the rear, swam the Red.

While the crossing seemed treacherous—especially once the sun set—Story could understand why the place had been used. The outcroppings of Rock Bluff forced the herd into what basically resembled a chute, which descended to a solid ford. Swimming proved dangerous and difficult, but once horses and longhorns reached the Indian Nations, the bank sloped north. The cattle just kept climbing up, on an easy grade, and Hannah's men kept them going, although Story wasn't sure how the men or horses could manage to keep standing, let alone go forward.

Story figured he had ridden his horse across that river at least a dozen times—and Jameson Hannah had more than doubled Story's total. Story's dapple had dodged horns and limbs, even trees that the wicked current propelled like torpedoes. He wasn't sure how many head they had lost, but Hannah sent Jimmy Titus and Ernesto Martinez, two of the regular drag riders, downstream. "Keep on this side of the river, boys. Any beef on the Texas side, let Texas keep. Our little present." He swung his horse around and called out to Fabian Peña: "Take advantage of the moon. Get us two more miles, then make camp."

Hannah dropped out of the saddle, urinated, and found a cigar in his saddlebags. "Are you partial to the weed?" he said. "I have an extra cigar. Straight from Havana."

"Don't you think between the moon and the glow from your cigar, you'd make a target?" He pointed across the river, toward the glow of torches.

"Two cigars might confuse them." Hannah laughed. He pulled his revolvers from a saddlebag, returned them to his sash, drew the Spencer from the scabbard, and left his exhausted horse on the muddy, dung-covered northern banks of the Red River, while he smoked his cigar and brought Story both Havana and match.

"You did well for a virgin," Hannah said.

Story dismounted, buckled on his gun belt, and accepted Hannah's offerings. The match flared, the tobacco burned, and Story felt the satisfying flavor in his mouth and throat.

Ten minutes later, the torches stopped on the southern side of the river. Hannah stood next to Story. Both men smoked. Story's worn-out horse hung its head and snorted. The two kept horses between them and the posse.

"Hannah." A voice roared from the Texas side. "Jameson Hannah."

"Is that you, Brock Ephan?"

"You know damn well it is. I have a warrant for your arrest."

Hannah tapped ash into the mud. "I don't think they allow you to do that, Junior. You're a far piece from Ellis County."

"And you also damn well know that I have a commission in the Texas State Police."

"Yeah. I don't think that'll do you any good up here."

"I'm telegraphing the law in Baxter Springs, Sedalia, and Kansas City. You'll have a hard time selling cattle—stolen cattle—anywhere, Hannah. And I hope the border gangs jump you and cut you to pieces."

Lightning flashed in the west. Those clouds moved pretty fast.

"You best find shelter, Junior," Hannah said. He crushed his cigar in the mud, nodded at Story, and led his horse north.

"You show up anywhere near Waxahachie, Hannah, and, by Jehovah, you'll swing."

Hannah did not answer until he moved behind an elm. "Don't give yourself a hernia, Junior. Tell your voters that you've run me clear out of Texas, that Texas and Ellis County and Fort Worth and Dallas and Jefferson and all those fine places will never see Jameson Hannah again. Rest easy, Junior, you've seen the last of me." He grabbed the reins, mounted the horse, and smiled at Story. "I'm going to . . . Montana Territory," he whispered.

The rains started around midnight. Stopped at one-thirty. Started again at two. Kept going. By morning, the skies showed no signs of relief, and the sun remained hidden.

Story sat in the back of the covered wagon, out of the steady rain, sipping lukewarm coffee with Jameson Hannah and the point riders, Fabian Peña and Sam Ireland. The trail boss had given the crew some extra sleep, although with no tents, and only cutbanks and trees for shelter, he doubted if many men actually slept.

"What we'll do," Hannah said, "is push on. Move on toward Fort Gibson, then trail up the Neosho toward Kansas."

"Baxter Springs?" Ireland asked.

"Story here wants to sell at Kansas City. Maybe Westport."

The lie made the coffee seem extra bitter, and Story tossed it out through the opening in the canvas.

"All right," Ireland said. "But Kansans have been as tetchy as Missourians lately."

"Well, I figure to swing a bit farther west than usual. Take longer, maybe, but you boys are getting paid by the day. Grass should be green, too, with all this rain."

"And the rivers will be higher," Peña said.

Hannah nodded without comment, turned toward the front of the wagon, and called out, "José, ring that triangle and get those sons of bitches up. Coffee only. But I want a full meal of bacon, biscuits, and beans for supper."

Story studied the supplies in the wagon. Cookware lay scattered about in boxes, and he found enough coffee to last two months. But the flour wouldn't get them to Kansas, and the bacon was getting low.

"We'll outfit at Fort Gibson," Hannah said after the two cowhands had climbed out into the misery. "Get your boys some fitting duds for a trail drive, too. You could use better clothes yourself."

Story let his head bob.

"Speaking of money, I guess it's time for you and me to settle up," Hannah said.

"I thought you wanted to do a head count."

"No need. I am a man of my word, same as you." He sipped coffee. "You said a thousand head, and that's what I got you. So ten dollars a head, I'll take ten thousand dollars."

Story dropped his cup in what the Texans call a wreck pan.

"Ten dollars for a bull," Story told him. "Eight-fifty for a steer. Seven-fifty for a cow."

Hannah laughed. "I don't seem to be able to find an abacus in José's wagon. That math might take a college professor to figure out, anyway."

"I happen to have attended college," Story said. Which was true. He hadn't finished, but that didn't really matter, and math had never been his best subject, either, even when he had been teaching school.

"You really want to count that way?"

"It seems fair to me."

Hannah drew in a deep breath, held it, and slowly exhaled. He opened his mouth to protest, but Story was already talking, "You have plenty of time to get this herd counted." He looked out the opening to make sure no man remained in earshot. "It's a long way to Virginia City. Your dilemma is when do you count the herd. Do it now, and maybe we haven't lost that many head. Wait till Kansas, maybe we pick up some by accident and some from mamas dropping their babies. Which reminds me. Calves, five dollars."

Hard raindrops began pelting the canvas. Story glanced up, found his hat, and placed it atop his head before the canvas started leaking.

"Well, let's say I get you a tally by the time we hit Fort Gibson. And we can dicker over those figures you came up with over some Chock beer. We settle that, we shake hands, and then you pay me. So . . . how do you plan on paying me? Gold? Scrip? I really don't care much for checks."

"You get the herd's count, and that's what you'll be paid for. But you'll be paid like all the rest of the men." He smiled, and quoted Hannah from that hillside just north of

Fort Worth: "'Paying in full at the end of the drive.' That being Virginia City." He was standing now, moving to the opening, ducking, and climbing out and into the rain. He pulled the brim down lower, looked up, and nodded at Jameson Hannah. "Minus, of course, the hundred and fifty dollars I advanced you."

CHAPTER THIRTY-TWO

The sun reappeared, disappeared, and after two days, Story began to wonder if it would ever reappear.

"At least we ain't thirsty," Jordan Stubbings said.

After Bill Petty reined in the farm wagon on a knoll overlooking the camp, Mason Boone pulled up his dun and said, "What is it?"

The rain had slowed into a drizzle as they rode back from a trading post at Boggy Creek, where Story had bought India rubber ponchos, flour, salt pork, beans, bedrolls, chaps, and just about everything the grizzled old half-breed had in stock—all now piled into the back of the wagon—which Story had also bought—except for the new clothes Boone donned.

Petty pointed. "It just isn't what I thought it would look like."

Staring below, Boone saw what he had been seeing daily. Beef. Horses. Puddles that became lakes. A gray horizon. He wiped his face, sniffed, and asked, "What?"

"That." Petty shook his head. "It didn't look anything like that in Ma's Bible."

A weary sigh left Boone's mouth and he shook his head, waiting to hear the joke.

"Just not what I figured Noah's ark would look like." Allen laughed, looked at Boone, and explained with a grin. "It's the wagon. See. José's wagon. Ark. Wagon." His chuckling stopped sooner this time, and he sighed, turned away from the unsmiling Boone, released the brake, and drove to camp.

Story dreamed again.

He's a boy, digging in the Ohio farm. Digging a grave. A grave for a dog. He doesn't see the dog, can't even know which dog it is. He just digs.

Digs.

Digs.

Story flinched, eyes shot open, and in the darkness he made out the face of the Mexican.

"Patrón," José Pablo Tsoyio whispered. "It is time. I have coffee ready."

Story threw off the blanket, sat up, watched the cook moving toward the fire. He could smell coffee. He stared at Tsoyio's back, wondering if the cook had heard him muttering something, sobbing, anything, but Nelson Story could not ask. And he wasn't about to start thinking dreams meant something, like a god telling him something, foreshadowing, bullshit like that.

He knew what the dream meant. Hell, he even remembered the dog's name.

* * *

The weather refused to break. Dark clouds hid the blue sky. Rain fell. And fell. And fell. The Clear Boggy Creek looked just as muddy as the Muddy Boggy, only substantially higher. Water levels at crecks and streams revealed that it had been raining upstream for a long time. Not spring thunderstorms, those treacherous displays of roaring winds, pounding hail, and driving rains—and, sometimes, destructive twisters—but steady, cold storms with no end. One cloud passed, another appeared. On and on, wet misery followed soggy melancholy.

"How many miles did we make today?" Story asked, standing in line behind most of the water-soaked drovers for coffee.

"Seven." Rainwater ran off Jameson Hannah's hat like a waterfall.

"This normal for this time of year?"

Hannah looked at the man in front of him, Fabian Peña.

"No," the point rider said.

"I don't like it," Sam Ireland said. "Too much rain can mean disaster up the trail."

Story ran his toes back and forth inside his boots, feeling his soaked socks.

"The beeves will have plenty of grass to eat." Dalton Combs walked toward them, smiling though practically waterlogged, but holding a steaming cup of coffee and a bowl of beans in his hands. "Fattening up."

"Till come the drying winds," Peña said, staring at the puddle at his feet.

"Right." Ireland pulled the makings from his shirt pocket, looked at the drizzle, shook his head, and shoved the pouch back out of the weather.

"What does he mean?" Story asked.

"That the grass will grow high," Hannah said. "And you'd think that's good, and it is good, till it gets hot, and that wind starts blowing. Then you've got dried-out grass. Tons of it." He snapped his fingers. "Lightning strike. Prairie fire." His head shook. "It's not a pretty thing."

"Good thing for us," Stubbings said, "is that we'll have this herd delivered and off to Chicago before it gets hot."

Story stared at his boots, no longer moving his toes.

"Yeah," one of the men closer to the cook said.

The rain made the lie he had told these men feel heavier, but that passed quickly, when he stepped under the tarp, out of the weather for just a moment, and got a bowl of beans seasoned with chile peppers, and coffee with even a cube of sugar to drop into the cup.

Dark clouds hung low that morning, but no rain had fallen since just after midnight, when the wagons driven by Bill Petty and José Pablo Tsoyio stopped in the soggy sand.

"What's that?" Petty pointed ahead.

"The Canadian River," the Mexican said as he pulled out his crucifix from a jacket pocket and brought it to his lips.

"That . . . that's . . ." Petty pushed back the brim of his hat, just beginning to dry out. "Hell's fire, that was nothing more than a ditch when we crossed it."

"Thus you see the power of God," the cook said. "He turns your ditch into an ocean."

Mason Boone stopped his dun between the wagons. He guessed one of the riders halfway in the river had to be Sam Ireland, who had left Boone to ride point. The other had to be Tom Allen. At least, he thought, their horses were standing, not swimming. On the near bank, Story and Hannah kept talking, pointing northeast and northwest, while the riders began to mark quicksand.

"Shouldn't you be back with the herd?" Petty asked.

"Fabian sent me ahead."

"Nelson won't like that."

"Fabian Peña," José Pablo Tsoyio said quietly, "can do the work of *dos* riders."

"What are they doing?" Boone pointed to Story and Hannah.

"They argue," José Pablo Tsoyio said. "To determine who gets to part the Red Sea."

Which is exactly what the Canadian resembled, a roiling mass of reddish water that reached the upper parts of trees at least a hundred yards from the normal banks. Uprooted trees shot down the river, too, driven by a current. Boone glanced at the sky to the west and frowned at the flash of lightning well off in the distance.

Boone started to find a plug of chewing tobacco, but saw Story waving his hat, so he touched his spurs against the dun's ribs and loped into water that came up to the gelding's hocks.

The water reached over Boone's saddle, but the dun's feet found firm ground in the center of the river. At least here. Sam Ireland had marked the quicksand just about twenty yards downstream, and Story had put Boone here to make sure none of those precious longhorns drifted into what Ireland called "the dangersome part of the river."

Dangersome? Ask Mason Boone, the whole damned ocean looked treacherous. Yet here came the cattle, Ireland and Peña back at point, Nelson Story riding on the other side with Tom Allen, Jameson Hannah on Boone's side near the northern banks.

Both wagons had made it across and kept right on going. "Boone."

He turned in the saddle and saw Hannah pointing toward the far bank. "Drift back. Keep them moving. Don't let the current take them."

Orders that meant little to Boone. His priority was to stay mounted, and now he cursed himself for not removing his .44 or poncho. Fabian Peña had stripped down to his socks and summer undergarments. Even his boots had been tied together with a thong through the pulls and draped over the saddle horn.

"Do not let them drift," Peña ordered, motioning with his hand downstream, before moving his horse closer to the steers following the leader.

That's what everybody kept telling Boone—even Luis Avala when he came alongside later—but nobody took time to explain how the hell anyone could stop a bull or heifer or steer from doing what it damned well wanted to do.

Back and forth, back and forth, from just about to the swollen banks, then riding alongside hooves and horns, bawling longhorns—even one struggling calf, crying for its mother. Boone wondered when it had been born. Northeast to southwest, but never once touching dry land, which caused him to picture Cody Hannah, Jameson's brother, talking to him somewhere in Tennessee after a long, hard ride. "If I had to do it again, I wouldn't have signed up to be no horse soldier," Cody had said as they passed a jug of corn liquor around the campfire. "Navy. Navy. That's what I'd like to be doin'. Sailin' in some riverboat."

"You can have it," Boone said aloud, and went after that

struggling calf before the current swept it to the Arkansas border.

The sky offered no help at all. No sun to see. No shadows, just a permanent dusk. He couldn't even guess the time, so the thickening darkness might mean sunset or more rain. Yet he sucked in a breath and almost shouted a hallelujah when he saw the drag riders nudging the last of Story's herd into the river.

Jimmy Titus waved his hat. He started singing, riding this way and that, though Boone could not make out the words or even the tune because of the blubbing cattle and splashing of water. Not until Titus drew near did Boone recognize the song:

The wee birdies sing and the wildflowers spring,
And in sunshine the waters are sleeping . . .

The youngster stopped abruptly at the scream on the other side of the herd.

Ernesto Martinez's horse reared, and he pointed at something in the water.

Snake?

No. In a current like this, no one would be frightened by a snake that likely was scared out of its skin trying to stay alive. Horns flashed. Cattle began to mill. Finally, Boone thought he saw something, but couldn't . . . A canoe?

"Shit." Suddenly, he knew. On the northern banks, Jameson Hannah cursed and plunged his horse into the stream. Story rode up toward the bank, but Boone paid no attention. He tried to swim his horse closer to the herd, not knowing exactly what to do. He heard—at least thought he heard—the sound of the uprooted tree as it slammed into a long-horn. Then the straggling, sore-footed cattle turned in the middle of the river, trying to escape the tree. And Boone realized his mistake.

A horn jabbed. His gelding reared. Boone's boots slipped out of the stirrups. He lost a rein, and the horse started to roll. Grabbing for the horn, Boone missed, only to realize the last thing he wanted to do was hold on to a horse that was going underwater. Another horn raked his side. The pain told him that wasn't water running down his shirt.

Suddenly, he realized he was in the water. His head went under. Came up. He started to gasp, only to feel a hoof clip his thigh.

"Boone."

He saw Jimmy Titus, lariat in hand. Jody Barley forced his black horse through the panicking steers, trying to cut a path toward Boone.

"Grab a tail," someone shouted.

A snake shot across the back of a brindle bull. No. Not a snake. Jimmy Titus's lariat. He reached for it, lost it as it slid on the far side of the bull's back. He ducked underneath a massive horn. Snatched at a tail, found only water. Barley cursed.

Then, Boone went under.

CHAPTER THIRTY-THREE

He vomited, so hard he must have busted up his insides, because he yelled and felt blood rushing out of his body.

"He shall need stitches, señor," a voice he thought he recognized said.

"If . . ."

The second voice belonged to Nelson Story, but Boone didn't hear what the tough man said because he was puking again, then rolling onto his back and . . . Jesus . . . he was breathing. Actually breathing. Sucking in air. Not muddy water. He gasped, breathed, sweet, sweet, merciful, glorious oxygen. His side burned. His left hand started to reach across his body, only to be knocked away.

The dark face of José Pablo Tsoyio bent forward, eyes probing, water dripping off the soggy hat's brim. Boone felt chilled. Wet. His eyes shot upward and he felt the cold drizzle.

Christ Almighty, it had started raining again.

"Cesar," José Pablo Tsoyio said, and the wrangler stepped over Boone's legs. Naked legs. Boone raised his head as much as he dared and realized he was stark naked, his legs covered with sand, leaves, scratches. His manhood all shriveled up to nothing in front of all the men he rode with. Son of a bitch. José Pablo Tsoyio spoke in rapid Spanish and the little wrangler answered and ran out of Boone's sight.

"You're lucky," Story said as he squatted beside Boone.

Boone didn't feel lucky.

"What happened?"

Jordan Stubbings's lean black face somehow showed up on Boone's right. Stubbings answered Boone's question, most of which Boone started to recollect.

"Who pulled me out?" Boone asked, then screamed.

José Pablo Tsoyio, Lucifer's top hand, had poured whiskey over the hole in Boone's side.

"Can I have some of that?" Boone asked when he could open his lips without yelling or cursing.

The cook glanced at Story, who nodded, and Stubbings lifted Boone's head as José Pablo Tsoyio, that angel of mercy, let Boone swallow a bit of forty-rod that tasted like his mother's applesauce.

His head lowered, he repeated his unanswered question, but this time adding, "I'd like to buy him a bottle of rye."

"He don't drink ardent spirits." Boone looked at Stubbings, who grinned wearily. "Steer done it, boss. You latched on to his tail. Got a couple of dallies around your wrist. Probably swallowed half the river getting out."

Boone almost laughed. He recognized another face. "Thanks," he said, nodding at Jody Barley.

Hoofbeats sounded, and Story rose, turning, and taking a few steps.

"How about another sip?" Boone asked the cook.

José Pablo Tsoyio did not answer because Story called out to a rider. "Did you find him?"

The answer came silently. Boone couldn't read Story's face. Then the voice of Jameson Hannah said, "Combs and Ward are still looking. Peña, Stubbings. Fetch some coal oil out of Petty's wagon. You two ride downstream. Might need torches. Dark's coming fast."

That's when Boone understood, and he turned his head, hoping to throw up again, hoping he could close his eyes and drown. But nothing happened except Cesar Lopez returned and handed the cook hairs freshly plucked from a horse's tail.

"The wound in your side requires stitches, señor," José Pablo Tsoyio explained as he began to thread one of the hairs through a wicked needle meant for leatherwork.

Story squatted beside him again. "I'll hold his shoulders." Story nodded to someone out of Boone's sight. "You two grab his legs." Then to the cook. "Give him another belt, and let's get this done before we lose the light."

The jug came into the hands of Kelvin Melean, who had replaced Jordan Stubbings. Boone jerked his head back to Story.

"Who was it?" he demanded, although he already knew the answer.

"That's not coffee," Boone said weakly.

"A broth," José Pablo Tsoyio said. "I make it. It will help you heal. From the inside." He reached up with his left hand, grabbed a spoke to the wagon wheel, and pulled himself into a seated position. The Mexican cook made no effort to help, perhaps realizing Boone wanted to do this himself. Although now that he had proved himself, Mason Boone wished that the cook had assisted just a little.

He stared into the blackness of morning and took the cup from the cook's hand. Other cowhands gathered by the fire, sipping coffee, eating biscuits, talking.

"Why is it," Dalton Combs drawled, "that we have to

wake up at first light when there ain't no light at all? All we do is sit around and sip coffee till it's light enough to saddle our horses."

"It's written in the book," Kelvin Melean said.

Boone wanted to smile, but his eyes turned toward José Pablo Tsoyio.

"Did they find Jimmy?" he asked.

The cook's head shook.

"Is there any chance . . . ?" But José Pablo Tsoyio rose and walked to the cookfire, leaving Boone with broth and guilt.

"We could rest the cattle and horses another day," Jameson Hannah tried.

"No."

"Leave a man, one man, and have him catch up with us at Fort Gibson."

"No."

"The men won't like it."

Story tossed the rest of his coffee into the soupy ground, and nodded west. "It's still raining. We sit around here looking for a dead boy and we'll never get out of the Nations."

"It's not right. Titus deserves a decent burial."

"It's right in my book." Story rose. "That boy could be ten miles or twenty downstream. He could be hung up on a submerged tree, feeding catfish. He's dead, and I don't think he cares one way or tother if he's six feet under sod or sixteen feet underwater."

Spitting and wiping his mouth, Hannah looked at the fire where the men ate breakfast. "And folks in Texas say I'm a hard man."

"You took the job knowing I'm boss. We've burned

enough daylight, and you told me that the Verdigris and Neosho are going to be hell if we don't put those rivers behind us mighty quick. Or maybe you'd rather lose one or two more men trying to cross those."

"All right." Hannah stepped closer. "But when you try to persuade these cowboys to stick with you all the way to Montana, they're gonna remember that you didn't give one of their own—a kid, and a damned good kid—a Christian burial."

"We'll be burying him," Story said. "He just won't be in the grave. I had Luis Avala fashion a cross. We found the boy's spurs in his saddlebags, and they'll be draped over the cross. It's a burial. It'll be Christian as we can make it. He just won't be laid to rest—like maybe a hundred thousand soldiers North and South. Maybe more."

Story started moving to the fire to break the news to the men. "I'll read over his grave, too."

"The hell you will," Jameson Hannah said. "Sam Ireland will. He actually believes in God."

"That's good to hear." Story kept walking, thinking— and smart enough not to say it aloud: *Because on this drive, I'm God, and he damned well better believe in me. You might want to learn that, too.*

Boone looked at the spurs on the cross, then twisted his head and stared at the expanding Canadian River, wondering where the body of Jimmy Titus might actually be. He wanted to believe that soon, when the waters receded, maybe some Choctaws or Cherokees—depending on which side of the river the body washed up—would find poor Jimmy and bury him. Maybe sing a song about him. "Loch Lomond"? He could hear Jimmy's voice just before . . .

"It wasn't your fault." Sam Ireland squeezed Boone's shoulder.

Blinking back tears, Boone turned and tried to think of something to say. No words came. His gut twisted. His side ached. José Pablo Tsoyio's broth was taking its good sweet time to start the healing.

"Freak accident. That's all. Maybe it was his time."

"You believe that?" Boone asked.

"I believe the boss man's right," Ireland said with a sigh. "We have to get this herd moving." His jaw jutted to the west. The drizzle had become steady, harder.

Boone felt like an idiot. He was dressed in clothes that didn't fit—a shirt that had belonged to Jimmy Titus, found in his saddlebags along with the spurs and a tintype of a woman. The boy's mother, sister, girlfriend? No one would ever know. They had buried the tintype in the grave, along with one of the boy's boots that had been washed up about a mile downstream.

Boone still had his own boots. The current hadn't swept those, or his trousers, off him, but the trousers had been ripped apart, so now he wore his extra pair of drawers covered by Kelvin Melean's chaps. Sam Ireland tossed in the vest. Cesar Lopez provided a scarf. Story had loaned Boone the hat, saying they'd get some new duds at Fort Gibson.

"You up to ride?" Story asked.

Boone rubbed the sleeves of the shirt, which didn't fit, but would keep the sun off him—if the sun ever returned.

"I'm not up to walk," Boone answered.

"I mean riding."

Boone looked into Story's heartless eyes.

"I'm down a drag rider," Story said.

"Nelson," Bill Petty called out from about ten yards away. "I figured Boone could drive my wagon, and I—"

"I'll do the figuring, and Boone rides better than you do." Story's face, damp from rain, remained hard, and the eyes unrelenting. "We'll hire another rider. In Gibson. Baxter Springs. Somewhere. But I need you on drag till then."

There had been no question since Story's *You up to ride?*

"Yeah. I'll ride."

Hell, had he said he couldn't, or wouldn't, he'd be walking back to Tyler, Texas. Boone felt certain of that.

"If the side opens up," Story said, "just mosey up to Allen or José, and ride in the wagon with one of them. We can go shorthanded at drag if we have to. Or I can send Tom Allen to spell you, though Tom's been acting as a scout a bit, and I was thinking about sending him out today to see if he could bag us a deer or turkey."

Boone made himself nod, but all he wanted was for Story to shut up and leave him alone. Instead, Story took Boone's empty cup. "Best catch yourself a horse," Story said. "We're moving north. I'll dump your cup in the wreck pan."

"That's mighty damned decent of you," Boone whispered as Story walked away.

CHAPTER THIRTY-FOUR

It would be faster just walking to Montana.

John Catlin sighed. His wagon moved at the exhilarating speed of two miles an hour. The scenery never changed, maybe because the wagon—filled with three tons of sugar, flour, coffee, and bacon—never really moved. He had learned the commands on the first day, but it wasn't like you needed to know a whole lot about oxen. *Ghee* meant "turn right"; *yaw* meant "turn left"; *whoa* meant "stop." It was getting and keeping the beasts moving that worked up the sweat, tried the patience, and increased the use of profanity among bullwhackers. And Catlin had beaten himself to hell more than he had popped that stiff-shanked whip against the hide of his team.

Though he was getting to like his oxen. And he had to thank Major Coushatta John Noah for patience, and the chance, and for teaching him a little bit about positioning the animals that had to pull three tons across a dreary, sun-baked, windblown country.

A pair of longhorns went in the lead yoke. Though nowhere near the size of the other oxen, these two steers just plodded along and wouldn't stop for hill, cliff, river, or mud bog. Catlin didn't need to try to crack his whip over the lead pair's ears. He just had to yell *Whoa!* loud enough to get them to stop.

Closest to the wagon, on each side of the singletree, were big Durhams, the one on the right mostly white with black spots, while the left one shone a deep reddish brown. Each animal weighed more than a ton. Between those two yokes were three pairs of Devons—Ruby Reds—not as big as the Durhams, not as reliable as the longhorns, but with quick temperaments. Back in Nebraska City, the major had told Catlin that he would be better off with all longhorns and Devons, but this would test the new bullwhacker, and if the wagon overturned, well, then Captain John Catlin would have a long, hard job, and a fine stretch of the legs walking back to Indiana.

So far, Catlin had not wrecked. He walked alongside the wagon—for a man in the volunteer infantry knew how to walk. Some bullwhackers rode on the back of the nigh wheeler. A few had found a way to sit on the left-hand side of the wagon, but Catlin did what he had spent three years doing. He marched.

A rider appeared ahead, legs bouncing out and back as the black horse galloped, kicking up clouds of dust. It had to be Coushatta John Noah. "Stop these . . ." The pounding of the horse's hooves faded the curse. ". . . miserable oxen."

"Oh, hell," Catlin said, and remembered the easiest of the commands, "Whoa. Whoa! Whoa, you . . ." He grimaced and did not exhale until he saw his two longhorns stop a good two yards behind the freight wagon immediately ahead.

He felt like sighing in relief until the major reined the black into a sliding stop right next to Catlin.

"Where's that boy extra?" the major roared.

The boy extra would be Steve Grover—at least twelve

years too old to serve as a boy extra on a wagon train, but Major Noah wasn't about to take a chance with two greenhorns driving wagons to Montana's goldfields.

"Boy. Hey, Boy Extra?" the wagon master called.

The call went down the train from bullwhacker to bullwhacker, and, at length, Steve Grover slipped between Catlin's wagon and the one six feet ahead.

"You need me, Major?" Grover said, out of breath, but he had been farming instead of marching for months now.

"Yeah. Fetch two saddled horses tethered behind Farley's wagon. Bring them here. Quicker than I can skin a coyot'. Move. And bring them fancy muskets you two soldier boys brought along." Grover had already disappeared. "With powder, lead, and caps, boy," the major called after him. He turned to Catlin. "You say you're pretty good shots with those smoothbores?"

Catlin stared blankly. "They're rifled muskets," he corrected. "Not smoothbores."

"I don't give a damn what you call them, can you shoot them?"

"Pretty well."

"You'd better."

Two miles ahead, they saw the remains of the wagons. Two of them, or maybe one double-hitched. The oxen were gone. The fire was out. The men, both of them, were dead.

Three years of war—well, not even three, about four months shy of that—had hardened Catlin and Grover. They had seen men blown in half by canister, ripped to shreds by grapeshot. They had seen how much damage one minié ball could do to a human body. But nothing could prepare them for the scene on the Nebraska plains.

"My God," Steve Grover said.

One body resembled a porcupine, pinned to the blood-soaked ground with dozens of arrows, the top of his hair ripped from the skull, throat cut, hands hacked off and tossed aside. A wolf had been seen running from the body when Catlin, Grover, and the major had ridden up. The scene was so horrible, the stench overpowering, they had hobbled their skittish horses fifty yards before the massacre site.

"He was the lucky one," Major Noah said.

For the other poor soul was staked out, naked, arrows piercing his feet, his hands, thighs, even his manhood. His head, blackened and charred and gruesome, lay on a pillow of ashes. Roasted alive.

"What's that . . . ?" Grover had to turn his head and spit. "In his . . . mouth?"

"His dick, boy," the major said. "Or his pard's. No telling. Cheyennes." He yanked the arrow from the corpse's right foot. "Yeah. Cheyenne." He pitched the arrow into the sand. "Cheyennes have a peculiar sense of justice."

"Barbarous bastards." Grover spit again. "Damned savage red-skinned sons of bitches."

"You reckon so, boy?" The major walked ahead. "It's payback, fellows. And the Cheyennes didn't start this fight." He pointed southwest. "Ever hear about Sand Creek?"

"No." Catlin shook his head. Grover spit more bile and wiped his mouth with his hand that didn't hold the Enfield.

"A bunch of your Union volunteers attacked a peaceful camp of Cheyennes in southeastern Colorado. Even the chief in the camp was known as a peace chief. Colorado boys, same group that had turned back the secesh down in New Mexico Territory back in '62, killed a hundred, maybe two hundred old men, babies, women. And what the Cheyennes did to these poor bastards ain't nothing compared to what your white comrades done to the women and kids at Sand Creek. Late November, maybe early December, don't rightly remember. In '64. Surprised you didn't read about it."

"We were a little busy," Catlin said. He couldn't find enough spit in his mouth to swallow.

"If I was President Johnson," the major said, "I'd give all of Colorado Territory back to the Cheyennes, Utes, and Arapahos. Tell them to do whatever they wanted to the residents there. Because those boys in blue turned this whole part of the territories red."

"I thought you preferred 'Liberty and Union Men,'" Grover said.

"I do." He started walking back to the horses. "But I abhor a butcher."

When the hobbles had been returned to the bags, and the three men sat in their saddles, Major Coushatta John Noah pulled tobacco from his pocket, tore off a hunk with his teeth, and offered the twist to Grover and Catlin, both of whom declined.

"If you remember . . ." the major said as he worked the chaw with his teeth. His eyes trained on Catlin. ". . . you allowed that you weren't teamsters, mule skinners, or bullwhackers during the late war."

The chaw shifted to the other side of his mouth. "But you said that I might be needing men of your particular talents. So we're about to see how good you and my boy extra are." He pointed. "Give the dead a wide berth, then cut back to the trail. Just follow the wagon tracks. Slow and easy. I'll be riding back to the train. You just take a slow walk, steady, till you come to where you'd think a wagon would barely fit between the Little Blue and some formidable bluffs. We call it 'The Narrows.' Don't ride through. We'll camp on this side. Do a little scouting in the morn and keep pushing on toward Kearny. I'll drive your wagon, Catlin."

"You don't want our Enfields with the train?" Grover asked.

Noah's head shook. "Indians find trains rather curious. Rarely will they attack them. Those two damned fools yonder are dead because they rode out alone. Strength in numbers, boys. That's how you all whipped the rebs. But . . . those Dog Soldiers might attack a couple of foolhardy wayfarers traveling alone." He pointed toward the remnants of the wagons, and the remnants of what once had been men. "This was a small party. Six. No more than eight. So most likely they had their fun and rode off without another thought. But, since Sand Creek, it pays to be careful. So this could be the work of some scouts for a big war party. If that's the case, and you boys are as good as you claimed you were back in Nebraska City, well, I figure they'd have to bring in their pals. So if they jump you, and I find that it's a hell of a lot of Cheyennes, we'll fort up at Fort Kearny till things get more peaceable. But if you make it to The Narrows, then I'll figure that the Cheyennes got what they needed, scalps and plunder and oxen and all, and it's safe to keep going west."

He turned the horse, kicked it in the sides, and loped off toward the wagon train.

"What do you think?" Grover asked after the major vanished in the emptiness.

"That I never should have read advertisements in the *La Porte Herald* in the dead of winter."

"Huh?"

"Nothing."

"Well, what do we do?"

Catlin shifted the Enfield into his other hand and climbed into the saddle of his horse. "Follow the major's orders," he said. "We're good at taking orders. Do what he said. Go nice and steady, around that . . ." He did not look at the corpses. "Walk slow and easy. Keep our eyes open for any cloud of dust, any bird call, or bark of a coyote. Hell, the major's likely right. Probably just some young warriors, eager to get revenge for that massacre the major was talking about. We'll get to The Narrows, rest our horses, wait for the major and the others to arrive. Have a few stories over Freezing Creek's jug tonight."

Grover mounted his horse, and they turned the animals westward, upwind, curved back to the trail, and moved slowly.

"You know, John," Grover said after a mile or two, "I'll admit that I was so scared I almost pissed my pants before Perryville. But after that first fight, I really wasn't scared before we went into battle. Figured if I got killed, I got killed, and you just couldn't fret over that."

"That's what made you a top soldier," Catlin said.

"Yeah, well. Maybe so. But this is just damned different. It just scares the hell out of me. I mean, what the hell would all the folks back in La Porte be saying, if some total stranger was to find my pecker in your mouth, or vice versa?"

Catlin had been reaching for the canteen, but now he stopped, looked over at his friend, and said, "Jesus Christ, Steve, shut the hell up."

CHAPTER THIRTY-FIVE

"*Osiyo*," said one of the riders, raising his hand in greeting.

"Cherokees," Jameson Hannah whispered to Story as they sat around the fire that evening. "Probably tribal leaders. Damned Indians. You talk to them . . . I'll mosey over to some of the boys and have them ride off to help the boys circling the herd. These sons of bitches will steal anything that's not—"

"Shut up," Story said. "And keep your ass on that log."

Sitting his coffee cup on the ground, Story rose, grimacing at the tightness in his legs, and raised his own hand, "*'Siyo*," he returned the greeting, and caught the look of surprise in Hannah's cold eyes.

They had come dressed in their best, and that impressed Story. The oldest man, with silver hair that hung past his shoulders and a face savaged by smallpox years earlier, wore a long-tailed green coat with brown velvet trim that had probably been in fashion a decade or two ago. His cotton shirt was a billowy crimson, and the silk cravat hung tight across the collar, with three medals hanging from buckskin thongs. One of the medals depicted the image of the late Abraham Lincoln, so he must have been a Union man. The trousers were buckskin, and the boots the style of the cavalry, complete with military-issue spurs. A Cherokee turban topped his head.

The other man was much younger, probably around Story's age, wearing moccasins and trousers of a Confederate soldier. Story guessed that he had ridden with Stand Watie's Cherokees during the rebellion. *A Yankee Cherokee and a Cherokee reb . . . riding together,* Story thought. *Much like we have in this outfit.* A fringed hunting shirt of orange and blue stripes, made from trade cloth of wool, covered his white dress shirt. His flat-brimmed hat had been tilted back at a rakish angle.

The third rider was a woman, in a silk skirt of gold, a cotton blouse of multiple colors and dozens of buttons, and a shawl. Her raven-black hair reminded Story of Ellen.

"Please." Story waved his arm. "Light down. Join us. Would you care for coffee?"

The old man turned to the woman for translation, although Story thought this might be an act, that the silver-haired devil understood English perfectly. He smiled, as did Story at the woman's voice, and after a short nod, the men and the woman, the latter riding sidesaddle, dismounted.

"Martinez," Story said. "Ward. Take their horses. José, fetch . . ." The cook had already poured three cups. He set two on the other side of the fire, and returned to bring the third. That one he placed in the hands of the Cherokee woman, bowing while removing his hat, before returning to the wagon.

The old man tested the coffee, smiled, nodding his approval, and spoke. The woman translated, "My grandfather is called Percy Gunter. He asks if you had any difficulty crossing the river today."

"The Verdigris was very, very high," Story said. "As well

you know." He smiled. The woman spoke to her grandfather in Cherokee. "I asked one of my men if he might build a ferry, only to be told that it would take too long."

Upon hearing this, the old man grinned and clapped.

Story raised his tin cup in toast and said, "It honors us to pass through your country. Do you know how the rivers are farther north?" He pointed toward the North Star.

"You will find no dry ground for many miles." The younger man spoke, only to be rebuked by the woman.

The Cherokee glared at the woman and waited for the old man to pretty much say the same thing.

Sipping coffee, they exchanged pleasantries, talked like folks did back in Ohio and Kansas, about the weather and corn, horses and cattle. Talked like every man in Ohio and Kansas, hell, even Montana, and the Cherokee Nation—except Nelson Gile Story. But here, in a camp before a tribal leader of the Cherokees, it was Nelson Story who showed his restraint, his patience, even something of an understanding, while Jameson Hannah had to bite his lower lip to keep from blowing up and demanding that the old man get to the point.

Which, the old man did at last. The empty mug went onto the log, and Percy Gunter said, "Many Texans have walked across our country this year with hundreds and hundreds of longhorns."

"Speaks English, that sneaky . . ." Hannah whispered. Story spoke loudly to drown out Hannah's anger.

"I think our cattle swim more than they walk." He smiled. Old Percy Gunter's eyes brightened.

"You have more swimming to do," he said.

"Go on." Story nodded.

"This land was not always our land. My land . . ." He gestured east. "Was there. It was where I was born. This is not the land my father wanted, nor is it the land I wanted, but your government made this our land. Now, it is my land, my home." He gestured to his son and daughter. "Their land. The land of our people."

Story sat patiently. "The Texans who drive the longhorns through our country have hurt our lands. Our fields. Even our water. For you to swim . . ." Percy Gunter grinned widely. ". . . your longhorns across Cherokee lands, we ask that you pay a toll of ten cents for each head of cattle. Horses and mules, we will not charge."

Leaning toward Story, Hannah whispered, "Offer him two and a half—"

"We will pay you what you ask," Story said, and Hannah's fist clenched as he straightened and his ears reddened.

"I own many cattle," Percy Gunter said. "Many others own many cattle. The numbers of our herds drop when each Texas herd comes through our land. We ask that any Cherokee cattle that wanders into your herd be returned to our people."

"I would have it no other way," Story said.

Hannah spit between his teeth and slowly shook his head. The fists remained clenched, the knuckles whitening.

"Lastly," the old man said, "the Texas Road—the Shawnee Trail—whatever name you wish to call it, is well marked. But Texas cattle often move off this trail, to eat Cherokee grass. We ask that you keep your cattle on the trail, and not stray from it until you are out of our country."

The old man leaned back, waiting. Story shook his head slowly. "This last demand, we cannot accept." He gestured toward the cattle's bedding grounds. "Too many herds have passed through already, and cattle and horses need grass to eat. Grass does not grow on well-traveled roads. We must move our herds where they can eat." He stood, reached inside his pocket, and withdrew a pouch, letting the gold coins cling. "But I will pay the toll . . . one hundred dollars—you require for us to pass through your land. And know this: Any Cherokee cattle that we find will be driven back toward your people each morning before we push north." He undid the thong as he approached the three Cherokees, and felt glad when Percy Gunter nodded his acceptance of the terms.

Not that Jameson Hannah was happy after the Cherokees had ridden off.

"We could've gotten out of this a hell of a lot cheaper," he sang out. "You let them farmers buffalo you."

"It's their land," Story fired back. "They have a right to charge us for crossing their country, and ten cents a head seems dirt cheap."

"We could've whipped them so badly they would've paid us."

Story turned and came face-to-face with Hannah. He whispered so that none of the men—even the closest, the Mexican cook—could hear him.

"You save that fighting for when we need it. I'm not wasting men, powder, or lead on some Cherokees. I'm certainly not paying men to fight damned Indian farmers. We get out of the Nations, we'll have those rustlers and mad-as-hell Kansas farmers dogging us." He came even closer and dropped his voice even more. "And once we turn this herd toward Montana, we'll have Sioux and Cheyenne after our hair, buster. I guaran-damn-tee you that fighting them won't be near as easy as running roughshod over an old man, a hotheaded boy, and a young Cherokee maiden. That's when I'll pay you and your crew to fight."

CHAPTER THIRTY-SIX

Eleven days later, long before daybreak, even before José Pablo Tsoyio barely had the coffee warm, Story galloped off toward Baxter Springs, Kansas, with Mason Boone, leaving the rest of the crew and the cattle on the southern side of the flooded Neosho River. That morning, they passed one herd camped a few miles from town. Then another. On the outskirts of town, a dozen riders trotted out to meet them.

"Texan?" The white-haired gent with the flowing beard, and a musket braced against his thigh, demanded.

"Montanan," Story said.

Some of the riders glanced at one another, but the old man leaned forward and said, "Bullshit."

Story leaned back in his saddle and laughed. "Well, I guess that's one way of calling me a liar."

The men laughed. Then stopped. Story's Navy Colt was cocked and pointed at the old man. Two riders reached for belt guns, but the bearded man muttered, "Don't act like damned fools."

"My name's Story. I hang my hat in Virginia City, Montana Territory. The man with me I met in Virginia City,

Montana Territory. We aim to get back to Virginia City, Montana Territory."

"What's your business in Baxter Springs, Kansas, Mr. Story of Virginia City, Montana Territory?" The leader's voice had lost much of its firmness.

"My business . . ." Story nudged the black into a walk, but kept the Colt trained on the big man's center vest button. ". . . is my own."

He did not holster the pistol until he had pushed past the riders, and he did not slouch in the saddle or increase the gelding's pace. "Don't look back," he whispered to Boone.

"Grangers," Boone said softly ten yards later.

Story looked straight ahead but nodded slightly. "I'd call them thieves."

Two horsemen galloped south.

"They'll be looking for the herd," Boone said.

"River's too far. They won't ride past the first herd we saw. Not without a dozen more men."

Another horse began walking slowly behind them.

"What happens if they start shooting?"

"We get killed," Story replied.

After leaving both horses with the blacksmith for new shoes, Story let Boone outfit himself in the general store, bought enough smoking and chewing tobacco to satisfy the cowboys back at camp, posted a letter to Ellen, got a bath and a shave, and moved inside a place called the Jayhawker Saloon. The old man with the snowy whiskers and one of his riders, a red-mustached man carrying more revolvers than any of Quantrill's bushwhackers, followed them from place to place, though never dismounting.

"What's your pleasure?" Story pointed at a table near the window.

"Living," Boone answered.

"Let's make it a beer." Story moved to the bar and came back with two foaming mugs of pilsner. Story sipped. Boone stared out the window.

"From what I've seen of Baxter Springs," Story said after wiping suds off his mouth with the sleeve of his coat, "there's not much worth seeing."

Boone found his mug. "I thought you don't drink."

"I don't drink much," Story corrected.

"Why are we here?" Boone downed about half of his beer.

"Get you duds. You've borrowed something from just about every man I pay since . . ." He nodded at Boone's mug. "What are they doing?"

"Smoking a pipe and watching me."

"Still just two of them?"

"As far as I can . . ." Boone's eyes went past Story, who heard the footsteps. A moment later, a thin man in a plaid sack suit and bowler hat stepped to the table and smiled.

"Evening."

Story nodded.

"Name's Cromwell. Brian Cromwell. I'm a correspondent for Robert Tracy, editor and proprietor at the *Troy Reporter*."

"Where's that?"

"Fifty miles, thereabouts, northwest."

"Not enough news in Troy to fill Mr. Tracy's pages?"

"Well . . . more news down here."

Story nodded at an empty chair, and the correspondent

from the *Troy Reporter* quickly sat between Boone and Story.

"What brings you to town?"

Story lifted his glass toward Boone. "He needed some clothes and gear. I needed a shave. Our horses needed shoeing."

"Where you from?"

"Virginia City, Montana Territory."

Brian Cromwell had found a notebook and a pencil, but stopped flipping through his pages, and stared. "Honest?"

Story nodded.

"Where you bound?"

"Virginia City, Montana Territory."

"Well . . . how do you like the salubrious climate of . . . ?"

"Mr. Cromwell."

The reporter looked up from his notebook. "I don't think the editor of a Troy newspaper wants to publish an article about what a wayfarer from Montana has to say about the sunshine and health one finds in Baxter Springs."

Cromwell let the grin brighten his face.

"Are you cattlemen?"

Story tilted his head toward the two men leaning against the hitching rail across the street. "Who are those two gentlemen? . . . Don't turn your head, just nod again and move your eyes. There. Now . . . who are they?"

"The ruffian is Will Ethridge. Rode with George Todd, or so they claim. Killed forty men during the war. Maybe half that figure since. But it's Ben Fariss you have to watch, Mr. . . . ?"

"Story. Nelson Story." It made sense to give the inkslinger some information. "This is a hired hand, Mason Boone."

The reporter shook hands with both men.

"We ran into . . . I don't know if you'd call it a welcoming party or a road block outside of town," Story said, "and exchanged a few pleasantries with Ben Fariss."

"Then you have a herd of cattle."

Story started to explain that no cattle had been anywhere near them, but the reporter's head kept shaking and then he mumbled, "No, no, you wouldn't be here if you had cattle." He stared at his notes, tried to think of another question. Brian Cromwell, Story decided, was no Professor Thomas Dimsdale.

"Why don't you explain why your editor, fifty miles from here, sent you to Baxter Springs," Story said, and looked at Boone. "Walk up to the bar and bring Mr. Cromwell a . . . ?"

Cromwell blinked. "Rye. If . . ."

"Rye's fine. Two more beers, too."

They called themselves the Granger's Association. Like a number of Kansans and Missourians on the Shawnee Trail, they had grown sick and tired of losing cattle to Texas fever every time a herd of Texas longhorns came through. Now, quarantine laws were being enforced, keeping Texas beef out of the states from April through October. But Ben Fariss was no cattleman, no farmer.

"What about the Neutral Lands?" Story asked.

Cromwell shook his head. "They won't let you go through."

"Even if a toll were agreed upon?"

The reporter scribbled in his notebook, and Story reassessed the man. He had a way of finding out a few things even without asking questions.

"You can't afford a toll."

"My understanding is that the Neutral Lands aren't Kansas or Missouri, but Cherokee land."

Cromwell's pencil moved. Actually, Story knew that, years ago, the Neutral Lands, running about twenty-five miles east to west and fifty north to south, had served as a buffer, so to speak, between civilized white folks and the Osage Indians. These days the Neutral Lands were . . .

"It's more of a no-man's-land," Cromwell said. "Run by Ben Fariss."

"James Harlan might have something to say about that."

The reporter stopped writing. "James Harlan as in . . . the secretary of the interior?"

Boone delivered the beers and rye. He had made a quick exit out the back door to the privy, and as he set the drinks on the table, he said, "Two more men out back."

Story shrugged.

"Secretary Harlan . . . ?" Cromwell coaxed.

"We chatted when I was in our capital earlier this year."

The writer wrote furiously. Well, Story had shaken hands with the secretary, and both men had commented on the beauty of an actress as she sashayed down the aisle of a theater, but what Story had learned was that Harlan was working out a deal with some land company to sell the Neutral Lands. Cheat the Cherokees, probably. One of the reasons Story had paid Percy Gunter a hundred bucks for the right to pass through Cherokee lands. That would, the way Story figured it, put his herd fifty miles north into Kansas, past the grangers, quarantine laws, rustlers, and gunmen like Will Ethridge. But now?

"There were two herds camped south of town," Story said.

The reporter gulped down half of the rye, wiped his mouth, flipped to another page. "They gave up."

"Gave up?" Boone asked.

Cromwell sipped the rye this time. "Yeah. This is how

the Granger's Association works. They'll demand a toll that only a fool would pay. Then stampede your herd. Then offer you the same toll. Or they stampede your herd and say, *Want your beef back? Here's what it'll cost you.*" He smiled. "It's a pretty good story. If I can get it. Mr. Tracy thinks a lot of newspapers in the East and maybe even San Francisco would pick this one up. *Harper's*, too, perhaps."

Boone had finished about half his beer. "I don't think most Texas outfits would like that."

The rye disappeared. "You'd be right. And if you go to our cemetery, you'll find five new graves. That's what it cost the last crew that tried to drive a herd without paying the Granger's . . . ransom?" He pushed the glass toward Story and wet his lips.

"Barkeep," Story called out. "A bottle of your best rye." His eyes bored through Cromwell.

"Some crews just turn east. Try to make Sedalia. But the farmers in eastern Missouri are fed up with Texas fever, too. They just don't have the . . ." He paused, looking for the right word.

Story gave it to him. "Balls."

"Yeah. I guess that's right." He laughed, the whiskey going to his head. "Don't think Mr. Tracy would let me put that in the *Troy Reporter*, though. But, there's the chance those herds will get stopped, too. Fariss has a good deal going here. He was a lieutenant under Senator Lane's Redlegs during the war. They say he shot two of the men killed at Osceola."

Story sipped his beer, casting a sideways glance through the window at the two killers still leaning on the hitching rail.

"They've flogged some boys. Hung two or three. Gutted and scalped one. That would be Will Ethridge's doings, if you ask me, the Missouri ruffian. But here's what Mr. Salzer and Mr. Quackenbush don't know. They'll sell their herds to Fariss, but the drafts Fariss'll make out to both of them won't be good for anything except, pardon my bluntness, wiping their asses."

The bartender put a bottle of rye on the table. Story handed him a note, took his beer, and lifted his glass at the reporter. "I don't think Mr. Tracy will let you write that in his newspaper, either."

He drained his beer, slid the bottle to the reporter, and rose. "We best ride, Boone. I suspect the smithy has finished with our horses, and it's a long ride back across the Neosho."

"Sir." Cromwell was refilling his tumbler. "One last question, if you don't mind?"

Story waited.

"What are you going to do?"

"Drive my herd west," Story said. "Beyond the state's quarantine lines." And, he figured, a good way to get closer to Virginia City.

"They might follow you."

"Who?" Though Story already knew.

"Fariss. Ethridge. Not many herds have come through the past several weeks. Word's reaching Texas."

"If word had reached Texas," Boone said, "Baxter Springs would be rubble and ashes."

There might have been some truth to Boone's Texas sentiments, Story realized, and most of the delay in herds coming into Baxter Springs had to do with swollen rivers, not Kansas cattle thieves.

Cromwell emptied his rye and pushed himself up. He reached inside his sack coat and pulled out a newspaper.

"Here. This is my paper. Well, Mr. Tracy's *Record*. I don't have anything in that issue."

Story shoved the newspaper into his coat pocket.

"I'd like to ride with you," Cromwell said.

Story grinned. "I was hoping to hire some men, Mr. Cromwell. But I have no need of a scribe."

"I'd still like to ride with you, sir. I feel a great story will follow you." He burst out laughing. "Story's story. You get it?"

"I've never heard that joke before." Story glared, nodded at Boone, dropped another coin on the table, and said, "Let's go."

"Can I ride with you?" the reporter called out.

Story pushed through the batwing doors. "It's a free country."

CHAPTER THIRTY-SEVEN

Setting his cup of tea down on the bench, Dr. Seth Beckstead walked to the pole he had nailed to the sides of the cabin and the privy. Shirtless, Thomas Dimsdale hung over the poll, wheezing.

"I think that has been long enough, Professor," Beckstead said.

The *Montana Post*'s editor said something that Beckstead could not understand. He bent his knees. "Excuse me."

Dimsdale wheezed. "Help me . . . up."

Sweating profusely, clammy, pale, Dimsdale eventually stood in his stocking feet, leaned forward, and braced himself against "Beckstead's Torture Chamber."

"What good . . . does this . . . do?" the newspaperman asked.

"Professor, I'm not sure it does any good, but it might clear out your lungs." Beckstead walked back, grabbed the journalist's shoes and shirt from a rough-hewn chair, and returned. He held out the clothing. The doctor still worked his lungs.

"Some doctors perform surgery that allegedly reduces your lung capacity. There has been success with . . ."

"A cure?"

Beckstead's head shook.

"Do you have backaches?"

"I hurt everywhere, Doctor," Dimsdale said. "I'm a journalist."

"And your back?"

"When you bend over to read, and write, as much as one does in my profession, yes, your back hurts. So does my head. And my eyes."

"Bend over."

"Sir, I . . ."

Beckstead began to push, and, after an arrogant blast about English dignity, Dimsdale leaned over again. The doctor's right hand ran over the backbone, gently at first, stopping at each vertebra but focusing on the lower-thoracic and upper-lumbar areas.

Dimsdale wheezed. "What . . . are you . . . doing . . . now?"

"Consumption can destroy the spine," Beckstead said. "Have you heard of Pott's disease?"

"No . . . haven't you tortured . . . me . . . enough?"

"The lung illness can spread to other areas, usually the spine. Eventually, the vertebrae will collapse."

"So . . . I'll be a . . . crippled cougher."

"You may stand, Professor." Beckstead lifted his hand. "The good news, Professor, is that I find no protuberance or depression. So far, I feel I am able to say that Pott's disease has not taken root. You may put on your shirt."

"Your prognosis, Doctor?" Dimsdale asked as Beckstead found the bottle of brandy and began to pour.

"You have consumption." The doctor brought two cordials to the office desk.

"Astute." Dimsdale lifted his drink, the glasses clinked, and he sipped. "My parents had consumption. My grandfather had consumption. I was born to suffer and eventually die from consumption. It's in my lungs and my blood."

Beckstead sighed. "I am not certain of that."

"Meaning?"

"A professor said that his belief is that our preconceived notions to this illness are wrong, that one does not inherit this disease, but it spreads from a contagion."

Dimsdale's head tilted to one side.

"Others agree with him, but . . ." Beckstead shook his head. "There is so much about consumption that we do not know."

"But there is no cure."

"Exercise and—"

Dimsdale laughed. "And go to the West. Fresh air. Yes, Doctor, that is what brought me to Montana. And might I inquire as to what brought you here?"

"I desired to become a doctor."

"My understanding, sir, is that you were a doctor." He pointed his cordial at the red surgeon's box on a shelf. "In the late war." Dimsdale finished the brandy.

"I was no doctor, sir, no surgeon. I worked in construction. Deconstruction. A sawmill." Beckstead refilled his glass, shot down the brandy, and shook his head. "The number of limbs I removed could have filled a boxcar on a train. Possibly more than one."

Beckstead had lost control. He sucked in a breath, embarrassed, and slowly exhaled. Dimsdale stared at him, through him, as Beckstead tried to think of a way to apologize, to explain. The editor tried to do it for him.

"Which needed to be done to save lives, Doctor."

"Yes, certainly." Beckstead wanted to stop, but couldn't.

His anger, frustration, boiled over. Thomas Dimsdale wrote about death. Thomas Dimsdale admired vigilance committees—murderers like Nelson Story. "Ask my associate, Dr. Sparhan, how his life was saved . . . when he sobers up, sir, if you have that much patience." He rose, bowed, and moved toward his black satchel. "I must rush off, Professor. I have a house call."

"Missus Story, I presume." Dimsdale rose, withdrew a billfold from his pocket, and dropped a note on the table. He grabbed his hat and jacket and moved toward the door.

The comment, but more the way in which the journalist spoke it, gave Beckstead pause. Maybe it was his imagination. Maybe he should not have had that second brandy. He dropped his hat, stooped to pick it up, but by then Dimsdale was outside, about to close the door.

"I am her physician, sir. And the baby's."

"Of course." The door shut, and Seth Beckstead brushed the dirt off the brim of his bowler. Dimsdale was another one of his patients, he figured, about to return to Dr. Justice. But at least the professor had paid his bill.

CHAPTER THIRTY-EIGHT

He hired three men at Salzer's outfit, but only one at Quackenbush's. Four men. He had ridden to Baxter Springs hoping to find one man to replace Jimmy Titus, but the inkslinger's revelations made Nelson Story reevaluate what he was up against. Especially when he saw the leader of the Granger's Association, white-bearded Ben Fariss, following Story, the reporter, and Boone.

Austin Bell, from Quackenbush's drovers, was the youngest, wasn't even a Texan, but he packed a Sharps .50-caliber rifle with a brass telescopic sight, which trumped the kid's age. Luke Price's face still bore welts from the beating he had taken from Farris's men, and the other two Stan Salzer riders—one-eyed Andrew Shaps and the gimpy Drew Finley—looked pissed off at Salzer for not fighting to the last man. "I got a full crew of cowboys," Story had told them. "I'm not looking for cowboys. What I want . . . are guns." They knew what they were getting into.

As they rode, Story questioned his new men, learning that Bell and Shaps did the most talking.

"They hit us around midnight," Shaps said. "Most of us snoring. I remember jumping up, thinking *stampede*. Heard the gunshots, but there were too many for our two night herders. That's when I realized we were being attacked."

"Closer to four in the morn for us," Bell said. "We were in the Cherokee Strip. They drove the herd right into the Spring River. Left them there. Must have lost ten or twenty, stuck in the mud, about the same number drowned. Couldn't go after them, because we'd be sitting ducks trying to cross the river."

"They didn't steal your herds," Story said.

"They would've," Shaps said.

"They give you a warning twice," Bell added. "Maybe. That's what Ol' Perkins told us."

"What happened to your night herders?" Story asked.

Shaps frowned. Bell answered. "You know what a man looks like after he's been caught in a stampede?"

Story cursed.

"No way of telling," Shaps said softly, "if they were dead before the hooves flattened them like hotcakes."

About a furlong later, Story drifted back to the new riders and found Bell. "Which way did they stampede the herd?"

"Hell, mister, I don't . . . no, no, I reckon. Yeah, north."

Shaps twisted in the saddle, but it was Drew Finley, to Story's surprise, who answered first. "North. Last thing I remember seeing before those bastards give me this . . ." He patted his bad leg. ". . . was the North Star."

Back at camp, just as the sun began to sink, Story swung off his horse and handed the reins to Cesar Lopez with an order, "Fetch the best night horse in Dalton's string." Taking the cup the cook had just filled, Story turned toward the crew. Dalton Combs was already standing, dropping his dishes in the wreck pan and stopping in front of Story. Jameson Hannah moved closer.

"I have a chore for you," Story told the black cowboy. In the roughly four hundred miles they had traveled, Story had learned that the quietest rider, the best man at night, and one of the toughest men on the trail was the wiry Dalton Combs.

Combs nodded.

"Some grangers followed us out of Baxter Springs," Story said. "Maybe a dozen. Maybe even more. Only four, five kept in sight. I figure they'll camp somewhere, on this side of the river, but not that far away. They won't have a campfire. They will have several guards. If I'm right, they'll be coming after our herd. If another hunch is right, they'll be camped south of us."

Other plates and cups clanged into the tub of dishes the cook and wrangler would be washing on most evenings. A series of soft clicks revealed the rotation of several pistol cylinders, including Dalton Combs's.

"Who's on the first watch?" Story turned to Hannah.

"Luis and Ward."

He nodded, looked at the gathering. "Peña, Melean. Join them." Those two were veterans, and likely could handle a revolver on a running horse better than any of the remaining drag riders. "Martinez. I want you and Lopez watching the horse herd. Barley, you stay here with José. Make enough racket like you're a full crew. But not so loud you stampede the cattle." He dumped his coffee, untouched, onto the ground. "Rest of you, saddle a good horse. You new men, have my wrangler catch you good night horses. Pretend you're riding herd and the air's full of lightning strikes and electricity. Shuck your spurs. And anything else that's likely to jingle or give you away. Watches. Coins. Leave them with José."

"Mil gracias," the Mexican said.

Ignoring the joke, unless the cook was being serious, Story swung back to Combs.

"We'll meet you at the southern tip of the herd."

With a grim nod, Combs stepped over the wagon tongue, stopping when Boone called out his name. The black man turned.

"One of those men," Boone said, "rode with Missouri bushwhackers during the war. He's not likely one to care much for your kind."

Combs nodded. "That's all right. I probably won't like him much, either." His head bobbed, and he grinned. "I appreciate the warning, Boone. You take care. All y'all, take care."

The newspaper reporter scribbled notes, and when the men started for the remuda, he stepped in line with them.

"Mr. Cromwell," Story said, "you should stay in camp."

"But the story is with you, and I should follow the story."

Story let his head bob. He liked a man, even a fool, who showed grit.

In an arroyo due south of the cattle's bedding grounds, Story opened his saddlebags and pulled out strips of white cotton that he had cut from two shirts. "I want you boys to tie one of these around your necks," he whispered, "over your bandannas, and another over your left arm."

"Even if those clouds stick, as bright as that moon is, that'll give us away," Andrew Shaps said.

"That's right. And maybe that way Stubbings or I won't accidentally put a bullet through your breast. Tie them tight, boys. That's how we sometimes did things on the vigilance committee up north."

As the men came over to pluck out cotton cloth, Story heard the soft hoofbeats. Sam Ireland reached for his holstered revolver, but Story shook his head. He waited, and suddenly realized he felt chilled. Son of a bitch, he had started sweating. A coyote pup barked, but Story let out a breath. "It's Combs," he said, handed the saddlebags to Boone to continue passing out the markers, and nudged his horse up the banks of the arroyo.

The black rider eased his mount with such skill, Story didn't see him until Combs and his blood bay gelding stood maybe twenty feet away.

"Boss," he whispered.

"It's me, Combs," Story said.

A revolver's hammer softly lowered, and rider and horse covered the distance. "They're camped on a knoll. Mile and a quarter south of here."

"How many?"

"Couldn't get close enough to count, not with them on the high ground. Maybe a dozen. Maybe six more. Just no sure way of telling."

Jameson Hannah brought his horse up the arroyo and toward Story.

"Two riders left, though," Combs said.

"When?"

"Ten minutes." He moved his arm toward the west. "My guess is that they'll be making sure the cattle and boys are all comfortable."

"You couldn't kill them?" Hannah said.

"I could've killed one. But that would have ruined our surprise."

"Can you kill them now?" Story asked.

"It'd be better if I had a partner." He lifted his head toward the clouds. "Stubbings."

"Get him," Story said. "And go. Quiet, if possible."

"If possible." Combs's gelding had already started down into the arroyo.

Story looked at Hannah. "Get the rest of the men up here. You'll take half and hit the camp from the east. I'll take the others and hit them from the west."

"Good chance we will be outnumbered," Hannah said.

"But they won't be expecting us," Story said.

That's when the full moon began to move beyond the dark rain cloud, and Story whispered a curse that would have left Ellen fuming for a week.

CHAPTER THIRTY-NINE

Jameson Hannah took his men, including Story's new hires, on a wide berth to the east. That left Boone with Story, Petty, Allen, and the newspaper reporter from Baxter Springs, who wouldn't be any help. Maybe that's why Story had let him tag along, especially now that the moon bathed enough light on the Indian Nations so that anybody could see the white strips of cotton around their necks and arms. They could see their faces, hats, chaps, and the nighthawks zipping across the cool skies.

In a muddy buffalo wallow, Story swung off his horse. "On foot," he ordered, and saddles creaked as nervous men dismounted. Boone's new boots sank into a miserable soup.

"Cromwell," Story said. "You stay here. Keep our horses, and keep them quiet."

The newspaper reporter wet his lips. "How do I . . . do . . . that?"

Story swore, inhaled and exhaled, and whispered, "Try not to let them bolt when the shooting starts."

Minutes later, Story climbed out of the wallow, motioned Petty and Allen to his left and Boone to his right, and they moved toward what folks in these parts might call a hill.

One that, even if it had to be pushing ten o'clock in the evening, Boone could see as plainly as if he were looking through one of Oliver Wendell Holmes's American stereo-scopes.

Crouched, with revolvers drawn, already cocked, they moved through sweet grass and cactus. Heart slamming against his ribs, Boone tried to recall the last time he had felt this mixture of fear and exhilaration. He thought he saw the brief reddish glow from a cigarette or cigar. Seemed absolutely sure he saw a shooting star dash across the sky, only to realize that as bright as the damned moon was, he probably hadn't seen a damned thing. He heard someone snort, or fart. In the back of his mind, he revisited the predawn discussions of his friends in the Confederate cavalry.

Then, somewhere in the brightness of darkness, a gun roared, and suddenly Boone was footing it toward the enemy, and the blood-curdling rebel yell escaped from his voice.

"Give them tyrants hell, boys!" someone screamed.

Forty yards later, Boone realized that it was he who had shouted.

A man charged down the hill, right toward him, probably didn't even see him, and Boone felt the .44 buck in his hand, saw crimson spray out of the back of the man's head, then damned near tripped over him, would have if his shoulder had not slammed into another running man. Boone spun, somehow kept his feet, and within seconds found himself charging into the camp of rustlers.

The first blasts from revolvers boomed like cannon. Now Boone heard merely faint pops. If anyone else cut loose with a battle cry, Boone could not hear. A horse reared, a muzzle flashed, a man with hands held above his head, slammed back onto the hill, to be met with the hooves of the horse's forefeet. Orange flashes. Rising smoke bathed by moonbeams. A rider pursued a running man off to Boone's right.

His legs felt light, but for a man who had spent the past year or more trekking up and down the mountains of western Montana Territory, he ran through the air.

A man stumbled before him, righted himself, tried to bring a massive Dragoon up, but the barrel of Boone's Army Colt split the side of the man's skull, and he toppled to Boone's left. Someone behind him roared. The piercing scream of a man consumed by panic died quickly.

Two men dashed down the top of the rise, and Boone spun, thumbed back the hammer, squeezed the trigger. By this point, he felt no heat, no jerking in his hand, heard nothing but a peeling in his ears. Thumb eared back hammer, finger touched trigger, hammer fell. Boone glanced at the nipples on the cylinder, but saw only blurs. Yet he had felt nothing, so he knew his gun was empty. He slammed the barrel into a man's side, saw him tumble, and Boone's brain told him to stop. He shoved the Colt into his holster, reached down, jerked a double-action revolver from the man's waist.

He could see horses now, even sabers slashing—but figured the latter to be his imagination, his insanity. A man stumbled in the distance. Boone stopped, spun, dropped, just as a bullet whistled past his ear. He raised the gun that felt different in his hand than a heavy Army Colt. Realized from the feel of the trigger that he did not have to pull back the hammer with his thumb. He squeezed. The big revolver spoke. He saw flame, smelled smoke, watched the man twist, stagger, and bring up his revolver. Boone's next shot blew a hole in the gunman's arm, glimpsed the rustler's pistol spinning, sailing, flying from his right hand to his left. Boone stepped toward the man, fired again. The man dropped to his knees, and Boone squeezed the trigger, felt the buck in his hand, saw the man spinning to his right. By then Boone had lost count of how many rounds he had fired.

It did not matter. The man lay on the ground, his head propped up against the stump of an ancient, long-removed tree. Boone stared at the revolver and tried to remember where he had gotten this strange gun. He could remember Sergeant Thomas handing him the Army Colt, saying it was appropriate that a Yankee gun be used to take Yankee lives—just before Boone had started walking west.

A hand touched his shoulder. Boone turned, tried to shove the double-action pistol into his well-worn holster. The first two tries missed. The third left the gun in the mud. He just blinked and looked at the man.

The face seemed familiar. The voice sounded like Tom Allen's.

"Son of a bitch, Mason. We done it. We're still alive."

He looked at the man he had shot to pieces. The face was drawn; the body bloodied. Boone counted four holsters on the man's torso, all empty now, and the man's head had been propped up against a corpse's thigh. Blood seeped from both corners of his mouth. He appeared to grin.

"Done what I set out to do." The man whispered, coughed, spit out phlegm. "Died game."

"You ain't dead yet," one of Nelson Story's conglomerates, that Andrew Shaps fellow, said.

Boone moved over toward Story, who stood over that white-bearded son of a bitch, Ben Fariss, who sported no more than a bloody bandage wrapped over his left hand. Story, on the other hand, was looking down the ridge, cursing.

"That inkslinging bastard. I told him to keep the horses. And they're running seven ways from sundown."

"Shut the hell up." Boone turned toward the shout, found Jameson Hannah pointing to the north. "I don't hear hooves. Maybe the herd's not scattering."

"What about Combs and Stubbings?" Sam Ireland asked.

"I think that's them." Boone didn't know who answered, but after a minute, or ten minutes, two riders eased their mounts up the slope.

Yes, he realized, it was Combs. And Stubbings. Grim-faced black warriors. They rode up easily, and Combs swung out of the saddle and approached Story.

"Did you see that inkslinging son of a bitch?" Story demanded. "I told him to keep the . . ."

He saw the notebook Dalton Combs shoved toward him. He could see the bloodstains on the paper.

Story frowned, hung his head briefly, then raised his eyes and asked, "Dead?" Though everyone knew the answer.

"Yes, sir," Combs said. "Reckon one of the grangers run up to him, shot him. He tried to get a horse, but me and Jordan rode up. It was Jordan who killed him. Killed the man who killed that newspaperman."

Story took the bloodstained notebook and tossed it to the ground.

That's when the ringing left Boone's ears, and he could hear clearly, could even think like a sane man, and he turned to look at the dying bushwhacker, Will Ethridge, head propped up against a stump, being offered a cigarette by Tom Petty, and then the laughing old killer Ben Fariss.

"You boys dropped the ball," Fariss said. "All I gots to do is tell the judge that here we sat, minding our own business, and you Texans jumped us. Us camped all peaceable, planning to see what kinds of fish was biting in the Neosho."

Another voice, more wheezing than speaking, came out. "Die game . . . That's . . . that's what . . . I told Todd I'd do . . . for him."

Story stepped over another corpse and made a beeline for Will Ethridge.

"You figure you died game," Story said.

The mortally wounded bushwhacker looked up.

"You didn't." The Navy bucked in Story's hand. Ethridge's head slammed back, blood pouring out of the hole where his left eye had been. Story shouted, "Get my horse." He closed the distance and stood over Ben Fariss.

"You hold on, Montana," Fariss stammered. "I got rights. I got . . ."

Story aimed the Navy and pulled the trigger.

Fariss's "Jesus Christ" overshadowed the loud click Story's Navy made, the hammer striking an empty chamber.

"Listen to me," Fariss shrieked, as Story tossed his empty revolver to Jameson Hannah and spotted a saddle near a bedroll. He moved as though possessed, lifted the lariat from the horn.

"Now, you just wait a damned minute . . ." Fariss started to rise, but Sam Ireland's boot caught him under the chin and drove him into the soggy earth. When Fariss pushed himself up, Story slipped the lariat over Fariss's neck, cutting short the granger's prayer or curse.

Tom Allen had brought Story's gelding, and carrying the rope, Story moved to the horse, made a few dallies around the horn, and stepped into the saddle.

"Wait." Ben Fariss had scrambled to his knees. He tried to push himself to his feet, then realized how much time that might waste. His fingers clasped over the lariat's loop around his neck. His face turned whiter than the full moon. He started to scream just as Story kicked the gelding's sides.

Boone watched as horse and rider dragged the leader of the Granger's Association down the slope and toward the Neosho River.

CHAPTER FORTY

When the cell door opened again, Molly McDonald rolled over, squeezed her eyelids tighter, and groaned from the light.

"You two get up," the deputy called. "And get out of town."

Molly coughed, started to curl up into a fetal position, but the man's words slowly registered. Her eyes opened. Lowering her voice, she said, "You ain't got no wood that needs cuttin' at the sawmill? No limestone to be put down at that new schoolhouse? No shit you want us . . ."

"I want you two out of Marysville. Your sentence has been served. Both of you up. Now. And get out of my sight."

Molly rolled up and sat on the floor. Marysville's wasn't the worst jail she'd ever struck, but after six months a change of scenery would be nice. She punched Constance Beckett's shoulder.

"Get up, Cory," she growled.

Sweet, pure Constance Beckett answered with a vulgarity that caused the deputy to say, "I can add another week to your sentence for language like that."

"He's just dreamin', talkin' in his sleep," Molly said, and came to her knees, bent over, and whispered. "We can get out of this town, this jail. You savvy that? We're free. Now get up before I drag your arse all the way to the Big Blue."

Constance's eyes shot open. "What did you say?"

They sat underneath the bridge that crossed the river, washing without soap, and still wearing their duds in case some travelers or teenage boys might happen by and discover that the two horse thieves that had spent the past six months in the Marysville, Kansas, jail were women, not men. Constance Beckett kept bitching, as she had been doing since they had been caught at the stables trying to saddle a couple of fresh horses.

Molly moved out of the water, found a rock to sit on, opened her possibles bag she had left on the bank, and found what remained of her twist of tobacco.

"You don't realize how lucky we are, gettin' catched like we was," she said. "First, this is Marysville. Pony Express used to ride right through here, so with folks around here appreciatin' good horseflesh, they could have stretched our necks." She shoved the last bit of tobacco into her mouth. "Second, they could have tried us, convicted us, and sent us to Lansing. The state pen wouldn't have been as accommodatin' as they was here. State pen would've identified us as bein' of the fairer sex. That could've gotten you sent up to Fort Kearny and tried for murder."

Constance ducked under the water, came back up, and stood, walking slowly, her clothes hanging tight against her body, toward Molly.

"Third . . ." Molly looked up at the bridge. "Us bein' in jail, nobody lookin' for you would've figured to find you in a Kansas jail."

"So what do we do now?" Constance Beckett just didn't appreciate all that Molly had done for her.

"We find breakfast. A fittin' breakfast. Something that ain't the hog and hominy they been feedin' us the past six months."

"We don't have any money to buy breakfast."

Molly sighed. "Girl, you ain't learned nothin'. We beg for somethin' to eat. This bein' a Christian community, folks will take pity on a couple of tramps."

They had to endure a lecture by Captain Cottrell of the Sons of Temperance on the evils of liquor, and empty the chamber pots, sweep off the porch, and beat out a rug in the lobby of the captain's hotel, but Cottrell finally served Molly and Constance ham, eggs, biscuits, and coffee outside, in the back of the American House, which Cottrell owned. He even gave them last week's *Marysville Enterprise*.

"What do we do now?" Constance asked. A good meal and decent coffee had made her practically sociable.

"I don't know. You ain't gonna eat that last bite of biscuit?" She plucked the bread off the tin plate.

"Still try to find that wagon train in Nebraska City?"

"Child, that train pulled out weeks ago." She washed down the biscuit with coffee, reached for the pot Mr. Cottrell had left on the doorstep, and refilled their cups. Constance picked up the newspaper, started reading. Molly guzzled coffee and looked at the American House's corral, then at the stables and barn. The horses weren't bad at all, Mr. Cottrell was upstairs taking his nap, and temperance men usually being sound sleepers, well, the Kansas state line ended just a hop and a jump north of town, and Molly might be able to lose a posse that didn't care if the two horse thieves were in Nebraska Territory and out of Kansas jurisdiction. They could keep the horses in the shallows of the river for a while. Make their way to Nebraska City, hire on with another freight company.

The page turned. Constance read. Molly eyed the dapple, not for herself, but Constance. Her pard wasn't that good of a rider—truth is, she wasn't good at much of anything except sticking a knife into a bastard's ribs—but Molly felt they were kindred spirits. Women in a man's world, pretending to be men.

"On my God."

Molly turned as Constance, her face paling, lowered the newspaper. Her Adam's apple bobbed, she wet her lips, and with trembling hands shoved the paper toward Molly. Molly saw an advertisement for a drugstore in town. "There." Constance pointed to a paragraph without a headline.

> The bodies of two freighters for the
> Sublette & Dixon Company of Leavenworth,
> Kansas, were discovered south of The
> Narrows on the trail to the Platte River
> Road. Both men were riddled with arrows
> and brutally tortured by the savage red devils
> plaguing the territory. Mr. Dixon also said
> the oxen were stolen and wagons destroyed.
> The deceased, Mr. Dixon said, were
> H. Coleman of Kansas, and K. Shishkov, a
> foreigner.

"Well, damn, if we ain't the two luckiest folks around." Molly tapped the paper with her pointer finger. "Luckier than ol' Harv and the Bulgarian." She turned, grinning. "You realize what this means, pard?"

Constance blinked.

"We can go back to Leavenworth. Get back to work. Don't have to worry about those two connivin' dogs to turn you in for no reward."

"What if they told Mr. Sublette or Mr. Dixon . . . ?"

"I'm not a damned fool. I ain't going to work for those two crooks. Besides, they wouldn't hire us back nohow. But there's lots of outfits in Leavenworth that could use somebody who knows how to handle a whip like I do. And it's likely a hell of a lot safer goin' south than north right now."

"That's a horseshit plan," Constance said. She was coming along in the profanity department.

"No." Molly grinned. "It's genius."

CHAPTER FORTY-ONE

A bullet had grazed Andrew Shaps's side, Sam Ireland took a ball through his left hand, Dalton Combs's earlobe had been shot off, and a ball had lodged against Luke Price's thighbone. Those had been the only injuries—except for the death of the newspaper reporter. José Pablo Tsoyio cauterized the ear and side wounds with the heated blade of a butcher knife, pulled a whiskey-soaked silk bandanna through Ireland's hand, and bandaged the injuries with some sort of smelly poultice. He couldn't do much with the leg wound other than give the Texas cowboy a jug of the rustlers' whiskey.

Nelson Story read over the grave the boys had dug for Mr. Brian Cromwell, and carefully wrapped all of the personal items found in the newspaper writer's pockets in a spare shirt, announcing that he would mail the package with a short note to Robert Tracy—Story hoped he remembered the name right—editor of the *Troy Reporter*. Some of the boys fashioned a cross and stuck it at the head of the grave.

The rest of the dead were dumped inside the cutbank of an arroyo. Peña and Stubbings collapsed dirt to cover the bodies. No warning to other trail thieves, no marker, no bodies left swinging from tree limbs, and it would not take long for coyotes or wolves to sniff out the dead and get to feasting. Funeral over, the volunteers from the Baxter Springs herds rode out, pulling the drunken, singing Price on a travois. Story jammed the hat on his head and ordered his men to get their cattle and crew moving.

They rode not toward Baxter Springs, but northwest, following the wandering course of the flooded Neosho River.

"How long we gonna keep goin' this way?" Ryan Ward griped.

"What difference does it make?" Ernesto Martinez said.

"Because Kansas City is thataway." He jabbed his finger across the river.

Jameson Hannah rode up and barked, "You get paid by the month. Longer we ride, more you earn."

"And the less time we have to drink whiskey," Jody Barley said.

Boone couldn't understand that logic.

Nor could he understand Nelson Story, when the iron-willed man told Jameson Hannah the next morning, "I'll catch up with you in a day, maybe two. Keep them along the river."

When he rode off, Boone turned and asked Kelvin Melean, "Where do you think he's going?"

"Why the hell would I care? Maybe the hard-rock bastard won't come back."

He swam the black across the river, rode casually, uncertain, and recognized that rare feeling of nervousness. Eventually, Story spotted smoke coming out of the chimney in a soddy, and he rode up easily, hands in clear view of the open door, and called out, "Hello, the house."

"Yeah."

All Story could make out was the muzzle of a shotgun.

"Looking for Centreville Township."

"Turn you horse north, mister. You should come across a wagon track. Follow that three miles, you'll find your township."

"Would you happen to know where a family named Trent lives?"

"Can't help you. But it's not much of a town."

The farmer hadn't been kidding, but Story didn't need to ask directions, for he saw a little girl rolling a hoop in front of another sod hut on the outskirts of what some might call a village. He turned the black east and rode to the soddy, noticing how little of the quarter section had been broken by plow. The hoop wobbled, spun, and toppled, and the girl stepped back.

"Ma," she called out. "Pa. We got . . ." The grin brightened her face. "Company."

Story removed his hat, but stayed in the saddle. "Do you remember me, Jeanette?"

Suspicion quickly darkened her sunburned face, and she stepped back to what was beginning to resemble a garden. A milch cow brayed and moved aimlessly over the prairie, its red-tinted bell clanging. A dog growled from inside the house of earth, and Story had to grab a firmer hold on the reins as the black snorted, twisted his head, and flattened his ears.

The man stepped out of the sod house, holding a rifle, which he leaned against the mound of dirt, shook his head, and withdrew a pipe from the rear pocket of his denim trousers. "Frances," the balding man said to someone inside the house. "Make yourself presentable and say hello to our son-in-law. Theodore. Hush."

The growls stopped. The girl, maybe five years old, stepped around the hoop.

"Are you . . . Ellen's beau?"

Story almost smiled. Beau. Well, that was something. After wrapping the reins around the handle of a plow, Story moved closer to the sod house, where Matthew Trent brushed his hands on his dirty jeans. Frances stepped out, followed by two other young'uns.

"Where's John?" Story asked after shaking the farmer's hand. John was the oldest of the Trent brood.

"Got a job." The man's grip remained as hard as ever.

"Would you like coffee, Nelson?" Frances called from the soddy.

Story wasn't about to drink up these poor folks' coffee. Besides, he had grown accustomed to the Mexican cook's brew.

He remembered those first meetings with Trent, trying to sell him some firewood.

"That wood's green, boy."

"Yes, sir, but it'll be dried out by the time hell's moved on."

"This be Kansas, boy. Hell don't never leave."

"I've been in Kansas enough to know that here, hell gets mighty cold, especially come January and February." Nodding toward the stack of wood. *"Oak and sugar maple, sir. Burn hot and long. Give you a good bed of coals, too."*

"What the blazes would a boy from Ohio know about oak and sugar maple—other than what you might've read in books?"

"There are trees in Ohio, sir. Lots of them."

Mr. Trent: "Uh-huh." The long stare would follow.

That had led to Trent hiring Story to do some chopping

and hauling of wood on Trent's own spread, then on Little Stranger Creek. Breaking sod, chopping timber, hauling wood. And he remembered seeing the black-haired girl with the haunting eyes, which diminished the sweat, and cuts, and aches from the bottoms of his feet to the back of his neck, but mostly in his back and shoulders, and the blisters on his hands despite working with thick gloves.

He did accept well water, brackish and hot, for himself and the gelding, and they found a place in the shade. The mutt of a dog stared warily at Story.

"New dog," Story said.

Trent stared at the mongrel. "Had him about a year now."

"What happened to the old one?" Story asked.

"Dead," Trent said. "Kiowas."

"You don't know that for certain, Matthew," Frances said.

Story swirled his cup, watching the grains of sand dance in the funnel.

"You wouldn't happen to have a tintype of that baby girl?" Frances's voice was hesitant, maybe fearful. "Of . . . our . . . grandbaby?"

He shook his head, made himself sip the water. Hell, he hadn't seen his daughter himself. He tried to think of something to say, something about the girl, or Ellen, or even Virginia City, but he kept thinking about the cattle, and those damned grangers.

"What's your plan for here?" he asked the old man.

"Prove it up. Sell it to some big dreamer with plans of a million acres of wheat or barley. Retire with servants and shade trees."

"And a swing for me," Jeanette said.

"And a swing for you," her mother said.

He realized, although he had known it before he even left the herd, that he never should have come here. He didn't know how to talk to these people, or any people, any . . . family. And the old dog was dead. He thought about that dream. Nelson Story digging a grave for a dog. After making himself finish the water, he handed the cup to Frances, and rose.

"What's Montana like?" Jeanette asked.

Story stared at the girl. "Cold in the winter. Nice enough in the summer. Mountains all around. Not like here."

She giggled. "I meant my . . . ?" Her head turned to her mother.

"Niece. Montana's your niece. That means you're her aunt."

"I can't be an aunt, Mama. I'm only five years old. Aunts are old."

They laughed. Story tried to smile. The black looked like he wanted to run, and Story longed to feel the wind in his face.

"We'd love to have you stay for supper," the old man said.

"And spend the night," Frances said. She looked bone-tired, worn to a frazzle, and now he knew why he was so determined to get this herd to Montana, to make his fortune, to put Ellen Story in a house not made of dirt, and where she could have servants cook for her, clean the damned house, and, hell, wash her feet if she wanted her feet washed. Like Ellen would ever allow that to happen. But she wasn't going to work herself to death like Frances Trent. Story didn't mind working himself to death. In that regard, he wasn't a whole lot different from Ellen's old man.

"Well, ma'am." Story made himself stand. "I've got to

be moving on. I'm eager to get back to Virginia City. See my baby girl."

"Can I come with you?" the girl asked.

Frances smiled. The cowbell clattered. The wind kicked up dust. The dog growled.

Story did not look at the kid, or any of the Trents. He gathered the reins, swung into the saddle, and debated if he should offer the old man money. Like Matthew Trent would have accepted any handout, especially from his son-in-law.

"I want to see my sister," Jeanette wailed. "I want to see Ellen. I want to see my . . . my . . . cousin."

"Niece." He could picture Frances smiling.

Story kicked the black into a walk. He turned the horse west, toward the Neosho. Behind him he heard Jeanette's screams, begging for him to take her with him, to see Montana—the territory or the baby, maybe both, Story didn't know. He gave the black his head, tugged the hat tighter on his head, and rode away. He did wave, just so they couldn't say he was rude. Though he never looked back.

Blue skies replaced the gray clouds. The rain stopped. The wind blew. They left the river and turned west.

"Now where are we going?" Ryan Ward asked at supper one evening.

"San Francisco, by God," Sam Ireland said. "I bet they're dyin' for beef there. Ain't nothing else to eat in San Francisco except seals and Chinamen."

"We're riding around the quarantine line, you knuckleheads." Jameson Hannah pointed at Ireland's bandage. "Unless you want a matching hole in your other hand."

* * *

The sun turned the skies more white than blue. Mile after mile, day after day, they rode into the wind. Wind that never ceased. It burned faces worse than the sun. Irritated noses, eyes, chapped lips. All they knew were cattle, saddle sores, and that son-of-a-bitching wind.

Moving north now. Bawling cattle. A blistering wind. Waving tall grass of fading green but a massive sea of brown to the west. The brown moved like ocean waves. Mountains? Mud? The men shielded the sun from their eyes and stared.

"Buffalo," Story explained.

"I've seen buffalo in Texas," Jordan Stubbings said. "But nothing like that."

Story laughed. "That's not even a big herd."

"I hear buffalo tongue is tasty," Ryan Ward said, "if it's pickled."

"I don't want no pickled tongue, but some meat would settle in my stomach better than more beans," said Kelvin Melean.

"What do you think, Mr. Story?" Dalton Combs called out.

"You want to shoot a buffalo, go ahead. But wherever you find a herd of that size, you'll probably find an Indian. A lot of Indians. Comanches. Kiowa. Cheyenne."

The banter stopped. Replaced by cylinders on revolvers being checked.

Pushing north, they skirted a wide loop around the buffalo herd.

Chapter Forty-two

The clouds to the southwest looked ominous, and after all that rain, a twister at this time of year—even one monster hailstorm—would be bad for farmers in Greenwood County. Just ten minutes ago, Mrs. Hartly explained how her dream last night portended a bad day, even though the crazy old bird hadn't told R. R. Turner exactly what she had dreamed. Everyone in Eureka knew Mrs. Hartly to be mad as a hatter, but that cloud could mean trouble. Still, Sheriff R. R. Turner smiled.

The children inside Fort Montgomery were hard at work, and Turner could picture Miss Withersteen inside the big building, waving her hands, trying to get these young'uns to sing and not shout. The old fort—green logs covered with dirt built up to the gun ports—had been put to good use since the old schoolhouse burned down. Fort Montgomery hadn't seen any action when it had gone up during the rebellion. Just a couple of scares—especially after the butchery over at Lawrence in '63—but nothing really ever happened in Greenwood County. That's why R. R. Turner didn't mind being sheriff.

These days, Eureka boomed. Folks had started talking about incorporating, taking over as county seat since there wasn't much to Janesville, and Eureka already had a jail. Even a post office. By next year, the schoolhouse they were putting up with limestone would be complete—and this one wouldn't burn down. Folks talked about adding a hotel one of these years. People kept coming in, putting down roots, either farming or trying to make a living in some type of enterprise—always the sign of a town with a future.

It was good country. Plenty of box elder and cottonwoods on the riverbanks, even some soft maple. Fine farm country. Good land in general.

Doc Reynolds had hung up his shingle. A new smithy— McCain, McConnell, McCartney . . . something like that . . . Turner had better learn that name and make friends, because a blacksmith was a good person to have on your side come next election—pounded away on his anvil down the street. His hammering seemed to be about as musical as the bellowing schoolkids. Since April, Eureka had managed to open a store, though it was closed today because old Jim Kerner had to get back to his farm. You couldn't blame a man for that in prime, fertile country. When the wind didn't suck out all the moisture, or a tornado didn't destroy your crops and sod house. But R. R. Turner didn't farm. He was sheriff, duly elected, and with the rebellion long over and no bushwhackers roaming about, he could spend most of his time smoking a pipe and imagining sweet Miss Withersteen trying to herd those schoolkids.

"Sheriff."

Sheriff. Not R. R. Not Turner. Sheriff. Never a good sign. Removing his pipe, Turner sighed out a stream of smoke and found Myrock Huntley kicking his mule like Quantrill rode after him. Stepping out of the shade of the old fort and away from the screaming-singing kids, Turner opened his mouth but didn't get a chance to speak.

"Sheriff, there's a damned herd of Texas longhorns moving north."

Turner blinked. One of the first white men to settle in Greenwood County, Kansas, Myrock Huntley came from good stock. Never one to be in his cups, and if the wind and weather and rebellion and Indians hadn't driven him loco in nine years, then . . .

"What?" Turner hadn't meant to say anything, but . . . cattle? Texas? Longhorns?

"I saw them with my own eyes."

Turner looked at that damned black cloud.

"Sheriff, I got two good milch cows and the last thing I need is to watch them die of Texas fever."

"I know, Myrock. I know." He didn't see anyone on the street except Doc Reynolds, and he couldn't bring the town's new doctor with him in a posse. What if the Texans killed the doctor? They'd have to patch up bullet wounds themselves.

"How many cattle?" He felt electricity in the air, or maybe it was just his nerves.

"I don't know, Sheriff. The line stretched on forever. Wagons. Horses. I couldn't count the number of men, either. I just hopped on Bruce's back and kicked him as hard as I could."

Turner appraised the farmer. No musket or shotgun with him, but Huntley had made it from his farm without falling off the mule's back and breaking an arm or neck. Still, Turner didn't think Myrock Huntley would make a good posse member.

"You say they were south of town, moving north, off by your place?"

"Right through the far side of the pasture I planned to clear next spring."

"Thanks, Myrock."

"Sheriff, those cattle aren't supposed to be here. We've got a quarantine—"

"I know that. I'll take care of it."

Already, Turner had started walking across the street toward his office, but he stopped and looked back.

"Go find Leander Bemis," he told the farmer. "Tell him I just deputized him, and have him bring his rifle and a belt gun. And not to dillydally."

Long strides took him across the street to the fire bell, which he immediately began ringing, drowning out Miss Withersteen's students and that smithy's hammer. It brought Edwin Tucker out of his post office and stopped just about everything in Eureka, Kansas, that morning. The circuit-riding Methodist, Preacher Stansbury, stepped out of the blacksmith's lean-to.

Colonists from Mississippi first settled here, but most slavery men left before the rebellion, before Kansas became a free state. Forming a posse shouldn't be hard, as farmers in town and the solid stock of Eureka started approaching the fire bell. Sight of McKeag, old Gow, the Reeves brothers, and Dave Smyth reassured Turner that he might live through this day. He hoped like hell Huntley could find Captain Bemis, who had led the Greenwood County militia during the rebellion. If Turner could turn back a bunch of Texas cowboys, no one would even run against him come the next election.

Suddenly, Turner smiled. Miss Withersteen had stepped out of old Fort Montgomery, a few of the boys and girls peering around her long skirt.

Despite crazy old Mrs. Hartly's dream, today might shape up to be a fine day—if Turner didn't get killed.

CHAPTER FORTY-THREE

Lightning came with the clouds long before the sun set, distant at first, and just bats of lightning as they had often seen. But when the storm reached the herd, the wind picked up, and while only a few hard drops of rain fell, flash lightning ripped across the sky, soon replaced by forked lightning. That's when Boone removed his spurs and revolver, collected the same from his fellow drag riders, and headed off to the wagon driven by Bill Petty, depositing the load into the back.

"If I get killed by lightning," Petty grumbled, "I'll haunt you for the rest of your life."

Boone made no comment. He rode a white gelding, which he quickly dismounted, unsaddled, and took his black horse from the remuda. Dalton Combs had already ridden off on his new horse, a blood bay; Fabian Peña came trotting up on his dun. Boone didn't know if he really believed that a light-colored horse attracted lightning, but he didn't feel like risking his life. Once he had the cinch tight and the reins to his liking, he swung up, and moved back to drag.

Ernesto Martinez brought his crucifix—wooden—to his mouth, lips moving in silent prayer. Tom Allen came back on a brown gelding to help out at drag.

"Cattle seemed spooked," he said.

"Cattle aren't alone," Boone replied.

The air smelled of burning sulfur. Ball lightning rolled across the tall grass. Sore-footed cattle began turning back, forcing the riders to work harder to keep them pointed north. Boone's horse fought bit and rein, whipping Boone's arms one way, then the other. The horse, like the longhorns, wanted to run. Hell, so did Boone, especially when the electricity in the air seemed to settle down over the prairie like a fog in hell.

Jameson Hannah loped back, reining up, and spinning his horse around. He spoke to Jody Barley, the most experienced of the drag riders. "We're bedding them down. No coffee. No supper till this storm passes us. Stay in the saddle. Circle the herd. If you haven't gotten rid of any iron, dump it now." He started back, reined up slightly, and looked at Boone. "If I was you, boy, I'd slouch some. Lightning hits the tallest point, and these other boys are damned short." He laughed.

No one else did.

Circling the herd, Boone saw it first. A blue flame rose from the tips of the horns on a dark-colored steer, as if someone had doused coal oil on the sharp points and lighted a match. Then he saw another glowing light.

The stink of sulfur intensified. Blue light glowed across the herd, and Boone leaned back when he saw the same glimmering on the ears of his gelding.

His mouth turned dry.

"Criminy," Ryan Ward said as he rode toward Boone. He pointed. "Your damn hat's got it, too."

Boone reached up, fingers tingling, hands shaking, wondering if the felt would burn. He lowered his hands and looked at the young Texan.

"So does yours." His voice sounded muffled from the strong current running through the air. He couldn't see Ward's face, but noticed the wiry kid leaning back in the saddle. The horse jumped, but Ward shifted in the seat, took a better grip on the reins.

Boone moved his gelding in and nudged the cattle back. "Easy," he said. "Easy." Ward's nervous voice wasn't quite a harmony, but the steers did not run, just blubbered, turning their heads, pawing the earth, crapping and pissing all over the ground. Boone prayed his bowels wouldn't loosen.

He looked up, trying to see how big this storm might be. He wished it would rain. Maybe that would eliminate this . . . evil.

"Fox fire." Dalton Combs, usually a swing rider who rarely night-herded on the same shift with Boone, rode by. He still wore a bandanna for a bandage over the ear that had been mangled by one of the Kansas ruffian's bullets. The bandanna was a yellow faded to almost white. The white stood out.

"What?" Ernesto Martinez said.

"Fox fire. Sailors used to call it St. Elmo's fire. Maybe they still do. They'd see it on the masts."

"What is it?" Martinez asked.

Combs shrugged. "Other than what I told you, I don't rightly know." He grinned, pointing. "Look at that."

Boone saw the blue light floating, sparking, waving. Even long blades of grass glowed with bluish illumination. The cattle bawled louder as the sulfuric scent turned heavier.

Boone realized he was cold, shivering, his shirt drenched in sweat.

"Never seen fox fire like that." Combs nudged his horse forward. "Keep them easy, boys. This drive has been finer than split silk. I'd sure hate for hell to break loose now, us bein' closer to Kansas City and a hatful of money."

The last man to ride into the camp and unbuckle his revolvers and spurs did not surprise José Pablo Tsoyio. On the other hand, the fact that Nelson Story finally rode in, stepped out of the saddle, and unbuckled the belt and spur traps, and deposited those items—even a pocketknife and a watch—made the cook think that the hard-ass might be halfway human.

"Coffee, *patrón*?" Tsoyio nodded at the fire.

Wind whipped the flames so much that Tsoyio could not say the coffee was hot, even lukewarm, but it was black, and strong. Story turned from the wagon, stared at the cookware. He said, "Shit."

When Tsoyio turned, blue light sparked off the top of the cast-iron tripod holding the big pot over the fire.

"In all my years," the cook said, "I have never seen it this bad, or last this long."

"I've never even seen it." Story came closer to the fire. "Seen the northern lights. Twice. Never this." He nodded at the pot, and José Pablo Tsoyio knelt, found a tin cup, and, using a towel to protect his hands from the heat, poured coffee. Still kneeling, he held the cup out toward his boss, who took it. José Pablo Tsoyio also filled a cup for himself. He was about to stand when he saw the glow of the fox fire, on brims of hats, ears of horses, and what, moments later, he understood to be the barrels of rifles, shotguns, and revolvers.

"Who the hell is running this outfit?"

The riders fanned out. Story's horse stutter-stepped, and he quickly grabbed the reins before the gelding bolted. Blue waves moved about the strangers. The wind blew so loudly, José Pablo Tsoyio had not heard the riders. He counted ten, but it was dark—even with the freakish wild light.

"I am." Story had the reins in his left hand, the cup in his right, and his weapons inside the wagon.

"You're breaking the law," a man said, jabbing a long gun toward Story, sending blue fire stems crazily, spooking not only Story's horse, but several of those carrying riders.

"Allan," a calmer voice said. "Let me handle this."

This rider's weapon remained holstered on his left hip, with the flap fastened. The stranger dismounted, keeping the reins in his right hand. He would be so easy to kill, José Pablo Tsoyio knew, but Story had no weapons, and there were too many for José Pablo Tsoyio to kill alone. Besides, José Pablo Tsoyio had seen two stampedes, and on a night like this, anything might send the herd running—straight for this camp.

"My name's Turner," the calm man said. "Sheriff of Greenwood County. There's a law against the shipping of Texas cattle this time of year. You're coming up from the south. I don't think these are . . ."

"They're my cattle," Story said. "And they're from Texas."

"I have to place you under arrest."

"And the cattle?" Story asked.

"We'll kill them," a man to Story's right said. The fox fire bounced off his stirrups.

"Enoch," Turner said. "We're not killing any cattle. There are no farms in this area . . ."

A hammer cocked. Then another. A voice in the darkness said, "Sheriff, maybe you best go back to town. We can take care of . . ."

"By all means." Story even smiled, though José Pablo Tsoyio did not believe most of the riders could see the Montanan's face. "Go back to town, Sheriff. Let your boys start shooting my beeves." He drew in a deep breath. "Smell that. See that." He pointed to the glowing ears of the sheriff's horse. "Fox fire. First shot'll send cattle stampeding all across this country. You won't be able to find them till first frost. By then, no telling how many milking cows you'll be burying."

Lightning flashed. Thunder almost immediately followed. José Pablo Tsoyio saw the tension in Story's face, his hands wrapping the reins tighter. The wind carried the anguished cries of frightened longhorns, but not the rumbling of hooves. José Pablo Tsoyio made the sign of the cross.

"I'm riding to my herd." Story turned to the horse, found a stirrup, and grabbed the horn. With his back toward the unwelcome visitors, he said, "You want to shoot me in the back, now's your chance. You'll notice I'm not wearing a gun. And that shot will send a thousand Texas longhorns every which way from Sunday." Now, slowly, he pulled himself into the saddle.

"If I were you boys," he said, "I'd ride out to the herd with me. Because on this night, we're going to have to work together. One bolt of lightning too close. One thunderclap too damn hard. One match striking. One stinking fart. Anything might send this herd into a run. All you boys have to do is sing softly and call out nice prayers to my beef. Once this storm passes, if we're still alive, we can talk about your laws."

The horse stepped forward.

"He makes good sense," said a rider.

"He's a damned Texas . . ."

"I'm from Montana," Story said. "And before that Leavenworth. I'm a businessman. Right now, my business is cattle."

The sheriff stepped back to his horse, easily mounted it.

"One more thing." Story nodded at the wagon. "You boys had better shuck all your hardware. Guns. Knives. Spurs, if you have them. Anything metal that might bring a bolt from the sky that'll light you up brighter than fox fire."

He eased the horse away from the wagon, past the sheriff and the bravest of the men, and reined up, waiting.

"He's bluffing," one farmer said.

Another streak of lightning blinded them, as though summoned by this godlike man, or Satan's captain, Nelson Story.

The sheriff moved to the wagon, unfastened his flap, and laid a big revolver inside. He even unpinned the badge on his lapel, and gasped when even the tin star began sparking with eerie flames. One by one, farmers and townsmen rode up to the wagon to rid themselves of metal before disappearing into the night that was alive with blue light practically everywhere.

With the wind, the ferocity of the storm, and as much electricity as the storm carried, Story expected a burst from hell at every flash of lightning, every roll of thunder. He also expected the storm to move past the herd quickly, but this one dragged on slowly. Every minute took a millennium. Each second, he expected the longhorns to bolt. A night like this, he thought, almost made him believe in God, or, at least, Lucifer.

That nightmarish scent of sulfur faded, as did the ball lightning and the fox fire. Clouds took the lightning—plus the rain those damned farmers wanted—east and south. To the west, and soon above the herd, Story began to see stars. He let out a long sigh.

The night, the danger, might be over, but he knew better than to jump ahead. Those cattle remained skittish. Even the horses in the remuda pranced around, nickering and moving in circles. Sam Ireland had sent most of the drag riders to help the wrangler keep the horses from scattering.

Jameson Hannah rode up.

"Well," he said.

Story nodded. "Well."

Hannah let out a half chuckle, half prayer. "That was something."

"It was." He made out the outline of another rider approaching slowly. The size of the horse revealed the rider as a Kansan. Story also had to deal with that.

Hearing the hoofbeats, Hannah twisted in the saddle.

"Hell," he whispered.

The rider stopped near Story. "You think it's over?" He couldn't see the man's face, but recognized the sheriff's voice.

"Storm's passing. Cattle are still ticklish."

"Then maybe we can talk."

"Sure. How about some coffee, Sheriff . . . ?"

"Turner. R. R. Turner. Coffee would hit the spot."

"Good. Let's go back to camp. Our cook makes some fine coffee."

As Story brought up the reins, the sheriff raised his arm.

"If it's just the same with you, sir, I'd rather serve you town coffee." Story heard the metallic click.

Hannah whirled, but Story said, "Don't." He leaned forward in the saddle. He couldn't see what was in the lawman's hand, but he knew it was a gun.

"You're under arrest. You and I are riding nice and easy back to Eureka. Tell your man here to stay with the herd till dawn. After all we've done to help, it would be a damned shame if those cattle stampeded. We'll work this out. Like the gentlemen we are. I've sent one of my men back to your camp to get our guns. I've told my men to ride out slowly. We don't want any trouble. We just want none of our cattle to die of Texas fever." Whatever he held in his hand, he waved.

"You brought a gun anyway," Story said.

"It's a four-shot derringer."

"You pull the trigger and that herd's running."

"And if I pull the trigger, you're dead. Last time I shot this hideaway gun, all four barrels discharged at once. Fellow I hit looked like he'd taken a blast of buckshot. Let's ride. Tell your man to go easy."

"You heard him, Hannah," Story said, and eased his horse in front of the sheriff's. "Which way?"

"North."

"You could've been struck by lightning," Story said.

"I aim to be reelected," the sheriff said.

CHAPTER FORTY-FOUR

John Catlin had not shaved in weeks. Now he knew why practically every man in the West—at least those traveling on the Overland Trail—sprouted whiskers. It kept the wind and sun from scalding your face. The trees they came to, almost always along creek beds or in canyons, leaned in one direction, and Catlin figured that if any damned fool tried to homestead in this country, he would find himself tilted. Probably his kids would be born bent by the wind.

"We were too damned cocky," Steve Grover said. On this day, the train's boy extra had nothing to do, so he walked alongside Catlin.

"How's that?" That was another thing about this country. A man had to shout to carry on a conversation with a fellow no more than five yards away.

"I said we were overconfident."

He made no response. All these years together, Catlin knew he didn't have to say much of anything to keep a conversation going with his friend.

"Cocky. Too sure of ourselves. Hell, we had whipped the rebs. Saved the Union and freed the slaves by ourselves. Then we up and join some bullwhackers." Grover turned and spit. The wind carried his tobacco juice like a missile, luckily for the freighters behind Catlin's wagon, in a southeasterly direction.

The oxen moved . . . better than the mules Catlin had owned back in Indiana. The sun, sinking low, made Catlin tug the brim of his hat down. He noticed the teamsters ahead of him looking at something on the side of the trail, sometimes craning as they kept the pace. Steve Grover kept talking. One of the men, a foul-mouthed German, removed his hat. Catlin looked ahead across the rolling plains, west and south. He sighed.

"What is it?" Grover asked.

Catlin pointed. They walked, the wheels turning, the hooves digging into the earth, the wind blowing. Ten minutes later, they saw the grave. A fresh one . . . only . . .

"God almighty," Grover said.

"Just keep walking," Catlin said.

"Wolves?" Grover asked.

Catlin tried to find a way to get water into his mouth, just enough so he could spit out the bile. Wolves? No. Wolves wouldn't have done that to a corpse. He wondered how the man had died. An accident? Killed by Indians? Disease? Then buried along the side of what Catlin now figured had to be the longest graveyard in the United States and her territories. He could picture the poor bastard, buried, maybe a psalm or some scripture read over him, planted with respect. Perhaps even a marker of some kind, even just a stick with a bandanna tied to it. Ready to wait out eternity till Judgment Day. Only to have some Indian come by and dig up the grave just to mutilate the body. Confederates didn't do that. No one would do that. But then, Catlin remembered what Major Coushatta John Noah had said the white men had done to a peaceful Indian camp in Colorado.

"What . . . ?" Grover fell silent. He saw the dust, and Catlin heard the commands of the men ahead of him.

"Whoa," he said, and watched the oxen slow and stop.

The major rode a blood bay this evening, and he did not slow his lope till he yanked hard on the reins beside Catlin's wagon.

"Get your long guns," the wagon boss ordered. "Both of you." Over the weeks, Noah had learned that Grover could shoot better than most men. Sometimes, Catlin figured his friend would hit his mark more than Catlin could. Hell, Grover had gotten more practice during the rebellion—especially after Catlin's promotions.

"What is it?" asked Shultz, leading the wagon right behind Catlin's.

Noah did not answer. Catlin found his rifled musket and his haversack. "Horses?" he asked.

The boss's head shook. "That would just make them bucks braver. Scalps aren't worth that much in the long run. But a horse is like whiskey or a willing tit to a Dog Soldier."

They walked on either side of Coushatta John Noah, across one arroyo, past a buffalo wallow, and through wind-blown grass.

"Your bluecoat buddies have been putting up some forts," Noah said. "On the Montana trail. To protect us entrepreneurs. Problem is, the Indians don't like having forts put up in their country."

"This isn't their country, is it?" Grover asked.

"Hell, boy, it was all their country before we stepped into it. Cheyennes and Sioux get along. And if you haven't noticed all them boys grading track for that railroad Mr. Lincoln thought was a good idea to build, well . . ." He reined up, withdrew his revolver, and checked the percussion caps on the nipples. "The one in the headdress is Talking Bull. Good name. Short for Talking Bullshit."

After shoving the pistol into his waistband, he breathed in deeply, slowly exhaled, pulled his hat down tighter, and looked down at Catlin.

Only then did Catlin realize about six or seven Indians were mounted on horses at the top of what passed for a knoll in this country. He could just make out the feathers.

"They want to parley," Noah said. "Probably will demand some toll I'll have to pay to pass through their country. We'll do some bartering. If it's like olden times, we'll pass through here and tell us all kinds of damned windies tonight. But the way things are, well, boys, once again . . . that's how come I hired you idiots."

He pushed the gelding ahead about a rod or two. Then looked back. "One thing I want you two to remember. They don't attack my train because they think I have powerful medicine. If I'm dead, they'll think they can swoop down upon the wagons and you boys'll reap the whirlwind." After turning back, he kicked the horse into a slow, deliberate walk. "So if you boys want to keep your topknots, you better make damned sure I stay alive."

Catlin and Grover stood, long guns in their hands, bracing against the wind, and watched. The knoll had to be about a half mile away. Once, Catlin knelt, scooped up a handful of dead grass, rose, and released the debris into the wind, making a mental note of the direction the grass blew.

After a lengthy talk with the Indians, Major Noah turned his gelding around and trotted across the prairie.

"Well . . ." Grover began.

The Indians, mounted, watched from the knoll, not riding away. Catlin thought he heard singing, though could not be certain. He watched his boss, who slowed the blood bay into a walk, disappeared into a depression, came up. Noah kept his back straight. His head high. Never did he look back.

"Oh . . . hell . . ."

Hearing Grover's loud whisper, Catlin looked at the Cheyennes. One of the warriors, in a headdress, kicked his pony and charged after Noah.

Catlin stepped forward, uncertain. During the rebellion, orders were orders, and orders were clear. As a private, you did what the sergeant told you to do. As a sergeant, you did what the lieutenant, or the captain, or what any officer told you to do. But Major Noah had issued no direct orders, just general suggestions. Was this a test? A challenge? Breach of etiquette or act of war? Catlin cursed.

Noah looked back, kicked the gelding into a hard lope. Again, the prairie swallowed both Noah and Talking Bull, or whoever the pursuing warrior was. The well-mounted Indian lifted a lance. No. Smoke blossomed, though Catlin never heard the musket's report. The gelding went down, hurtling Major Noah into the tall grass. He came up, crumpled, righted himself. And ran.

"Son of a . . ." Grover never finished. He lifted his weapon.

But Catlin reacted quicker. He drew in a breath, let it out, tried to guess the windage, the elevation, and saw that the running Noah and hard-riding Talking Bull lined up almost directly in single file.

"I don't have a clear shot," Grover said.

I don't, either, thought Catlin as he touched the trigger.

* * *

"You should have seen the son of a bitch," Major Coushatta John Noah said at camp that evening. "In fact, I wish to hell I had. Talking Bull goes catapulting off his pony's back. I keep running my sorry ass off, not looking back, fearing I'd find I had been dreaming, and that that Cheyenne brave was about to count coup and then do me in."

"What happened?" the Swede asked.

"I'm alive, ain't I?" Noah pointed at Catlin. "This son of a bitch killed Talking Bull dead. Deader than dirt." He took another slug of forty-rod. "I kept running, mind you, till I got to these two soldiers. Turn around. Grover's lifting his magical gun, but I tell him to hold it, let them boys carry off their warrior. Talking Bull was full of shit, but he was a brave son of a bitch. And we just stand there, watch the warriors gather poor Talking Bull, carry him off."

Noah tossed the jug to Catlin, who let it fall in the grass by his boots.

"Catlin," Noah said, "you just earned yourself a partnership in my company. I'm not sure how much of a partnership, but it's something. I'd be dead and scalped and hacked to pieces if you hadn't done what you done. And don't you try to talk yourself out of it. Ask anybody on these trails, and they'll tell you. Major Coushatta John Noah is a man of his word." He let out a hurrah. "But how the hell did you make that shot, bubba?"

Catlin did not like being here, in the camp, every damned eye staring at him.

He shrugged. "I was aiming at the brave's horse," he said.

Noah let out a belly laugh of approval. Even Steve Grover slapped Catlin's shoulder, chuckling and nodding. But Catlin had not been joking.

CHAPTER FORTY-FIVE

He dreamed again. The same damned dream. *He's a boy back in Ohio, digging a grave. It's night, but he's sweating. Clouds hide the stars this time, and he looks up from the grave and sees the dog. But he can't tell which dog it is, which one he's burying. So he digs.* Until he woke up.

Boots sounded on the stone floor, metal jangled, and the sound of the heavy iron key in the lock grinded as Nelson Story lifted his hat off his face and pushed himself into a seated position on the thin, straw mattress. Sheriff R. R. Turner pulled open the door. Two townsmen from the posse stood on either side of the lawman, each holding a shotgun, one a single-shot, the other a double-barrel.

"How dangerous do you think I am?" Story said.

"Dangerous enough to have gotten a herd of beef from Texas to this far in Kansas," Turner said. "In this weather. And with herd thieves all around Baxter Springs."

He wondered if what had happened along the Neosho had caused lawmen to send word out across the state.

"Judge is in my office." Turner stepped back, scraping the door on the stones.

Story pushed himself to his feet, brushed off straw and dust, pulled on his hat, and left the cell, giving both guards a *good morning* nod. Sunlight beamed through the open door as he walked down the hall and into the light.

"My office is down the street. Next block."

He walked, stiffly, all night in a saddle after all day in a saddle, and then the rest of the night with only a thin layer of ticking and straw between his body and hard, cold rocks left him feeling like an old man. He looked across the street at this monstrosity of a building, part fort, part redoubt, amazed at the singing going on from inside.

"That's our school," Turner said.

One of the guards muttered, "Wish to hell she'd teach them young'uns something other than singing songs. That's all my boy wants to do when he gets home, and, God, that kid can't carry a tune."

The streets were muddy. It must have rained in Eureka, while the prairie had gotten just a few hard, cold drops last night. He crossed over and stopped at the first building, a frame structure painted blue. The citizens expected great things from Eureka—if they were hauling in wood to build businesses.

Turner stepped around Story to open the door. "You all go in," he told his guards. "Tell the judge I'll be in in a moment. I want to have a word in private with Mr. Story." When the guards frowned, Turner told them, "I'll be fine." The men lowered the hammers on their shotguns and disappeared inside the small office. Turner closed the door and stared at Story.

As if planned, the singing stopped.

"One thing I hope you'll remember, Story, is that we helped you keep that herd from running last night."

"What I remember," Story said, "is you pulling a hideaway gun on me. In front of my men."

"That's right. To keep you, your men, my men, from doing something stupid."

Story waited.

"Where are you taking your herd?"

"Most of my men hired on to get this herd to Kansas City."

"You're a long way from Kansas City. And you didn't answer my question."

Story smiled in spite of himself. He had to give Sheriff R. R. Turner credit. He was smart, a wily son of a bitch, and a peace officer. *Peace* officer. Not some hired killer with a gun and a badge.

"Montana," Story said.

"Montana." Turner stepped back.

"If I can get there. I figured to drop that plan on my men's shoulders . . ." He let out a dry laugh. "I don't know when. But the time's getting sooner."

"Think they'll quit you?"

"Some will. Maybe all of them."

"Don't underestimate them. From what I saw last night." Story waited.

"I figure most of your men will come riding in soon. To get you out of jail. I don't want this to turn ugly." He pointed at the schoolhouse. "I hope you don't want this to turn ugly."

The sheriff opened the door and motioned for Story to step inside.

"Take a seat there." Story sat. Turner pulled a newspaper off the desk, tossed it to Story, and moved to the stove, where a man wearing a black suit and somber countenance poured coffee into a crude cup. The deputies had placed themselves at the office's corners, holding shotguns in one hand, coffee cups in the other. Story opened the paper and began to read. If he knew Jameson Hannah, the herd would be moving north by now. If he had figured Sheriff R. R. Turner right, some county men would be trailing that herd. At some point, Hannah would turn the herd toward Eureka. The thing was, Story didn't know how far Jameson Hannah would go. Stampede the herd through town? Turn Eureka into another Lawrence? Nor did he know how far Turner's watchdogs would go. Last night's storm had passed, but things remained ticklish.

And these bastards had not offered Story a drop of coffee.

"Story." Turner and the judge walked to a desk.

Story tucked the paper in his pocket, rose, and met the two men.

"Plead guilty," the judge said.

"To what?"

The judge sighed. "Just plead guilty. So I can fine you seventy-five dollars and order you and your damned cattle out of Greenwood County."

"You paid those thieving Yankees?" Jameson Hannah spit out coffee and disgust.

"It's my money. And my cattle." Story refilled the cup with some of José Pablo Tsoyio's coffee, which, after drinking Eureka coffee, revived him.

"I would've wiped that town off the face—"

"And my cattle would've been scattered all across the prairie, those that weren't butchered, and you and I would be heading to Lansing for life, at best, or dangling from a cottonwood branch on some creek bed."

Laughing, the Texan pitched his empty cup into the wreck pan.

"We're heading toward Topeka," Hannah said, changing the subject. "Then you've gotta make a choice." He lowered his voice. "Either give up this folly about driving a herd to Montana and turn east and find a buyer in Kansas City or . . ." He shook his head. "See how many damned fools we have that'll play out your hand."

Story did not respond.

"You turn west at Topeka and these boys'll mutiny."

"We're not turning west. We're moving to Leavenworth."

Hannah let out a sigh of relief. "Well, although I fancied seeing this Montana Territory, I will admit that . . ."

"I have supplies waiting for me in Leavenworth," Story reminded him. "To take to Alder Gulch along with this beef. And there's something else I want to get in Leavenworth." From his pocket, Story pulled out a page torn out of the newspaper he had been given by the Eureka lawman. He had balled up most of the *Burlington Patriot* and tossed it in the garbage.

E. REMINGTON & SONS
Manufacturers of Revolvers, Rifles,
MUSKETS *and* CARBINES,
for the United States Service.
Also, Rifle Canes, Revolving Rifles,
Rifle Barrels,
Shotgun Barrels, and Gun Materials,
Sold by GUN DEALERS *and* TRADE
throughout the Country.
In these days of HOUSE BREAKING
and ROBBERY,
Every House, Store, Bank, and Office
should have one of Remington's Revolvers.
Circulars containing CUTS *and*
DESCRIPTIONS *of our Arms*
will be furnished upon application.

E. REMINGTON & SONS, Ilion, N.Y.

Moore & Nichols, *Agents*
No. 40 Courtland St., New York

L. M. Rumsey & Co., *Agents*
No. 141 North Second St., St. Louis, Mo.

The advertisement included a drawing of a Remington revolver at the top.

"You plan to sell Remington revolvers in Virginia City, too?"

"I'm a Colt man," Story said. "But the rifles interest me. Breechloaders. Not muzzleloaders. They fire .56-50 Spencer rimfire cartridges. From what I've heard, you can fire one of these five, six, even seven times in one minute. A rifle like that will come in handy if we run into Indians. Or more herd thieves."

"If you got men who can shoot them. You turn west, you might have a bunch of Remingtons and nobody to pull a trigger but you."

"And you."

Hannah laughed. "And me."

"I lived in Leavenworth," Story said. "There were several gunsmiths and gun dealers when I left a few years back. Town's grown, from what I've been hearing. So I suspect there are more dealers and traders in town now."

"Those rifles won't come cheap."

"Boone and I saw some in Philadelphia for thirty-five bucks. In Leavenworth this spring, they sold for a hundred dollars. But you spend money to make money. And you spend money to stay alive."

"Yeah. That's a businessman talking. But how about I offer you a suggestion, from one businessman to another." Hannah's eyes gleamed with delight. "You let me and Sam and Combs ride off. I'll get you those guns. It might cost you more than thirty-five bucks, but not a hundred or more. You use your money for grub and wagons and maybe more men. And to pay off the quitters we'll have when you turn west."

"I don't want the army or a posse chasing us out of Kansas," Story said.

"Now, Nelson, do you think I'd do something dishonest?"

Story stared without blinking. Then asked, "How much money do you need?"

CHAPTER FORTY-SIX

The Cottonwood River roared like a Montana mountain stream during early summer runoff. Only deeper, wider, deadlier.

There would be no quicksand to worry about here. The remuda crossed first, helped by Stubbings and Peña while Allen and Petty chopped down young cottonwoods, then with sweat and muscles from the cook and Story, roped the logs to the wheels. The mules swam. The wagons floated. The drivers cursed between prayers. Horses and wagons reached the far side, worn out, drenched, but alive. Afterward, Stubbings and Peña began pushing the lead steers into the raging Cottonwood, while Story rode back to urge the crew to drive the cattle in fast and keep them swimming.

Flooding had turned the prairie into a quagmire. The bay's legs sank into the mud up to its cannons, causing a sucking sound with each step. Longhorn cattle churned up the slop into a path of filth. The stench of mud reminded Story of Ohio, only here the piss and excrement of horses and beef mingled with the odor. He reined in, yelled at the men to keep the cattle moving, warned them of the river's depth and current, and waited for the drag to arrive. The trench widened and deepened. Twisting in the saddle, Story looked back down the line of beef that led to the river. He could see cattle on the far bank, moving through more mud, and keeping on north.

"This work is shit," Kelvin Melean called out, slapping his hat against his horse's rump. Globs of mud clung to the cowboy's boots and stirrups. Story couldn't even see the man's spurs.

"The river will wash you clean," Story told him.

"If I don't drown."

Story shrugged. "There's a pontoon bridge at Topeka."

"If the floods haven't washed it away."

How many men will quit me? Story wondered. Here he sat, his horse sinking in mud, and he hadn't gotten out of southern Kansas. Summer would officially be here in a day or two—or maybe it had already come—and he hadn't made it to Leavenworth. He had a bet to win, to get a herd to Virginia City in December. He pictured Ellen. What kind of husband leaves a wife carrying his child in the dead of winter in a savage frontier where blizzards could bury an entire town? By thunder, he had a daughter he had never seen, yet here he was, with a thousand Texas longhorns and a crew ready to mutiny. A crew that had signed on to bring cattle to market in Kansas, not to follow a damned fool's dream of starting a ranch and making another fortune in the wilds of Montana.

He thought again of the dream. That damned dream that kept coming to him once or twice or even more times a night, two or three times each week. Nelson Story. Digging a grave. His own grave? The grave for the men he had killed? The grave of the boy who had drowned so many miles back while helping Story see his dream come true? The graves of men who would die in the coming months?

He tugged hard on the reins, pressed his spurs, and

nudged the bay closer to the beeves. "Move," he barked, slapping his own hat against mud-splattered leggings. "Move."

Hooves sucked, though not as deep this far from the Cottonwood. The gelding moved down the line, slugging through the bog, till Story could see the last of the riders, the cattle. He waved his hat over his head, and yelled, "River's up ahead. Half a mile or so." Turning the bay, Story rode down with the cattle, his cattle, hurrying the animals through deeper mud, soggier ground, all the way until they plunged into the water.

Stubbings and Peña swam fresh horses—they had already swapped out the mounts they had been riding—on the eastern side of the river, back and forth, keeping the cattle swimming with the current. Story could make out Luis Avala and Mason Boone on the other side. White smoke wafted over the tops of waterlogged cottonwoods on the far bank. José Pablo Tsoyio must be cooking coffee to keep the men fortified. Story's stomach growled. Damnation, he would almost swim that river from hell just for one cup of the old Mexican's brew. Instead, he spurred the bay and moved back down the herd.

Two of his men were well behind the last of the steers, one mounted, one on the ground. That left two men pushing the slowest cattle, and one of those he recognized was Tom Allen, a good man, but far from a top cowboy. Cursing, Story kicked the horse into a lope, until the deepening swamp slowed him to a series of lunges through a stinking soup of manure and mud.

"What the hell's going on?" he yelled at Allen.

"Calf." Allen pointed.

Allen might have said more, but Story kept on, leaving Allen and Ernesto Martinez to push the cattle through the marsh. He could see the men, and the calf now. Ryan Ward struggled, up to his thighs in filth, while Jody Barley had roped around the calf's neck. "It's no use," Barley kept repeating.

The calf could not be more than a few days old, stuck in the bog, struggling, crying like an infant. Story looked back, only to realize that the mother had to be near the river now.

"It's no use."

The calf bawled.

Kelvin Melean slogged through the slop. "What the bloody hell is this? You dumb sons of bitches. Shoot that calf if it can't get out of the mud, and get those beeves moving."

Barley and Ryan looked at each other, hoping for someone else to volunteer.

"Jesus Christ. I'll kill it." The revolver's hammer clicked as Melean urged the horse closer.

"No."

It took a moment for Story to realize he had spoken.

"What?" Melean turned.

"You're not killing that calf," Story said.

"I don't like it no more than you do," Melean argued, "but it's got to be done. Unless you want to leave it to the wolves. Or have it starve to death."

Story swung down into the stink, moving to young Ryan Ward and the frightened calf. He came to the other side, nodded at Ward, then at Barley, and reached both arms into the foulness until he grabbed the belly of the bawling, smelling, calf. Barley began spurring his horse. The newborn cried out. Story and Ward tried lifting.

"You crazy bastards." Melean swung out of the saddle and moved into the muck until he was behind the calf. "There's no point to this." He cursed, pushed.

The calf lunged into some sort of vacuum, and suddenly

it was free enough that Barley managed to drag it to firmer ground. Melean slung mud off his hands. Ward laughed, tried to find some way to get the globs and stink off his hands, arms, and face, and Barley let out a whoop and yelled, "We done it."

"And just what the bloody hell have you done? That runt's so puny and tired it'll drown in that river just like—" He stopped, spat, moved back to his horse.

"It won't have to swim." Story slogged through knee-deep thickness until he reached his bay, then pulled it through the channel the herd had created. He handed Barley the reins.

"Give me a hand," he told Ward.

They lifted the kicking, screaming brown and white baby onto the saddle, just behind the horn. The calf kicked. The horse whinnied, and almost bucked. Barley struggled with the reins, but Story swung into the saddle. By then, Barley had stepped off his horse, whispering or humming—Story couldn't tell—to the bay. Barley carefully handed Story the reins.

"Have you gone mad?" Melean said. "You'll drown yourself, your horse, and this bastard of beef trying to swim across that current."

"It's my calf," Story said.

"You're the greediest, craziest son of a bitch I've ever worked for."

Ignoring the insult, Story turned the horse toward the river. The calf pissed, then crapped.

"Jesus, Mary, and Joseph." Melean spit, and hurried back toward his own horse, clawing the mud off his clothes. "I've had my say, and you two squirts will be my witness."

Story was already easing the horse toward the river.

He entered upstream, more than a hundred yards from

the last of the herd. The bay snorted, and Story took the reins in his left hand, tight, and pushed his right hand hard against the struggling, bawling calf. The coldness of the water shocked him, and even though he knew the current would be powerful, its intensity almost swept him out of the saddle. Three jumps into the river, and the bay was swimming, moving like a missile toward the herd. He probably should have ridden farther upstream or tried crossing farther down the Cottonwood.

The calf bawled, almost slipped over, but the speed of the river worked in Story's favor. Jordan Stubbings and Mason Boone plunged their mounts into the river from the far bank, moving toward him and the calf. An instant later, the baby slipped out of Story's grasp. He twisted, turned, tried to grab it, then lost balance and stirrups, and plunged into the river.

He came up, spitting, and felt a rope loop over his outstretched arm and head. Suddenly he was being dragged, but only a few feet. His boots felt something firm, and the tightness of the lariat loosened. He rose, knee-deep, freezing. Stubbings kicked his gray toward him and collected the rope as Story removed the lariat. On the banks, Story's horse began shaking savagely, spraying water everywhere.

Mason Boone swung out of his saddle.

And there stood the calf, bawling in panic, but beside Boone's horse. A moment later a brindle cow rushed to her calf.

Shaking his head, Boone pulled his horse away.

Kelvin Melean rode up to Story, his horse dripping wet, and he leaned down and extended his hand. "I won't take back what I said," Melean said. "You're greedy, crazy, and a son of a bitch. But damn it all to hell, you're a man to ride the river with."

"Swim a river with," Boone called back. Someone laughed.

The calf began to suckle. Turning north, Story started walking. "Where the hell is that coffee?" he said.

CHAPTER FORTY-SEVEN

Trying to get Montana to burp, Ellen Story gracefully moved around the furniture to the cabin's door and pulled it open to find Dr. Seth Beckstead standing, black satchel in one hand, his fine hat in the other.

Montana burped, loud for a baby.

"And good morning to you as well, Montana Story, and to your lovely mother."

She looked a fright, and now here she stood on a fine June morning, with spittle on the napkin she had placed on her shoulder. Montana cooed. Ellen stepped back and pulled the door open wider. "I'm sorry, Doctor . . ."

Beckstead's head cocked to one side, and he frowned.

"Seth," Ellen corrected.

"Much better . . . Ellen."

"I am such a scatterbrain," Ellen said. "I had forgotten that you were coming for a checkup."

Beckstead entered the cabin, the windows open, the air fresh, and he shook his head. "Your brain functions at full capacity, my lady. I called without invitation. I have been told, by none other than Professor Dimsdale himself, that such visits are allowed. It is considered western hospitality."

He started to close the door, but Ellen stopped him.

"Please. Leave it open for a while. The breeze is so nice. It is such a beautiful day."

Nodding, he set his hat and satchel on the table.

"How is Montana?"

"Full." Ellen laughed. "And contented. For now. She can be a handful."

"And how are you?"

"Exhausted."

"Then have a seat."

They sipped coffee while Ellen bounced the baby on her knee, held her to her shoulder, rocked her gently, kissed her forehead, and counted her fingers over and over again. Five on each hand. She couldn't help herself. Ellen just had to make sure she had not miscounted, that Montana was not deformed in any way. She usually counted the girl's toes, as well, but not in front of company.

"You work too hard, Ellen," Seth Beckstead finally said.

"Well, I have been told by several of our most respectable ladies in the Fourteen Mile City that my work will be done as soon as Nelson and I marry Montana off."

"I do not jest, Ellen." She studied the doctor closely. "You should have a night for yourself."

"And who would look after Montana?"

"Not your husband, I dare say. Have you heard from him?"

She did not answer.

He made himself laugh, as though he had been making a joke, but she knew he had been serious.

"Allow me to give you a prescription," Beckstead said. "Montana needs a healthy mother to grow up to be a strong girl and fine woman, but the mother needs something that does not mean changing diapers and feeding a baby and rocking and catching a minute of sleep if she can."

She waited.

"Professor Dimsdale assures me that Missus Martin's daughter has looked after babies all across Alder Gulch. And Missus Martin has assured me that Grace is free this evening." He glanced out the open door. "It is a lovely day." Turning back to Ellen, Beckstead said, "You have often mentioned how much you love the theater."

She looked down at Montana, now sleeping, and knew better than to move. The girl had this devilish way of waking if you moved her to the crib either too early or too late after the knee rocking. Virginia City had two theaters these days. The Montana Theater had opened in a cabin two years earlier and had staged a number of dances, burlesques, recitations, some concerts, one ax-throwing contest and an arm-wrestling match. No Shakespeare. The other, The People's Theater, had only recently opened its doors—in what had been one of the town's myriad billiard parlors. And Con Orem had renamed his Champion Saloon to Melodeon Hall, but his idea of theatrical entertainment had been a prizefight, London Prize Ring rules, in which young Con himself, all 138 pounds but packed into a hard, small frame, went up against Hugh O'Neil, older, heavier and a whole lot meaner. Nelson had dragged her to that one. All three hours and more, 185 rounds of blood and sweat and profanity before O'Neil called it quits because of darkness.

"Theater." The word came out as a sigh. Leavenworth . . . even Denver had staged *Our American Cousin, Hamlet,* and *Richelieu; or, The Conspiracy*.

"Perhaps you have not heard that The People's Theater tonight is staging *The Poor of New York*."

She stared in disbelief.

"Jack Langrishe's company is in town with his troupe. They are quite—"

"I am quite familiar with Colonel Langrishe," she said.

She rose, carefully, and carried the baby to the crib, kneeling, praying that Montana would not wake in a screaming fit, and turned. Her knees felt weak. Her heart raced. "Colonel Langrishe . . . is here . . . really?"

"With his wife—do you know Jenette?"

"Just from seeing her perform." She sat heavily in the chair across from the doctor.

John "Jack" Langrishe. In Virginia City, Montana Territory. She had seen him and his Langrishe-Allen St. Joseph Theatre Company performing in Missouri and Kansas, and even briefly in Denver. From *Ten Nights in a Bar Room* to *Uncle Tom's Cabin*. From *Hamlet* to *Othello*. The last she had heard, Langrishe had found a new partner and had taken over the Colorado Theatre in Denver. He was a true theater man, even if Nelson had told her that his theater company operated on the second floor of the building in Denver, while the first ran twenty-four hours nonstop, seven days a week, with performances of faro, roulette, chuck-a-luck, and monte.

"I would like you to accompany me to tonight's performance, Ellen." His eyes held her. "For your own good. Do not think I ask with improper intentions. Professor Dimsdale will be with us. You will have an evening out, Montana will be cared for, it will do the both of you good, and I will beg your leave after the performance and let Professor Dimsdale escort you to home."

She could not speak.

"If Montana proves inconsolable, Miss Grace will send a runner to The People's Theatre to fetch you."

Her mouth moved, but all she could do was breathe.

I will be delighted.

She realized she had not spoken the words. After swallowing, her eyes brightened and she told him. His eyes beamed, and he sprang from his chair, said something about dinner at six, and hurried through the open door. Five minutes later, he came back, apologizing, collecting his hat and grip, his face bright red. Then he left.

Montana slept peacefully.

She sat between Professor Dimsdale and Seth Beckstead, on the front row, staring at the closed curtain, aware of the bustling of the crowd behind her, and the energy, the jitters, the excitement behind that curtain. Ellen Story loved theater, always had, and as she had told Seth a few weeks earlier, how she had once dreamed of running away from home, then in Platte County, Missouri, to join a theatrical troupe. Seth had laughed and said that he had dreamed only of running away to join a circus.

As the crowd settled and the lights dimmed, a man slipped from between the curtains, removed a wide-brimmed hat, and bowed. She recognized Langrishe immediately, the long, angular face with the prominent nose and solid chin, a big man who moved with grace, dressed out in boots, black trousers, a fine vest of silver brocade, black coat, and silk shirt of a rich purple.

"Ladies and gentlemen . . ." The crowd broke out in applause. Ellen clapped excitedly.

The impresario laughed. "Well, we shall see if you shower us with applause or rotten fruit after our performance this evening in this wonderful and exotic city. But first, I have to make a sad announcement. One of my poor, sweet actresses, the incomparable Lenore McKee, is a little off her feed. Must be the altitude—although we hail from Denver, and that's a mile high. And that leaves us without a Lucy."

The crowd fell silent. Ellen feared her evening on the town would soon end, without a performance.

"But I understand this is a city of thespians, that citizens in this very theater performed *Ingomar the Barbarian* just last year."

Professor Dimsdale shook his head and whispered, "How well I know, having to sit through all four wretched acts."

"Be quiet," Ellen admonished.

"So . . . if I may be so bold and brave, might I ask for a volunteer. There are no lines to remember. I—Not you, sir. Your beard does not fit my interpretation of sweet, pure Lucy."

More laughter. A few hoots.

"There are no lines to remember. You will have a copy of Dion's play in your hands. Just follow along with us, and read your lines . . . *with feeling*." He stepped back.

Seth Beckstead turned in his chair and said, "Ellen, here is your chance. To see what your dream would have been like."

Her face flushed, and Langrishe stepped to the edge of the stage, as if he had heard the doctor or read his lips.

"Madam." The colonel bowed. "Would you do us the honor? As a thespian, as a production manager, and leader of a troupe of rascals and vagabonds, I can promise you nothing other than . . . that greatest of all treasures— applause!"

"Get up there, girlie," someone yelled.

"Yeah. I paid seventy-five cents to see something."

Dimsdale nodded, Beckstead stood, offering her his hand.

Hers, trembling, reached up, and he lifted her from her seat, guided her to the steps at the side of the stage. There two other actors helped her up, and the curtains parted. Someone placed the drama in her hands, turned the pages, showed Ellen her first appearance, and then flipped back to the beginning. "Just stay here," he whispered. "Read along. And when your line comes up, read. Enunciate. Have a blast. We sure will." He left, leaving behind the scent of his rye-soaked breath.

So she stood there, trembling, afraid she'd drop the book or rip the pages, listening to the young man playing Mr. Badger talk to the outlandish and energizing Mr. Bloodgood, played by the great Langrishe. And when act 2, scene 2, began, she saw the stage instructions for the first time:

Enter LUCY, *with a box.*

She thought: *What on earth am I doing here?*

But there was no piano or orchestra to play, and the actor playing Livingstone nodded at her, grinned, and whispered, "You're on, lassie."

Her mouth opened, and she heard herself say, hearing every tremble at every syllable, "My dear mother."

Followed by a deafening roar of approval.

They cheered. They hissed. They gasped at the fires the evil Bloodgood had set, even if the flames were orange-painted wooden cutouts with a few actors not involved in the scene blowing smoke from cigars and holding up lucifers. They cheered when Badger slapped the manacles on Bloodgood's wrists. And the applause hurt Ellen's ears when she stepped onto the stage, hands locked with Langrishe and the actress who played Mrs. F, stepped toward the edge of the stage, and bowed.

"You are a natural actress, Ellen."

"Bosh." But she so enjoyed the compliment.

"I am surprised you did not accompany Langrishe and his troupe to Birmingham's eating house," Beckstead said.

She pushed open the door. Grace Martin stepped to the door, smiling. "She's asleep, ma'am," the young blonde said.

"Any trouble?"

"None whatsoever."

"Let me get your payment, Grace. How is your mother, by the way? I was so rude not to ask. We were in such a hurry."

"Ma's fine. She says come over and show off that sweet little girl you got. She's adorable. Don't bother with the money, ma'am. Doc Beckstead's already taken care of it." She got her shawl and bonnet and hurried into the night.

Ellen turned, found herself alone with Seth Beckstead.

Her heart skipped, and her throat turned dry.

But Seth Beckstead bowed, smiled again, his eyes bright, and said, "It was a lovely evening, Ellen. Now get some rest. I will call on you, officially, two days from now."

Like a gentleman, he pulled the door shut.

PART III
Summer

CHAPTER FORTY-EIGHT

Kansas winds and the summer sun quickly dried out ground, grass, and men. They found the Santa Fe Trail, and followed it east till near Dragoon Creek Crossing, turned north along the Fort Riley Military Road to Topeka, rode over the Kansas River on that pontoon bridge—where it seemed like half the town came out to watch in awe—and eastward to Leavenworth. A few miles before reaching the fort and the town, Story had the herd bedded down.

"Boone," Story said as he halted his horse beside the two wagons. "Catch yourself a fresh horse. I want you to ride into town with me. See if Jameson Hannah is dead or in jail."

The lean Texan did not appear overly excited about climbing into a saddle again, but he nodded without comment and moved toward the remuda.

"You planning on selling this herd to the army?" Kelvin Melean put his hands on his hips. "Or maybe you figure to drive this herd all the way to Chicago."

"I heard tell of a fellow who took his cattle all the way to New York City," Luis Avala said. "In the '50s, I think."

Tom Allen and Bill Petty looked at each other, then at Story. Ernesto Martinez dropped his saddle on the ground and stared. Fabian Peña stopped rolling a cigarette, and Jody Barley stopped gathering dried buffalo dung for the fire. Boone would be with Cesar Lopez now at the horse herd, and Jordan Stubbings and Ryan Ward remained with the cattle. Standing to the right of, but not offering to help, José Pablo Tsoyio set up a coffeepot and stewpot over a fire pit.

"We've been shorthanded since you sent Sam, Hannah, and Combs off," Melean said. "And I ain't rightly sure why you sent them away. Hire some new men, I figured, maybe stock up on coffee and salt pork. But how many men does that take?"

"We have been taking a roundabout way to get this herd to market," Jody Barley said.

"And now you take Boone into town." Peña spit in the dirt, paper and tobacco still in the fingers of his right hand.

Melean. That came as no surprise to Story. The Irishman had always displayed a temper, and Barley rode drag, and Story had yet to find a drag rider in a good mood. But Peña? Story had figured the Mexican would ride forever and never question where they were going or how long it would take. Petty and Allen knew Story's intentions, as did Boone. And the two men with the cattle, Stubbings and Ward, probably would not have complained, maybe would have even backed Story.

Story said, "You want to quit, quit." He looked at the cook. "How much longer till coffee and chuck?"

José Pablo Tsoyio rose and leaned against the wagon. "Supper," he said, "can wait."

So here it was. The mutiny. Well, Story knew it would come to this at some point.

At that point Boone led a dun horse into the camp, oblivious to the rumblings.

Story walked to his tethered horse, grabbed the reins, and stepped into the saddle. "There's a good café in Leavenworth," he said. "Coffee's better there, too. If any of you are still around when Boone and I get back, we'll talk."

"What the hell was all that about back there?" Boone asked when they had trotted a hundred yards out of camp.

"If it were any of your business, I'd tell you," Story said.

His mood had worsened by the time he stepped inside the Leavenworth city jail. The deputy, an old gimp holding a shotgun, hammers cocked, stepped into the corner of the narrow hallway. Inside the only occupied cell, Jameson Hannah lifted his black hat off his face, grinned, and sat up on the bunk. Fresh scratches on his knuckles, one missing thumbnail, a swollen bottom lip, a bloody scratch through the beard stubble on his left cheek, and a deep shiner surrounding the right eye.

Hannah grinned. "You might not believe this, Story, but I won the fight."

"I didn't send you to Leavenworth to whip the whole damned town."

Hannah tested his jaw. "If I'd whipped the whole damned town, I wouldn't be here." He nodded at the jailer. "He used the butt of that cannon on the back of my head when I was just getting started."

The gimp spit tobacco juice into a bucket in the corner. "If there weren't so many people around, I would've given you the other end," he said.

"How long have you been here?" Story asked.

"Three days."

"Eighty-seven more to go," the jailer said. "Or two hundred dollars."

Hannah stood. "The judge was generous," he said. "I'm ready whenever you are."

"To stand your bail?" Story shook his head. "I could let you rot for three months."

"But you won't. I got something you want. That's why I was celebrating. It was the Fourth of July. I just told the bartender what I thought of that damn Yankee holiday. Some Kansas boys took exception."

"Where are Ireland and Combs?"

"Guarding your purchase."

Story turned to the jailer. "I pay you, Deputy?"

"You pay the court," the gimp said. "I'll walk you to the courthouse."

"Well, hell," Hannah said, "that'll take you a week and a half."

The gimp spit tobacco juice on Hannah's shirtfront as he limped past. Hannah just laughed.

Dalton Combs pried open the crate and withdrew one of the Remington rifles, handing it to Story. "Just like you asked for. Fires a .56-50 Spencer rimfire," Hannah said as he sipped coffee on the camp two miles outside of town. "Sam tested one. Managed to get off five rounds in a minute, and that's with Sam's bum hand."

Story looked at Sam Ireland, with his hand still bandaged from that ruction with the herd thieves south of Baxter Springs. "Kicks like a damned mule," Ireland said, "but it'll put down whatever it hits."

"You know why I want these rifles." It wasn't a question. Story looked at Ireland, then at Combs.

"I reckon we ain't fools, boss." The black cowboy raised his eyes and held Story's stare. "Man don't need this kind of protection to get a herd of cattle to Kansas City."

"There's a job for you in Montana Territory if you ride with me. At the ranch I plan to start."

"We got to get to Montana Territory first," Ireland said.

Story held out the heavy rifle. "These might help."

"You talked to the rest of the boys?" Hannah asked.

"Not yet. That's why I wanted to get to Leavenworth. Plenty of men to replace any quitters."

"I wouldn't call them quitters, boss." Combs stood and pushed back his hat. "You hired them for a job. Get your cattle to Kansas. They've done that. And more."

"Would you have hired on had I told you we were going to Montana?"

The black man smiled. "Maybe. I kinda like seeing the elephant. And Texas ain't exactly friendly to men of my color. Any folks up in Montana look like me?"

"Some." Story turned to Ireland. "What about you?"

Before he could answer, Jameson Hannah said, "Boys, this is your chance to make history. They'll write songs and books about what Story here plans to do."

"You going?" Ireland asked.

He looked at Story. "If I get an invite. Is there a job waiting for me in Montana, Story?"

"Most likely a rope." He handed the Remington breech-loader back to Combs. "You got a bill of sale for these guns and ammunition?"

Hannah laughed and nodded at Combs, who untucked

his shirt to reveal a money belt. He unfastened it, reached in, and handed a slip of paper to Story.

After glancing at the paper, Story stared hard at the grinning Hannah. "Sold by Dick Turpin," he said.

"It's a bill of sale, Story," Hannah said. "And you have to admit, I do have style."

"Just remember what happened to Dick Turpin in England." Story nodded at the mules. "Load these up. We'll see how Boone's making out in town."

Mason Boone, freshly shaved, wearing a new shirt, stood in front of the general store, leaning against a hitching rail and cleaning his fingernails with the blade of a pocketknife. The Texan wasn't as stupid as Story had figured him, for he had visited one of Leavenworth's tonsorial parlors instead of a saloon—though he might have visited one of those, too—and now waited in front of two loaded freight wagons.

When Story and his men reined up, Story asked, "Room in those wagons for what the mules are carrying?"

Boone folded the blade and slid the knife into his trousers pocket. "Yeah."

"All right." A nod at Ireland and Combs sent the cowboys swinging out of the saddles and moving to the mules. "I'll put Allen and Petty on these wagons," Story told Hannah. "Then we'll hire another man to drive our extra wagon."

"What about him?" Hannah pointed his jaw toward Boone.

"He's an old horse soldier," Story said. "I want him on the back of a pony." He continued speaking to Hannah. "Then we'll see how many men I have to replace, other than the dead one. With Combs and Ireland sticking with us, it might not be as bad as I thought. They carry some weight among the boys." Boone stood at Story's side. "You got an aversion to getting that store-bought shirt dirty, Boone?" He pointed at the crates strapped to the mules.

Boone reached inside his vest and pulled out a folded sheet of paper. "You're gonna need more men than you figured," the Texan said. "A lot more men."

Story snatched the notice from Boone's hand.

CHAPTER FORTY-NINE

General Order No. 27
Headquarters Department of the Missouri,
St. Louis, Missouri, February 28, 1866.

For the security of trains and travellers crossing the great plains during the coming season, the following rules are published and will be enforced by all commanders of military posts in that region:

I. Fort Ridgley and Fort Abercrombie are designated as points of rendezvous for all trains or travellers pursuing the routes from Minnesota to the mining regions of Montana, by way of Fort Berthold, Fort Union, and the valley of the Upper Missouri and Yellowstone rivers; and to the same region by way of Sioux falls, Fort Pierre, the Black Hills, and Powder river. This latter route is believed to be safe to travel as far as Fort Pierre or Crow creek, on the Missouri river, even for small parties. Beyond the Missouri river all precautions herein indicated must be taken.

In like manner, Fort Kearny is designated as the point of rendezvous for all trains destined for Denver City or Fort Laramie, by way of the Platte River route; and Fort Riley and Fort Larned as the rendezvous for trains for New Mexico and for Denver City or other points in Colorado, by the Smoky Hill or Arkansas River routes. These points can be reached from the Missouri river without danger.

II. At the posts above designated all trains will be organized for defence by electing a captain and other officers, and organizing the teamsters, employes, and any other persons travelling with or belonging to the train, into one or more companies. Every person who accompanies a train must be properly armed for defence, and must submit himself during the journey to such regulations as the captain of the train shall lay down, and perform such duties, as guards, sentinels, herdsmen, &c., as may be designated by the same authority. No train consisting of less than twenty wagons and thirty armed men, organized as above indicated, will be permitted to pass into the Indian country; and during the transit across the plains these trains will be held responsible for the faithful observance of the rules and regulations laid down and the treaties with the Indian tribes through whose country they are passing.

III. The commanding officer of each military post on any of the routes west of the posts herein indicated as rendezvous is directed to inspect each train which passes his post, sufficiently to assure himself that the military organization herein specified has been made, and that the usual precautions against Indian attacks or surprises have been carefully observed. When it is found that the provisions of this order have not been complied with, the train in which such neglect occurs will not be permitted to pass beyond the military post where it is discovered until it is made manifest to the commanding officer that such neglect will not occur again. The commanding officer who discovers this neglect will also report the facts to the commander of the next post on the route, in order that careful examination of the train may again be made at that post.

IV. All persons travelling across the plains, except those belonging to the military service of the United States and such as are transported in the mail coaches or other conveyances on the overland routes, must join themselves together in a military organization, consisting of not less than thirty armed men, or must connect themselves with some train.

V. No persons will be permitted to enter the Indian country unless they comply with the provisions of this order; and commanding officers of the military posts, as far west as Washington Territory, the State of Nevada, and the Territory of Arizona, will arrest and hold all persons attempting to cross the plains in any other manner than that herein specified.

VI. Whenever a military escort is thought necessary, the commanding officer of the military post beyond which such escort may be required will notify the captains of trains of the fact, and will furnish a sufficient escort in addition to the force with the train to protect it to the next military post, when, if necessary, another escort will be furnished; and these escorts will be supplied from one post to another in this manner until the point of danger is passed.

VII. Whenever an attack is made by Indians upon any train pursuing the overland routes, or travelling elsewhere on the plains, the commanding officer of the nearest military post will furnish prompt assistance, and will immediately report the facts in the case to these headquarters, specifying particularly whether the party attacked had complied with these rules, and had made as good defence as could be expected.

VIII. These regulations will be enforced in like manner upon all returning trains, which will be organized in conformity thereto at the military post nearest to their points of departure from the settlements.

IX. All commanding officers of military posts on the plains are charged with and will be held responsible for the faithful execution of this order; and on no pretext should they fail carefully to inspect every train or party of travellers which passes through or within reach of the posts under their command. While every assistance at their command will be furnished by the commanders of military posts which may facilitate or render secure the transit of emigrants or supply trains across the great plains, these officers are also charged with the responsibility of exacting from these parties a strict observance of all proper precautions against Indians, and of requiring that such parties be prepared to protect themselves as far as may be in their power.

X. It is not practicable, with the military forces within this department, to render every foot of the overland routes entirely secure against Indian hostilities; and, whilst the military forces will be disposed and used in the manner which seems best adapted to protect parties of travellers, such parties must, between the military posts, rely much upon their own organization and means of defence. As the government provides such protection for emigrants and trains as it is practicable to do without ruinous expense, and as the military forces are held largely responsible for any misfortunes which may befall such parties from Indian attacks, they claim and will exercise the right to lay down rules for such journeys, made within the Indian country and the jurisdiction of the military authorities, as may be considered necessary to provide against danger, and at the same time not be oppressive or embarrassing to emigration or travel.

The above regulations are thought reasonable and easy to observe, and, if complied with, are considered sufficient, with the presence and aid of the troops at important points, to render travel across the plains reasonably secure. They are therefore published for the information of all concerned, and will be strictly enforced.

By command of Major General Pope:

J. P. Sherburne,
Assistant Adjutant General.

CHAPTER FIFTY

After a full minute of blistering profanity that sent some of Leavenworth's residents crossing to the other side of the street, Story crumpled the edict and jammed it in his pocket. He cursed some more before looking at Hannah.

"You said thirty rifles?" Story asked.

"Yeah."

"I guess that's exactly what we need." He spit, kicked the water trough with his boot, and turned to the clerk who had left the store to see what had provoked Story's outrage.

"We'll leave the wagons here for another day, maybe two," Story said. It wasn't a request. Then back at Hannah, Story barked, "Let's get to camp and see how many replacements we'll need."

"You can cut your losses," Hannah said, "and sell the herd in Kansas City."

"The hell I will."

They watched Ernesto Martinez, Luis Avala, Cesar Lopez, Jody Barley, and Sam Ireland ride off. Story figured he knew why the Mexicans quit. Montana was a long way from Texas and their families, and there weren't that many

Mexicans in the Montana gold country. Sam Ireland was a disappointment, having changed his mind perhaps after hearing General Order No. 27 and how serious the army thought about the danger of traveling through Indian country this year. Ireland claimed he would have stuck, but not with his bum hand after the fracas with the trail thieves. Fabian Peña remained—Story hadn't expected that, especially after the other Mexicans drew their time, though José Pablo Tsoyio also agreed to ride north. So had Kelvin Melean, and Story thought for certain he would have quit. Jody Barley? Well, riding drag for five more months, and perhaps even longer, wasn't appetizing to a young rider, although Ryan Ward decided that he, like Dalton Combs, Jordan Stubbings, and Peña would like to see that elephant.

"They ride for the brand," Jameson Hannah said. "Although I never figured Ireland for a quitter."

Story started to comment, but Tom Allen walked over, and Story knew from his face what his colleague would tell him.

"Nelson . . ." He sighed.

"You knew we were going to Montana before we even rode south to Texas," Story reminded him.

"Yeah, I know. And I thought I was up for the adventure and all. But being here, home, and seeing . . ." He shrugged. "I guess I'm not as brave as I thought. You understand?"

"No."

The response shocked Allen, but he straightened, hardened, and said, "I'll gather my gear, walk into town."

"You can ride in the wagon with me," Boone said.

"No." Allen already turned and walked back to the bedrolls. "I wouldn't want to inconvenience anybody."

Story watched him go. His mouth opened once, but no

words, no apology, no reconsideration came out. Instead he emptied his coffee cup and looked at Hannah. "Well," he said.

"Combs will move up to point with Peña," Hannah said. "Stubbings and Melean can ride swing. Your friend's quitting means you'll need a scout."

"I'll scout," Story said. "I know the country from here on out."

"Then you need a wagon driver. Boone here . . ."

"Like I said, Boone's a horse man. He's yours."

Hannah glanced at the Texan. "Swing. Don't botch the job." He shifted the tobacco to the other cheek and said, "Melean stays on flank. I don't think Ward's up for anything but drag. That means we'll need three drag riders and a good hand for flank. And a wrangler."

"That gives us fifteen men," Story said. "We'll need fifteen more." Cursing, he shook his head.

Bill Petty would drive one wagon. The Mexican cook drove the other. They had two wagons waiting at the store in town.

"Sixteen more wagons then," Hannah said. "Or we don't get past Fort Kearny. There might be an outfit that'll be short of men needed to continue thanks to this bluebelly horseshit."

"No." Story pitched his cup into the wreck pan.

"You gonna try to get past the army? They'll be over you before some Cheyennes lift all our hair."

"I pick the men who ride with me. We'll load up some wagons with grain. That way we'll have food for horses, mules, oxen, maybe even some cattle if we get an early snow. And I'll buy more supplies to sell in Virginia City.

Groceries. Saddles. Tack. Hell, maybe some china and silver candlesticks."

"You might go broke," Hannah said.

"And we might all get killed. But if we make it, what I can sell in the Fourteen Mile City will more than pay for what I'm about to shell out. You hire the cowboys, Hannah. Boone and I will find the wagons and men to drive them."

Connor Lehman was an Israelite. Nelson Story didn't hold that against him. But Lehman was about as puny as a lunger, and that gave Story pause.

"You don't think I'm up to it?" Lehman grinned underneath his thick black mustache and beard.

"You're the first freighter I've talked to," Story said. "I'll wind up hiring the best man—"

"Which will be me."

Story lifted the whiskey, nursing it, and reconsidered the man.

"I have four wagons," Story repeated. "I need three drivers." He ran through the figures again in his head. Ten men to herd the cattle—four drag, two each at swing, flank and point. Petty and Tsoyio driving the wagons for the herd. A wrangler for the remuda. Plus Hannah and Story. Two more drivers for the wagons Story had purchased and loaded with supplies—including Remington breechloaders and ammunition. Seventeen men. He needed thirty. But sixteen more wagons.

Again, he explained all that to Lehman, and again cursed General Order No. 27.

"You don't need sixteen drivers," Lehman said. "Eight will do." He lifted his hand to silence Story's argument before it even began. "I've read the army's edict, Mr. Story. Wagons. Twenty wagons. We'll double-hitch them. One driver. Six oxen. We can make ten miles a day. That's about as far as your cattle will go, I do believe. And I know my arithmetic, sir. You're still five men short of thirty. We'll put an extra rider on every other wagon. We will be riding through hostile Indian country, so that'll give us an armed presence. Add me. You've got your thirty armed men. Twenty wagons. All we have to do is elect our commander, and I believe that is you, sir."

"Can you get these men?" Story asked.

"I can." Now he put his right elbow on the table, spreading out the fingers on his hand. "Now can you put my hand down on this table, Mr. Story? Arm wrestling? I'm not big, sir, but I am one tough Jew bastard."

Story set the shot glass, practically untouched, on the rough table and slid it away from him.

"Sixteen wagons," he said. "Eight should be filled with grain, another two with some hay. Two wagons I want to be filled with supplies. Wooden axles and . . ." He stopped, for Lehman was shaking his head.

"Iron axles," the wagon boss said. "Less likely to break. And tallow. Not tar. For greasing. For wood, you'll want bois d'arc. It's hard, and it lasts. I'm guessing you've already out-fitted most of your boys with guns."

"Breech-loading Remingtons," Story said.

"Caliber?"

"Spencer .56-50."

"I think we might be able to agree to terms, Mr. Story," Lehman said. "You need me to hire drivers for your three wagons?"

"I got one of my men on that," Story said. "The other

wagons will be filled with supplies to sell in Montana. Or food we can eat."

"Whiskey?"

"No."

"You'll need some," Lehman said. "Medicinal purposes only."

"All right."

"When would you like to leave?"

"How long will it take you to double-hitch those wagons?"

Grinning, Lehman reached over and took Story's shot glass. He lifted it in toast, smiled, and killed the rye. "Mr. Story, let's finalize this contract."

At camp, Story looked over the men Jameson Hannah had hired. The wrangler, José Sibrian, looked just like Cesar Lopez. Story wondered if every wrangler was a Mexican. Drag riders Jess Williams and Sam McWilliams—with those names, and similar faces, Story would never keep those two straight—and George Dow seemed young and sturdy enough to swallow dust with Ryan Ward. Luke Beckner, missing his right ear, would ride flank opposite Melean.

"You boys know where we're going?" Story asked.

"Montana," either Williams or McWilliams answered. Everybody else nodded.

"Any of you have any idea where Montana is?"

"North," Dow said.

"Twelve hundred miles north. Northwest. I want you boys to understand that. Pay's forty a month. But you get paid when we get the herd to Virginia City. You quit, you'll get no money from me, but I'll make damned sure you get a flogging."

"What happens if you lose the herd?" the other Williams/McWilliams asked.

"That's not going to happen," Story said. "I won't allow that to happen."

José Pablo Tsoyio said something in Spanish. Story caught only the Spanish word for *God*, and he saw the new wrangler, Sibrian, grinning, so Story took a chance. "That's right, boys. On this drive I am God."

"Don't be sacrilegious," Luke Beckner said.

"You a preacher, Beckner?" Story asked. At least he would remember this cowboy's name.

"I know the Good Book, sir."

"Good. That'll come in handy. You keep your relations with your God, son, and pray all you want. But you remember what I say is the law. From here on out. Anybody want to quit now, this is your only chance."

No one moved. "Get some chow," Story said, and walked toward the dust. Mason Boone was riding in. Two men trailed him. One of the riders led a string of mules.

Story spit in the grass and cursed. He had sent Boone to hire three drivers, and the stupid Texas son of a bitch had come back with only two.

Boone reined in. Story glared, and looked at the first rider.

"This is Tommy Thompson," Boone said. "He'll take Allen's place."

"Where you from?" Story asked.

"New York State." Thompson certainly sounded like he wasn't from Kansas or Texas.

"All right. We need some more Yankees in this outfit."

Story looked at the other rider, young, yellow-haired, sunburned, thin, wearing clothes far too big for him.

"You know where Montana is?" Story asked.

"I know it's on the other side of Indian country." The voice didn't fit, like it was a disguise.

Story waited.

"My name's Bennett. Cory Bennett." His shirt was green with big yellow horizontal stripes. The pants were tan wool with thin vertical green checks. The tan hat was a shabby slouch, and the scarf was also green.

"I hope you drive a wagon better than you dress," Story said.

"I hope I do, too." He slid out of the saddle, ducked underneath the lead rope, and walked toward the mules.

Story forgot about the teamster and turned to Boone. "Can you count?" Then he turned back to Cory Bennett, who had reached the first mule. That's when he noticed that the package slung over the packsaddle wasn't a tarp, but a man, a short man with unruly yellow hair. Bennett grabbed the back of the man's buckskin collar and jerked him off the saddle. He landed with a thud, rolled over, and vomited.

"Son of a bitch, Const—"

Bennett's boot caught the drunk in the stomach as he was lifting himself up. Groaning, he fell to his side, gasped, gagged, and coughed. "What the fu—"

"Shut up, Mickey, and sit up. Meet our new boss, you dumb bastard. We've got a job, Mick. We're going to Montana." Bennett turned back toward Story. "This is my pardner, Mickey McDonald. He can't hold his liquor better than a sieve, but you won't find a man with a better touch with a mule."

Ignoring the newcomers, Story stepped toward Boone. "This is what you bring me?" he growled.

"Not many folks want to get scalped on the way to Montana." Boone nodded at Bennett. "That one had to get the other one drunk to agree to terms."

CHAPTER FIFTY-ONE

"My goodness, Seth," Ellen Story said. "This looks fancier than a Brewster phaeton."

Comparing the baby carriage to a fancy horse-drawn buggy from the New York carriage company pleased Dr. Seth Beckstead. Smiling, he held out his arms to take little Montana and lay the baby into the carriage, but Ellen insisted on doing that herself. The carriage was made of bent wrought iron, with four ten-spoked wooden wheels, quite large, and sat on a complicated suspension system. Once Ellen had her baby cushioned on the blankets and pillows, and covered up, Beckstead adjusted the fringed sun canopy. The wooden part of the carriage was painted a rich burgundy, with gold stenciling.

"Where did you find this?" Ellen said. She walked around the carriage like most men would do a horse they wanted to buy.

"People are leaving Virginia City all the time," Beckstead said. "This came from a patient. Her baby isn't a baby anymore, walking and all, so I accepted this carriage as payment instead of gold."

"How much do you want for it?"

Beckstead laughed. "It is a gift, Ellen. I have no need for a baby carriage."

"You might one of these days, Seth."

Stepping away, Beckstead pointed at the handle. "Let's take little Montana for a ride."

They crossed Wallace Street between the Pioneer Bar and the Stone Garden, and moved along the boardwalk past the Masonic Temple. Montana had fallen asleep.

"Have you been back to the theater?" Beckstead asked.

"Of course not." Ellen nodded at the baby as if offering her excuse. "And you?"

"They did *Hamlet* two nights ago," Beckstead said. "Of course, no one on the stage could match your performance."

Ellen's laugh sounded like a symphony. "I don't think Montana or I would have been up for that play," she said a long moment later.

"Well," Beckstead said, "what about *As You Like It*?" He gazed at her. "That's what they plan for tomorrow night."

"My favorite of all of Shakespeare's comedies," Ellen said.

"Mine as well." He slowed his pace and slipped in behind Ellen and the carriage to let pass a burly man carrying a box full of groceries and heading in the opposite direction. "I could see if I can get a similar arrangement, Ellen," he said. "Ask Missus Martin if Grace would be willing to watch over Montana."

"I could not impose and—"

"Colonel Langrishe's troupe will be in town for just two more performances. They embark for Helena for two weeks, then return to Denver. It will be your last chance to see them."

She pushed the carriage without comment, but appeared to be considering his offer, debating herself. Beckstead started to speak, but they had reached the offices of the *Montana Post,* and Professor Dimsdale must have seen them through the window, for he stood at the door.

"Good day to you, Missus Story." The professor spoke to Ellen, but his dead eyes stared at Beckstead.

"Professor Dimsdale." Ellen stopped the carriage, moved closer to the editor, and straightened when she saw how weak, how pale he looked.

He held a silk handkerchief in front of his mouth, stifling a cough, and tried to smile, but pain wrecked his face. "Have . . . you . . . heard . . . from . . . your . . . husband?" Every word sounded like a desperate struggle. This time he looked at Ellen as he spoke, but as soon as Ellen had shaken her head, Dimsdale stared at Beckstead. "Well . . . the mail . . . travels . . ." He coughed, just once at first, but then again, dropping the white cloth flecked with spots of blood, and falling back against the wood.

"Doctor . . ." Ellen brought her hand over her mouth.

The printer—Beckstead's bunking mate, Patrick Walsh—stepped out of the office and put his right arm, covered with a black cotton sleeve stocking, around the editor's shoulder.

"Ellen . . ." Beckstead looked at the woman. "Take Montana for the rest of your walk. I will call on you tomorrow evening unless Missus Martin tells me her daughter has another engagement." He had already hired Grace, so he knew that wasn't the case. "If Grace can't come, I shall send word to you. No, no, don't give me that look. I am your doctor, and Shakespeare has been prescribed. Fear not. I don't think you will be called upon to play Lucy again."

He watched her go, then stepped into the office, closing the door behind him.

* * *

"I asked . . . Patrick . . ." Dimsdale struggled with words and fought for breath. He must have lost ten pounds since Beckstead had seen him last. "To . . . tell you . . ."

"He told me, Professor," Beckstead said.

The editor coughed again, swallowed, then spit, and groaned.

"What have you been eating?"

"Rye."

"I said 'eating,' Professor."

The dying man tried to smile. "Rye." His head shook feebly. "All I . . . can keep . . . down. And I . . ." A full minute passed before he could finish the sentence. "Have . . . no . . . appe . . . tite."

Without his grip, there was little Beckstead could do. But . . . even had he a stethoscope or probe, there was nothing he could do.

"I can bring you a bottle of laudanum," Beckstead said after timing Dimsdale's pulse and listening to the wheezes, the coughs.

"No." Dimsdale again tried to smile. "The paper. It . . . requires . . . a mind . . . without . . . impairment."

"But you still drink rye?" Beckstead shook his head.

"Rye is . . . an . . . editor's . . . best . . . friend."

Beckstead looked across the newsroom at Walsh, who shook his head, and went back to setting type. "I'll call on you tomorrow morning," Beckstead said. He walked to the door.

"Doctor?"

With his hand on the doorknob, Beckstead turned back to the editor.

"How . . . long?"

Beckstead's frown worsened. "Months. If that. It depends

on your will. But whiskey and a newspaper office, those do not help."

"They . . . help me . . . Doctor." He coughed again, but turned in his chair, bent his head to a piece of paper, and his right hand moved across the desk, searching for a pencil.

Ten minutes later, Seth Beckstead knocked on that familiar door. Ellen answered it and stepped back in surprise.

Removing his hat, Beckstead asked, "Ellen, can I talk to you?"

He never planned on telling her this. Rarely even thought he would say the words out loud.

Three times Thomas Dimsdale had sent word with the printer that he desired Beckstead to pay a house call at the newspaper or Dimsdale's home. The first time, Beckstead had told Walsh, "He knows where I office. Have him come there," and laughed off the Irishman's reply, "He doesn't want anyone to know how sick he is."

Beckstead never went to the *Montana Post*. He wouldn't have gone by there this day but he had not been thinking about anything but Ellen, the baby, the new carriage, the beautiful summer day.

"Aren't you a doctor?" Ellen said, not angrily, though. She never judged anyone, not even that bastard she had married.

"I thought I was," he said. Almost got up and left, not just the Story cabin, but Virginia City . . . Montana Territory . . . the western United States. "Till Antietam."

It was not the kind of story you told a mother, or any woman. You might not even tell a priest. It was the story most doctors would take to their graves.

He remembered the dead on that warm afternoon. The

horses were bad enough, but the men . . . or what had once been men . . . in blue, in gray, in butternut. You could hardly tell what uniforms they wore because of the flies, the maggots. Gas hissed from their mouths, ears, nostrils, and the wounds caused by musketry, bayonets, cannon. But these men were dead, bound for burial—and none too quickly.

Dr. Seth Beckstead had other woes. He and two other doctors had turned a farmhouse, the barn, the lean-to, into hospitals outside of Keedysville. Ambulances still brought in the wounded, some two days after the rebs had retreated back for Virginia.

"We took command of two of the ambulances," Beckstead said. "Not to haul the wounded, or even the dead. To take away our trash."

Trash. Fingers. Toes. Limbs. Arms, from the forearm if they were lucky, at the shoulder joint if they weren't. Hands. Feet. Legs. A well-placed minié ball left a doctor with no choice but to amputate.

"Once I thought I was a doctor," he said. "Once I thought I could save lives. At Antietam and for the rest of the war, I ruined lives. I crippled men. I was no surgeon, but a carpenter. Sawing. Sawing. Sawing."

He remembered after one long stretch in what had been the formal parlor, the rugs and wooden floor now slick with blood, gore, water, he stepped away from the table to find coffee, good coffee, something that could keep him going, and found the floor littered with what he had taken off dozens of men. Before long, they had no quinine, no morphine, not even castor oil or adhesive plasters.

"I prayed for me to die before I stepped to the table to perform surgery. Surgery?" He laughed. "Butchery."

He stopped, realizing how much he was saying, and tried to pull away, to apologize, to run to South America or the

North Pole, but Ellen had her gentle hands around the back of his head, and she pulled him to her, let his head rest against her shoulder. And he sobbed without shame. He saw in Professor Thomas Dimsdale what he had seen in 1862 and for the years after that. A hopeless case. It was not what he thought he would see when he had left the University of Maryland.

His head rested against hers.

"It's all right, Seth," Ellen whispered.

He pulled away, just slightly, saw her eyes, filled with tears, and he leaned closer and kissed Ellen's sweet lips.

CHAPTER FIFTY-TWO

Wind, sun, dust. That's all they knew. Following the Smoky Hill Trail westward, then north and along the Big Blue. Just a short while back, Boone and others had prayed for the sun, begged for not one more day of clouds and rain. Now they thought it might never rain again. At least, Boone thought, they had water. The Big Blue still ran high.

He swung slowly, sorely, off the buckskin. Didn't even remember unsaddling the gelding, or leading it to Sibrian, the new wrangler. After slapping the dust off his leggings, he made his legs move him toward the wagon, where José Pablo Tsoyio's coffee told him that he was not in hell. Purgatory, perhaps. But not quite hell. When he saw Nelson Story walking back and forth, hands behind his back, shaking his head, Boone frowned.

If that hard-rock bastard tells me to take first watch on the herd . . .

Story didn't.

When he saw Boone, he stopped pacing. He didn't even glance at Jameson Hannah, riding in from the herd on his zebra dun. Instead, Story brought his hands to his sides and said, "Boone. Catch yourself a horse and ride back and find out what the hell is holding up those two cripples you hired

as wagon drivers." He pointed down the trail. The wind
had blown away the dust from the longhorns, and Boone
could see clearly in the darkening day the line of double-
hitched freight wagons moving toward camp. Four teams
of oxen, hauling two wagons each, with a bullwhacker
walking alongside the oxen and a guard riding in one of the
wagons, the sun reflecting off the Remington breechloader
he held across his lap or braced on a leg or sack of grain or
whatever.

The stragglers, not in view, would be the two drivers
bringing along the single wagons of mostly supplies Story
had ordered months before even beginning this damned
cattle drive. Boone looked at the pot of coffee. Laughing,
Hannah slid out of the saddle and extended the reins toward
Boone. "Take my horse, Boone," he said, and when Boone
was mounted and riding out of the camp, Hannah added,
"I'll try to save a cup of coffee for you."

"Boone." Story's voice stopped him. Twisting in the
saddle, he saw the ramrod moving toward his horse, tethered to the tongue of the second wagon being driven by
Bill Petty. Story reached into the driver's box and pulled
out one of the .56-50 Remingtons. He grabbed a box of ammunition, too, and started walking. "Better take these. Just
in case."

Two miles down the trail, he found the wagons. Moving
like infantry, maybe even as slow as artillery. No Indians in
sight. No busted axles or lame mules. Mickey McDonald
cursed, and the wagons crawled along.

Boone kicked Hannah's horse into a trot and rode up to
the wagon being driven by Cory Bennett. "You best hurry.
The boss is fuming."

"Tell him to bugger off," Cory said.

Turning the horse around, Boone rode alongside the wagon. "I don't think I want to do that." He looked back at Mickey McDonald, a good thirty yards behind Bennett's wagon, then leaned closer to the driver's box. "Why are you doing this?"

Bennett's head jerked to the side. "Doing what?"

"Dressing up like a man."

The eyes widened. Then Bennett laughed, used the whip on the mules, and shook her—not his—head. "Boy, you must be blind."

"Maybe, but I'm not a fool."

The head stared ahead, one hand on the whip, the other holding the lines.

"My name's Cory Bennett. I'm a mule skinner. That's all you need to know."

Boone swore underneath his breath. "All right, Cory Bennett. But if you and your pard don't get these wagons to camp soon, you'll be out of work by the time we reach Fort Kearny. Story will replace you two in a heartbeat." He kicked the gelding into a lope, but still heard Bennett's one-word whisper: "Kearny."

He didn't ride too far ahead, and somehow Bennett and McDonald picked up the pace, dragging the mules and wagons into camp after sundown. Sure enough, here strode Nelson By God Story.

He had been angry with the two skinners for at least a week, always the last to show up in camp—a long time after the other wagons had arrived. Even when Story had started Bennett and McDonald at point, they dragged in last by the day's end.

This time, he shoved Bennett against the wagon. "You keep dawdling like this and I'll drive the damned wagon myself, and you and your filthy pard can walk back to Fort Riley or Hades for all I care. I'm damned tired of this . . ."

"Then give them mules that aren't half-lame."

Story whirled away from Bennett.

Well, Boone figured, he couldn't blame anyone but himself . . . and his mouth. No sense in backing down. "You couldn't drive that team any faster."

"Boy, I'll hitch you to the harness and let you pull these wagons."

Boone laughed. "I believe we were at Ebbitt's saloon in Washington City when you told those senators and that banker about how slow your mules were when you and your wife came up to Montana Territory. And before that how you hauled wood with one mule blind and the other mostly lame."

"Boone." Cory Bennett stepped away from the wagon. Story whirled, shoved Bennett back, hard into the wheel. And Boone made a beeline toward his boss.

A shrill whistle stopped him, and Story, and even Cory Bennett.

Mickey McDonald spit tobacco juice into the grass, wiped his mouth, and said, "Mr. Story, you hired us to get your wagons to camp every day, and every day we've gotten your wagons to camp. And we will continue to get your wagons to camp, Lord willing and Indians finding better pickings. But my pard and me will drive these mules so they won't be slow-footed when we need them to run faster. They's slow-footed enough."

Boone waited. Story took his hand off the butt of one of his Navy Colts.

"Unhitch your mules, boys," Lehman, the wagon boss, said. "Supper's cold. There's some coffee left, though."

Boone started to take Hannah's horse to the remuda.

"Boone." This time it was Hannah who spoke. "Go ahead and keep Sad Sadie. You can spell Luke Beckner watching the herd."

"And give that Remington back to Bill," Story added.

CHAPTER FIFTY-THREE

In the three-plus years in which Virginia City had been, officially, a town, the log cabin on Idaho Street had been a home, a brothel, a saloon, a hotel (with its two rooms and summer kitchen), a billiard hall, a home again, an apothecary, a barbershop, and, since April, a café. The food could best be described as adequate, but people came for the excellent coffee. And the wine selection.

By the time Ellen Story stopped in for coffee, Colonel Jack Langrishe had poured two glasses of his third bottle of Madeira, so he and his wife waved her and little Montana to join them. Now at the neighboring table, Jenette played peekaboo with little Montana, who cooed and laughed with blessed content in her top-line baby carriage, while Ellen sat across from Langrishe, well in his cups.

"We hope you shall return to our small city," Ellen managed to say.

"Perhaps, dear Fluffy," Langrishe said. "Perhaps."

"Lucy," Jenette corrected, and put her hands over her eyes, grinning with the beauty of a fine actress, then jerking the hands away, her face radiant, and telling Montana, "I . . . seeeeeee . . . *youuuuuu*."

Sweet, precious baby Alice Montana Story giggled with a baby's delight.

The theatrical troupe's leader put his elbows on the table—Ellen's mother would have thrown a fit over that—and leaned forward, winked, his eyes suddenly lecherous. He said, "Well, little darling, I wish I could talk you into joining our jovial group of thespians. Helena in a few days. Boise. Salt Lake City. Then back to our base in Denver."

Ellen made herself smile. "I am a mother, Colonel."

After guzzling, he splashed more red wine into the goblet, spilling more onto the table, and slurped the Madeira. "Dear Missus Puf—Lucy. Did you not have a grand time reading lines with the greatest theatrical troupe west of the . . . some damned river?" His eyes lost focus, became glassy, finally locked on to Ellen again. Out of the corner of Ellen's eye, she saw Jenette turn away from the baby and beam vehemence toward her husband. Ellen knew that look. Jenette was telling John "Jack" Langrishe to close his mouth and not utter one more syllable. Ellen had given Nelson similar, silent messages, though not because her husband was intoxicated, just being an ass. She also knew the hopelessness of such tactics.

"Wasn't it, sweetheart?"

"Jack," Jenette whispered, trying to keep control.

"It was one of the highlights of my life, Colonel." Ellen wished she had stayed home and brewed her own coffee. "I do love the theater."

"You should start one, sweetheart. And you're damned right it was a highlight for you, appearing with my colleagues and me. God knows, honey, that fellow of yours . . ."

"Jack." Jenette's frigid eyes matched her voice.

But the colonel had his wine, a lot of wine, and his ears needed a good cleansing. ". . . hell, he paid enough for it."

"Excuse me." Ellen challenged Jenette's tone.

Red wine dribbled onto the front of the colonel's white silk shirt. He wiped his mouth with his right arm, staining the sleeve as well. His wife slumped into her chair and sighed. "You stupid bastard," she said.

Leaning into Langrishe's face, Ellen demanded, "What do you mean?"

"Why . . . nothing . . . child."

"What do you mean?"

The actor looked to his wife for help. Instead, he got this: "Tell her the truth, before she beats it out of you."

Colonel Jack Langrishe wet his lips, wiped his brow, and finished his glass of wine. He tried to smile, stopped quickly, tried to straighten, and finally leaned forward, resting his chin on the bridge he formed with his hands.

"It was merely a . . . a . . . a good . . . deed. Your . . . we . . . we thought it . . . considering your love for the boards . . . we thought . . . you see." He looked like an actor who had completely forgotten his lines and realized none of his friends on the stage was willing to help him through this nightmare. So Langrishe looked away from Ellen and at his wife.

"The son of a bitch," Jenette said, "took up your beau's offer. That doc paid the stupid prig to pick you to play the part of Lucy. Oh, Lenore was drunk enough. She always is. But she decided to let you take over the role. For the good of our troupe, and for the glory of your town." She smiled. "You were quite good, though."

"I see." Ellen bowed to the woman. "Thank you for your honesty and kindness." She did not look at Langrishe, but grabbed the handle to the carriage and left the café, bound for Dr. Seth Beckstead's office, until she remembered he would likely be paying a call on Professor Dimsdale. Good. That was closer, and more convenient.

Her timing had been impeccable, for Seth Beckstead has stepped out of the *Post* office door. Seeing her, he started to smile, but that vanished when she stopped the carriage, stepped around it, and said, "You paid them to choose me to play Lucy."

Quickly he pulled the door shut.

"I thought . . ."

"I do not care one whit for what you thought. I thought you were a gentleman."

He straightened. "I opened my heart and soul to you the other night."

"I did not ask you to do so. Nor did I ask you to take me to the theater, or to *buy* me a role on the boards."

His head turned toward the people passing on the other side of Wallace Street, and he looked past her down the boardwalk, probably seeing more people. Virginia City and the Fourteen Mile City had lost hundreds, perhaps thousands, of residents to Helena and the newer mining camps over the past months, but she still boasted a substantial population, especially of gossips.

"Perhaps we should hear one another out . . . in my office . . . or your home."

"I do not want you inside my home again, Dr. Beckstead. And the next doctor's office I visit will be Dr. Justice's." She spun quickly, moved to the carriage, and began to turn it around.

"Ellen," Beckstead whispered with urgency, "the other night, you kissed . . ."

She was already pushing the carriage down the boardwalk and spoke without shame, and without turning her head back to him.

"You kissed me. Uninvited and unwelcomed. If you remember, I did not return your kiss."

CHAPTER FIFTY-FOUR

Rather than turning onto the wide and rutted Oregon Trail, they stayed with the Big Blue River north, then westerly until reaching the Platte. The Texans, and some of the Kansans, could not believe the river.

"I thought it was an ocean," Ryan Ward said. "At first, I mean."

Molly McDonald thought the kid was horsing around, but quickly realized he was serious.

"You could see the other side," Molly said.

"I know that, Mickey. But . . . it's . . ."

"Wider than anything we call a river in Texas," Dalton Combs said as he rolled a cigarette. "That's certain for sure."

"Nothing that shallow in Texas," Jameson Hannah said. "Except most of the women I know." He laughed.

Molly spit into the fire and looked at Constance Bennett, who stared, coffee cup untouched, at Mason Boone's back. The cowboy was adjusting the stirrups on his saddle, and the unlacing and lacing that required would keep him occupied the rest of the night.

"He ain't gonna tell nobody," Molly whispered.

She didn't appear to hear, but she had, and slowly realized

Molly was speaking to her. Blinking, Constance turned around. "What?"

"You heard me."

"I didn't . . . well . . ." Constance sighed like she had just climbed a mountain—like you'd find any mountains in this country. "He . . . I really wasn't thinking . . . about . . ." Her head tilted toward the Texas cowboy. She rose, and moved closer to the fire, not to keep warm—not as hot as this day had been, but so no one would overhear the conversation. "I was thinking . . . about . . . Fort Kearny."

Shaking her head, Molly smiled. "No one recognized you, me neither, in Maryville when we went through that pebble of a burg. Nobody will know us from Adam's left ox when we get to Dobytown."

Tears began welling in Constance's eyes.

Molly scooted across the ground, tossing out her coffee onto the grass. Leaning forward, she spoke quietly but sternly. "Buck up. They see you crying, they'll suspicion you and me for sure. You know what a bastard Story is. Think he'll let a woman, or a couple of women, ride with him to Montana? Hell, no. He'll figure us to be deviants and turn us afoot, maybe tar and feather us. Wouldn't put nothing past that—" She stopped in midsentence and looked at young Sibrian as he came over to warm himself by the fire. How a Mexican could think he needed to stay warm in this infernal heat pestered Molly, but she painted on an idiot's grin and held up her cup.

"Hey, kid, would you mind runnin' over to that belly-cheater and gettin' me another cup?" She rubbed her knee. "All that sittin' in a wagon just aches an ol' hoss like me." Old hoss. Hell, she was just past thirty. But Sibrian likely figured thirty to be ancient, pup that he was. The Mexican grinned, Molly tossed the cup to him, and when he had moved twenty feet, she whirled back to Constance.

"That's right. Wipe your eyes. You can blame that on smoke. Trust me. That major you killed is buried and forgotten. And we get past Kearny, we're free." She laughed. "Unless we get killed by Injuns."

She made herself stand, squeezed Constance's shoulder, and faked a limp as she came out to get the cup of fresh coffee from the wrangler. After thanking him in her worst Spanish, she sipped some of the coffee and looked back at Constance. Who stared again across the camping ground at Boone.

"Shit." Molly gritted her teeth and heard one of the bull-whackers call out, "Mickey. How 'bout a story? Or a little Spanish monte?"

"How 'bout both?" She turned away from Constance, shifted the chaw to her other cheek, and limped toward the gathering of gamblers.

Maybe the Texas boy would be good for the girl. Keep her mind off Fort Kearny and the rotting corpse of that son of a bitch she had knifed.

CHAPTER FIFTY-FIVE

Dragoons, cavalry, scouts—whatever the hell they were—galloped past the wagon, and Steve Grover cheered them as the oxen slowed, and John Catlin breathed again. Fort Laramie, big, sprawling, dismal but suddenly the most beautiful sentinel Catlin had ever seen, lay 100 or 150 yards before them. A pistol shot echoed as the soldiers chased after the Cheyennes, and another group of soldiers rode out of the fort. Grover cheered them, too. Catlin probably would have, as well, if he had any voice left.

He leaned the Enfield against the freight wagon and looked into the pouch on his belt. Empty. No voice. No powder or lead, either. Damn, they were lucky.

Another rider left the fort, but at a walk, and not dressed in Union blue. Major Coushatta John Noah trotted down the line of wagons that made up his train till stopping beside Catlin and Grover. Swinging a leg over his horn, he grinned before nodding at the worst bullwhacker and boy extra he had ever hired.

"You can thank me with a whiskey at the post sutler's this evening," Noah said.

"For what?" Catlin had climbed into the back of the wagon, pulling Cheyenne arrows out of the sides of boxes and sacks of seeds and such.

"Putting you last in the train." Noah dropped out of the saddle and walked to the wagon, yanking out two more arrows. "Had I put you fellows anywhere else, a lot of us would be dead."

"We almost were." Catlin stuck his hand into the pouch and withdrew his empty fingers.

"You ought to play faro, Catlin." Noah dropped the arrows into the dirt and returned to his horse.

"They always attack this close to the fort?" Grover asked as he moved back to where he had made a seat of some sort at the front of the wagon.

"Never. I'll stand you two to drinks after I clean up. Find out where the idiot in charge here wants us to make camp. Wash up, empty what all you crapped in your britches, and be prepared to get good and drunk." He led the horse about ten yards before stopping and turning back after Grover called out his name.

"Good and drunk?" Steve Grover beamed. "That's redundant."

They sat on a bench, watching the sun sink, the soldiers march like men with purpose but not much order, and the civilians in tents, shelters, huts, or nothing at all. Catlin wasn't certain if a census taker would find more civilians or soldiers at Fort Laramie. There were slim pickings for grazing land—at least close enough to keep any Cheyennes from stealing livestock or slitting throats.

Catlin took another sip from the jug and passed it to Grover.

"You're blaming this on the new forts?" He studied Noah, who didn't look like he was that drunk.

"Damn right. Son, you look at this from a white man's eyes. You gotta take the Indians' point of view."

"Why the hell would I do that?" Grover said.

"First . . ." Noah didn't even look at Grover. "You got thousands of white folks coming through Indian country. Indian country given to them by our U.S. government. Nobody asked Red Cloud or anyone else if that was all right with the Sioux. Sioux got a little riled. But things weren't that bad till our U.S. government decided it was well and good to put up some forts on land we give, through treaty, to the Indians. Again, nobody asked Red Cloud or anybody what they thought about this."

"They're just digger Indians," Grover said.

"Boy." Now Noah turned to glare at Catlin's pard. "Only digging those Indians do is for graves."

"They put their dead on scaffolds," Grover said. He was drunk, Catlin figured. "I seen the drawings in—"

"Digging graves for those they kill," Noah said. His hand shot up. "I know, boy. I know. They don't dig graves. I was being facetious."

Catlin changed the subject. "What did the commandant say?"

"Enough to convince me that our best chance is to forget Montana."

The jug had returned to Catlin, who started lifting it to his mouth, but now lowered it.

"By my ciphering, I can make enough of a profit by taking these wagons to Salt Lake."

"What about Virginia City?" Catlin said.

"Making a profit don't mean a thing, son, if you're dead."

Noah took the jug, drank, wiped his lips, and tossed the Taos Lightning to Grover. "We'll rest here a few days. Let the soldiers chase the ornery Cheyennes away. We head west, not north, won't likely run into many hostiles. I'm not always a cautious man. But I am rarely suicidal." He started away.

"I had my mind on Montana," Catlin said.

Coushatta John Noah stopped, turned, and put his hands on his hips. "You hear anything I just said, boy?"

"I didn't leave Indiana to settle in Salt Lake. And I didn't quit farming to look at an oversized cow's ass for a thousand or more miles."

Noah's mouth opened, but before he could speak, Catlin asked, "How much to buy you out? Just this wagon." He chuckled. "That's likely all I can afford."

"Buy me out?"

"You got no contracts in Salt Lake, Major. No guarantee you'll sell anything. How much? For this rig, the oxen, and all she carries?"

The wagon boss walked back, took the jug, poured more whiskey down his throat, and shoved the jug into Catlin's hands. "You are loco."

"Just make me a good offer."

"You might be eating all that grain and shit till next fall, boy. The army has issued a law. You can't light out for Montana on your own. If you were dumb enough to try. Lakotas would have you scalped, gutted, and feeding ravens within a week. But there's a rule—and they sure are enforcing it here—that says thirty armed men and twenty wagons, at the least, for permission to travel through hostile territory.

Without you, I still got my numbers. But without me, you'd have to catch another train. And I don't think you'll find anybody wanting to go to Virginia City. Not this time of year. Not after me."

"I'm willing to take my chances."

"I think a night's sleep'll change your mind," Noah said.

Steve Grover took a pull from the jug. "I thought you knew John better than that, Major."

"You side with him?" Noah asked.

"Well, it sure as hell isn't boring riding with him." Grover wiped his mouth.

"Fools." Noah walked away.

The next morning, Major Coushatta John Noah handed John Catlin a bill of sale.

"Told you we was pards after you saved my hair back down the trail," he said. "Figured our partnership would last longer. Tell me you realized the error of what you was thinking."

"I'm going to Montana, Major."

"Then put that paper in your pocket. On the back I wrote out a letter of introduction." He held out his hand. "I'm glad to have known you." He nodded at Grover. "Both of you."

"We appreciate your taking a chance on us," Grover said.

Catlin used both of his hands to clasp Noah's.

"If you're here when we come back from Salt Lake," Noah said, "we'll let you ride back to Nebraska City with us."

"If we're here when you come back," Catlin said with a grin, "we'll be dead."

Noah grunted something unintelligible, slapped Catlin's

shoulder, shook Grover's hand, and strode toward the wagons.

"Not to worry you any," the wagon boss called out without turning around, "but if you aren't here when we come back, you will most certainly be dead, too."

CHAPTER FIFTY-SIX

Trail-worn longhorns and dust-caked cowboys trudged down Front Street in Grand Island, Nebraska Territory, not that many drovers would have called Grand Island a town. Irish railroaders stepped out of a clapboard boardinghouse and stood watching in silent awe. Telegraph poles stretched east to west, past a tent depot where stacks of railroad ties stood as high as the tent's ceiling, and more men, and a few women, observed the cattle drive from the shade of a tent saloon. Two empty flatbeds and a handcart were parked on a siding.

That was all there was to Grand Island.

Boone pulled away from the cattle, pushed back his hat, and stared—ignoring the slurred comments from the Irish railroad men, and the sarcastic beckoning from the whores.

Story reined in the claybank. "If you're thinking about dipping your wick into one of those virginal goddesses, I'd advise against it."

Boone wiped dust from his beard stubble and told his boss, "Just staring at that." He pointed at the westward-stretching rails, then glanced over his shoulder at the ramshackle buildings and wind-battered tents. "This place wasn't even here when we came through here last winter."

"Get back to work," Story said. "It's against my policy, but I shall see how much these thieves charge for what they call whiskey, and if I don't think it'll leave everyone blind, I might buy a couple of bottles for tonight's camp. To prevent a mutiny in the ranks."

Boone barely heard him. "It's history, you know." Pulling his hat back on his sweaty head, Boone looked at his boss. "Ever think about that? That what we're doing . . . what you're doing . . . will be part of history, that you're making history."

"I don't give a fig about making history," Story said. "I'm just interested in making money." He pointed. "I'll bring back some rotgut, maybe, but no chirpies."

Boone kicked the horse into a trot to catch up his position across from Jordan Stubbings.

At the campsite, José Pablo Tsoyio found the young wrangler, José Sibrian, at the edge of the great Platte River. There was much to admire in the young man, José Pablo Tsoyio knew. They had a common first name, they were true Spaniards, at least in the mind of José Pablo Tsóyio, unlike Fabian Peña, who was a mere *peón*. Sibrian had a way with horses, even better than the other wrangler who had started out in Fort Worth but had grown homesick by the Verdigris River and ran back to his mother on the Brazos after learning of Nelson Story's intention to push the herd all the way to the rough country near Canada. Sibrian, on most days, worked hard after he had the horse herd under control, and José Pablo Tsoyio rewarded him with sugar in his coffee. But on this late afternoon, he found the wrangler standing dumbly, bucket at his feet, looking at a barren island in the middle of the river.

"I sent you to gather dried buffalo dung so I can cook supper," José Pablo Tsoyio said in Spanish. "What do you think you will see on that island? A mermaid?"

The wrangler turned, blinking rapidly, and shook his head. Sibrian did not know what a mermaid was. He pointed. "What could have cut down the trees? Do you think beavers did this? I have always wanted to see a beaver."

The anger vanished from José Pablo Tsoyio. Smiling, he stepped closer and put his arm around Sibrian's shoulder.

"My young friend," he said softly, "beavers did not cut down those trees. That is the work of the men who lay the iron rails."

"For what reason?"

José Pablo Tsoyio shrugged. "Bridges. Poles for the white man's wires. Ties for the iron rails. Houses for the next stations. Who can say? But you will not find any buffalo dung looking at what the *norteamericanos* will do to all of this country. And our *patrón* will be angry."

"*El patrón* is always angry," Sibrian said.

Laughing, José Pablo Tsoyio squeezed the boy tighter, turned him west, and pointed his free arm. "Soon . . . but not very soon—we will come to the high mountains. When we get there, José, I shall show you a beaver."

The boy grinned, picked up his bucket, and walked along the banks, stopping to pick up dung, and José Pablo Tsoyio returned to continue preparing supper.

A blond-mustached lieutenant led a squad of soldiers to inspect the caravan at Fort Kearny, but spent most of the time damning the Union Pacific Railroad for putting the tracks so far—maybe five miles—from the fort.

The pup of a lieutenant finally reached the mule-driven wagons of Cory Bennett and Mickey McDonald.

"Is this the end?" the officer asked Hannah.

"Yep. These buckos always seem to be pulling rear tit."

The lieutenant almost laughed himself out of the saddle. "'Pulling rear tit'—that's a good one, sir."

Hannah blinked and shook his head. Molly McDonald spit tobacco juice onto the soldier boy's horse's nearest hoof, but the officer didn't even notice.

"Well, you've got enough men and wagons to proceed." The lieutenant nodded, scribbled something in his notebook, which he stuck inside his blouse. "It's one hundred eighty miles to Fort Sedgwick. You'll be inspected there." He started to turn his horse back toward the head of the column, but Hannah stopped him.

"Speaking of rear tit, Lieutenant, you know of any place around where me and the boys might find some?"

The kid's face flushed—undoubtedly Hannah's intent—and mumbled, "You might ask Sergeant O'Rourke, sir." And spurred his horse into a lope back up the trail.

Laughing, Hannah grinned at Molly McDonald and Constance Beckett and rode after the fleeing soldier.

Molly released the brake and slapped the lines. The mules started down the trail. "Well, gal, looks like Fort Kearny will soon be behind you."

Constance didn't hear. "'Pulling tit.' What an asshole."

"You're learning, gal," Molly called back to her. "You're learning."

Black smoke belched from the hissing engine that had stopped while men pounded spikes to secure the rails. An Irish voice sang out a melody, and the railroad crew worked in unison. The engineer and the fireman stood on the flatcar, loaded with ties and rails. They looked south as the longhorns, cattle, and wagons moved along. Then they turned their heads and stared north.

Story rode back from the crew boss and turned his horse alongside Boone's. Boone looked north, too. So did Jordan Stubbings.

On a small rise beyond the tracks, more than a dozen Indians sat on their horses. Cowboys and teamsters south of the tracks. Indians north of the tracks. The Irishmen trying to ignore both. Hammers sang out in time with the song.

"Brulé Sioux," Story told the two drovers.

"What do they want?" Stubbings asked from the other side of the cattle.

"Interpreter said they just want to see how this railroad building works," Story answered. He pointed to one wearing a bonnet and holding a lance, aboard a striking piebald stallion. "Says that one yonder is Spotted Tail, big man with the tribes."

"Some of them seem more interested in us." Boone reached for his canteen. His throat had turned dry.

"We'll put extra men on night herds till we reach Julesburg and Fort Sedgwick," Story said. "And I'll have Lehman pull the wagons into a tight circle. Tonight, every man sleeps with one of those Remington rifles next to him."

The Lakota Indians, however, vanished. A few days later, so did the rails and tracklayers, replaced by grading crews, then surveyors, and then the nothingness of the stark plains. Days dragged into weeks, weeks into eternity, but the country never changed. The river might narrow, or widen, and the wind might shift directions. Sometimes clouds appeared in the pale blue horizon. A buffalo, or pronghorn, might lift its head in the distance, and a hawk, raven, or turkey buzzard flew overhead. The land, though, stretched on with an unremitting endlessness.

"I think the Brulés have lost interest," Connor Lehman told Story at camp one night.

"I do, too," Story said. "But we'll keep the wagons circled tightly at camp, we'll keep more guards on night herd, and we'll keep the rifles handy."

"You'll wear these men out," Lehman said.

"But I might keep them alive."

They passed a westbound train of forty-five wagons—Constance Bennett counted them—with the bullwhackers shielding their faces from the dust. Maybe the boss and others had talked to Story or Hannah, perhaps asked where they were bound, but by the time the last of the wagons came down the trail, they were no longer staring with wonderment, or scratching their beards. Irritation had replaced curiosity.

Once, a stagecoach rolled along on the rutted trail. At first, the driver yelled at the passengers not to lean to the port side to see the spectacle of cattle and wagons. Finally he gave up, pulled hard on the lines, to stop the mules.

"Dumb sons of bitches," Boone heard the jehu say. "They'd topple Ol' Nancy over." The driver pointed his whip. "Where the hell did you come from?"

Boone jerked a thumb behind him. "Hell," he answered.

The bearded man shook his head and pointed west. "You ain't out of it yet."

CHAPTER FIFTY-SEVEN

They loped to the crest of the small rise north of the Platte.

"Son of a bitch," Jameson Hannah said as he wheeled his black to a stop.

Story's bay fought rein and bit, twisting, turning, trying to run south. "Lightning?" he asked.

Smoke filled the sky to the north, but beneath the billowing thickness of white smoke, orange and yellow flames raced across the prairie, as far as Story could see, driven by that damned never-ending wind.

His horse still jumping, Story called out again, "Lightning?" He hadn't seen a cloud in a week.

"Spotted Tail," Hannah guessed.

"Get the herd across the river," Story yelled, and let the bay run, away from the inferno. Now he knew why all that rain back in the spring had worried cattlemen. They were right. The grass grew, rich and thick, but when the rains ended and the sun and wind remembered it was summer, the prairie dried out quickly, turning thick grass into a tinderbox.

"I'll get the wagons."

* * *

Wide the Platte River might have been, but the longhorns easily trotted across it. So did the wagons, driven by Bill Petty and José Pablo Tsoyio, and once on the south shore, the cook set the brake, leaped over the side, and gasped. He had seen just the massive clouds of smoke. Now towering flames rushed across the prairie.

He wondered if the river would stop the flames, and José Pablo Tsoyio made the sign of the cross and prayed.

"Señor José. Señor José." Young Sibrian ran toward him, his nose bleeding, limping, crying, tears cascading down his cheeks. He pointed, and José Pablo Tsoyio could see the hundreds of horses galloping south, southwest, southeast. The wrangler's young colt, still saddled, took off more westerly, having thrown its rider.

"I could . . . not stop . . . stop them," Sibrian wailed.

"It is for the best," José Pablo Tsoyio told Sibrian. "You have work to do here." He walked to the wagon, reached inside, and found his apron. Handing what had once been pristine white to the young boy, Tsoyio said, "Take this to the river, let the water soak it through. Do not wring it out." He pointed. "The wind will carry sparks across the big river. Wherever you see smoke, you must beat out the flames. If fire catches here, we are doomed."

"But the horses . . ."

"Let the horses run. Go. To the river." He thrust the apron into the boy's shaking hands. "Go now. And go with God."

Hearing his name called, Boone pulled hard on the reins and turned in the saddle.

"Forget the damned cattle. Forget the son-of-a-bitching

horses." Jameson Hannah slid his horse to a stop and jerked his left arm toward the river.

"Shit," Boone said as he reached for his lariat and spurred his horse into the shallow river.

Once her wagon made it across the Platte, Constance Beckett wanted to let the mules keep running. They might be able to catch up with all those horses raising dust. Or even some of the steers bolting from the smell of smoke that burned Constance's eyes. But Molly was yelling something, and Constance saw her friend running back, afoot, toward the river.

"We gotta help them, Constance," Molly cried out, calling her by her real name and sounding like a woman, not the rough-hewn man she pretended to be. "Come on. For Christ's sake, come on. Lend a hand."

She didn't even remember stopping the wagon or jumping into the mud. The next thing Constance realized she was knee-deep in the Platte River, running back toward the orange and gray horizon, feeling the heat already against her face.

The Platte River was no barrier to horses, or longhorns, or light wagons. But double-hitched freight wagons sank to their axles in the mud.

The rigs driven by George Overholt and Kyle McPherson made it across easily enough, and those teamsters begin unhitching their teams, while their guards, Patrick Caulfield and Zack Hall, ran back into the muddy water.

* * *

At first, Boone thought he felt the ember burn his face. *Can't be,* he told himself as he swung out of the saddle. *I'm soaked through with river water and damned sweat.* He looked at the lariat in his hands, but while he was learning to throw a loop, he wasn't sure he could do it now.

The teamster on the wagon, David Mc-something, McKay, yes, McKay, barked something, grabbed one end of Boone's rope, and disappeared. Boone turned, realized he held the other end of the lariat, and hurried back to his horse. By the time he was in the saddle, making five or so dallies across the horn, he heard McKay screaming, "Pull. Pull."

Boone needed no encouragement. Neither did his horse. He spurred, feeling the water splashing on him, over him, behind him. George Dow moved on the other side of the big wagons, the lariat behind him straining, taut. The two wagon drivers—the woman who pretended to be Cory Bennett and her foul-mouthed pard—splashed through the river. Cory found a spot behind the lead wagon, began pushing. Tiny as she was, Boone didn't think she'd help much. His horse snorted. Boone dug the spurs in harder.

The sun disappeared behind the clouds of smoke, but the heat around them doubled, tripled. Men coughed.

One double-hitched wagon made it across, pulled by oxen from other teams. The wagons driven by Jake Rogers somehow found hard rock underneath the mud, and lurched forward, splashing onto the south side at such speed—for oxen—that Rogers didn't stop the team for another quarter mile.

But one remained closer to the north bank, and now all Story could see on the south side of the Platte was the savagery of flames and smoke. He kicked free of the stirrups and leaped into the mud. His horse bolted; Story did not care. He ran into the river, barking orders no one could hear. Before him, riders tried to keep their horses pulling, straining, grunting, cursing, praying, sweating.

The rope on the eastern side of the wagon suddenly popped, rifling back toward the freight, slicing into the river that reflected the images of fire and hell. The other end popped the rider, George Dow, in the back of the head, and sent him headfirst into the Platte while his horse rolled over on the side—luckily away from the struggling Dow—found its feet, and bolted out of the river and out of Story's view.

On the other side, Boone and his gelding worked hard. Story saw the intensity, the madness, in the faces of both man and horse. Then he staggered to the side of the wagon, found a spot he could grip on the rear wagon, just in front of the mule skinner named Bennett, one of the two who could never get into camp before sundown.

He pushed. He cursed. Even thought about praying, as though God would listen to an atheist. He imagined the heat on his back. Suddenly, the wagon moved, freed from the quagmire beneath the water. Cory Bennett fell into the water, pushed up, slipped, went back into the river.

Story forgot about the damned wagon, forgot about everything but Cory Bennett. He moved quickly, grabbed the mule skinners' left leg, and pulled, pulled, pulled until he fell into the water, and came up spitting, cursing. He saw the wagon moving to the bank, and to his relief, Cory Bennett sat up in the river, spit out water, ran his hands over his face.

Story glanced at the flames, pushed himself to his feet, and forded his way to Bennett, but the skinner's pard, Mickey McDonald, reached him first. "Them wheels would've gone right over you . . ." McDonald looked at Story and nodded.

"You'd be dead, or crippled for life." Bennett coughed, shook his head, and put an arm around McDonald.

But he did manage to look at Story.

"Thank you," he said, barely audible.

One of the bullwhackers had fished George Dow out of the Platte. They made their way to the south bank.

Story started that way, too. "Thank you," he heard himself saying. "You boys did all right today." Five paces later he added, "But we're not out of this fix yet. Get ready for a long night."

The night, Molly McDonald thought, would never end.

The night did not darken until the flames on the other side of the Platte finally had no more fuel to burn. But sparks fluttered into the dry grass for hours, sending cowboys, mule skinners, and bullwhackers with wet blankets, towels, shirts, bedrolls, slapping at the flames and putting them out as quickly as possible.

When morning came, Molly looked at the blackness that covered the plains across the river.

It took them three days to round up what they could of the herd, and a day more to catch the last of the horses from the remuda.

Even after passing the last blackened prairie, they remained on the south side of the river. "Keep the Indians on the other side of the river," Jameson Hannah explained.

"Like there ain't no Indians on this side of that river," Dalton Combs mumbled.

No more prairie fires. No more Brulés. Just the wind . . . and monotony. When they reached where the big Platte forked, they followed the South Platte, still on the southern banks, till eventually crossing to pick up the main trail that led to Julesburg and Fort Sedgwick.

Late as they were again, sure to summon Story's ire, Molly McDonald couldn't figure out why Constance Beckett stopped the wagon so quickly on the outskirts of town. Constance yanked the brake lever, fell to her knees in the driver's box, leaned over the side, and vomited all over the Julesburg road.

Swearing, Molly barked at the mules, popped the whip, and covered the thirty yards before bringing the wagon to a stop. After leaping over the side, she ran to the side of Constance's wagon, where her friend had risen to her knees, gripping the wide of the wagon. Her sunburned face had turned ashen, and, unsteadily, she tugged off her bandanna and wiped her lips and face, ignoring Molly's questions: "Are you all right? . . . What's the matter? . . . What has happened?"

Molly drew in a deep breath, exhaled, while Constance lowered the kerchief. Turning her head, Constance spit over the front of the wagon before staring glassy-eyed at Molly.

"You . . ." She swallowed. ". . . you said . . . Julesburg had become . . . tame."

All Molly could think to say was: "Huh?"

After a long sigh, Constance tilted her head toward the other side of the road.

Too short to see over the backs of the mules, Molly walked along the narrow road, past the leaders, and gawked.

The man's decapitated head, beginning to putrefy, had been stuck atop a post, standing five feet high after being driven into the earth. Molly stepped closer, tilting her head so she could read the sign knocked askew by the wind or the ravens that had pecked out the dead man's eyes.

Sloppily written, the sign read:

coddnt cheet WERTH a DAM

Slowly, she removed her hat and spit tobacco juice into the grass. "Son of a gun," she said aloud. "That's ol' Mike Tucker."

"You knew him?" Constance coughed out the words.

"Sure did."

"I'm . . . sorry." Constance said after another gagging fit.

Molly turned around, slapped the hat back on her head, and strode toward the wagons. "Don't be," she said. "Mike Tucker was a horse's ass. Wish I could've been here to join in on the fun."

CHAPTER FIFTY-EIGHT

North from Julesburg and Fort Sedgwick to the North Platte River. Then northwest, back on the Platte River Road, again following the ruts left by the emigrants from a decade, two decades ago bound for Oregon and California. Through pale bluffs and small patches of woods. Across trickling streams of water, barely deep enough to wet the hooves of livestock. Following the North Platte to their left, and the rolling, never-ending plains all around them. They moved slowly, yet steadily, letting cattle graze on the thick grass. Wind blew the grass. Wind blew the dust, the grime. Wind blistered their faces, chapped their lips. Wind blew, and blew, and blew.

Jameson Hannah rode into camp with a pronghorn draped over the back of his saddle, and slung the carcass onto the ground near José Pablo Tsoyio's wagon. "Fresh meat," Hannah said with a grin. "Antelope steaks for supper. Antelope stew for breakfast. You boys can thank me with whiskey once we get to the sutler's at Fort Laramie."

That evening, José Pablo Tsoyio served beans, biscuits, and salt pork.

"What the hell, Tsoyio," Hannah barked when he rode in from checking on the herd. "I bring in a meaty doe, and you serve the same shit we've been eating forever." He pulled his revolver, but kept the barrel pointed at the dirt. "You've known me long enough, cookie, that when I tell you to cook pronghorn, you cook pronghorn. And don't tell me you are drying that meat because my belly is as sick of jerky as it is of your beans."

José Pablo Tsoyio did not look up, but continued stirring the batter he was setting for the next morning's breakfast. Softly, without stopping his chores, he said, "If I thought the men wanted worms for supper, I would have cooked your doe."

A few spurs chimed. The fire crackled. The spoon ground against the bowl. Finally, Boone chuckled, and that set off nervous laughter. Even Jameson Hannah grinned until the bullwhacker named Gordon Beck slapped his thigh and hooted. "Hey, Hannah, did you put a Remington bullet through the worm's heart—so as to not spoil no meat?"

The revolver started to rise, but Hannah stopped about halfway up. "You think you can do better, go ahead."

"We passed a buffalo herd about a mile or two back," Beck said. He lifted the Remington rifle from his side, butting it against the ground.

"Could you hit a buffalo?" Ryan Ward asked.

"Couldn't miss," Beck said.

"I tasted buffalo tongue once," Jordan Stubbings said. "Liked it."

"How much would you pay for some tongue?" Beck asked.

Stubbings grinned, but Story came out of the bushes, grabbed a plate, and noisily loaded it with beans. "You eat what the cook puts on your plate," he said. "This isn't Ebbitt's place in Washington City."

"Now—"

Beck didn't finish. "That herd's a mile behind us," Story said. "We're not taking these wagons and cattle east. And how would you get that buffalo skinned and the meat back to us?"

"I'm just thinking about some tongue."

"Give your damned tongue a rest," Story said. "And finish your supper."

In the mornings, before sunrise and before José Pablo Tsoyio rang the hell out of that damned iron triangle to get the men up and moving, Story could stretch, and groan, and try to rub the stiffness out of his back, the soreness out of his thighs, and sip the first cup of coffee while wondering if he knew what the Sam Hill he was doing.

Kneeling by the fire, trying to return to life after another miserable night of dreams and rocks biting through the blankets, he sipped coffee and waited for daybreak.

"Story."

The wiry little wagon boss knelt beside him, frowning, not even holding a cup of coffee. "We're missing one of my men."

Story stopped hurting. He set the cup on the stone near the fire. Not even having to think, he said, "Beck."

Connor Lehman leaned back on his haunches. "How'd you know?"

Instead of answering, Story asked, "Did he take the Remington rifle?"

"It wasn't by his bedroll," Lehman said. "He didn't take anything else, though. Just the rifle and ammunition pouches."

Story was already making himself stand, and he crossed the few yards to the wagon. "José," he said softly, "rouse Sibrian. Have him do a quick count on our horses." Looking back at the wagon boss, Story said, "I bet that son of a bitch stole a horse, but if he took one of my men's saddles, I'll stake his hide across Chimney Rock."

As the sky began turning gray, the young wrangler, sleepy-eyed and confused, told Story that, as best as he could tell, the bay with two white feet—the one from Fabian Peña's string—was gone. All saddles had been counted, but that didn't make sense. Until Story understood. The thought struck Connor Lehman at the same time.

"Check Overholt's wagon," the wagon boss told Kyle McPherson, who had the misfortune of sleeping too close to the fire and conversation. "There should be six saddles and six bridles."

There were only five. A blanket was missing, too.

Then José Pablo Tsoyio began ringing that damned bell.

"Sibrian," Story told the wrangler. "Cut out my black and two other mounts. Use the tack we planned to sell in Virginia City." He nodded at McPherson. "Show him." He whirled, spotted Boone, told him to get a horse saddled and be ready to ride. "You'll ride with us," Story told Lehman. "You and McPherson." Then to Hannah, who stood sipping coffee, not knowing what was going on. "Get the herd and wagons moving west. We'll be bringing a horse thief and idiot back. And I'm going to flay the skin off his back."

"I don't think so."

Story turned, eyes burning, until Boone nodded toward the east. The sun was up by then, not high, but the light stretched out across the horizon.

Buzzards circled over a little knoll.

"That's about where that buffalo herd was yesterday," Jordan Stubbings said, and emptied his coffee onto the ground.

"Maybe he killed one." Ryan Ward sounded like he was trying to convince himself. "You know. For the tongue."

Boone rode into the noon camp first. No one asked him a word. They didn't have to. He handed the reins of his horse to the wrangler and shook his head when Dalton Combs offered to pour him a cup of coffee.

Connor Lehman and Kyle McPherson came in next, McPherson leading his horse and limping, but not wounded.

George Dow nudged Kelvin Melean and laughed. "That bullwhacker ain't used to riding horses."

"Shut the hell up," Melean said.

The men put down their biscuits and cups and watched the last rider coming in at a trot, a Remington rifle braced against his thigh, and constantly looking back. Jordan Stubbings drew his revolver and checked the percussion caps. José Sibrian took his crucifix to his lips.

When Story reined in at the edge of camp, he tossed the big rifle to the nearest teamster. "Lehman," he said.

The wagon boss turned around. "Your man stole a horse, a saddle, a bridle, a blanket, and a Remington rifle. Those will come out of your pay."

Lehman did not look angry or surprised. He simply nodded, and led his and McPherson's horses toward the young wrangler. But the teamster named Overholt called out, "Would that be Leavenworth or Virginia City prices, Mr. Story?"

Story didn't look angry, either. "Fort Laramie's closer. We'll see what the prices are at the sutler's." He looked back.

"Finish your coffee. Eat in the saddle. Let's cover some miles before dark." He spurred the horse, did not stop for a drink or another word, and rode the lathered buckskin to the remuda.

"What happened?" another bullwhacker asked Lehman, who tilted the pot and filled a cup with coffee.

"Did Beck really steal a horse?" . . . "And a rifle?" . . . "What were them buzzards doin'?" More questions went unanswered, till Jameson Hannah rode up from the herd.

"Dead?" Hannah asked.

Boone nodded.

Constance Beckett lowered her head. Beside her, Molly McDonald fingered the tobacco out of her mouth and tossed the chaw into the grass. Fabian Peña made the sign of the cross.

"Indians?"

"Yeah."

All banter ceased. Men rose, deposited the dishes in the wreck pan, and walked to the horse herd. Young Sibrian was already heading to the remuda to help.

"You heard the man," Hannah said. "Wagons rolling and cattle walking." He turned the horse and spurred it after Nelson Story. By then, Luke Beckner had removed his hat and bowed his head. "I would have liked to have been with y'all," he told Lehman. "If only to pray over poor Beck's grave."

"There was no grave." Lehman limped toward the wagons. "Nelson Story won't bury a horse thief."

CHAPTER FIFTY-NINE

About the time they crossed the North Platte, somewhere west of Ash Hollow? Constance Beckett tried to remember. Maybe the day, two days, before that bullwhacker got killed, scalped by the Indians. A week ago? She shook the cobwebs out of her brain. A mule skinner lost track of time in this sea of nothingness, but that sounded right. Yeah, that was the last time Constance had seen a cloud. Skies were supposed to be blue, she remembered, but these days the horizon turned a grim white. She could hardly pick out Courthouse Rock to the south a day or so back. Now she barely made out Chimney Rock.

She looked at the road, at Molly's wagon ahead of her. She heard the ox-pulled double-hitched wagons behind her, but did not bother to look back. That would be just the same country she had already seen.

After the death of that fool Beck, Connor Lehman had put one of his big-ass rigs at the rear of the column. "Nice of him," Molly had remarked after that first night. "So we won't die alone if the red devils jump us."

But they had seen no sign of Indians. Nor wagons, not even a solitary stagecoach coming from the west. Nothing to see here, but waving country, an occasional landmark, and that hot, overbearing endless sky. The Rocky Mountains were somewhere out there, if they hadn't fallen off the ends of the earth.

She brought the loosened bandanna to her face, wiped off sweat, and then flicked the lines just to do something. In front of her, Molly spit tobacco juice onto sage. Behind her, the teamster cursed and popped his whip. On days like these, Constance halfway wished she had been captured, tried, and convicted for killing that son of a bitch back at Fort Kearny. She wiped her face again and looked northwest, hoping the wind would cool her off. Her head tilted, and she blinked, closed her eyes and counted to five before prying the eyelids up.

A cloud? No, she must be hallucinating, having just been thinking about how many days had passed since a cloud had floated across the sky. She thought about calling out to Molly, asking her if that distant silvery cloud might be a mirage. But the thought of talking made her throat hurt.

"¿Es esa nieve lo que veo?" Cursing himself for talking to himself, José Pablo Tsoyio studied the horizon. As the wagon lumbered along, north of the herd of cattle, he pushed back his hat. Snow? White smoke from another prairie fire? He remembered the big grass fire along the big Platte River, recalled the heat, the filth, the hell. He studied the glittering, moving madness. No, that could not be smoke. Hail? Snow . . . in August?

The cattle bawled nervously, while the mules pulling his wagon balked at his commands, those spoken, those with his usual firm touch on the leather lines. Tsoyio glanced over at young Sibrian, who had so much trouble keeping the horses under control, the *segundo*, Jameson Hannah, galloped over to help.

Whatever that cloud might be bringing, it spooked the animals. *Madre Bendita,* Tsoyio thought, and shook his head. *It troubles my nerves, as well.*

Cursing the mules, he found the whip and made it bark, returned it to the holder, and pulled his gloves on tighter with his teeth. Now, while he had time. Once he had a firm grasp on the lines, he reexamined that strange *fantasma.* The apparition grew larger, higher, eddying and twisting like a macabre *danza del venado.*

No, no, that could not be smoke, hail, or snow. But it might be hell.

"If that's a dust devil, it's the damnedest and biggest one I ever seen," Dalton Combs told Story.

"It's not dust." Story rode away from the approaching cloud. Dust devils rolled across the ground; this specter remained high in the air, like a tornado that had not touched down. "Sing to them, Combs. Sing something soft. Keep them calm, keep them moving."

Looking over his shoulder, Story continued southeast, down the trail. This angle soon gave him a different view of the swirling gale of what resembled dead leaves dancing in the wind, but there could not be enough trees on the Great Plains to produce that many leaves. And autumn felt like an eternity away. Not one cloud, or one . . . whatever the hell it was . . . no. Two. Three. Four. The dun fought rein and bit, jerking Story's arms one way and the other. On the other side of the herd, Fabian Peña and Jordan Stubbings kept their horses running alongside the longhorns, turning several steers, even one bull, back into the herd.

"Ain't sure how much longer I can keep them from bolting, Mr. Story," Stubbings called out.

"Keep them moving west," Story said. "Maybe this . . ." What the hell was it? "It's high enough, as long as it stays that high, it'll pass right over us." He cursed under his breath. "A snowball's chance in hell."

The wind blew harder now, leaving Story to fear that maybe these were twisters, but the air felt hot, and no dark clouds appeared anywhere. Just these silvery, whirling funnels. Then, a faint drumming reached his ears, growing louder as the strange clouds moved with the hard wind. Minutes later, the first cloud went over, and his horse bucked again, wanting to run, but Story pulled the reins tight and to his left, twisting the head.

He swore, struggling to keep the horse under control. The hum intensified, and he noticed the wild clouds began descending. One, a few hundred yards to the north, unleashed its torrent to the earth. Another cloud passed overhead. The concert of buzzing and droning and a numbing *clicking* reached a crescendo.

Whatever this was, it began to swallow everything in its path.

Out of the corner of his eye, Story saw Mason Boone's head snap back—Story heard the impact—and Boone, swearing, brought his left hand up to his face, cursing, blood rushing from his nostrils. A moment later, amid the insane buzzing, rasping, something popped against Story's hat. Hailstones? No. These were alive. Then one slammed into the back of his head. Hurt like a son of a bitch. The horse bucked again, harder, more determined. Story turned. Boone cursed, spit out blood, shouted something, but that constant drone drowned out everything as the funnels closed all around him, the cattle, the countryside.

The deluge began. But not rain, not hail, but thousands and thousands of . . .

Another pop in his shoulder, and a blur that slammed into the horse's withers, caused Story to look down just as a fat insect fell onto the grass.

"Grasshoppers," Story shouted, trying to bring the bandanna up over his mouth and nose, as the cloud unleashed its fury with a storm of living insects.

Locusts. Wings unfolded. Bugs covered the grass. The deafening buzz grew into such a roar, Story barely heard the thundering hooves as the cattle stampeded. His horse reared as Story slapped at the insects. He felt the breath rush from his lungs, the pain in his back, knew he had been thrown. The ground trembled around him, and he rolled over, covered his head, and thought not about his wife and daughter, but his legacy. To die in a stampede was one thing, but to be killed by bugs? Jesus, the professor would have a story in the *Montana Post* that would be reprinted everywhere, and the whole world would be laughing at Nelson Story.

The mules snorted as the roaring, whirling cloud of insects enveloped Constance and the wagon. She screamed, felt a bug in her mouth, could not stop herself from biting down, and the gall spread across her tongue, down her throat. Insects fell like rain. She tried to spit, tried to keep her hands on the leather lines. A rut, a man, a rock, a horse . . . something jolted her off the bench and into the floor of the driver's box. Her eyes opened to a whirling world of madness. Locusts covered her hair. Panicked mules carried the wagon off the trail, down an embankment, away from the rise of blurry dullness of Chimney Rock.

No longer encumbered with the lines, she swatted at the bugs. Screamed again. The mules carried her and the wagon toward the North Platte. Suddenly, the wagon lurched, and she felt herself flying, sailing with the swarm. Dimly, maybe she made out the crash of the wagon as it catapulted its supplies in all directions. She hit the ground, rolled into more sand and weeds, as breath exploded out of her lungs. She tried sucking in air, only to feel more locusts cover her. Rolling over, she wanted to keep rolling, squishing as many of her tormentors as she could. Reach the river, go under, drown the sons of bitches, drown herself. Instead she slammed into the embankment. She had rolled the wrong way.

Her hands swatted, slashed, combed away bugs. All around her, the insects clicked, tapped, buzzed, whirled, devoured grass—and buried her. They covered her shirt, her pants, her soul. Well, God had to punish her for killing that bastard.

Constance wanted to cry. Maybe she was. Bugs would soon eat her flesh, and her soul. She bit through another insect, and finally relented, bringing arms over her mouth and nose, squeezing her eyelids shut, feeling and hearing the madness of *click, clack, click, clack, click* . . .

The nightmare deepened, and at last she understood that God was not punishing her for taking a life.

This had to be Armageddon.

Boone found her. He swung off the claybank, but did not let go of the reins, keeping the leather wrapped tightly over his gloved left hand. Given a chance, the gelding would not stop running till reaching Texas.

Once locating the overturned wagon, he tied the gelding

up short. He would have hobbled him, too, but somewhere during the stampede he had lost his saddlebags.

"Cory," he called out, and wished to hell he knew her real name. "Cory."

Nothing. His boots trod over the remnants of grass-hoppers, locusts, whatever the hell they were, crunching their bodies, and he came to the first mule.

"Son of a bitch." Boone tugged the Colt out of the hol-ster, eared back the hammer, and touched the trigger. The noise shocked him, and he realized the stillness, the fright-ening quiet that had descended over the plains after some Old Testament nightmare. Stepping around the dead mule, he found the rest of the team in the river, up to their knees, alive, frozen in panic or stuck in the mud. Drowned insects floated downstream, attracting schools of hungry fish. Much of the grass had vanished, and even the trees along the riverbank looked as though an early fall had struck.

"Bennett," he tried again. "Cory Bennett."

The remaining locusts answered with mocking snaps and ticks. He turned back from the river, heard something that sounded almost human. Then he saw her. Boone ran to the cutbank, dropped to his knees, and reached out for the woman's shirt.

"God," he whispered, quickly dropped the revolver, pulled off his vest. His hat came off next, and desperately he yanked the shirt over his head. The woman sobbed, but her eyes opened, darting this way and that, and she slapped Boone's hands as he pulled her up. She screamed. Boone handed her his shirt.

"Put this on," he told her.

Her cry pierced Boone's soul.

Another voice came from behind him. "Get away from her, you jackass." Mickey McDonald's boots crunched over the carcasses of the swarm before Cory's pard fell onto his knees and stared. "God A'mighty," Mickey said.

Most of Cory Bennett's outfit had been devoured, her shirt reduced to yellow horizontal stripes—the green cotton gone. Her green bandanna hung in threads. The green checks on the tan pants had . . . vanished. Locusts, either hungry or crazy, consumed anything resembling grass or leaves. Even cloth that wasn't green had been chewed. Bark, Boone noticed, had been stripped off trees.

"Sons of bitches eat everything," Boone said, realizing his shirtsleeve was chewed in places with more efficiency than moths.

Constance screamed again, and McDonald reached down, put his arms around Cory's back, and lifted her as the remnants of the shirt slid off her pale body. She must have rolled over and over trying to escape the attacking horde, and that had loosened the linen wrappings used to keep her breasts hidden. Blood trickled down her back, her stomach, her sides, from the sand and hard weeds. "Get that shirt on, boy," McDonald ordered. "Be damned quick and—"

The girl sobbed on McDonald's shoulder. Boone wanted to be gentle, but felt clumsy, tried not to see her nakedness, her breasts, the pale skin, the cuts and scratches, the remnants of bugs. He had no idea how to get the shirt over her. Maybe he should just use the vest.

Too late. A shadow crossed Boone's face, and he looked into the wrath of God.

Nelson Story, hat gone, a cut over his forehead, clothes covered with dirt, bug guts, and flecks of grass and leaves, swore vilely. "A woman?" he roared. "A damned woman?"

CHAPTER SIXTY

One wagon lost, though the contents, at least what could be salvaged, had been loaded into some of the freight wagons and the cook's Studebaker. Eighteen head of cattle dead, or missing. One mule dead. Nine horses gone.

Story stood by the campfire, listening to the reports from Connor Lehman and Jameson Hannah. When both men had finished, Story had not moved.

"Where's your hat?" Lehman asked, just to fill the silence.

Shrugging, Story looked at the men—and the woman—all dazed, exhausted—while the Mexican cook kept checking the coffeepot, waiting for it to boil.

"There are a few you bought to sell in Virginia City," Lehman said. "Maybe one will fit you." Getting no response, the wagon boss explained, "Hats, I mean."

"Those are to be sold in Virginia City." Story thought, but did not say: *And I might need the profits to pay off you bastards.*

Someone—Story couldn't recognize the voice, for rasping locusts echoed in his ears—yelled at the cook, "What's for supper?"

"Grasshopper," José Pablo Tsoyio answered.

"You serve bugs, Mex," one of Lehman's teamsters said, "I'll gut you like a fish."

"In parts of my country, it is considered a delicacy," the cook said.

"Hey." Ryan Ward rode into camp, pulling a roped calf behind him. "We can eat this for supper."

He did not recall moving, but Story found himself walking past Ward and the buckskin, to the brown calf with the white face, and then he dropped to his knees, working on the noose, saying, "You're not eating this calf." He flung the end of the lariat away from the bawling calf.

"Boss," the young cowboy pleaded, "his ma is dead. There—"

Story's glare silenced the kid. The calf bolted, stopped, cried. Story rose, saw Boone walk to the calf, drop a loop over its head, tighten the noose, and pull the bawling orphan toward a wagon.

A moment later, the woman, Cory Bennett, or whatever her real name was, stepped out of the line of Lehman's bull-whackers and came to the calf, kneeling beside it, calming it. "I'll take care of him," she said.

"Just like a good mama." Jameson Hannah laughed.

She wore George Dow's trousers and Luke Beckner's plaid shirt.

"What do we do with her?" Lehman asked.

"Leave her at Laramie," Story answered.

"You might think that over," Lehman said. "Beck's dead. Without her, we don't have the number of men we need to keep heading north. And she can drive a wagon."

"Like the one she wrecked?" Story kept staring at the calf.

"Well, you know what a stickler them bluebellies are for numbers," Hannah said. "Besides, she might come in handy."

"That's enough." Story moved toward the coffeepot, never taking his eyes off the woman, who, with Boone's assistance, led the bawling, orphaned calf to the wagon Mickey McDonald drove.

Then Kelvin Melean rose, pointed at the river, and yelled. "I know what we can eat." He laughed. "Fish. Fish."

The cook rose from the coffeepot, looking toward the river.

"Yeah," another bullwhacker said. "Those sumbitches are fattening up on bugs but . . ."

The boys stampeded toward the North Platte.

Five days later, they reached Scotts Bluff and let the livestock graze on grass that had not be shaved by thousands of locusts.

Young Ryan Ward hurried to the wagon, carrying a beer bottle in his hand. Constance laughed when he tripped over a rock, but he kept from falling, and slid on his knees in front of her. "Here." He jutted the bottle toward her. "It's . . . milk." He spoke so fast, she could barely make him out. "There's another mama cow with a baby. Actually, golly, ma'am, must be six or seven that've dropped on this drive. I milked him myself, ma'am."

"Him?" Constance grinned.

He stared dully before a wide grin stretched across his young, dirty face. "Oh. Right. We drew lots. I got the short one, but not really. I broke it off in my hand. Didn't want Luke Beckner to . . ." His face turned crimson. "Well. It's for . . . what are you calling him?"

"Hobo," she said.

"Huh." His head bobbed. "Yeah. He sort of looks like a hobo. Where'd you come up with that name?"

"I didn't." She took the bottle. "Mr. Story named him."

Ryan's face reminded her of a boy from the school—though his name escaped her—and the look he would have, utterly lost, completely overwhelmed, whenever the schoolmaster began arithmetic. "Thank you, Ryan." Constance's smile seemed all the payment Ward needed, or perhaps the mention of Nelson Story's name frightened him. Springing to his feet, the cowboy tipped his hat and raced across the campground.

"There's a dress," Story said, "in one of the wagons. Might be short, but I'll have it brought to you." He stood, still hatless, his face burned by the sun where the beard offered no protection.

Constance looked at him as she let Hobo drain another bottle of milk. This one had been brought by Dalton Combs. Yesterday, one of Lehman's bullwhacker's, David McKay, managed to milk a cow, and apparently had a black eye to go with the novelty.

"And how much will that cost me, Mr. Story? Fort Laramie prices?"

The ears reddened to match his sun-blistered forehead and cheeks. "What is your name?" he demanded after about half a minute.

"Constance Beckett," she answered without hesitation, "Mr. Story."

"You may call me Nelson."

"I think not."

"Then just plain Story. This *mister* gets damned annoying."

She focused on letting the calf suckle.

"We shall leave you at Fort Laramie," he told her.

Which she had expected. "No, you won't."

"I am sure I can hire men to replace you and . . ." He left Gordon Beck's name unsaid.

"You won't be able to replace all of us." Good old Molly McDonald, still dressed in men's duds, still chewing tobacco, and always as uncouth as a Tennessean from the hills, strode into camp with a plate of supper for Constance. "Cory and me been pards too long for me to break in some other dumb bastard."

She squatted, put the plate at Constance's side, and scratched Hobo like one might do a dog.

"You had to know she was a . . . woman," Story told Molly's back.

Molly looked into Constance's eyes, and sighed.

"Was she your . . . ?"

"Don't go there, *mister*." Apparently, Molly had been eavesdropping on the conversation before storming in with supper. "She's my pard. You're just the sumbitch that pays us, and I skin mules for bosses till I grow sick of them." She turned. "And I've gotten me a bellyful of you."

"I can replace you, too, McDonald."

Molly rose, laughed, spit, and walked right past him. "Fort Laramie's a big post, mister. How many you reckon you'll have to replace? Couple of your cowboys is moonstruck. So is some of Lehman's boys. Besides, you lose Cory yonder, who's gonna be nursemaidin' your little baby?" She kept walking, and did not look back.

Story looked at the calf, then at Constance. His face remained burned but unreadable. Finally, he nodded at her. "Ma'am," he said as he turned, "you're doing a fine job with that calf." He started back toward the main camp.

The compliment stunned her. She had to try twice before she called out to his ramrod back, "Nelson."

He stopped, but did not turn around.

"Who was Hobo?" Constance asked.

"A dog I had when I was a kid." Story resumed that intense, strong stride. "Pa made me bury him. After he shot him."

CHAPTER SIXTY-ONE

On the far side of the Laramie River, Fort Laramie sprawled across the flats before them: tents and teepees, soldiers and civilians and Indians, wagons and cannon and livestock. Beyond the post, trees lined the bank of the bending river and a canal on the southern edge of the military post, and a handful of wolfberry trees rose like sentinels on the rolling plains of wheatgrass. Past that, hills, barren mesas, sandstone outcroppings, the occasional stand of soapweed yucca, and in the distance, the bluish-gray outline of mountains, including towering Laramie Peak—looking so close, even though the mountains lay some forty miles west.

After weeks of endless prairie, seeing the Rocky Mountains brought a semblance of life back into the party. So did the sight of people and civilization: civilian wagons—mostly freight rigs, a few farm wagons, even a couple of Conestogas—were parked outside the open compound near a trading post, where smoke rose from a chimney. A makeshift corral held dozens of oxen, mules, and horses. Tombstones and crosses filled a small graveyard next to scaffolds holding the Indian dead.

And the smells: coffee, broiling meat, beans, bacon being cooked at campfires, and in the fort's kitchens.

Molly McDonald hadn't seen a stranger in so many weeks, she had joked that the world had ended when those grasshoppers came by—Nelson Story's party just hadn't realized it, yet. Maybe Fort Laramie even revived any remaining humanity in Story's soul, Molly thought, for he rode up alongside the wagon Molly shared with Constance Beckett.

"How's Hobo?" he asked.

Constance tilted her head toward the wagon's tailgate. "See for yourself."

The calf was tied up behind the wagon, though if he got tired, they would stop and Molly—not Constance—would have to lift up the smelly bovine and put him inside.

"Well, keep your hat pulled down and your voice low," Story said. "You're Cory Bennett."

Molly and Constance stared at that stiff-backed, hard-rock tyrant.

"I've lost a wagon, cattle, horses, one man, supplies, and time," Story said. "No need to hire more men and waste time teaching them what I demand from men I pay." He started to turn the horse back to the herd, but stopped and pointed his finger at Constance. "But, by thunder, when we reach Virginia City, you're dressing like a woman. Or I'll run you out of town as a pervert or have you burned at the stake as a witch."

He loped away, and Molly spit tobacco juice. "Girl," Molly said, "watch yourself around that man."

"He's married," Constance told her.

Molly flicked the lines and muttered a stream of indelicate words.

"Every man here wants me, Molly," Constance said. "Even that cute wrangler and sweet Ryan Ward. I can handle myself."

Molly started to say something like Major Warner Balsam could attest to that, but dropped the subject when Constance patted her thigh, and said, "But thanks for looking after me, pard."

James Van Voast ran his fingers through his receding, prematurely graying hair. Although the major probably hadn't reached his fortieth birthday, wrinkles creasing his face and rheumy eyes made him look closer to sixty. Massaging his temples with elbows on his desktop, he shook his head and sighed.

"My advice to you, Mr. Story," he said, "is to find another destination."

"My destination, Major, is Virginia City."

Van Voast released his head and looked into Story's eyes. "You might reach your grave before your destination, Mr. Story." He pointed at the window, though the shades were drawn tightly, allowing not one ray of sunshine into the office. "Red Cloud stormed out of here earlier this summer, refusing to agree to any peace terms the commissioners put before him."

"I have a wife and child in Montana," Story said.

"But you are aware of the restrictions placed on travelers on the Bozeman Trail." Van Voast raised a paper from his cluttered desk. "Mr. Michener reports that you are short one man and one wagon."

"Your lieutenant is a good counter."

The major's head shook. "Then you know I have no recourse but to deny you permission to continue north."

"I figure I can get another wagon and another man here."

He raised the black hat he held in his left hand. "Already replaced the hat I lost." He did not grin.

Nor did Van Voast. "Mr. Michener also says you have more than two dozen Remington rifles, supplies, ammunition, grain, and . . . hundreds of longhorned cattle?"

"All bound for Virginia City, Major."

"The Sioux would love to get their hands on that," Van Voast said.

"They'll have a devil of a time getting it, sir."

Their eyes locked, and Van Voast almost grinned. "You are a stubborn man."

"Major, I just want to get home."

"Once you have your extra wagon and your extra man, you may pass, Mr. Story. All I can do is advise you of the risks involved, but . . . well, sir . . . we have had no fresh meat, no beef, I mean, in more than a month. Would you be willing to sell steers here?"

"What's your price?"

"The army commissary has . . ."

"Army prices? No thank you, Major. I'll sell them in Virginia City, keep some for myself."

The major's face darkened. "Good day, Mr. Story."

Story nodded, put his hat on, and turned toward the door.

"Story." Van Voast dropped the *mister*.

"Yes, Major?" He looked back at the tired commander.

"Camped among those ten or twelve stranded emigrants you'll find a freight wagon and two men. They stayed behind after another wagon train changed its destination from Montana's goldfields to Salt Lake City for safety. Union veterans, sir. Both of them. The kind of men you'd need, and with their wagon, you'd be able to continue north, at your earliest convenience."

Story stared for a moment, finally nodded, and thanked the major.

"Your thanks are neither necessary nor desired," Van Voast said as he opened a drawer and withdrew a bottle. "My wish is for you to reach your home, and, from what I hear, those two men would give you a better, if still slim, chance." He uncorked the bottle and splashed three fingers of amber fluid into a tumbler. "Finding anyone willing to join your caravan might prove fruitless, which means that eventually you would sneak out on your own. That, in turn, would force me to order a detail after you. This has been an ugly summer, sir. Fall shall not cool down any hostilities. Already, too many dead men are on my conscience." He raised the glass in a toast. "I would dislike very much to report losing any men I had to send after you."

The major had drained the whiskey by the time Story closed the office door.

Sitting in front of the fire, John Catlin sipped coffee from the tin mug as this fellow named Nelson Story made his offer, after which Catlin looked at Steve Grover.

"You understand," Catlin said after setting the cup on the ground, "that what is in our wagon belongs to Grover and me. We plan to sell it in one of the gold camps and use the money to . . ." He shrugged.

Grover finished: "Do anything but grow wheat."

Catlin tried smiling, but Story's face remained unreadable. "If we decided to sell our goods in Virginia City," Catlin said, "we'd be competing with one another."

"It's a free country," Story said.

"It's also a dangerous country," Grover said. "Around here." He nodded at the cemetery.

"I have twenty-nine breech-loading Remington rifles," Story said.

"Can your men shoot them?" Catlin asked.

"They can. Can you shoot one?"

Catlin shook his head. "Never owned a breechloader, Remington or otherwise." He pointed at the rifle leaning against the wagon.

"Muzzle-loader," Story said.

"That's right," Catlin said. "Enfield. English-made."

"Can you shoot those?"

Steve Grover chuckled. "A passel of Johnny Rebs might say we could, if they weren't six feet under."

Story's head bobbed. "You might not want to mention that to the men trailing my cattle. They're Texans, and still smarting after the war."

"And you?" Catlin asked.

"Ohio by birth, Kansas for a few years, short while in Colorado, Virginia City since '63."

"So," Grover said, "you need a couple of Yankees for company . . . and protection."

"I'm no Yankee," Story said. "I'm a businessman. And I protect myself. You'll be protecting your wagon, your investment. I don't pay you. Your pay's in that wagon. You ride along because you need me to get to Montana. And I need you to get to Montana. That's my offer."

"What's the chow like?" Grover asked.

Story held up the coffee Catlin had poured him and dumped it out. "Better than what you cook for yourselves." He tossed the empty cup across the fire to Grover, who caught it and set it on the ground.

"You're a wee bit ornery," Grover said with a smile.

Story had no reaction. "If you don't want to join me, I'll bid you good evening. If you do, let me know. I need one man and one wagon, and I'll be making my rounds. First man with grit, rifle, and wagon I find, I'm moving north." He nodded. "Thanks for the coffee and time, gentlemen."

As Story strode away, Catlin looked quickly at Grover, who shrugged.

"Story," Catlin called out.

The man stopped and turned.

"We'll move over to your camp first thing in the morning," Catlin said. "Leave whenever you're ready."

"I'll be ready tomorrow morning." Story walked into the evening.

"That man's meaner than any son-of-a-bitching officer we ever had in the 87th," Grover said when Story was out of sight. "Present company excepted."

"No," Catlin said, "he's meaner than I ever was. But that son of a bitch, I warrant, gets things done."

CHAPTER SIXTY-TWO

When Jameson Hannah swung out of the saddle and led his horse a few rods off the trail, Story spurred the black into a lope, reining up when he found Hannah kneeling beside a grave, probably two or three weeks old.

Hannah rose, put his hat on, and led the bay back toward the Bozeman Trail. "You ever think we should have listened to those bluebellies at Laramie, took the long way to Virginia City?"

"You ever been snowed in in the Rockies?" Story answered. "Without a cabin or dry wood?"

"Nope."

"I haven't, either," Story said. "And don't intend to."

Having turned north off the Oregon Trail, they followed Sage Creek. The country hadn't changed much, but the Bozeman Trail had more fresh markers than the Oregon Trail had. Markers like this grave . . . the charred skeletons of wagons . . . and what was left of dead oxen, horses, and mules.

Hannah mounted the gelding. "Well," he said, "at least we haven't seen any Indians."

"We will," Story told him.

* * *

The first frost usually made Ellen Story smile, but this September morning just felt gloomy as she pushed the carriage, little Montana cooing underneath her blankets. She stopped at the newspaper office, opened the door, and came in, offering a quick "Good morning" and frowning when she turned to find an empty desk. On the other side of the office, the printer and one of the *Post*'s publishers, Benjamin Dittes, proofread a page. "Where is the professor, Mr. Dittes?" she asked.

Dittes looked at the desk as if noticing the editor was not there for the first time, then he glanced at Patrick Walsh, who busied himself studying the proof. Finally, after drawing a deep breath, he turned back to Ellen. "He's . . . sick, ma'am," he said after exhaling.

"Oh." Ellen failed to hide her disappointment.

The publisher managed a smile. "I'm sure that new wife of his is taking real good . . ." He did not finish.

The baby laughed. Dittes grinned at the carriage. "How is Montana?"

"A handful." Ellen turned toward the printer, who did not look up. "Mr. Walsh?"

Patrick Walsh raised his head slightly, and his eyes above the rims of his spectacles. "Missus Story," he said.

"How is . . . Dr. Beckstead?"

Walsh turned toward Dittes, looked at the page he held, finally straightened, and told Ellen, "I wouldn't know, ma'am."

"Does he not still share living quarters with you?"

"No, ma'am. He's bunking with Doc Sparhan."

"Oh. I passed the office, a couple of times."

"I don't think either of those docs have been practicing medicine much, Missus Story." Walsh returned to his page.

"Well." Ellen made herself look happy. "I look forward to reading the next edition on Saturday, gentlemen."

"Have you heard from your husband?" Dittes remembered he ran a newspaper.

"Not since that letter from Julesburg," she said. She turned the carriage around and opened the door. "Good day, gentlemen."

"Missus Story," Walsh called.

Ellen looked. "You being real close to the professor, it might be a good idea, ma'am, if you wanted to see him . . ." He swallowed. "To do it soon."

For all John Catlin had heard about Dakota Territory and the Bozeman Trail, he figured September would feel like winter. Instead, sitting on the rumbling wagon, clammy hands gripping his Enfield rifle, sweat trickled down his forehead. And he had been sweating before Steve Grover said as he drove the wagon, "You see them?"

"I see them," Catlin said, and pried his fingers from the rifle to wipe his right hand on his trousers.

Mounted on horses, a dozen warriors watched from a ridge to the east, silhouetted by the morning sun. Catlin looked to the west, wondering if more Indians might be there, and he studied the terrain, just in case those men might be trying to distract them from a real attack. All he saw were grass, rocks, a few cacti, hills, and mesas, so he focused on the ridge. The Indians began riding along the top, paralleling the caravan. The mesa ran another five hundred yards or so. If they left the high ground, would the Indians be harder to find in the rolling prairie?

Clopping hooves caused Catlin's heart to skip, and he whirled around. Riding at a hard trot and pulling a saddled horse behind him, Nelson Story reined up alongside the wagon.

"You said you were infantry," Story said. "How are you in a saddle?"

"I've ridden," Catlin said, "but I'm no horse soldier."

Story held out the reins. "Take this horse. Ride to the remuda. I've got Overholt and Collins already off their wagons. You help them guard the horses. Indians would rather steal horses than attack a train such as ours."

"And the cattle?" Catlin asked.

"Indians like horses better than beef. Besides, they know my drovers are armed."

Catlin lowered the rifle into the box and took the reins. When Grover started to pull back on the lines, Story barked, "Don't stop. Keep moving, and pick up the pace." He turned to Catlin. "Get on from there. And take that Enfield." He spurred his horse and rode down the line to the trailing wagons.

"I hope that hard-ass is right," Grover said. "If they hit us, it'll be the horse herd, not me." Without looking away from the road, he grinned.

Catlin just handed Grover the Enfield. "Hold this for me till I get on this beast . . . And if I break my neck, write Ma and Pa."

"Tommy," Nettie Dimsdale whispered. "Ellen's here. Ellen. Ellen Story. Hey, handsome. How are you feeling? Ellen Story's here. Do you feel like talking to her? Would you like me to sit you up?"

From the doorway, Ellen heard Thomas Dimsdale mutter

a hoarse "No," and his wife stepped from the bed, nodded grimly at Ellen. "He probably won't be able to talk more than a few minutes," she whispered, and walked out of the bedchamber. Her eyes looked as though she had been crying for weeks.

Ellen summoned some strength, made herself smile, and walked to the bed that reeked of urine, blood, rot, and opium. Moving her skirt, she sat on the stool and reached up and took Dimsdale's cold, feeble hand in her own. "Good afternoon, Thomas," she said.

His gums had receded, his face held no color, and his eyes dulled. The hair was slick from sweat, thin, gray, and his drooping mustache looked absurd, as though someone had pasted a theatrical mustache on a skeleton.

Dimsdale drew in a shallow, ragged breath that pained Ellen.

"Is Nelson home?" he whispered.

"No. Not yet."

"Any word?"

He would always be a newspaper journalist. That made Ellen feel somewhat better. "Not since the last letter. With Bozeman's Trail being what it is, I doubt if I shall hear from him till he walks through our door."

"Tell him . . ." His eyes closed, and stayed closed, and Ellen made herself look at the blanket covering his chest, saw it rise and fall in shallow, struggling breaths. When his eyes opened, his right pointer finger moved toward the bedside table.

Ellen found the bottle and brought it off the table, then looked for a spoon.

"Just." Dimsdale swallowed. "Pour some in . . ." He grinned again.

After he had swallowed a bit of the medicine, he sank

into his pillow. "Tell Nelson . . . I am sorry . . . I didn't get . . . the story of the . . . century."

"You'll write it," she told him, and repeated, "You'll write it."

"Maybe," he said, and fell asleep.

She corked the laudanum, returned it to the table, looked at the poor, dying man, and left the bedroom. Nettie stood staring at the fireplace.

"He's sleeping," Ellen told her.

She didn't appear to hear.

"Do you need anything?"

Nettie shook her head.

"If you do, please call on me." Not wanting Nettie to see her cry, Ellen found her shawl and darted for the door, but once she had it opened, Nettie's voice stopped her.

"How long have you been married?"

She turned, but Nettie kept staring at the fire. Ellen had to think, wet her lips, and replied, "Four years . . . on the twenty-eighth."

The head bobbed, but did not turn. "Four and a half months," she said. "Do you ever wonder?" Now she turned, fresh tears flowing down her young face.

"Wonder . . . what?"

"What it will feel like to be a widow?"

CHAPTER SIXTY-THREE

Conversation, curses, clinking glasses, and balls rolling across felt stopped shortly after Ellen Story stepped inside Sabolsky's billiard hall. When she started waving a handkerchief over her nose, men promptly snuffed out cigars in ashtrays or tossed them into spittoons. Stepping out of the gray haze, Reuben Sabolsky took off his hat, which prompted those standing with shot glasses or pool cues to use their free hands to remove their hats or caps.

Someone whispered something, which prompted a sharp rebuke from a nearby pool player: "Shut your trap, Timmons, or I'll shut it for you."

Sabolsky shouted at the patrons in a thick Polish accent, turned to Ellen, said, "Ma'am," and for the moment, appeared to have forgotten any more English.

Ellen coughed slightly. "I am looking for Dr. Beckstead. Dr. Seth Beckstead."

Sabolsky realized he held an unlighted cigar in his other hand, and dumbly handed it to the burly miner at the closest billiard table. His mouth opened, closed, and kept repeating that operation for five or six seconds.

"I was told he frequents this establishment," Ellen said firmly, and coughed. Tears welled from the potent smoke.

An Irish voice in the darkness called out, "Take her to him, Rube."

Sighing, Sabolsky motioned with his hand, and Ellen followed him, weaving through the gawking men, young and old, her eyes burning, until the rear door opened, and Sabolsky tilted his head down the alley. Outside, the moon, not full but close, bathed light, and Ellen saw the figure among the trash.

"Most he drink," Sabolsky said. "Sometime he drink, fight. Tonight he fight. You friend, tell him not come no more. No man I want killed here." She stepped around him without another word, and heard the door close.

Once his eyes fluttered open, Ellen tossed the blood-soaked handkerchief among the beer bottles and busted crates. Dr. Seth Beckstead did not notice her at first, for he was too busy rolling over, throwing up, before collapsing in his own vomit. He groaned, laughed, turned to his side, and lay on his back, wiping the filth off his face with his torn shirtsleeve.

"Seth," she tried.

He heard, froze, and eventually sat. "Well." He fought another wave of nausea. "Good morning . . . good . . . evening, Ellen."

"Professor Dimsdale needs medical attention," she told him.

He laughed. "I told you I could do nothing . . ."

"Seth," she begged. "He needs help."

"Find a doctor."

"Yes." Face flushing, she rose. "There is a new one in Nevada City." When she walked past him, he lunged, grabbed for her skirt but missed, and rolled into busted bottles, cursing from the cuts the shards made.

"I told you," he yelled to her back. "All I know how to do is cut men to pieces." He laughed and lay back on the refuse. "I haven't saved a life in years. Ellen. Ellen, if you ever see that heartless bastard you married, thank him for me." Another cackle. He found a beer bottle, shook it, tossed it behind him, where it shattered. Ellen walked steadily, with a purpose. "Before he lynched some ruffians, I told him he must let me amputate the limb of one of the wounded miscreants," Beckstead said. "I must amputate, I pleaded. And when he told me there was no need, that the man would be dead directly, I protested." The laughter resumed. Ellen saw the main street just a few steps ahead. "But deep down, when he did not listen to me, damn his soul and mine to hell, I could have kissed him." He coughed, spit, and rolled over, now sobbing. "Could have kissed him. Could have kissed him. What a fool I was to come here. What a fool to become a surgeon. What a fool to fall in love . . ."

Reaching the corner, she turned back to the wastrel. When he stopped gagging and rolling amid the trash, she said, "I thought, as a doctor, you took an oath."

He rose, again wiped his bloody face, and said, his voice suddenly quiet, but steady: "Drunk and wretched as I am, Ellen, the best physician in the world could do nothing for the professor, I regret to say. Like there is nothing to be done for me."

She turned the corner, did not stop, did not look back.

"Fill every barrel, every canteen, every bottle we have, every flask," Story barked. "Filled to the brim, and then drink your fill." He pointed northwest. "It's sixty miles to

Fort Reno, and unless it rains, we might not see any water till we hit the Powder."

Holding his dust-covered hat, Jameson Hannah wiped the sweat off his forehead with his arm, and barked, "You heard the man. Get to it." After pulling the hat back on his head, he nodded at Story. "Sixty miles? No water? Honest?"

Story had uncorked his canteen, and now submerged it into the stream. "Yes," he said. "Maybe a shallow pool here and there. Maybe just sand."

"Didn't know there was desert in Dakota Territory."

Rising, Story corked the canteen, and slung it over the horn on his saddle, and wiped his face with his moist hands. "It's not desert. It's just dry."

Rolling prairie swept out before them, seemingly as endless as the sky, the browning grass waving like ocean waves, broken up by islands of rocky hillsides of sandstone and sage, and at the end of the ocean, the distant purple outline of the Rockies, which looked like it would take forever to reach. No antelope, no birds, no Indians. No trees, no prairie dogs. The Dry Fork of the Cheyenne meandered through this Spartan country like a weaving drunk, but cowboys and teamsters obeyed Story and began kneeling on the banks or wading into the shallow water. Others ran to the rocks to relieve themselves.

Connor Lehman dipped his hat in the water, dumped it over his head, and put the hat on his head, then barked orders at his men. "When your team has cooled off, take them downstream and let them drink. While they're cooling off, get our water barrels filled."

"We'll rest them here," Hannah told Story, "take them through the country slow and steady."

"No," said Story. "We'll move them hard and fast. Twenty miles a day."

Hannah stepped back and looked at the wagon boss for help.

"Story." Water dripped off Lehman's face and fingers. "That can't be done."

"It will be done. Three days, no more than four, we need to be at this new post, this Fort Reno."

Hannah wet his lips. "If it's Indians you're worried about, we haven't seen—"

"I'm worried about Indians, I'm worried about winter, I'm worried about lots of things," Story said. "Right now I'm worried most about getting across Thunder Basin and the Pumpkin Buttes to the Powder River. Once we get there, I'll worry about something else."

"An oxen can't make twenty miles a day for three days, Story," Lehman said.

"And cattle can't cover that much ground, either," Hannah said. "Especially when there's no water to be had."

"I say it will be done," Story said. "By God, we'll do it."

Lehman glanced at Hannah and started to speak, when someone shrieked from the rocks on the other side of the river. Hannah drew his revolver, and Story stepped back toward the bank.

A boy sprinted, stumbled, came up, holding his right arm. José Pablo Tsoyio hurried across the stream and raced toward the fallen kid. "It's . . ." said Boone, who had been kneeling in the stream, letting the water cool his feet. Now Boone splashed across Dry Fork.

"Sibrian," Story whispered. He scanned the rocks for Indians, for anything. The cook reached the young wrangler, lifted him into his arms, and ran back, meeting Boone along the way. When Boone offered to help, the cook did not stop, reached the stream, crossed it, and laid the boy in the closest shade he could find on the bank.

"Madre de Dios." Tsoyio stared at José Sibrian's left forearm. "He has been bitten . . . by a rattlesnake."

That evening, after Tsoyio had cut Sibrian's arm and sucked as much blood and poison as he could manage, after the teamster named Rogers had given the wrangler a little brandy, after Constance Beckett had held his hand and kissed his forehead good-night, Story found Luke Beckner at the campfire.

"Preacher," Story said. "What the hell are you doing here, sipping coffee and talking horseshit with Stubbings and Melean?"

Beckner looked for help, found none, and Story went on: "You're a man of the cloth, aren't you?"

"Mr. Story, I know some scripture, I've read the Good Book cover to cover a dozen or more times but . . ."

"Get off your ass, damn you, and get over to Sibrian. Pray for him. That's your job for tonight. It's your job for as long as it takes. And I'm holding you and your damned God accountable." Story turned, went back to his horse, mounted it, and rode out to night-herd.

Luke Beckner blinked, glanced at Stubbings, Melean, then at others who stared at him, and quickly rose, went to his saddle and bedroll, found the Bible, and walked to the Studebaker where the cook sat with the young wrangler.

PART IV
Autumn

CHAPTER SIXTY-FOUR

Little Montana squalled no matter what Ellen tried. The baby didn't want to eat. Her diaper remained dry. She would kick and bawl when Ellen tried to rock her; she fidgeted when Ellen tried to hold her. And now someone knocked on the cabin door. Probably, Ellen thought as she laid the baby in the cradle and crossed the rug, someone complaining about the noise—likely all the way from Summit.

The door opened, and color drained from her face. Patrick Walsh, printer for the *Montana Post*, stood solemnly, hat in hand, head bowed.

It wouldn't be Nelson, she thought. The new editor would come for that, along with the mayor and a group of women. "Missus Story," the Irishman said. "He has gone to Glory."

Nodding, Ellen balled her fingers into her hands.

"Mr. Blake, ma'am, you know, my new boss at the *Post*, he thought maybe . . . maybe you'd like to sit with Missus Dimsdale." Then he seemed to hear Montana's shrieks for the first time. "Ummm . . . well . . . if it's not . . . ummm . . ."

Relief swept through her, but the same feeling also troubled her. "Yes, of course. As soon as this little tigress calms down. Patrick, can you find Missus Martin, see if Grace can sit with Montana? I don't know how long I shall be away."

"I'll find her, ma'am."

"When did he pass?"

"Around two-thirty this morn. Mr. Blake's getting something in today's paper. Won't be much. And the paper will be late. Funeral's tomorrow. Masons are planning something special."

"I'll be there."

"Yes, ma'am. I'll find Missus Martin." He put his hat on. "It's a blessing, really, ma'am. He won't suffer no more."

"I know, Patrick." She smiled faintly. The printer left, the door closed, and Ellen leaned against it, drowning out Montana's wails.

It was a blessing. Consumption was a curse. Professor Thomas J. Dimsdale finally found peace. Ellen breathed in deeply, exhaled, brushed away a tear, then shivered. For a moment, she feared Walsh would say that Seth Beckstead was dead.

"I never got to see a beaver." Tears welled in José Sibrian's eyes.

Smiling faintly, José Pablo Tsoyio jutted his jaw toward the distant mountains. "When you have healed," he said quietly in Spanish, "I will show you a beaver." He brought his right hand to his lips and extended the first two fingers, wiggling them. "Their teeth will bring a smile to your lips. And their tails make a beautiful noise." He placed the wet rag over the wrangler's forehead and drew back the blanket covering Sibrian's arm. Nodding, he returned the blanket and started to rise.

"How does it look?" Fear showed in Sibrian's eyes.

"You are a lucky young man, José." Tsoyio chuckled. "I have known many men, and some women, four horses, and more dogs than I can count in Texas that have been bitten by rattlesnakes. All, except a few dogs and one horse, a mare, old, too, have lived. You are not a dog or an old mare, but you, my young friend, are the first I have met to have found a rattlesnake in the Dakota Territory. There are not as many here as back in our homeland. Was he hard to find, José?"

Sibrian tried to laugh.

"I will bring you some tea. Can you eat?"

The wrangler's head shook.

"Tea is better for you than food." José Pablo Tsoyio walked away, ignoring Luke Beckner, who looked up as Tsoyio passed.

"How's he doing?" Beckner asked quietly.

Tsoyio did not stop, did not answer.

Residents from the Fourteen Mile City filled the new cemetery, and more trailed all the way back into Virginia City, bundled up against the cold, Free and Accepted Masons looking resplendent, army veterans in their uniforms, women, children—some whom Dimsdale had taught, others who never knew him—every minister, hundreds more than even read the *Montana Post*.

Three-thirty in the September afternoon felt like dawn in February, but the weather did not stop the band from blowing on cold, brass instruments. Strangers crowded together, the nearness keeping them warm, listening as Justice Hosmer, a brother of Montana Lodge No. 2, read the resolutions: ". . . with dignity to himself, and with profit to his brethren. Favored alike by nature and culture, with a well-disciplined mind and a ripe scholarship, he was a wise counselor, an intelligent lecturer, and a most affable and genial companion. In friendship . . ."

Two other Masons steadied Dimsdale's sobbing widow. The priest and other ministers bowed their heads. Henry Blake, the *Post*'s new editor, who realized he could never replace the professor, scribbled notes. And Ellen Story kept looking down the hillside, into Virginia City.

"You and your damned God." Story reached for the worn Bible Luke Beckner clutched, but the cowboy jerked it back, holding it tightly against his chest. "I should have asked the damned Jew to pray."

"I did pray," Connor Lehman said, and Story turned away from the cowhand, took one step, and stared at the wagon boss. "Sometimes God's answer is no," Lehman spoke respectfully.

"Believe what you want," Story said. He looked down at the blanket covering the body of José Sibrian. His head rose, he searched faces, all solemn, mostly bowed, though Story figured half of those were in mourning, the other half just scared to death of catching Story's glare. "Peña," he barked, and when the Mexican looked up, Story ordered: "You're wrangler. I know, but you're better with horses than anyone else. Boone, move up to point. Melean, you're across from Stubbings here at swing. Ward, that means you're up to flank. That means the rest of you on drag are shorthanded. Don't make a mistake."

Another look at the draped corpse.

"Bring me a shovel," Story said.

"Jake," Lehman said. "Bring a pick and three shovels. We'll—"

"One shovel," Story said. "I'll dig the grave. Then you can say whatever you want over the kid."

"*Con permiso,* I shall get stones to cover his grave, *patrón,*" José Pablo Tsoyio said.

"You can't," John Catlin whispered.

"*¿Qué?*"

"He's right," Story said. "Peña, you'll have to drive the remuda over him." He nodded to the east. "Make it harder for any Indians to desecrate . . ." After spitting, Story raised his head. "I'm still waiting on that damned shovel."

Brother Hosmer concluded the Masons' resolutions, and the Baptist minister stepped forward, taking over for the Catholic, announcing he would lead everyone in prayer. Before bowing her head, Ellen Story looked down the hill, at every building draped with black crepe, at the men on the boardwalks staring up the hillside. Ellen dabbed her eyes. She wondered if Seth Beckstead were among them watching below.

"It's not your fault."

Story turned from the Dry Fork to find Constance Beckett, still dressed in men's duds, at the top of the embankment. "I never said it was my fault," Story said.

"You're not as hard as you think you are," Constance said.

"I'm hard enough." He nodded toward the circle of wagons. "If you're not going to pray over the kid's grave, hitch your team. We're pulling out as soon as they finish." He looked west. "Got a few hours of daylight."

"People die every day," she said.

Story kept staring at the blue mountains, so far away.

"I never thanked you," she said.

His reply came instantly. "Don't. I don't want your thanks. Just do your job."

She let out a mirthless laugh and started toward the grave of poor, unlucky José Sibrian. "What kind of woman would marry you?" she said.

"A good one," she heard him answer after a long while. That stopped her, and she glanced over at him, still looking toward the mountains, and he let out a mirthless laugh. "If you can believe that."

Again, she started to leave, but he called her name, and once more, she looked at him. This time he stared at her.

"Put Hobo in the back of your wagon. Don't let him walk. We have three, maybe four, damned hard days ahead of us."

Ellen walked to Nettie Dimsdale, took her hand into her own, squeezed it, leaned forward, and kissed the widow's cheek. She thanked all the preachers, and the Masons, and the director of the band.

Justice Hosmer asked if she needed him to escort her to her home, but she smiled kindly and shook her head.

She walked with the throng down the hill, no longer wondering if Seth Beckstead were on the streets. She looked east, biting her lower lip, trying to stop any tears from forming, praying to God to keep her husband alive.

Luke Beckner prayed. Some men crossed themselves. Fabian Peña, Kelvin Melean, and three teamsters knelt. José Pablo Tsoyio reached down, picked up a handful of sand, and dropped it onto the covered body.

"We ought to sing," Dalton Combs said. "Before we cover him up."

"We ain't exactly harmonic angels," George Overholt said.

"And that hard-ass is eager to move," McPherson said.

"Anybody got any suggestions as to what we ought to sing?" Beckner asked.

Molly McDonald heard herself laugh, but when she looked at the grave, she frowned, pulled the tobacco out of her mouth, and she stepped to the grave's edge. "I remember this one, boys," she said, and began.

What a friend we have in Jesus,
All our sins and griefs to bear.
What a privilege to carry
Everything to God in prayer.

She made it through the third verse before stopping, knowing she had loused up a few words, and realizing she couldn't remember anything past "Blessed Savior" of the final verse. When she lifted her head, she jammed the hat on her head, saw the faces of cowboys and teamsters, and she cackled before starting for the wagons.

"That ain't nothing, boys," she said. "You should've heard me back when I could hit them high C notes."

CHAPTER SIXTY-FIVE

Since nobody could see him, Story took a long time dismounting, then stretched his back before Jameson Hannah rode up on his worn-out bay. "Bed the herd down here," Story ordered. "Have Lehman keep the wagons in a circle, the oxen on the inside."

Moonbeams sneaked through the clouds, illuminating the dry bed of Antelope Creek.

"Your longhorns are thirsty," Hannah said.

Story nodded at the dry sand. "They'll be thirsty till we hit the Powder."

Traces jingled and the wheels squeaked as José Pablo Tsoyio's wagon pulled into view, stopping at the edge of the dry creek bed.

"Coffee for supper," Story said. "The men'll have to eat hardtack and jerky, but fill them up for breakfast. We move at first light."

He walked down the sandy creek bed, trying to get the blood flowing in his legs again, not letting anyone see how much he hurt. His horse was worn out, too, and when he figured no one could see or hear him, he groaned, bent over, and massaged the backs of his thighs, flinching at the touch.

Twenty miles. Even after covering a few miles the day

before, today had been brutal. The calendar might have read autumn—Story wasn't entirely sure about the date—but the weather still felt like summer. When he finally straightened, he wiped his eyes, feeling the grit on his face. The horse snorted, and Story rubbed its neck.

Wagons, cattle, horses, and riders arrived at the camp, bringing with them moans, curses, sighs, and, once they learned they would get just a few hours of sleep—unless they happened to be assigned night-herd or sentry duties— and push on at daybreak, the grumbles and oaths grew louder. The last person they would want to see was Nelson Story, so he grabbed the horn, tried for the stirrup, missed, tried again, and finally lifted himself back into the seat.

The gelding's head hung, until Story lifted the reins. "I know." He patted the dun's neck again. "But we aren't done yet."

He found Fabian Peña first, decided against changing horses.

"*¿Hay agua aquí?*" the wrangler asked.

"No water," Story replied. His Spanish kept improving. If he didn't watch out, people might start mistaking him for a Texan, answering a Mexican's question, spoken in Spanish, in English.

"We might find some pools tomorrow—today, I mean— on the trail. But don't count on it." He hooked his thumb toward the glow of the campfire. "Get some coffee. Then stay with the horses. I'll make sure Lehman sends some guards."

His next stop came when he met up with the two night-hawks, Boone and McWilliams, told them they wouldn't get any sleep this night, and rode to the wagons, where Lehman ordered the drivers to grease the axles, grain the oxen, then get their coffee and hit their bedrolls.

"What about water?" McPherson asked.

Story answered before Lehman. "Maybe tomorrow. But don't count on it." He told Lehman, "I want two sentries with the horses."

"We didn't see any sign of Indians all day or all night," George Overholt snapped.

Story turned to the bullwhacker. "Well, George, since you've got such damned good eyesight, and since you're familiar with our horses from riding along with them the past few days, I guess you'll be right for guard duty. Pick his partner, Lehman."

Overholt's face flushed, but he turned to his wagon and pulled out the Remington, put his thumb on the hammer, and let his malevolent eyes tell Story what he thought.

"You want to use it, make your play," Story said.

"I ain't that pissed off." Overholt moved toward the horse herd, calling back, "Just yet."

Lehman turned to the teamsters. "Go with him, Collins," he said. "You know the horses, too. I'll send somebody with some coffee in an hour or two." As the bullwhacker grabbed his rifle and walked away, the wagon boss walked to Story's side, looked up, and said in a quiet but firm tone: "Push anything hard, it breaks. Including men."

"They're well paid."

The smile did not match Lehman's eyes. "They haven't been paid yet."

"They knew the terms. Payment at end of trail. Virginia City." Lehman's head kept shaking, and Story leaned low. "If we don't get there, nobody gets paid. Including you."

He rode back to the cook, climbed out of the saddle, and saw most of the cowhands guzzling down coffee. Stubbings rode in after scouting the back trail, but before he could swing out of the saddle, Story called out, "Not yet."

Lehman had given him an idea, not that it would prove to the men that Story did have something resembling a heart. "Take some coffee to McWilliams and Boone. They'll be watching the herd while you boys get some sleep."

Stubbings looked at Combs, and the cook, then back at Story. "There's a small coffeepot in the wagon. Fill it up." He spoke as if explaining this to a child. "Bring two cups with you—three, if you'd like to be sociable and drink with them. And try not to spill any on your horse." He turned to the others. "Drink down your supper quickly and get as much sleep as you can. We move out in four hours."

Finally, he eased the dun toward the remuda.

The pounding never ceased, grew louder, until Seth Beckstead rolled over, pressed his hands against both ears, and screamed—and still someone hammered until the door gave way, and someone jerked Beckstead off the floor.

"Doc . . ." The breath stank of whiskey. "Doc . . . you gotta help. My two girls . . . they's sick."

He felt like laughing. What damned fool would come to "Doc Forty-Rod"—the moniker anointed him in the Fourteen Mile City—at this time of . . . ? His eyes opened, darted past the walking whiskey vat, to find blackness.

"Get someone else," Beckstead managed. He and Sparhan had hung their shingle in a one-room hut that was more lean-to than home, but the owner had run off to Helena, like so many others, and while the logs didn't keep out most of the wind, a man could walk to Iverson's Saloon—if he had money, which Beckstead did not.

"Please, Doc." He coughed, and Beckstead again caught the scent of alcohol. He had been sleeping on the floor here for . . . it didn't matter. What mattered was he hadn't had a drink in more than a day, and this man smelled like John Barleycorn, perhaps he had some, and if not, he would have to pay for a doctor's visit.

"Where do you live?"

"Corner of Fremont and Broadway."

Damn. Couldn't it be closer? That was a haul. Rough hands lifted Beckstead off the floor. When he stood, he brought his arms up hard, knocking his captor aside. "Unhand me, sir," Beckstead said, surprised to find himself standing without support. "I shall be with you directly. Let me find my bag."

The man staggered to the door, coughing, spitting onto the dark street. Fumbling, Beckstead found his hat, Doc Sparhan's bag, grabbed a stethoscope, some pills and balms, let the wave of nausea pass, and tried to smile. "Lead the way, sir."

CHAPTER SIXTY-SIX

A hand squeezed his shoulder, and Story's eyes flashed open. His left arm swung up, knocked the hand away, while Story palmed the Colt on his lap with his right hand. He cursed himself for falling asleep, heard a sharp gasp, then, "It's me."

He did not recognize the voice until she repeated the words, and in the moonlight, he saw her sprawling on the sandy creek bed. By then Story had come to his knees, his thumb cocking the .36. He cursed again, lowered the hammer, shoved the revolver back into the holster.

A hundred yards off, the cook prepared breakfast, though from the moon's position, they had an hour, maybe more, before the men would be roused. Turning, he stepped toward Constance Beckett and held out his right hand. "Take it," he told her. When she did, he pulled her up, and waited.

"You were dreaming," she said after brushing off her trousers. "Sounded like a nightmare."

"It wasn't. You shouldn't be out here."

"Nature's call."

"Oh." He turned around, studied the graying sky. "It'd be better to stay closer to camp."

"For you," she said.

He made himself look at her and almost smiled. "I see your point."

"I heard you when I was walking back." She shrugged, then laughed. "I don't think I'll be going back to sleep. Maybe I'll see if José has coffee ready. Want some?"

He tried to say *no*, but a *yeah* came out.

A few minutes later, he took the steaming mug from her hand, thanked her, and stood in the predawn darkness like an oaf.

"What was the dream?" she asked.

He studied the steam of the coffee. "Same. I'm burying a dog. Digging a grave."

"Hobo?"

His eyes raised. Maybe he made a slight nod.

"You said your father shot him."

He tested the coffee, but it was too hot, even for Nelson Story the Blackhearted Son of a Bitch to drink. "Dog was old, had the mange, suffering." He kept looking at the cup.

"Oh," he heard her say, followed by her soft footfalls.

"I thought . . ." He stopped. Slowly, she turned.

"You know much about dreams?" He moved the cup closer to his lips, made himself look at her. "I thought . . . the dream was a warning. Then I buried Sibrian. What the hell did that mean? That Sibrian was no better than a dog? That I worked him like a dog?" He felt his head shake. "Now I'm still dreaming that same damn dream. What's it mean?"

Constance shook her head. "I'm sorry," she said. "I know nothing about dreams."

She returned to the wagons, and Story cursed himself for being half-asleep, talking flapdoodle to a woman, revealing just a sliver about himself to a damned stranger. He almost pitched the coffee into the dirt, but knew better than to waste water. His head lifted, and he said, "Constance."

Although she stopped, she did not look back.

"Keep Hobo in the back of the wagon," Story said. "Give him some water. Yesterday was hell. Today will be a damned sight worse."

Again, she started, again Story spoke. Maybe because he remained half-asleep.

"I don't know about dreams, either. I had one. To get a herd of cattle to Wyoming, make my pile, keep my wife from working herself to death like her ma's doing, and my mother did. Had dreams off and on about me burying my dog. Hell, I don't know which one is crazier."

Ellen sat up, gasping, eyes darting, recognizing Montana's cries and what must have been a battering ram on the door that made the entire cabin shudder. Muffled shouts came from outside, but Ellen couldn't make out much of anything with the pounding of the door and the ear-ringing wails of her baby. Flinging off the blanket, she found a robe and stormed to the door.

"I'll be there, honey," she snapped at her daughter, grabbed the latch, and . . .

"Nelson?" Her face paled. News? Bad news? She pulled the robe tighter, tried to breathe, and opened the door.

The wild-eyed man in front of her almost made her scream. "Ellen. Are you all right?"

His breath stank. The body reeked. He had not bathed in weeks. Beard covered his face, but the voice. Dear God.

Montana wailed.

"Seth Beckstead," Ellen snapped. "How dare you."

The impertinent drunkard pushed past her and looked across the room at the cradle. "Montana? Is she sick?"

"No, you dumb son of a bitch," Ellen barked. "You woke her up. And scared the life out of me." She hit his chest with a balled fist, then again, and yelled—not caring who heard— "Get out of my house, damn you. Get out."

He grabbed her wrists, pulled her close, and now fear replaced Ellen's anger.

"Are you all right?"

Wretched breath made her turn away. She trembled.

"Sore throat. Cough? Is Montana all right?"

The baby cried louder.

"Let me see my baby," Ellen cried.

"Are you all right?"

"Yes. Yes. We are fine. Please, let me care for my baby."

When the vise released, she wanted to rake his flesh with her nails, but he started backing toward the door. "Stay here. Stay with Montana," he said. "You should not leave the house until I tell you . . ."

The anger returned. She stepped to him, and spit venom. "This is my house. You will not tell me what I shall and shan't do." She started to gouge him, but he struck first, the slap stunning her, staggering her, and she might have fallen had he not caught her arms and pulled her close to him again.

He whispered urgently. "Ellen. Listen to me. It's . . . diphtheria." He let go, ran for the door, stopping once and turning. "If you or Montana cough. A sore throat. Even if you think it's just a cold, for God's sake, find me. Please."

And vanished into the early dawn.

The brown gelding moved close to the brindle cow, and Story lashed out with the lariat. "Move." He struck again. Breathing through a dust-caked bandanna, he coughed, tried to blink the grime out of his eyes, and heard his name called. Turning the gelding away, he rode through dust and haze and bawling cattle, away from the cow, realizing she would never make it, not even to the Pumpkin Buttes, let alone the Powder River.

The cowboy waved his hat, and when Story got close, he realized it was George Dow, on his feet, holding the reins to a bay gelding. Story swore, thinking the horse had gone lame, only to realize this was worse than a lame horse.

"I can't get him up, boss," Dow said.

Story stared at the calf lying in trampled grass. He swore again, the weak bawling of cattle echoing all around him in the haze, and nodded at the cowhand. "Finish him," he said.

Dow's eyes widened, but Story just stared harder. "Now," he said, but when the drag rider reached for his revolver, Story shook his head. "Not with that."

"Oh." Dow bowed his head. "Right. Stampede."

Let him think that, Story thought. *Stampede? These cattle are too sore, too tired, to run ten yards.* But he waited until Dow had drawn the knife from his vest pocket and unfolded the blade. When the cowboy knelt by the dying calf, Story turned his horse away and moved into the dust.

Story traveled less than a hundred yards before he had to dismount, to slit the throat of a straggling year-old steer.

* * *

"I don't believe it is diphtheria," Mayor J. M. Castner said. "It can't be. Not in Virginia City. In our existence, this city has seen no outbreaks of scarlet fever, no typhus fever, no cholera." He pointed a long finger at Beckstead and continued to scold the doctor from his perch on the boardwalk in front of the *Montana Post.* "We sit at more than five thousand seven hundred feet above the tidewater, sir, and our climate is the healthiest in the territory, certainly better than Helena's."

"What do you think, Dr. Yager?" the newspaper editor, Henry Blake, asked a balding man wearing bifocals and a long plaid coat.

"I have not examined Dr. Beckstead's poor family, but I have found no signs of diphtheria among my patients." He smiled the smile of a jackass. "A boy with the croup, two girls with tonsillitis. Mostly, my patients have been—"

"A boy? Girls?" Beckstead interrupted. "Did they attend the new school?"

Yager's smile vanished. "Doctor, those are my—"

"Were they at the school, damn you?"

Yager became flustered. "I don't know. I suppose . . . maybe . . . but I tell you this is not . . ."

"Oh, it's diphtheria," said the old man with a missing right hand who sat with his legs crossed on the other side of the street.

"And how would you know?" The mayor let out a humorless sigh and painted a grin as he waved toward Beckstead and Dr. Sparhan, then spoke to the gathered crowd. "Our two most accomplished drunks are diagnosing diphtheria and trying to spread fear throughout our community." He whirled toward Henry Blake. "I tell you, Henry, these men have been bribed by the nefarious scoundrels in Helena who want to steal the territorial capital from us."

A few men whispered, and Blake started to ask a question but the old man across the street stopped everyone.

"I lost my wife to diphtheria." Sparhan's soft voice carried across the street. "My son. My mother-in-law." He lifted his gaze. "I may be a drunk, gentlemen, but I have seen that family on Fremont Street. And it is diphtheria. And if you don't listen to my colleague, you will see the wrath of God— as I saw . . . ten years ago . . . in California."

Chapter Sixty-seven

That Indiana farm, John Catlin found himself thinking about once more, couldn't have been all that bad. He had a town to go to, a church when he felt like it, women to fancy, some even to talk to. Newspapers to read. Fresh milk. People. Yet here he was, in the middle of nowhere, with a linen rag over his mouth and nose to keep from choking, on the back of a skittish Texas cow pony, pulling guard duty to keep a bunch of unseen Indians from stealing a bunch of other bony, wiry, half-broke horses. Bracing the butt of his Enfield against his thigh, he felt autumn's first bite.

A rider appeared, loping hard toward the remuda, and Catlin tightened his grip on the Enfield. No Indian, he decided. At least, he didn't see any feathers. Black horse. He relaxed, recognizing the figure as Jameson Hannah, who slowed to a trot and spoke to the Mexican wrangler, Fabian Peña, pointed northwest, then rode to Isaac Collins, another teamster turned guardian of horses, and finally reached Catlin, who reined up.

"Water up ahead," Hannah said. "You boys will hold the horses here till Peña says they've cooled off. Then let them drink."

That was all. Hannah loped off to tell Overholt, riding rear guard, the same thing.

Ahead, Peña began stopping the horses, letting them graze. Catlin watched the longhorns keep going, and the wagons, including the one he should be riding in with Steve Grover. They followed the Dry Fork of the Powder River to the big river—*big* as you might find in this country, anyway—and Story had told them pools of water might be found before they hit the Powder. His canteen was empty, his throat ached, and he knew those cowboys' horses, teamsters' oxen and mules, and a thousand Texas longhorns . . . hell . . . they'd drink the water first, and what would be left for the ponies, and Catlin, would be mostly mud.

After Tibbetts's hearse stopped at the cabin on the corner of Fremont and Broadway, Seth Beckstead stepped out of the cabin and nodded at the undertaker. That fancy rig had been shipped in all the way from Rochester, New York, back in '64, when ten thousand people crammed into Alder Gulch. Or so Beckstead had been told. Tibbetts must have spent a fortune on the hearse alone, what with its bouquet holders, white curtains with gold fringe and tassels, and black-and-white plumes.

"The girls are inside." Beckstead's voice was hoarse.

Old Tibbetts nodded at the burly miners who had been walking behind the hearse. Bundled up with heavy coats, gloves, caps, and bandannas, the men grimly walked to the cabin.

"I'll likely send for you in a day or two," Beckstead managed. "For Missus O'Ryan." Hell, he could use a drink today. "And Mr. O'Ryan's in bed now."

"Dr. Mathews has two cases," Tibbetts said. "Dr. Justice, three."

"How about the rest of the Fourteen Mile City?" asked Dr. Sparhan as he stepped out of the cabin.

Sheriff Andrew Snyder, mounted on a white stallion that trailed the hearse, snorted. "Doc Whitford in Nevada City won't let anyone from Virginia City come through town."

"Bring the sick here," Beckstead said. "Then you'll have just one place to burn when the last of the dead is buried."

"Bring them to my cabin," an Irish brogue rang out across the street, and a tall, well-dressed man stepped into the dirt.

"Meagher, you can't do that," the sheriff said. "You just can't."

"As acting governor of this territory, I can do whatever I want to do." Thomas Meagher stepped off the boardwalk and walked around the matched pair of gray Andalusian stallions, stopping at the edge of the O'Ryan cabin. Despite the chill, Meagher wore no hat, and the wind whipped his unruly dark hair. Probably in his forties, he wore a silk cravat and Gaelic cross, and stuffed his hands inside the pockets of a Union blue greatcoat, and walked toward Beckstead.

Meagher stopped a few feet from the cabin. "I hear you served in our late army," he said.

"Second Baltimore, General."

"Governor." The laugh brightened Meagher's face. "Acting governor, my rivals will point out, or dictator. Secretary if you prefer. Drunkard if you wish to be accurate."

"Then we are brothers-in-arms." Beckstead smiled.

"My cabin is yours, Doctor." Meagher turned serious.

"Thank you, but there's no need."

"What can be done?"

Now Beckstead sighed. "We know so little about diphtheria. What causes it. How it spreads. Treatments range from calomel to bleedings, and they are all worthless. The only way to stop it is to catch it early." A thought seized him, and he stepped aside as the miners carried the shrouded body of the first girl to the hearse.

"The school," he yelled. "Have you closed the school?" The new public school had just been built, opened this term. Before that, school had been held in one of Virginia City's churches.

"School just opened," the sheriff snapped.

"Then close it. And if any of the children feel sick—sore throat, cough, cold, anything—they must be treated immediately."

"But . . ." someone started.

Meagher spun around, and roared, "You pimps and poltroons can either help this valiant surgeon or you can watch what's left of Virginia City become a morgue. Close the school." He pointed at the *Post* editor, busily taking notes. "Blake, print notices and have them posted all across the Fourteen Mile City."

"You can't do that," J. B. Chapin, owner of the Planter's House, thundered. "You'll send this city into a panic, and no one will come here."

"Meaning no one will stay in your first-class hotel," Tibbetts said.

"He's not the governor," Chapin preached to the men across the street. "He's a damned secretary who has become a despot. I'll write President Johnson, sir." He turned back, waving a finger, either at Beckstead or Meagher or both.

What brought men out like this, Beckstead wondered,

in the cold, to stare across the street at a house filled with sick people? As the sheriff dismounted to open the door to the hearse, Chapin and Tibbetts continued their bitter banter until Beckstead lashed out with profanity that left everyone silent, and staring at him.

"That's an eight-year-old girl," Beckstead said. "*Eight.* Have you any decency? Any respect for a child? My God, I thought I saw the worst of mankind during the rebellion."

He disappeared inside the cabin.

When the lead steers broke into a run, Boone spurred his chestnut gelding. Bawling, the rest of the longhorns stampeded. "Let 'em run, Boone," Dalton Combs shouted across the herd, waving his right hand forward. "They smell water. It's the Powder."

Loping alongside the cattle, sweating despite the cold, Boone thought he could smell water himself. The herd hit the water at a run, wading in, drinking, splashing, and Boone and Combs rode in with them. Boone cheered. Combs whipped off his hat, leaned in the saddle, filled the crown with water, and dumped it over his head. It didn't matter that the temperature might have been in the fifties. Boone laughed harder and tried to copy Combs's actions, but slipped, and got a frigid Powder River bath.

Rising out of the cold water, he laughed, spit water out, found the stirrup, and pulled himself to his feet. He didn't even feel the cold—yet.

"You needed a bath," Combs yelled at him.

"Feels damned good," Boone said, and climbed back into the saddle, urging the chestnut downstream, letting the rest of the cattle drift into the water or move along the banks, drinking their fill.

Twisting in the saddle, Boone watched the rest of the caravan, the running longhorns, the remuda, the wagons. Then the cold hit him, and he shivered.

At the edge of the river, Story sat in the saddle on his blood bay gelding, letting his horse drink.

The son of a bitch, Boone thought, *looks just like Moses.* He wiped his soaking face with his wet hand, then reached back to find the coat strapped behind the cantle.

José Pablo Tsoyio stepped back from the pot of beans and the coffeepot and watched the riders come toward the camp. All banter, all joking ceased, replaced by metallic clicks of hammers being cocked.

"Easy." Story had been going over tomorrow's plan with Hannah and Lehman. Now he stood. "Keep the rifles out, and make a show of loading them. Same with the revolvers. Show them our arsenal, but no one fires a shot." Before he stepped toward the old-but-grim warrior in the long, feathered bonnet, Story nodded at Tsoyio, who followed the tall man to about a dozen Indian warriors, well mounted, formidable, and scary as lost souls in purgatory.

Story stopped a few rods in front of the leader, but Tsoyio walked straight to the Indian—Sioux, Tsoyio figured, though he had heard they did not care much for that name, preferring to be called Lakota.

When Tsoyio made the sign, the tall man with bold features, black eyes, and a Roman nose seemed impressed. After handing his lance to the rider on his right, he raised his hands and began signing to Tsoyio.

"He says his name is Four Elks," Tsoyio said.

"Tell him mine."

A moment later, Tsoyio said, "He says he likes his name better."

"Tell him I never thought much of mine, either."

That, Tsoyio was pleased to see, made Four Elks grin.

"They're peaceful," Tsoyio called back to Story after the next round, and whispered, "For now." None of the Lakotas' faces had been painted for war, nor did their horses wear paint. The leader's hands moved again.

"We are in his country," Tsoyio translated. "His hunting grounds. We are trespassing."

"Tell him we have hunted no buffalo, no antelope, not even rabbits or birds. And taken no fish from this river."

"Don't think they eat fish," Tsoyio said. "Same as Comanches." He moved his hands and fingers, and waited. Then: "Four Elks says you may move through his country at peace, as long as you move fast, but he would like twenty-five beeves."

Story answered immediately, "No."

Hannah whispered, "He didn't bring all his men with him. No telling how many he has backing his play."

Lehman added: "And he is right. This is his land. He has a right to ask for a toll."

"He's not talking to either of you," Story said without looking back. "He's talking to me. And he sees our fire-power." He cleared his throat. "Tell him we will pass through quickly and that we will not come back. Tell him I need these cattle to feed my family, my child. They are hungry, too."

Tsoyio's hands moved. Four Elks's did not.

"He is welcome to coffee," Story said, but the Lakota turned his horse around before Tsoyio could make the sign, and the rest of the warriors followed him into the darkness.

Chapter Sixty-eight

"Four drops of carbolic acid," Dr. Mathews said. "Milk punch. Ice." Sighing, he lifted the tin cup to his mouth, only to realize he had not refilled it with coffee. "No one has any idea how to cure this terrible illness."

"Eat fish," Doc Sparhan said with a smile. "That's why folks don't get sick on Fridays."

The fire burned furiously, but the chimney sucked most of the heat with the smoke out of the cabin. Six more patients had been brought in during the day, though Dr. Justice and others decided to keep theirs either at the homes of the sick or in the office.

And the first day was just ending.

"I read in *Scientific American*," Dr. Mathews said, "that we should heat pitch tar on a flat iron, and blow the smoke through a funnel into a patient's mouth for several minutes. Six times a day, more if necessary. After that put ice pieces all the way to the roots of the patient's tongue." He sighed. "That was in *Scientific American*. Humans and doctors, for we are not human, will grasp at anything."

Seth Beckstead shook his head. "I knew a man in Baltimore who said breathing fumes from burning sulfur deeply would cure him." Beckstead heard the braying mule and jingling trace chain and knew someone was bringing in another patient, so he pulled himself to his feet and walked to the door.

"Did it cure him?" Mathews asked.

"Oh, yes." Beckstead opened the door. "We buried him." He saw the torches, a lantern, and stepped out, pulling the door closed to keep at least some semblance of warmth inside.

Two newly appointed deputies moved to the back of a buckboard and pulled a stretcher from the back. A lantern in the front of the wagon moved toward Beckstead and the cabin. When the arm raised, Beckstead recognized the face of Thomas Meagher.

"Governor." Beckstead nodded.

"Doctor. Two more. A thirteen-year-old boy from Pine Grove." That was the settlement between Virginia City and Summit. "And Miss Bass, the schoolteacher."

"It might have started at the school," Beckstead said. "Ask Dr. Justice and that nuisance in Nevada City to check all families of children in the new school. We might be able to stop this . . . if that's how this monster spreads."

Beckstead stepped back to open the door, letting the stretcher-bearers bring in the child. Like the war, all over again, except instead of bringing in men to scream as a saw cut through bone, these were children and ladies, too. The girl, he saw at a glance, already suffered from bull throat. She would likely require a tracheotomy to avoid paroxysmal spasms, violent tossing, gasping, suffocation.

Two other men unloaded Miss Bass, but one swore, whispered something, and they slid the stretcher back into the Studebaker. "This one's bound for Tibbetts," a man said.

When Beckstead stepped into the street and started for the wagon, those two men hurried away. Even the wagon driver stepped down and grabbed the harness to the mule. Meagher followed Beckstead, but kept a cautious distance.

Beckstead found his stethoscope, and when Meagher raised his lantern, the woman's eyes, staring but not seeing, and her mouth, open in desperation to suck in one more breath, told Beckstead everything. "Yes." Beckstead lowered the stethoscope. "She is gone."

"War," the Irishman said, "was never like this."

Oh, but it was, Beckstead wanted to tell him, to remind him of the dysentery, measles, cholera, and diphtheria he had seen, in addition to the savagery and agony of battlefield deaths—and the ceaseless amputations.

He started back for the cabin, but stopped and turned back to the acting governor.

"Governor, have you seen Missus Story?"

"No. Not in some time," Meagher whispered. Raising his head, he must have read Beckstead's face. "I guess she's well, Doctor. She and the little girl. But I shall check on them both before I retire."

Beckstead smiled.

"Doctor?" Meagher asked. "How do we fight this?"

"Like we fought the rebels," Beckstead said. "Like Nelson Story fought the banditti. Attack without delay." His voice faded as he spoke. "Without mercy. Don't overlook a cough, a cold, croup. The only way to beat this is to catch it early."

Sighing, Beckstead nodded at Meagher and returned to the cabin, hospital, morgue.

Molly McDonald leaned against the makeshift pillow jammed between the spokes of the wagon wheel and let out a contented sigh.

"Your beau might not have a heart," she told Constance, who lounged underneath the wagon, "but he does have a soul."

"He's not my beau, damn you," Constance said.

Molly laughed. The sun moved overhead, yet they remained at the Powder River, cattle scattered, a few boys fishing downstream. Nelson Story had promised those Indians that they wouldn't hunt game, but the Sioux didn't eat fish, so what the hell. Oh, Story still had the remuda well protected, and the oxen and mules were kept in camp behind the wagons—stinking up the place—but he had given the men at least half a day off.

It would soon be ending. Bill Petty started dragging the harness for his team from underneath his wagon.

Yeah, they'd be making their way to Fort Reno, which Story figured it couldn't be that far up the river. That, Molly knew, was why Story had let the men relax. Indians wouldn't be dumb enough to attack this close to a military post.

Petty dragged his rig, straightened, turned, opened his mouth, and slammed against the front of the wagon, tripping over the tongue, screaming before he hit the ground.

"Son of a bitch," Molly roared, realizing an arrow jutted out of Petty's shoulder.

All had been so peaceful—except for the stink of mule dung and Molly's incessant babbling—when Constance Beckett's world plunged into chaos. Hooves thundered, someone shrieked, Molly cursed and scrambled to her feet. A rifle roared. As Constance rolled over and crawled from underneath the wagon, she heard the cries, yips, singing. A mule brayed. Oxen snorted. Something thudded against the wagon.

The cattle ran.

Constance rose, tried to take everything in. Molly struggled to unfasten one of her bags, so she could fetch a pistol. Copper-skinned men with black hair and braids—bodies painted in myriad colors—rode about the camp, and around the longhorns. Last night, she had counted maybe a dozen, perhaps not even that many, Indians. Many more than that now struck the camp.

"Get down." . . . "Kill that red-skinned thief." . . . "Jesus Christ, save our souls." . . . "Look out." . . . Mostly, she heard profanity.

Her head swung. Indians drove longhorns across the Powder. One of the fishermen dived into the river and stayed down, out of sight. A red ox kicked the freight wagon. A riderless horse, saddled, bolted toward the distant buttes.

"Get down, Cory." That was Molly, still calling her by her alias. Constance moved her eyes. Molly had found that gun of hers. She raised the barrel, squeezed the trigger, cursed percussion caps.

Through thickening dust, Constance spotted Story, guns in both hands, one pointed at the ground, the other trying to catch up with a warrior who raced a pinto pony across the camp. Seeing something else, she ran.

Praying. Legs, still stiff and sore from riding in a miserable wagon for half of forever, carried her. Smelling gun smoke, dust, horses, oxen, her own stink despite what passed for a bath, clothes and all, in the river earlier this morning. Story's Navy barked once, twice, then he shoved it into the holster and tossed the weapon in his left hand to his right. It never got there.

Because Constance leaped, turning sideways, letting her body catch the back of Story's thighs. He cursed as he fell backward, and Constance hit the ground, felt the air rushing from her lungs as she rolled over, glimpsed the warrior on the skewbald, its tail tied up short, saw the spear—lance— whatever the hell Indians called those things—coming right at her, following her as she rolled toward Tsoyio's fire.

Story jerked the lance hard, and Constance Beckett gasped and placed her right hand against her side. Blood streamed between her fingers, but Story figured she'd live.

"That was a damned fool thing to do," he told her.

"Yes." Tears streamed down her cheeks. "It was."

He nodded at Boone. "Cauterize it. Get her patched up." Then yelled, "Catlin. Hannah. Tsoyio. Thompson. Overholt. Mount up. You're riding with me."

"Overholt isn't going anywhere," Connor Lehman said.

Story whirled to the wagon boss. "Dead?"

"No, but he wasn't as lucky as the girl. Lance got him in the thigh."

"All right. Collins, you're with us. Rest of you, get the horses, cattle, and wagons to Fort Reno. Have the sawbones there patch up the girl, Petty, Overholt, anyone else who needs it."

"Where's the fort?" Boone asked.

"How the hell would I know? It wasn't here last time I came through. But from what the boys said at Laramie, it's just up the river. Not far. Shit. I shouldn't have stopped till I got there. Get moving. The rest of you. Mount up and come with me."

"Where are you going?" Constance managed to ask.

"To get my damned cattle back."

CHAPTER SIXTY-NINE

The thieves, José Pablo Tsoyio knew, would be easy to follow. Twenty or thirty longhorns, the many unshod ponies of the Lakotas. One did not have to be Kit Carson to follow such a trail. It was the catching up with the Indians that worried José Pablo Tsoyio, and might explain why he kept reaching into his coat pocket and fingering the crucifix of poor young José Sibrian.

Tracks led northeast, but this country remained brand-new and strange to José Pablo Tsoyio. Texas was vast, Mexico, big. Yet the sky in this Dakota Territory reached from one end of the world to the other, making you feel you rode underneath a bowl. Still, as flat as the land seemed, there was no hiding place for—

The mule's ears flattened. Which is why José Pablo Tsoyio told Story he would ride a mule, not one of the skittish Texas cow ponies. Mules were tough, dependable, reliable . . . and they could smell an Indian or an Indian pony.

He jerked the reins, heard the shot to his left, and felt the rush of a leaden ball as it passed in front of him.

Raising his revolver, he spotted the warriors rising to his left. How they had remained hidden, keeping their horses lying on their sides and silent . . . well, the Lakotas could teach José Pablo Tsoyio many wonderful tricks, if they did not kill him. He snapped a shot, finding more Indians rising like Lazarus on the other side of the trail.

He kicked the mule's side, turned the jack, rode hard after dust raised by the horses of Story and his men as they bolted for the rocks. A feather flashed to his left, struck the ground about twenty yards in front of the mule. No, not a feather, but an arrow. Behind him came yips, war songs, crashing hooves. The rocks lay a hundred yards ahead.

It would be wrong, José Pablo Tsoyio told the Blessed Mother, for a man like him, brave José Pablo Tsoyio, who had lived with honor, who had killed no innocent men, especially those who had insulted him or his honor, to die with an arrow, lance, or musket ball in his back. Besides, José Pablo Tsoyio had made a promise to a dying boy, a fine Catholic, a believer, a child. José Pablo Tsoyio hoped the crucifix did not fall out of the pocket of his coat.

The rocks neared. So did the Indians. Then Nelson Story, his *patrón*, stepped out of the natural redoubt, firing two Navy Colts. Story stepped toward the mule. Smoke and flame belched from the Remington rifles behind them, the charging warriors slackened their pace, and José Pablo Tsoyio rode into the rocks, dismounted, and joined the fight.

Ellen Story stared at the crowd surrounding an odd wagon, painted yellow, green, and tan, parked in the middle of Wallace Street.

"Twenty drops in one tumbler of water," the barker called from the wagon's rear. All Ellen could see was the top of the man's tall silk hat. "That's all you need, folks. Give it to your little ones, your loved ones, give it to yourself. Folks, there's no need to suffer when Coldsmith's Ready Relief is a cure for every pain. Inflammation of the kidneys, inflammation of the bladder, inflammation of the bowels, congestion of the lungs, sore throat, palpitation of the heart, croup, diphtheria, catarrh, ague . . . Folks, this is better than French brandy or bitters as a stimulant."

Men and women, young and old, rushed to the wagon with paper money and coins.

"Dear Lord in heaven," Ellen whispered, "have they all gone mad?"

"Boss . . ." Tommy Thompson lowered the binoculars and slid slightly down the rock perch that served as a lookout tower. "They're pulling out. Riding north."

Story turned to José Pablo Tsoyio.

"Likely one, maybe two, remain behind," the Mexican said. "To see what we do."

"And what do we do?" Collins asked.

"Tighten your cinches." Story moved to where Catlin held the horses. "We ride back to the herd."

"You're letting them take your beef?" Hannah said.

"I'm letting them think that," Story said, nodding at Catlin before taking the reins to his mount. "There's a coulee a mile south. We'll hide in there till night, then follow their trail."

As he worked the cinch, he looked over the saddle at Catlin.

"You know why I made you wrangler?" Story did not wait for an answer. "It's because you're the only one big enough to hold all five animals. I know you're a hell of a shot, but you're also the only man here I'd trust not to let our horses hightail it out of here."

* * *

After turning up the lantern, Ellen looked at her sleeping baby while tapping continued on the cabin's door. Ellen hadn't been this timid, or scared, since during the rebellion, when Kansans feared any night visitor might be a Missouri bushwhacker. She drew in a breath, let it out, and said, "Yes?"

"Missus Story," the thick brogue announced. "It is I, Thomas Meagher."

"Governor." She opened the door quickly, and the Irishman stepped to the light, hat in his left hand, a leash in his right. Beside him, a dog began yapping.

"Hush," Meagher told the hound. "You'll wake Montana." He dropped to his knee and began scratching the skeletal dog's ears, leaving Ellen standing there with a lantern at ten in the evening wondering if Meagher might be in his cups.

He lifted his head, smiled, and said, "Missus Story, this poor pooch is an orphan, I am sad to say. Dr. Beckstead asked me to see if you and your baby would like a watchdog." The dog whined, and Meagher laughed. "Though I dare say he would not be good for that particular assignment." Again, he looked up, and his eyes saddened. "Mr. O'Ryan died this night. The doctor thought you would be so kind." He sighed. "I fear, we fear, all other residents would kill this noble hound, thinking it might carry the diphtheria." He sniffed in the cold. "The good doctor says there is no chance of that. Though how anyone knows . . ."

"He knows," Ellen said. She made herself say: "I trust Se—Dr. Beckstead." Glancing again at the dog, she asked, "What's his name?"

Meagher rose. "No one knows."

"I'll let Nelson name him when he returns." She reached out with her right hand to take the leash.

No one held the horses this time.

Catlin fired the Enfield, saw the warrior with the buffalo headdress spin around and drop into the dirt. He kicked the sides of the horse, and heard the cannonade of pistol and rifle shots. Another Indian rose from the ground, and Catlin swung the blistering hot rifle barrel like a war ax, feeling the stock crash against the brave's forehead. The jolt jerked the Enfield from his hand, almost pulled Catlin out of the saddle. He held the reins, heard guttural shouts, drowned out soon by the ringing in his ears.

Sliding out of the saddle, Catlin drew the Remington from his waistband. Dropped to his knees, still gripping the reins no matter how desperate the gelding tried to pull him all the way to Canada.

All around him sparked muzzle flashes in the night. Something moved to his left. He snapped a shot. The earth trembled. He shot at a shadow. Fired again. Now he felt blinded, and all he could smell was brimstone. As though he had stepped into hell. At length, he realized he kept triggering an empty revolver.

Moments later, a stillness replaced the thundering in his ears. His vision returned, but all he saw was a dying campfire.

A face flashed before him, but he couldn't quite see straight or clear.

"You all right?" At least, Catlin could hear. "Damn fine job, Catlin."

As quick as it had appeared, Story's face was gone.

Catlin blinked, turned, saw the figure moving into the

Indian camp, and Catlin did what those years in the infantry had trained him to do. He followed his commander.

As Tommy Thompson stoked the fire, Jameson Hannah reloaded his revolver, pulled the hammer to full cock, and aimed at the wounded warrior's head.

"Leave him be," Story said.

Hannah looked up, but did not move the barrel. "He's a damned cattle thief and Indian to boot."

"And when Four Elks and the others come back, they'll have to tend to him and the one whose face Catlin smashed," Story said.

"They won't come back," Hannah said. "They've disgraced themselves by leaving their wounded and dead behind."

"They'll come back," Tsoyio said.

Hannah whirled. "What does a Mexican cook know about a Sioux brave?"

"I know they are men," the cook said.

"Holster it," Story ordered. "We got what we came for. Get on your horse, Hannah. Round up the steers that strayed and let's get out of here before those sons of bitches realize they outnumber us eight to one."

Swearing, Hannah lowered the hammer, shoved the revolver into the holster, kicked the Indian's ankle, and climbed into the saddle.

John Catlin picked up the Enfield he had dropped and looked at the nearest warrior, who covered his bloodied face with both hands. "Hell," Catlin whispered. "He looks punier than a starving squirrel."

Walking by, Story glanced at the Indian, then back at the

herd, and at the roasting quarter of one of his steers on the fire. "Thompson," he said. "Don't bother with that heifer and that steer back there. They're so sore-footed, they'd never make it to Montana." He kicked his horse into a walk and rode to the other grazing longhorns.

Smiling, Catlin mounted his horse.

"One of these days," Hannah said, still staring at Story's back. "I'll kill that uppity son of a bitch."

Catlin nudged his horse closer. "Over my dead body," he told the ramrod. Their eyes met. "He's a son of a bitch, all right," Catlin whispered. "But I'd follow that son of a bitch anywhere."

After spitting to his right, Hannah looked back at Catlin. "If you like following sons of bitches, you might as well follow me to get the rest of his damned longhorns, and let's get the hell out of here."

CHAPTER SEVENTY

Boone knelt, glanced at the sleeping girl, at the steaming bowl he held, then looked around the camp and realized he was surrounded by cow shit.

"Hey." The voice came out weakly, and Boone looked back at Constance Beckett.

He almost spilled the soup. "José made you some soup." He shoved the bowl toward her, spilling about a fifth of it onto the cold ground. He apologized.

"That's all right, Boone," Constance said weakly. "You can just set it beside me. I'm not hungry right now."

"Oh." He still held the bowl.

She smiled. "Maybe later."

"How do you feel?" he asked.

"I've felt better." She tried to sit up, and that cost her another few spoonfuls of soup as Boone tried to help her. "It's all right, Boone," she said. "I'm not dying."

He managed to put the bowl on the ground without losing any more contents. Wet his lips. Looked around the campground, then back at her. "You can . . . you can call me . . . Mason."

"Is that your first or last name?"

He seemed to have to think. "First," he said. And laughed.

"Once upon a time, if somebody called out, 'Boone,' I'd have turned around to look for Daniel Boone."

"Mason." She tested the name. "I like that."

His face brightened, then the moment was gone, and Story stood over them. "We're moving out," Story said. "Get a horse. I want us at Fort Reno as soon as we can get there."

Boone said nothing, just rose, didn't even look back at Constance, and walked away. Story squatted where Boone had been, looked at the bowl, the spoon, then at Constance. His lips moved, but never formed a sentence.

So she said, "Mason Boone's a good man."

Story's eyes bored through her, then tried to melt the soup bowl, finally followed Boone toward the remuda. "He'll do," he said, and looked back at her.

"He's the type of man who doesn't know how good he really is."

Story just stared.

"You all right?" he asked after a long pause.

She just nodded.

Just thank me, she thought. *Just thank me for saving your life, and go away. It's all right. I don't even know why I did it.*

"Well," he said. He rose, pointed at the soup, and said, "You should eat. We're pulling out." Standing, he looked down on her, and that made her turn her head and stare at the grass, until she heard his spurs fading away.

She brought her hands to her eyes and tried to stop from crying.

"Reckon Tom Allen had the right idea." Bill Petty managed to grin. He lay on one of the cots in the picket house that passed for a hospital at Fort Reno. A few cots away,

George Overholt groaned. The rest of the patients were soldiers, though Story doubted if anyone in this ramshackle building other than Petty and Overholt deserved being called soldiers.

Attempting his best smile, Story pulled a few greenbacks out of his vest pocket.

"No," Petty protested. "You pay at the end of the trail, Virginia City."

"Fort Reno's the end for you, Bill." Story realized what he had just said. "Hell, that's not what I mean. You know . . ."

Petty laughed. "Nelson, you ain't much for passing time with conversation." He lowered his voice. "You need more men. I mean . . ."

Story's head shook.

"There's no fight in these men." He tilted his head toward the allegedly sick soldiers. "All I've seen them do is lay around, play cards, and steal from emigrants, though none has guts enough to steal from me." He let his voice fall to a whisper. "As far as I know, they've never heard of General Order Number Twenty-seven." He slipped the money under Petty's pillow, and stood, nodding grimly. "Take care of yourself, Bill." He started to extend his arm for a shake, remembered at the last second, and shoved the hand into his coat pocket. Then he turned, leaving the recently one-armed man inside the post hospital. Once Story stepped outside and felt the chill of the afternoon, he looked back at the roughhewn door and cursed.

He looked at the child with the tube in her windpipe, sat on the edge of her bed, and held her hand, smiling gently, though she never looked at him. The door opened, the men from Tibbetts's undertaking outfit took the girl's mother outside, and a deputy sheriff closed the door. Seth Beckstead felt the girl's forehead, a little warm, and watched her chest rise and fall.

She kept improving. Would probably live. Tears started down her cheeks, and Beckstead rose, still silent, and stepped away from the row of makeshift beds and cots until he reached the fireplace. He held out his hands, coughed, spit into the flames, sniffed, and tried to feel warm.

A moment later, Doc Sparhan stepped beside him.

Two drunks had become doctors again. "What would . . . ?" Beckstead couldn't finish, so he nodded at the teakettle on the table. He had meant to ask Sparhan, *What will history have to say about us?*

"Seth," Sparhan whispered, "I think I should look at your throat and tongue."

Beckstead smiled. "Too late, my fine colleague." Even that much hurt like hell, but Beckstead made himself heard. "The tongue's black. Like my soul."

Shorthanded, they pushed north. So shorthanded, Constance Beckett now drove Bill Petty's wagon, since Petty and George Overholt remained at Fort Reno. The temperatures dropped, and they gained elevation, now in the hills, the mountains, following the Emigrant Trail.

For the first time in years, she thought about Nashville.

The prairie, the plains behind them now, climbing up. She breathed in deeply, looking at the trees—not stunted trees, not cottonwoods along riverbeds, but tall conifers. The wind brought to her the scent of pine. Sweet, tall, beautiful pine.

And for a moment, she dreamed she had never left Tennessee, never met a louse of a major at a dreary place called Fort Kearny. Yet then the dream ended, and Constance saw that she drove a wagon in the Dakota Territory, bound for Montana, and she glanced behind her, looking for Molly McDonald's wagon, but it would be too far back. And she liked the feel of the leather lines in her gloved hands, and she imagined the scar she'd have on her side when the stitches—made from horsehair—were out.

This country was so wonderful, and for the first time in long memory, Constance Beckett felt alive. To her surprise, she kept catching herself looking at the trail herd, not for the cattle, or even at Nelson Story riding in front of the column, but at the point rider, Mason Boone.

At length, she knew why she felt so happy, so alive. She had found her home.

Riders topped the treeless ridge, briefly halted, and loped toward the herd. Seeing the guidon one rider carried, Story slid the Navy into the holster, told Hannah to keep the cattle moving, and spurred the dun into a gallop. When maybe a hundred yards separated them, Story raised his right hand and pulled gently on the reins, slowing the gelding to a trot, then a walk.

The soldiers stopped first, and Story slowly approached them, stopping in front of the patrol of six men. He hoped these bluecoats were better men than those at Fort Reno.

"Name's Story," he said. "Nelson Story. Got a thousand longhorns and wagons of supplies bound for Virginia City."

"Lieutenant Colonel William Fetterman," said the soldier on Story's left. "Eighteenth Infantry out of Fort Phil Kearny."

Story grinned, and pointed at Fetterman's blood bay stallion. "Infantry?"

The bluecoat's face flushed. His hair was dark, wavy, with a mustache intersecting with long, well-groomed sideburns. He held a Colt's revolving rifle across his lap. He had announced himself as a lieutenant colonel, though the bars on his shoulder ranked him a captain. Brevet colonel, probably. Story would never understand soldiers or their massive egos.

"Captain . . . *Colonel* Fetterman requested to join us," the other captain said, and he introduced himself as captain, not major, colonel, general, or senator, James Powell, 2nd Cavalry.

"We were hoping to find some red Indians," Fetterman said. "They've been dogging us for weeks."

"We found some." Story gestured southeast. "Just south of Fort Reno."

"They attacked you?" Powell asked.

Story shrugged. "We sort of attacked each other."

"How many? Indians, I mean," Fetterman asked.

"Thirty. Maybe more. It was dark."

"And how many men did you have?"

Fetterman sure had an inquisitive nature. "I have thirty-five with me now," he said, hoping they wouldn't check his math. "Twenty-two wagons."

"So, it was an even match, you and those red devils?" Fetterman asked, while his friend, the captain of cavalry, just stared blankly at the infantry officer.

"Not exactly." Story decided to be honest. "I had five men with me. They took some of my cattle. I wanted my cattle back."

Fetterman laughed, slapped his thigh, and looked at Powell. "See, Jim, what did I tell you? These Sioux are no better than digger Indians. Give me eighty men, and I'll ride through the whole Sioux nation."

Story waited a moment, then looked at Captain Powell. "Captain," he said. "I was hoping to bed down my herd at the fort. For a day or two. Have some horses shod, some injuries attended to, then get home to Virginia City before the snows hit hard."

The captain nodded. "You will have to address your wishes to Colonel Carrington, Mr. Story. We'll be glad to escort you back to the fort."

Fetterman might have been a glory-hunting fool, but Henry B. Carrington was a jackass. The colonel's brow knotted, sending canyons of wrinkles stretching from the corners of his eyes to his slicked-back hair, and stroked his thick mustache and chin whiskers, and finally shook his head.

"The grass near this post is needed for army livestock, Mr. Story. You may camp three miles from the post."

"Three miles." Story studied Carrington.

"My men are here to protect you. Trained horse soldiers can cover three miles quickly."

"So can Cheyennes and Sioux."

Carrington folded his arms across his chest and leaned back in his chair, but did not speak after feeling the bite of Story's insult.

"Then I'd like to move on," Story said. "Winter's coming, and I have miles to go."

"That I cannot allow," Carrington said. "The Indians are devilish. They maraud, torment, frustrate, and kill. You must stay here under our protection until the Sioux realize they cannot best the United States Army."

"Protection," Story said.

"Correct, Mr. Story."

"From three miles away."

Carrington lifted a silver bell off his desktop, rang it, the door opened, and a gaunt sergeant major stepped inside.

"Is there anything else, Mr. Story?" Carrington asked.

Without answering, Story walked past the sergeant major, through the anteroom, out the door, mounted his horse, and waited for the sons of bitches to open the gate to their damned fort so he could get back to his outfit.

CHAPTER SEVENTY-ONE

It had become a daily game. In the morning, Story sent a request to Carrington that he be allowed to leave for Virginia City, and with prompt efficiency the colonel would deny the proposal. In early afternoon, Story asked to be allowed to move closer to the fort. That, too, would be rejected.

"The way I see it," Catlin said, "the army needs all that pasture for the one saddle horse the Sioux haven't stolen yet."

Sitting on a stump and sipping his coffee, Jameson Hannah snorted. "Well, I think they have a few more horses than that."

"How about us?" Catlin turned away from staring at the fort. "We lose any horses last night?"

"No horses. We keep them well guarded." Last week, the teamsters had finished two large corrals, one for the remuda, the other for the oxen and mules, and four men guarded both corrals day and night. "But we might have lost two more steers. Peña, Dow, and Boone are following some tracks."

Standing a few yards from the center of the camp, sipping his coffee, waiting for Connor Lehman to return with Colonel Carrington's latest denial of Story's request, Story turned around, "You told them—"

Hannah cut off Story's comment. "I told them not to go more than a mile. If the tracks keep going, they know to turn back. Two steers aren't worth dying for."

"But we can't let them pick us clean," Dalton Combs said.

"That's a peacetime army for you." Catlin spit and looked across the pastures. A squad of infantry marched along two mule teams pulling wagons with men in the back ready to cut hay. Yesterday, they had dragged logs for firewood or to help fortify the palisade walls that surrounded the fort. "They put up these forts to protect travelers like us. All that did was piss off the Indians and make it damned hard for travelers like us."

"Here comes Lehman." Lying in her usual position with her head against the wagon wheel, Molly McDonald pointed her tin cup toward Fort Phil Kearny's wooden palisade. Connor Lehman trotted on the back of a mule to the edge of the campground before reining up. "He said no. Again."

Story spit, and Lehman turned the mule toward the corrals.

Rising, Hannah emptied the dregs of his cup and crossed the ground till he stood beside Story. "You gonna stay here till you don't have one head to sell in Virginia City or stock that ranch you're planning?"

"No."

"It's getting colder every day."

"It's that time of year."

Hannah sighed. "A corpse is a better conversationalist than you," he said, and walked back to the coffeepot.

Story almost grinned. Back when they had been courting, Ellen once told him the exact same thing.

* * *

She sat on the top rail of the horse corral, whittling and wondering what the folks back in Nashville would think if they could see her now, short hair, sunburned to a deep bronze, wearing men's duds, and still answering half the time to a man's name, whittling a piece of pine while watching three riders come trotting in. She let one of the teamsters on guard duty get ready to open the gate.

Three riders. Constance Beckett let out a sigh of relief. They kicked their mounts into a lope and covered the last quarter of a mile quickly, reining up and swinging out of the saddles as though they had been doing this all their lives. Which, she figured, two of them probably had. But Mason Boone? She wasn't sure.

Boone stared at her, holding the reins to his brown gelding, and asked, "Story got you on guard duty?"

She laughed. "Not hardly."

Boone waited, but saw just her smile, and he shrugged and turned to unsaddle his horse. She pitched the stick, folded the knife, and leaped to the ground, waving at George Dow and Fabian Peña, and stopping a few feet behind Boone.

"Did you find the cattle?"

"No. About a dozen pony tracks with them. Guess they'll be feeding Indians directly."

"Yeah." She toed the earth. "I suppose they're hungry."

"Not half as hungry as me."

"Let me fix you a plate," she said.

Boone turned, wet his lips, his face a mask of bewilderment. She shrugged, grinned, tilted her head. "Well, I never paid you back for all you did when the locusts attacked."

"I didn't do much."

Constance sighed. "You also never told anyone . . . How did you know?"

Boone blinked, turned to work on the bridle, and muttered, "I got sisters back home."

A grinning Peña came over and took the reins to Boone's horse. "Let me take him for you, Boone," the cowhand said, taking the reins with his left hand and grabbing Boone's saddle with his right, and led the gelding away.

"Come on." Constance crooked her finger. "José has some beans and biscuits, even got some bacon from the post commissary." She started away.

From the gate, Fabian Peña called out, "Boone, if you don't go, I will."

Boone hurried to catch up with Constance Beckett.

Boone excused himself from Constance, told her he'd be along in a jiffy, and walked to Story. "No luck," Boone said. "About a dozen tracks, unshod. Two steers." He pointed. "Heading up over that tall ridge there."

"I figured," Story said, and looked back at the fort.

When he turned a few minutes later, he saw Constance Beckett handing Mason Boone a plate, then filling a cup of coffee. Like a damned homemaker.

"You son of a bitch," he whispered to himself. "You're jealous." And from the looks on the faces of the other cowboys and bullwhackers around the camp, Story wasn't alone. A few minutes later, Peña and Dow walked to camp, but Constance did not fix their dinner.

Story strode to the center. "Boone." He made sure Boone looked away from Constance. "Peña, Dow." The bullwhacker Kyle McPherson happened by so Story called out his name, too. "You all will have guard duty on the horse corral. So if you need sleep, get it this afternoon." He turned, called out four other names, told them that they would be guarding the oxen and mule corral. Then he looked at Hannah. "You and me will take first watch on the cattle."

Hannah didn't like that. Boone wasn't happy. Nor was Constance Beckett, but Story felt like he had done a good deed for the night. *Hell, boy,* he thought as his eyes locked on Boone's, *I might have just saved your life.*

Throwing off the covers, feeling the bitter predawn cold, José Pablo Tsoyio cursed the day he learned how to cook. Yet he rose, bones aching, blew into his hands to warm them, and moved to the fire. He jammed it relentlessly with the piece of charred wood, then added kindling to the hot coals. Eventually, he had the fire going, and the coffee boiling, and soon started tossing thick slices of bacon onto the skillet. Fort Phil Kearny wasn't much, but the commissary and Mr. Story's money could be a blessing.

Bacon would get cowboys up quicker than a *puta*.

Yet the first person to come to the fire was the girl in men's duds. She knelt, held her hands to the fire for warmth, and finally asked, "Is there anything I can do?"

José Pablo Tsoyio sighed. He wasn't about to send a woman to gather firewood, even if it was real wood, not dried dung they had used for so damned long on the plains.

"There is a small pot," he said at last, and slid the bacon into a plate. He nodded. "There. Fill it from the big pot."

She worked eagerly. Most cowboys, and a few bull-whackers, would do this for an extra biscuit or two. He did not know what he should pay a woman. He wondered if she could cook. Not as well as he could, he decided.

The woman set the smoking pot on the rocks. She was smart enough to use a big rag to hold the handle. Most cowboys burned themselves because they did not think.

"Can you fry bacon?" he asked.

"Sure."

He rose, nodded at the skillet and the thick slabs. "Do this." He pointed to the side of bacon and the knife. "Till I return. I must bring the guards some coffee." He picked up a wheat sack that rattled with tin cups. "They have been up all night." *And better be awake,* he thought to himself, *unless they want to have their manhood kneed into their stomachs.*

"I can do that," the girl cried out, and almost spilled the smaller pot into the flames, which caused an obscenity to escape from José Pablo Tsoyio's lips, but it was in Spanish, so perhaps the señorita did not understand.

"I'll do it," she said, and this time lifted the pot, again using the rag, and extended her left hand for the sack of cups. But her eyes betrayed her as she looked toward the corrals.

José Pablo Tsoyio smiled. Ah, to be young, and in love. It was a good thing. He said, "Let me fry some more bacon first. They will be hungry, too." He forked the meat in the skillet, looked up, and laughed.

"It will not take long, señorita. The fire is hot."

CHAPTER SEVENTY-TWO

Ellen thought she had prepared herself for this, but the tears ran down her cheeks the moment she stepped into the room. Dr. Sparhan squeezed her and whispered that she could come back later, but she shook her head. "I'm all right," she told him, and stepped forward, slowly, smelling the death and foulness, and managed to sit on the stool by the cot.

For some undeterminable amount of time she sat there, uncertain, and finally found the rag in the bowl on the nearby table. She wrung it out, placed it on Dr. Seth Beckstead's head, reached down to his arm and squeezed it gently.

He struggled for breath.

A shadow passed over Beckstead's face, and Ellen lifted her head.

"He refused to allow a tracheotomy," Sparhan whispered. Tears welled in the old man's eyes, too. "I am not certain it would have helped. In his case." He moved closer, leaned, and held out a pad and pencil. "If he regains consciousness," he said, and walked to another patient.

When the eyes opened hours later, after the lanterns had been turned down and morning light filtered inside the cabin, Ellen swallowed and tried not to cry, but her lips kept trembling. Beckstead's eyes found hers, widening, his lips tried to part, he sucked in air, and must have seen the pencil and paper on her lap, for he wiggled his pointer finger.

Understanding, she slid the pad under his arm and placed the pencil in his hand.

He struggled to speak, couldn't, and she found the rag again, wet it, and let water trickle over his lips and into his mouth. She looked for the Adam's apple to move, but just couldn't tell. He scratched with the pencil, which left him exhausted, and his eyes closed.

U shldnt hve com

When he looked up at her, she smiled. "After all you've done for me?" She pointed to the bunk a few feet away. "You and Jessie Baker are the last patients, Seth. Dr. Sparhan says Jessie should be sewing dresses in a week. You saved a lot of lives."

The lips moved, but no noise came out. The hand worked again.

Go hom

"Grace is with Montana, Seth. We're all fine. Dr. Mathews says he believes the contagion is gone." She repeated. "You saved a lot of lives."

He wrote: *GO!*

The sluice opened, and she cried, trying to find a handkerchief, giving up and using the cuffs of her sleeves. When she had some composure, she saw he had written again.

Dont want U 2 se me die

Tears came harder this time, and the sleeves were no help. She prayed, even cursed, and tried to be like that hard-rock husband of hers. When she could see again, he had written more.

Its al rite. I stil no how to spel.

His lips barely mouthed, "A joke."
She smiled. He wrote.

Plez. Go. 4 Me?

Her head dropped, but she managed to nod, and she whispered something, though she could not remember what she had said, and doubted if Seth Beckstead heard. The pencil scratched again, and she made herself look again.

I love you

She sighed, and mouthed, "I know," and thought: *And I wish I could have loved you but* . . .
"*Go.*" Somehow, he choked out the word, and gasped out, "*Please.*"
Nodding, she asked, "Is there anything I can get you?" And not waiting for a reply, she leaned over and kissed his forehead and gingerly traced his lips with her fingers. She felt his arm moving, heard the scratching, and when she rose and saw what he had written, she tried to laugh, but couldn't.

Ry Wisky

She blew him a kiss, and said, "Rest, my sweet prince."

She left the O'Ryan cabin, knowing that the next time she came down this street, if she ever did, she would find ashes in its place, and that Dr. Seth Beckstead would lie in the cemetery, perhaps next to another brave man, Thomas J. Dimsdale.

And she wondered if her husband were still alive.

Story sat bolt upright, flung off the blanket, and cursed the wailing coyotes or wolves and himself for sleeping so damned hard when he hadn't done anything for the past eternity except sit around and play some kids' game with an idiot army officer. The sons of bitches would scatter the herd. He found his hat, started to rise, and stopped. That wasn't a coyote, or a wolf, and he didn't think it was an Indian brave.

The cowboys in the early dawn stood at the cookfire, some pointing, some staring. The cook moved away from the skillet. Every one of them looked at the corrals, and Story swore again, grabbed his rifle, and ran.

Others began to roll out of their bedrolls, and seeing Story, they rushed for their guns. The cowboys by the fire drew their revolvers—those that had already buckled on their rigs—and began to run.

"Not all of you," Story roared as he reached the camp. "Half of you stay here. In case this is some Indian trick." Could be, he thought, that the warriors might want to ransack the wagons, which could also, if not bankrupt him, leave him broke one more time.

The cook, well ahead of them, moved fast for an old man.

* * *

"Dear God in Heaven." John Catlin lowered the Enfield, dropped to his knees, hung his head over, and vomited. Something he hadn't done since before the second battle of the rebellion. The first time, the soldiers said, you don't know any better, and all you do is piss your pants. The second time, you puke up all you've eaten and drunk for a month. After that, it wouldn't matter.

The cook slid to his knees, crossed himself, and began praying in Spanish. Wiping his mouth, Catlin saw tears streaming down the man's dark face. He started to look at the girl, stopped, and had to use the Enfield to push himself to his feet.

Coffee cups littered the pasture, as if the Indians had flung them in all directions, like they were playing a game. The pot Constance Beckett had been bringing to the guards was gone; the warriors must have taken that, along with Constance's scalp. Arrows, more than Catlin wanted to count, pinned the poor woman to the earth, blood pooled all around her. Mason Boone cradled her head in his hands, lifted his head to the breaking dawn, and let out sounds Catlin never had heard in all the battles he had lived through.

Then Story stood over Boone and the girl. Catlin waited for him to talk, but the man of iron will paled, and he sank to his knees, letting his rifle fall into the grass.

The whispers began. "What was she doing out here?" . . . "Did you hear anything?" . . . "Nothing." . . . "They didn't rape her." . . . "Too dark to see, I reckon. And her in men's duds." . . . "God, I never seen nobody scalped before." . . . "Maybe we ought to get back to the camp."

"Shut up," Catlin barked. "All of you, shut the hell up." He stood, wiped his lips, moved to the girl, her eyes wide open, her throat cut, her shirt drenched in drying blood, the topknot of her blond hair jerked off. "Sons of bitches," Catlin swore.

"Boone." Catlin touched the grieving cowboy's shoulder. "Boone." He had cried his voice hoarse, but the tears flowed like water from a busted dam. "Boone, we need to get her out of here. All right? We'll take care of her, son. I'll take care of her. Come on. Come on."

Story stood then, breathed in deeply, watched the latecomers arrive. Most of them removed their hats. A few turned around, unable to look at the dead woman. Then Beckett's pard, Mickey McDonald, ran forward, ripping off the hat, sliding to the knees, slamming fists into the dirt, and roaring louder than a dozen coyotes. And all the while, for five minutes or more, Story stared at the pale, bloody face of Constance Beckett, and instead of seeing her, he saw Ellen's face. And he wondered as he cursed himself for not making Constance Beckett stay back at Fort Laramie. Was this what that damned dream about him burying a dog meant?

"We can ask permission," Connor Lehman said in the compound. "I'm sure the colonel will let us bury her in the post cemetery. The chaplain—"

"Like hell you will." Boone hadn't said a word that anyone could understand until that moment. "You're not burying her with a bunch of damned Yankees."

Silence covered the camp like a shroud.

"We'll bury her on the trail," Story said after a long pause. "We're pulling out. Tonight."

"With the Sioux brave enough to kill one of us this close to camp?" George Dow shook his head. "Let's think this through."

"I said . . ."

But Lehman cut Story off. "We should put this to a vote." Story whirled, but Lehman raised his hand. "You're the boss, but this is dangerous. Extremely dangerous. You can't force these men to commit suicide."

Story stiffened for a minute, finally nodded, looked around, and said, "All right. All in favor of leaving tonight, raise your hands." His hand was already up. So was Boone's.

One by one, the hands raised. There was no question this was the majority, and it stunned Story. Would it be unanimous?

"Anyone object?"

George Dow stepped out into the center and raised his hand. "Mr. Story . . . this just . . ."

The revolver barrel held against Dow's head silenced the lone dissenter. When Boone cocked the trigger, Story cleared his throat.

"Boone." The wild eyes came up, and Story shook his head. "Shot'll bring the troops down on us."

"We can't leave him behind," Hannah said. "Yellow as Dow is, he'll tell Carrington and those bluebellies."

"We're not leaving him behind. Tie him up. Gag him. Throw him in the back of . . ." Story spit. "A wagon with room." He spun around to Lehman. "You want to object, too?"

Lehman's head shook. "No, I think you're right. Dow would talk."

"We'll need another driver," Story whispered, and nodded toward the wagon Constance had driven, and before that, Bill Petty. He spit. Dow started sobbing.

"Make a show. Do the same damn thing we've been doing for the past few weeks. But get ready. Build big fires tonight. And then we leave this damned place. We're three miles away from the post, so nobody should hear us, but keep the noise down. We'll swing a wide loop, pick up the trail, move on."

"What if Carrington sends troops to bring us back?" a teamster asked.

"He won't. He's too scared of leaving his fort unprotected. And if he does, we'll kill the bastards."

CHAPTER SEVENTY-THREE

The Milky Way and a bright half-moon guided them across cold, desolate country, and once the moon disappeared behind the peaks, they stayed on the trail, moving slowly, cautiously, shivering from cold and dread. At dawn, they breakfasted on coffee and the last of the bacon, after which they continued, slowly, steadily, cowboys and bull-whackers alike watching the Lakota warriors that followed them along the ridge line before disappearing a few hours before dusk.

That morning, they held Constance Beckett's funeral.

Connor Lehman read from the Old Testament, Story stood in the back with his hat in his hand, Boone bowed his head, and Luke Beckner led the assembled in prayer, while most of the men stared up the ridge, waiting for the Indians to return. When they didn't, Beckner looked at the gathering and said, "It strikes me that we should sing."

Men exchanged glances, a few looked at Boone, who did not look up, only sniffled and absently rotated his hat by the brim with his hands.

"Well," Beckner said after a moment, "I guess . . ."

The gasp stopped him. Whispered profanity caused him to raise his head as the mule skinner they knew as Mickey

McDonald walked from the parked wagons, wearing a dress that didn't fit all that well but certainly revealed the cleavage previously kept hidden with tightly wrapped linen. She had washed her face, combed her hair, and even scrubbed her tobacco-browned teeth with paste.

Isaac Collins said, "Shit," that everyone heard, though he had not meant to say it so loud.

Mickey, née Molly, stood by the blushing Beckner, whose mouth hung open, and smiled. "She was my pard, and a body to ride the river with. And if any of you bastards say something demeaning her character you'll answer to me." That hushed the whispers, but what silenced them was when Molly McDonald began singing "Tarry with Me."

Now the shadows slowly lengthen,
Soon the evening time will come;
With Thy grace, O Savior, strengthen,
By Thy help I would go home.
Tarry with me, O my Savior,
Tarry with me through the night;
I am lonely, Lord, without Thee,
Tarry with me through the night.

She started the second verse, only to fall to her knees, then forward, stopping herself with hard arms and hands, sobbing without shame or control. Men gawked. Only José Pablo Tsoyio walked over, put his hands on Molly's shoulders, and let her cry.

She stopped when a male voice picked up the song, out of tune, out of key, broken by sobs.

Thou art with me, O my Savior,
On Thy bosom calm I rest;

Thine anointed, Lord, Thou savest,
Now I know Thou givest rest.

When Boone started the chorus, the others joined in. Even Molly McDonald mouthed the words. On the far side of the clearing, Story watched in silence, hands shoved deep inside his coat pockets, his face stoic, mouth closed, eyes impenetrable.

It would not be right for Mason Boone to see teamsters dig alongside the trail, where the remuda and herd would march over the young woman's grave to keep it hidden from Indians. While the men dug late that afternoon, Tsoyio found Boone leaning against a pine tree, drumming his fingers against his thigh.

Clearing his throat, he waited until the cowhand lifted his eyes, then Tsoyio gestured. "Follow me," he said.

Boone stood as though by rote, and walked behind the Mexican cook for two hundred yards before he finally asked, "Where are we going?"

Tsoyio stopped, turned, and said, "I want to show you something."

Without comment, Boone followed. At length he asked, "Aren't you worried about Indians?"

"Are you?" Tsoyio answered. By then, they had found the stream, and they moved along its banks till finding the pond.

"Wait here." Tsoyio moved to the massive dam of twigs, branches, limbs, and logs. He reached into his pocket, withdrew a shining chain and ornament, draping the necklace over a log. After maneuvering his way across the drifts of wood, not seeming to mind the cold water, he pulled himself onto the bank beside Boone.

"What's this all about?" Boone asked.

The cook smiled. "A promise." Which was just partly true. Tsoyio also wanted to steer Boone away from the grave of Constance Beckett, where the horses would be flattening the mound as Fabian Peña and his guards started the remuda on the trail. Again, they would travel at night, hold up in tight confines the following day. They would have to get back to the camp soon, so Boone could take his spot with the herd, and Tsoyio would drive his wagon, but the *patrón*, Nelson Story, had agreed to Tsoyio's scheme, and would be waiting back at camp.

Tsoyio smiled. "Have you ever seen a beaver?"

Boone shrugged.

"Well, we shall wait here awhile. They are funny-looking animals. But beautiful. Hard workers. Yes, we shall wait awhile." Boone did not seem to hear. "Many years have passed since I last saw a beaver, but this is for you. *Y mi amigo* José Sibrian."

Bullwhackers untied George Dow and hauled him out of the wagon. Jameson Hannah loosened the gag, jerked it down, and shoved the cowboy forward.

Story handed Dow the holstered revolver, the belt wrapped around the rig.

"You're free," Story told Dow.

"Free?" Dow stared.

"You can ride with us. Or make your way back to the fort."

Dow let out a humorless chuckle and held out his hands to accept the gun and rig. "That's some choice, Story."

"It's yours to make."

"I'll stick with you," Dow said.

Story nodded. "Catch yourself a horse. Take over point till Boone gets back with the cook." He nodded at the revolver. "If you want to use that, now's your chance."

Dow strapped the rig on, but shook his head. "You wouldn't even feel the lead ball, Story. You don't feel nothing."

After a slight nod, Story walked away.

The trail led west, through mountains, but only the nights proved frigid. The days were just damned cold. Numbed by cold, wet from frost and snow flurries, men and animals moved west for days, weeks, millennia. They had done nothing but this for so long, maybe they knew nothing else. Later, however, the Gallatin Valley protected them from most of the weather. When José Pablo Tsoyio and Story decided they were out of the range of the Lakotas, they stopped moving at night—it was too damned cold anymore to travel without the sun's warmth. Thanksgiving passed without notice, and by the time John Catlin figured Christmas would come and go, Story stopped the caravan.

"You want us to do what?" John Catlin asked.

"Two cabins," Story said, and began sketching a blueprint with a stick in the dirt. "Bunkhouse. Main house. Nothing fancy. Just something to get us through the winter." His mind and the stick continued to work. "We'll put up a lean-to here. Corrals there. Barn will have to wait till spring or summer."

He raised the stick and pointed. "Plenty of grass, and this valley will protect the cattle most of the winter."

George Dow let out a dry, mocking laugh. "I thought we were going to Virginia City."

"We are," Story said. "Those who want to draw your time, we'll take two hundred beeves into Virginia City."

"I know you want to keep your bulls and cows for your ranch," Jameson Hannah said, "but you got more than two hundred beeves."

"That's just what I want to sell now," Story said. "In Virginia City. I bet the army at Fort C. F. Smith will like meat. We'll see what they'll offer in the spring."

"How about Fort Phil Kearny?" Luke Beckner said with a chuckle.

"To hell with them," Story said.

The corrals were built first. Then the cabins. Story said he'd pay the carpenters two and a half dollars a day. That's what they were doing, when the log slipped, and a man screamed.

Teamsters McPherson, McKay, and the drag riders Williams and McWilliams managed to roll the log off. The others removed their hats as José Pablo Tsoyio knelt, closed the eyes, then placed his fingers on the throat. Snow started to fall. Nelson Story hurried over from the woodcutting detail. He stared down at the body, looked south, shook his head. "See if we can make him a coffin. We'll bury him in the morning." He turned, walked away, but a few men swore they heard him curse.

Connor Lehman watched Story for a long while, then looked at the body and said, "Blood for the foundation?"

"What?" Boone asked.

"Nothing."

And for a long while, they just stood over the body of Jameson Hannah.

"I never thought the son of a bitch could die," Dalton Combs said.

"I did," José Pablo Tsoyio said. "But not this way."

Boone stood. "Get him inside the lean-to. We've got work to do."

Story nodded at Connor Lehman. "We'll bring the wagons in to Virginia City. You can take your money, wait out winter here, or move on wherever. Stagecoaches run to Salt Lake. Helena's a hard ride in winter, but you can go there, too. And there are business opportunities in the Fourteen Mile City, to hang your hat in the winter, or stick it out as long as you can."

The funeral of Jameson Hannah, obviously, had officially ended.

"I'd like to get back to Texas," Kelvin Melean said. "See if I can remember what heat feels like."

Story's head bobbed. "I'll pay you off in town. But first, we ought to get some roofs up."

CHAPTER SEVENTY-FOUR

This was how Story had imagined it, but it wasn't how he thought he would feel.

He rode in front of the steers, while men, women, children stepped out of their homes or businesses, watching the procession in silent awe all the way down the Fourteen Mile City. He had left seven cowboys, including Mason Boone, back at the ranch. The others pushed the two hundred beeves, followed by the wagons led by Connor Lehman.

As they neared Virginia City, Story turned his bay gelding around. "Combs," he told the black cowhand, "keep them moving. There will be a newspaper office, the *Montana Post,* up on the right. We're taking these to the Eagle Corral. At Jackson and Cover. Tell the owner, Foster, that he owes me a thousand dollars." He did not smile. "The pens won't hold them all, but I figure these cattle won't wander off."

"No, sir," Combs said. "But some of these city folks might try throwing a wide loop. They look hungry."

Story coughed. "Let them," he said. "If they're that hungry."

He spurred back to the wagons, reining up at the wagon driven by John Catlin. Behind him, Steve Grover drove another wagon, with Molly McDonald riding in her wagon, still in her dress. The professor would not know what to think about this, Story thought, or how to write about it.

Story reached behind the cantle and tossed the money belt into the driver's box at Catlin's feet.

"Pay off the men," Story said. "You'll find the ledger in there." He started to turn the gelding around, but looked back at Catlin. "You figured out your plans yet?"

Shaking his head, Catlin jerked a thumb back at Grover's wagon. "We're still talking about it."

Story nodded, and loped back, passed the cattle, swinging down in at the newspaper office, where he tied the gelding to the hitching rail. A stranger stepped through the door.

"By God," the man said. "You did it, Story. You did it." He held out his hand. "I'm Henry Blake, Nelson, editor . . ."

"Where's Professor Dimsdale?" Story interrupted.

The man's face turned waxen. "I am sorry, but the professor passed in September." He withdrew pencil and pad as Story turned.

"How many cattle?" the journalist asked.

"We started with a thousand Texas longhorns," Story said. "We're bringing in two hundred beeves. The rest are back in the valley, though we lost some on the trail."

"How many men?"

Too damned many to count. And a woman.

He didn't speak, didn't even hear Blake repeat the question, because now he ran, in front of the cattle and cowboys, across the street, until he wrapped his arms around Ellen, swung her around in front of an abandoned cabin, feeling the wind take off his hat, knowing the men stared at him as they rode past, whispering, cracking jokes.

Let them, Story thought. He didn't give a damn.

* * *

"She's sleeping," Ellen told Nelson as he stared down at little Montana in her crib. "Who do you think she looks like?"

His head shook, and he walked away, raising the filthy bandanna to his face. "Got dust in my eye," he said, and sat down on the chaise he had never liked a whit. Ellen moved to the rear entrance, opened the door, and a dog bounded inside, leaping, yipping, then bolting across the cabin and jumped, pressing its paws against Nelson's chest.

Baby Montana did not even stir.

"Down," Ellen whispered. "Get down."

The dog wagged its tail, did not obey.

Story looked at the dog, which turned around and ran back to Ellen. "What's this?" he said.

"A dog," she said.

"What's his name?"

She shrugged. "Montana and I figured we'd let you name it." When the dog barked, Ellen hushed it, walked past the table, grabbed a bone she had bought from the butcher, and tossed it through the open door. The dog raced out, and Ellen closed the door. By the time she came back, Story had stretched out on the chaise. His eyes were closed.

Outside, Ellen heard the bawling of cattle.

"Hobo," Story whispered.

"What?"

"Hobo," he said. "We'll call him Hobo."

"All right, Nelson." Slowly, she knelt beside him and began stroking his nearest hand. "Hobo."

His eyes opened, locked on hers.

"Hobo," he said again. "I don't have to bury him. I've buried too many already."

She stared blankly. "Nelson?"

His eyes closed, and she thought he was asleep, but he

drew in a deep breath, exhaled, and the eyes opened again, found hers, and he whispered, "I love you. I don't say that enough."

She thought: *You've never said it*. Smiled. *But I love you, too*.

The eyes closed, and he said, "I'm so tired." A moment later, he was asleep.

She leaned down, kissed his forehead, looked at Montana, still asleep, and walked back to the front door, opening it, seeing the last of the cattle come down Wallace Street, followed now by a caravan of wagons, jingling traces, bone-weary men. Hobo ran back inside, found a spot by the fireplace, began working on the butcher's bone. She told herself to remember to close the back door, but for now, she watched the parade, thinking history was being made this very moment, and her husband had done it.

Yet her eyes gazed up the hillside, toward the new cemetery, and she breathed in slowly, and she thought about what Nelson had said, more to himself than to her, and she wondered if he would ever tell her about it.

Finally, she whispered to herself, "Yes, we have buried too many already."

Then, Ellen closed the door.

AUTHOR'S NOTE

This novel is a blend of fact and fiction—and a whole lot of legend. In 1866, Nelson Story drove a herd of cattle—the number of cattle ranges from three hundred to three thousand—from Texas to Montana. John Catlin and Steve Grover, both Civil War veterans from Indiana, did join him at Fort Laramie. The army at Fort Phil Kearny did order the caravan of cattle and wagons to stop, and Story, at least according to legend, did take a vote; George Dow voted not to continue and was silenced and basically kidnapped. Story reportedly used some of the cattle to start his own ranching empire and sold the rest in Virginia City.

Thomas Dimsdale was the editor at Virginia City's *Montana Post* until his death in 1866. Ellen Story did give birth to a daughter while Story was away; Alice Montana Story died in 1869, but the Storys had several more children, with three sons living well into the 1900s. And by most accounts, Story could be a downright nasty man.

The participants on the cattle drive and wagon train and other characters—with the exceptions of Catlin, Grover, Dow, Jack and Jenette Langrishe, George Overholt, Tommy Thompson, Thomas Meagher, Fort Laramie's Major James

Van Voast, Fort Phil Kearny's Henry Carrington, William Fetterman and James Powell, and many of the Virginia City townspeople—are fictional. But all are used fictitiously. The diphtheria epidemic is also my creation, loosely based on other outbreaks in Montana during the 1870s and 1880s.

In the spring of 2019, I followed the route most historians believe Story would have taken—in a rented car, not on horseback. The flooding, thunderstorm, and hailstorm scenes were developed on that drive. The idea of the locusts came about on follow-up trips that summer and fall in Dodge City, Kansas.

Sources for this novel, listed alphabetical by the author's name, include Laura Joanne Arata's May 2009 thesis, "Embers of the Social City: Business, Consumption, and Material Culture in Virginia City, Montana, 1863–1945," for her master of arts in history at Washington State University's Department of History; *Empire Express: Building the First Transcontinental Railroad* by David Haward Bain; *Gold Camp: Alder Gulch and Virginia City, Montana* by Larry Barsness; *Fort Phil Kearny: An American Saga* by Dee Brown; *Cowboy Culture: A Saga of Five Centuries* and *Frontier Medicine: From the Atlantic to the Pacific, 1492–1941*, both by David Dary; *The Vigilantes of Montana* by Professor Thomas J. Dimsdale; *Great American Cattle Trails: The Story of the Old Cow Paths of the East and the Longhorn Highways of the Plains* by Henry Sinclair Drago; *Montana Mainstreets Volume 1: A Guide to Historic Virginia City* by Marilyn Grant; *Montana: High, Wide, and Handsome* by Joseph Kinsey Howard; *The Bloody Bozeman: The Perilous Trail to Montana's Gold* by Dorothy M. Johnson; *Fort Worth: Outpost on the Trinity* by Oliver Knight; *Fort Laramie: Official National Park Handbook* by David Lavender; *Railroad 1869: Along the Historic Union Pacific Through Nebraska* by

Eugene Arundel Miller; *Golden Gulch: The Story of Montana's Fabulous Alder Gulch* by Dick Pace; *Fort Worth: Outpost, Cowtown, Boomtown* by Harold Rich; *Treasure State Tycoon: Nelson Story and the Making of Montana* by John C. Russell; *Virginia City and Alder Gulch* by Ken and Ellen Sievert; *Following Old Trails* by Arthur L. Stone; and *The Trampling Herd: The Story of the Cattle Range in America* by Paul I. Wellman.

I also read through many period newspapers in Texas, Kansas, Maryland, Nebraska, and Montana on Newspapers.com and NewspaperArchive.com, as well as articles in *America's Civil War, True West, Wild West* and the Texas State Historical Association and Remington Society of America websites.

The text of Major General John Pope's General Order No. 27 in Chapter 49 comes from *Senate Documents, Volume 242, Indexes to the Executive Documents of the Senate of the United States for the First Session Fortieth Congress, and for the Special Session, 1867* (Washington: Government Printing Office, 1868).

Thanks also to Micki Fuhrman Milom of Nashville, Tennessee; Michael Zimmer of Roy, Utah; and Steve and Candy Moulton of Encampment, Wyoming, for answering questions and steady coaching; Denise Beeber and Cindy Bagwell for lunch in Dallas, Texas; Max and Kim McCoy for lunch in Emporia, Kansas; Monty and Ann McCord for supper in Hastings, Nebraska; Charles Rankin for lunch at Wheat, Montana; Mary Hedge of the La Porte County (Indiana) Public Library, and Tom Lea and Lori Van Pelt at WyoHistory.org for helpful background research; and the staffs at the Greenwood County Historical Society in Eureka, Kansas; Kansas City Public Library's Missouri Valley Special Collections; Frontier Army Museum at

Fort Leavenworth, Kansas; Wyoming State Museum in Cheyenne; Fort Kearny State Historical Park in Kearney, Nebraska; Dawson County Historical Society in Lexington, Nebraska; Fort Laramie National Historic Site in Fort Laramie, Wyoming; Fort Phil Kearny Historic Site in Banner, Wyoming; Gallatin History Museum in Bozeman, Montana; Montana Historical Society in Helena; and Thompson-Hickman Museum in Virginia City, Montana.

Special thanks to Lisa and Jack for putting up with me through another historical novel.

—Johnny D. Boggs
Santa Fe, New Mexico

Connect with
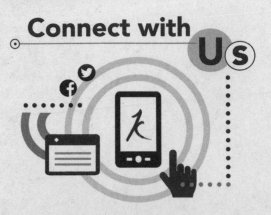
U s

Visit us online at
KensingtonBooks.com
to read more from your favorite authors, see books
by series, view reading group guides, and more.

Join us on social media

for sneak peeks, chances to win books and prize packs,
and to share your thoughts with other readers.

facebook.com/kensingtonpublishing
twitter.com/kensingtonbooks

Tell us what you think!

To share your thoughts, submit a review,
or sign up for our eNewsletters, please visit:
KensingtonBooks.com/TellUs.